IN FOR A
POUND

TITLES BY SG WONG

Lola Starke Series

Die On Your Feet
Out Like A Lion (2016)

Crescent City Short Stories

"The Fix"
Sleuth Magazine (August 2015)
"Movable Type"
AB Negative (*anthology*)

IN FOR A POUND

A LOLA STARKE NOVEL

Murder!

SG Wong

SG Wong
PO Box 67064 Meadowlark RPO
Edmonton, AB T5R 5Y3
www.sgwong.com

Publisher's Note: This is a work of fiction. Names, characters, places, and incidents are a product of the author's imagination. Locales and public names are sometimes used for atmospheric purposes. Any resemblance to actual people, living or dead, or to businesses, companies, events, institutions, or locales is completely coincidental.

Book Layout ©2013 BookDesignTemplates.com
Cover Design by little h design works

In For A Pound /SG Wong. -- 1st ed.
ISBN 978-0-9940880-1-7

For my mum
with much love
because she gave me a name I'm proud to live up to.

In for a penny, in for a pound.

—English aphorism

ONE

W hy, hello stranger." Ria looked up at Lola, gave a lazy smile. She patted the shoulder of the man in whose lap she sat. "This is my new friend Charlie. Charlie, meet my best friend, Lola Starke." She switched to a stage whisper. "I bet she's here to take me home."

"I'm here to take you home," Lola said, deadpan.

Charlie smiled and nodded. He had a dimple in his right cheek and a jaw shadowed with dark stubble. "A pleasure to meet you, Miss Starke." His gaze measured her from head to toe—and back again.

There might have been an awkward pause then, but the trumpet player chose that moment to blow for all he was worth. Lola turned to face the stage. The club patrons were out of their seats, clapping, jumping, and shouting encouragement. Ria bumped Lola's right hip as she straightened up. Lola threw her a sidelong glance. Ria winked.

The trumpet player reached his apogee, his body a taut arc, his eyes squeezed shut. The cheering grew. Tables were bumped. Glassware tumbled with clinks and crashes. The crystal chandeliers rattled and Lola felt pressure building in her eardrums.

Just as she started to cover her ears, the trumpeter's high note cut out and the rest of the band slammed to a halt. The calls of the crowd became a wave of sound and energy, cresting as the band members collapsed into their chairs, and breaking into laughter as the bandleader swept a spotted kerchief across his forehead and fell onto his seat at the edge of the stage.

1

Lola turned to Ria. They grinned at each other like fools.

Ria whirled around to face Charlie, kissed him soundly on the lips, and pushed away, laughing. She grabbed Lola's hand and led the way around smashed glass, tipsy people, giggling cigarette girls, and potted palms. Lola glanced back to see Charlie wave languidly at her, dimples deepening and eyes glinting.

The women burst through the beautiful etched doors of The Supper Club. Lola was laughing so hard, she could hardly stand up. Ria was little better.

They stumbled away from the doors and the startled doorman, turned right on the pavement, and made for the beach. Lola drew a deep breath, only to dissolve into more laughter at Ria's continued mirth. It went that way, back and forth for another half block.

As the sun lightened the sky in the East, its long rays cast themselves across the ocean waves. Glimmers of white appeared as the waves crested and broke. Lola breathed in deeply and craned her head, stared straight up. She felt Ria's hand tighten on her own. She pressed the soles of her shoes into the pavement and vainly searched the sky for the moon as the dim stars seemed to fly away from her.

A screech of tires broke the spell. Lola whipped her head around, back toward The Supper Club. A dark Packard idled at the curb, its front passenger window wound down. A small whirl of dust rose around the car. She caught her breath and willed her heart to calm. She shook her hand from Ria's grip.

"Someone's hubby, I bet." Ria's drawl was lazy, throaty. "Come to see what wifey's up to."

Lola watched the car.

The Packard remained still. Lola narrowed her eyes, but the windshield gave nothing away, its glass reflecting the overhead streetlamp. No one came strolling over to it, and, indeed, the street behind the car was empty of people.

"I bet the doorman's gone inside to fetch them," said Ria.

A blur of activity at the club doors suddenly deposited four women and two young men in rumpled evening wear on the sidewalk. Lola recognized the immaculate posture and elegant bearing of Gillian Gee, the Club manager. The cigarette girls with her were as fresh now as they'd been at nine o'clock. Black, black and bleached blonde. They gleamed from their upswept hair to the short excuses for skirts on their costumes. Even half a block away, Lola could read the genuine affection in their smiles for the two men.

Ria gasped, poked Lola in the ribs. "Lola, do you see him?"

"Elbows to yourself, doll." Lola turned her gaze back to the Packard.

"It's Tommy Chu!" Ria paused, made a noise of disappointment. "He's shorter in real life."

"Aren't we all."

"That must be Stuey Lim, then. What a dish. C'mon, let's go say hello." She gave Lola a little shove.

They neared in time to hear the famous comedian's signature chuckle. Lola felt a sudden intimacy, a joyful laugh bubbling up in response.

Tommy Chu looked up at them, his eyes sparkling with mischief. "The gods have answered my prayers at last," he said, using English. The cigarette girls tittered quietly. Lola nodded to Gillian, who bowed and hustled her employees back inside.

Ria stopped just in front of Tommy Chu's companion. "He's got to have better lines than that," she said, her Cantonese smooth and lilting.

The other man shrugged, smiling. "He's been up two days." His reply was in Cantonese. He looked at Lola and grinned. "Hiya, ace."

"Stuey." Lola smiled as he bussed her cheek. She felt the faintest scratch from his whiskers, couldn't help herself from taking a deep breath. Sandalwood, cigarettes and other women's perfume.

"Stu, you sneak, you know these sirens," said Tommy.

Lola caught Ria's look of surprise. She lifted a corner of her lips. Ria glowered at her.

"We share an Auntie," said Stuey. "Uncle Stanley's wife, Vivian."

Tommy's face was blank for a few seconds. Then he punched his friend in the shoulder. "The Mei Triplets? That Vivian? Vivian Mei?" He punched his friend again then turned to Lola. "You're the Mei Triplets' niece?"

Lola automatically searched for any hint of sarcasm or disbelief, but Tommy's expression was open. Excited and eager, in fact. Lola eased her shoulders. "The Aunties were close friends with my father. From the silent era. They practically raised me."

Rubbing his shoulder, Stuey lifted an eyebrow at his friend, then turned back to Lola and Ria. He said, "Tommy's a student of the Old Theatre. He always said Vivian had the biggest—"

"Laughs," Tommy said. "She always got the biggest laughs. That's why she's my favourite Mei Girl."

"Well," said Lola, "I'll tell her you said so. She'll be thrilled."

"I'd love to tell her myself." He used his thumb to indicate Stuey. "This one keeps hedging." He grinned at Lola. "But I see you're a much better prospect."

Stuey gave a snort. "I keep telling him it's a bad idea, but he won't believe me."

Tommy splayed his hands out, his face arranged in a mock plea.

"Yes, but you've never explained *why* it's such a bad idea, old man."

Stuey ignored him. He said to Lola, "Perhaps you could...?"

Lola shook her head. "You're on your own with that one, I'm afraid."

Stuey's eyes crinkled at their edges as he grinned back at her. Lola's heart sped up. She was suddenly aware of the soft breeze along her bare shoulders. She shivered.

"Well *someone* oughta tell me." Tommy gave a theatrical sigh.

Lola gave herself a mental shake. She smiled politely. "Not my story to tell. Sorry. Besides, I stay well away from Auntie Viv's feuds. I like my life peaceful."

Now it was Ria's turn to snort.

Tommy grabbed Lola's hand. "Life is too short to live peacefully." He twirled her in a smooth circle, ended with an elegant dip. Lola laughed as Tommy straightened back up. He stepped away and bowed formally. "I don't believe we've been properly introduced."

"Now we're talking," muttered Ria. She glared at Lola, who grinned. The men bowed elegantly and kissed the women's hands in the European fashion.

Lola hesitated, cleared her throat. "May I give my regards to your Ghost, Mr. Chu? My father was close to a mutual friend, Nicky Lo."

Tommy's expression froze. Lola wondered if she'd overstepped. His eyes remained on her as he cocked his head slightly to the right, listening to his Ghost.

Tommy's mouth tightened just before he said, "Yes, of course." He paused. "Lucky says hello. He, ah, sends his regards to your father, of course." Another pause. A tight smile. "He says you should pay your respects to Nicky more often."

Lola considered explaining that her father had passed on almost a dozen years ago. She nodded instead. "I'll do that. Thank you."

Stuey said, "Don't *you* have a Ghost, Lola?"

"Long story." She put on a rueful smile. "A bit of a recluse."

"Aubrey?" said Ria, eyebrows raised. "I doubt that."

Tommy waved his hand impatiently. "If he doesn't want to talk, let him alone. The gods know, don't they, Miss Starke, how precious privacy is to Hosts and Ghosts alike?"

Lola made a noncommittal noise.

Tommy turned to Ria, expression thoughtful. "Monteverde. You don't happen to write for *The Herald*, do you Miss Monteverde?"

"Why yes. I run the City Desk."

"Any chance you're on good terms with Walter Yee? I've got a new show in the works and he's always been my most, ah, stringent critic."

"Oh Walter, of course. He's a real pussycat when you get to know him."

"I've been thinking of holding a preview and inviting the City's top critics, including Walter naturally."

Ria smiled. "I'm afraid my information can't be bought, Mr. Chu. I've got to work with Walter every day, you see. Wouldn't do for him to think I'd sell his darkest secrets so easily."

Tommy grinned, shrugged. "I didn't get this far just because of my good manners, Miss Monteverde. I'm sure we can find a middle ground, don't you?"

Ria shook her finger at Tommy. "No disrespect, but that's entirely too glib. I believe I'll err on the side of caution. Just this once, you understand."

Stuey hid a smile behind his hand.

Tommy opened his mouth, about to argue, Lola was certain. Instead, he put on another charming smile. "How about a drink before we greet the dawn?"

Ria turned to look over at the ocean. "Oh, let's just stay out here. It's too gorgeous to go back inside."

Tommy inclined his head. "Of course. Whatever my lady desires." He offered Ria his arm.

Lola found her own hand being tucked into the crook of Stuey's elbow.

"Shall we?" he said.

She looked into his eyes, so close now. Thick black lashes, deep brown eyes. And that crinkle again as he smiled warmly at her. He led her slowly down the sidewalk. Ria and Tommy talked animatedly as they strolled a few paces ahead. Lola felt the soft breeze growing as they neared the beach.

"Here," said Stuey, "let me get that for you." He gently tugged her wrap up and around her shoulders. "It's always cooler near the shore." His fingers skimmed her skin. Lola shivered as goose bumps appeared on her arms.

"Do you know if Walter happens to enjoy the duck at White Crane?"

Lola had to admire Tommy's tenacity. She saw Ria shake her head, smiling, even as Tommy continued. "Do you know if he has a particular favourite dish?"

"I'm sorry," Stuey said.

"About what?"

"Lucky not knowing about your father."

"I wouldn't expect him to know. 'Butch Starke' was hardly a household name even when he was in the business."

Stuey smiled gently. "I'm not sorry about his mistake. I'm sorry if it brought up an old sorrow."

"Oh." Lola cleared her suddenly thick throat. She knew there ought to be words she could say, something facile and cool. She found that she didn't know any. Or perhaps, she didn't think it a fair repayment for this man's genuine concern.

"I'd forgotten that about you," she said. "Your ability to always say just the right thing."

He chuckled. "Well, I remember your ability to deflect conversation you didn't like."

Lola couldn't help smiling. "Caught in the act."

He shook his head. "No, no, that's fair. It was a gamble." He looked out at the water, breathing deeply.

"Well then, since we're being so terribly gracious, I'm sorry I couldn't help your friend with Auntie Viv."

Stuey laughed. "*My friend.* You may be the only person in the entire world who'd refer to him like that."

"I knew you first."

Stuey patted her arm. "Loyal to a fault." He made a face. "As for Vivian, ancient history. I'm happy to follow my parents' lead. Besides, now that I'm older and wiser, I'm inclined to agree that Viv and Uncle Stanley married too young. No fault in that, surely?"

Lola thought of her own status, now five years a divorcée at twenty-eight. She grinned at the thought of her ex-husband, Martin. They were better friends since their parting and she was content that they'd made the right choice.

"Has anyone told Vivian that?" She kept her tone light.

Stuey slid a sideways glance at her. "Not me. Public enemy number one, remember?"

Lola winced. "Sorry. Put my foot in it again." She cursed herself inwardly. What was the matter with her? The infatuated twelve-year–old girl she used to be seemed determined to rise again. She flushed, imagining how fifteen-year-old Stuey must've seen her then, a gawky girl with knobby knees and sharp elbows making calf eyes at him.

Stuey shook his head. "It's not even personal, strangely. I mean, I know she shoots dagger-eyes at me, sure, but it's not *me* she sees, y'know?" He shrugged. "I don't hold grudges. I can't say I understand Vivian." He paused. "But I guess I can feel some sort of compassion. Stanley was an ace of an uncle, but I can see how he might not have been a great husband or father, with all his travelling."

Lola nodded, took a deep breath of salt-tinged air. The breeze brought freshness with it even as it crept along the nape of her neck, creating tingles. She felt the softness of Stuey's jacket fabric along her arm and resisted the urge to squeeze. She imagined corded muscle beneath and turned her face away slightly, hiding her grin. Her shoes dangled in her hand. She swung them in a lazy circle.

Stuey nudged her. "I'm afraid Tommy's doing his best impression of a steamroller."

Lola laughed, returning her attention to the pair ahead. "Ria's a tough cookie. She won't let herself get flattened. Even if it is the fa-mous Tommy Chu."

Stuey chuckled. "Aha. Your contempt for fame reveals itself."

"Contempt is rather strong." She grinned. "Let's call it a jaundiced view, shall we?"

This time, he laughed outright.

Ahead, Ria stopped and turned, pulling Tommy back along with her. She pulled a face.

"You two are having entirely too much fun. I want to walk with you. Mr. Chu here only wishes to talk business."

Tommy bowed. "My abject apologies, Miss Monteverde. I'm a terrible man. Can I make it up to you back inside the Club? I happen to know Gillian keeps a beautiful bottle of cognac for special occasions."

"Are you saying I warrant a special occasion, Mr. Chu?"

"I am indeed, Miss Monteverde. A very beautiful, very special occasion."

"That's much better." Ria allowed her arm to be recaptured and secured in the crook of Tommy's arm.

"Um," said Lola.

"Don't say it," said Ria. "I don't wanna hear it, *Mother*."

"Doll, you made me promise."

Stuey cocked his head. "A previous engagement?"

"I promised to remind her that she has to be at the office for an eight o'clock meeting. And that we don't have the luxury, as men do, of showing up in whatever shape we happen to be in." Lola gave Ria a weighted look.

"Surely, you can reschedule?" Tommy grinned impishly.

"I'm afraid not," said Lola, gaze still locked with Ria's. "I'm certain Ria said something about a big meeting. With her editor." They stared at one another for a few silent moments.

"Time to retreat gracefully, old man." Stuey grinned. "You're not gonna budge her, not if she's the same girl I remember."

"If you're suggesting I'm stubborn," said Lola, "it's beside the point, although you'd be correct. However, she made me promise and I don't break my promises."

Ria heaved a dramatic sigh. Tommy patted her hand.

"Now that we've made friends, I assure you we'll be seeing one another again." He waggled his eyebrows and exaggerated his grin.

Ria laughed.

Lola felt amiable and light, tucked into Stuey's side neatly, as they were of a height. She flushed again, surprised at the strong pleasure that realization gave her. Just a rarity, she told herself, Chinese men being on the whole so much shorter than she was. It was a relief to be able to look a man directly in the eyes rather than having to avoid looking at his hair pattern. She suppressed a snicker.

The men graciously served support as the women replaced their strappy sandals on their bare feet and the four of them walked slowly up the few wooden steps to the pavement. Tommy began expounding on the unfathomability of women's shoes. Ria countered with the ancient Chinese tradition of feet binding and they were off. The four argued good-naturedly until they found themselves in front of The Supper Club doors.

"I'd very much enjoy continuing this discussion tonight." Tommy bowed over Ria's hand, kissed it. Ria murmured something meant only for his ears.

Stuey pulled a card from his inside pocket and held it out to Lola. She caught the scent of musk and cloves.

"Friends should keep in touch."

She nodded, slipping the card into her clutch purse. Stuey gently arranged her wrap around her shoulders once more, kissing her on the cheek.

"Looks like the valet's missing. I'll run in and roust someone, shall I?"

Lola smiled. Stuey pushed through the glass doors. Lola caught herself staring after him and shook herself. She turned away.

Tommy Chu was whispering into her best friend's ear. Lola steeled her jaw and closed in.

"Excuse us a moment, if you would, Mr. Chu." Lola took Ria by the elbow and herded her down the sidewalk. She stopped about five feet away, manoeuvred so that Ria's back was to Tommy. He grinned at Lola as he patted his pockets. A cigarette case and a lighter were soon in hand. He winked. Lola refrained from rolling her eyes. She turned her attention back to her friend.

"What are you doing?"

Ria sighed contentedly, looked up at the slowly brightening sky.

Lola sighed, impatient. "He's trouble with a ca–pi–tal, Ria, and you know it."

Ria smiled broadly. "The best kind and *you* know it. Anyway, that's all beside the point. You've been holding out on me."

Lola tamped down her exasperation. She answered carefully. "I haven't seen Stuey in years, not since the Old Blossom retrospective. Auntie Viv complained of a headache as soon as Stuey and his parents showed up. We left." She paused. "I was still married then."

"Ah," said Ria. "Still, how could you forget to mention you grew up with Tommy Chu's best friend?"

"We were never *close*." Lola felt heat rising to her face.

"Well, if I'm any judge of character, he's certainly worth getting to know now."

"Oh, was it his *character* you were assessing then?" Lola flushed, glancing at the Club doors as movement caught her eye.

Stuey stepped out, his handsome face alight with laughter. He held out a handful of keys. "No sign of the valet, but I've discovered his treasures. Guess we'll have to hunt them out ourselves, ladies. Let me guess, Lola, something beautiful, speedy, and red, yes?"

The doors behind him exploded in a shower of glass. Lola instinctively flattened herself on the pavement, pulling Ria down with her. She raised her head in time to see a blur of movement on the street. It was the car, the black Packard. She cursed herself for an idiot. She'd forgotten all about it.

The big black car caromed into a sharp turn, its tires screeching, and sped away. Lola pushed herself up off the ground and grabbed Ria's hand, hauling her friend up roughly.

"Are you all right?" she shouted.

Ria nodded. "Fine. I'm fine. What happened?" Her gaze caught on something behind Lola. She gasped sharply, pushed away. "Oh dear gods."

Lola's scalp prickled and a chill spread down her spine. She faced The Supper Club doors fully.

Shattered glass speckled the grey pavement. Stuey's black hair and evening jacket glittered with it as he lay prone, one arm flung against the door frame. Lola felt her face go cold. She took a halting step forward, stepped crookedly on her heel and stumbled. Her knees didn't seem to be working properly, but she pressed on.

Ria was shouting into the interior of the club. Lola dimly noted shapes in her periphery. A scream sounded, piercing and shrill. Lola stared at Stuey's hand, outstretched on the pavement. A jumble of keys lay scattered around. Clenching her jaw, Lola looked into his face. She held back a sob. Stuey's dark eyes stared upward, wide and blank.

Lola turned then, the dark edges in her vision receding, sound returning in a crashing wave. She heard crunching footsteps, an urgent voice. She watched Ria snatch a bit of cloth from the wide-eyed doorman.

Tommy lay motionless on his back, his head almost touching Stuey's shoes. Ria was kneeling in the blood next to Tommy, pushing the kerchief against his neck. The white cloth darkened under Ria's fingers. Blood spread across the pavement, relentless, quick.

Lola couldn't stop herself glancing once more at Stuey. She felt her gorge rise. The shards of glass in his hair were mingled with bits of white bone and dark matter. Lola swallowed, hard. She heard Ria curse, trying desperately to stop a man from bleeding to death with nothing but a square of fabric and her fierceness.

Lola knew it was useless.

Tommy Chu, the most famous comedian in Crescent City, was dead.

TWO

Lola stared at the uniform staring back at her, wondering if she could get away with grabbing his ears and shaking his head. Repeatedly. She clenched her hands into fists, then slowly took a deep breath. She released her fists and laid her hands deliberately on her thighs.

"He wasn't there. There aren't any other ways I can say it, so can we just skip to the next one? Asking me a dozen more times isn't gonna change my answer." She clamped her lips together.

"What do you mean, he wasn't there?" The copper's baby-smooth cheeks contrasted sharply with the cynicism in his black eyes. "Last I heard, Miss Starke, you're stuck with your Ghost day and night."

Lola bit the inside of her cheek and silently counted to ten.

"Yes, I'm well aware of that, Officer Chin." He narrowed his eyes at her. Lola forced herself to soften her tone. "I can't explain anymore than this. My Ghost takes a hike now and then. I don't know where he goes. I don't care. He's gone and that's good enough for me."

Chin wrinkled his brow. "I ain't never heard of someone wantin' their Ghost to disappear. You signed up for a haunting, didn't you?"

Lola clenched her jaw for a moment. "Frankly, Officer, that's none of your business. I've told you over and over again. My Ghost was not with me tonight. It doesn't matter why. He wasn't with me, so he didn't see anything. End of story."

Chin stared at her. "I'm asking, Miss Starke, because I'm hoping your Ghost saw something about the car you mentioned. Something more than 'it was a black Packard.'"

Lola shook off the sudden prickling in her eyes, the roiling in her stomach. "Yes, I forgot about the gods-damned car. I stood six feet away, and I completely forgot it was there. Satisfied?"

Chin considered her, seemingly oblivious to the sudden silence around them. "Well you see, Miss Starke, the way police work runs is that we have to corroborate witnesses' statements. So you and your Ghost will have to present yourselves to a station Catcher." He laid a business card on the table. "Today."

Lola clenched her hands again.

"I think Miss Starke is entitled to a break, eh?"

Lola jumped at the stranger's voice. She turned sharply in her chair. Ria's friend, the tall one with broad shoulders. He smiled at her, then at the copper.

"C'mon, Officer. The lady's in shock, can't you see it?"

Lola stared up at him blankly. She turned back stiffly to face Chin. Her head felt stuffed with wool. Chin's black gaze wavered in her vision. She gripped the table's edge so tightly the wood beneath creaked.

"C'mon, I'll just take her over there—" the tall man pointed "—to the bar. Fix her something that'll help. She ain't going anywhere 'til you coppers say so. Deal?"

Chin eyed the tall man warily, then gave a curt nod.

Lola felt herself lifted gently by the elbow. She followed Ria's friend across the crowded room. Her gaze bounced around, unable to settle. She absently noted other club patrons, huddled around tables in wilted finery. Some smoked and stared at the police standing at the entrance to the main room. Others talked in whispers, casting furtive looks over their shoulders, eyes wide and unnaturally bright.

"Thanks, Charlie. I owe you."

Lola startled at Ria's voice. She blinked rapidly, trying to clear the cobwebs from her head. Charlie. The tall man's name.

"You don't look much better," he said to Ria. Kindly, he helped Lola onto a stool, then went behind the bar.

Lola blinked.

Ria returned Lola's blank stare with a tired sigh.

Lola shuddered into sudden wakefulness.

"He must be right," she said. "You look like I feel." She rubbed her eyes, squeezing her lids tight.

"Thanks a lot, sister." Ria's tone was strained. "Keep rubbing like that and you'll look like a raccoon."

Lola grimaced. "I already feel like a zoo exhibit."

Charlie placed two cups of coffee on the bar before them. Lola saw the rough hairs on his bare forearms. She breathed deeply over her coffee cup.

"You're aces." Ria took a quick sip then coughed, red-faced and spluttering.

Charlie reeled back, eyes wide. Lola rubbed her friend's back. She looked back at the big man. "She hates brandy."

"Dear gods, I'm sorry, Ria." Charlie rushed back around the bar. He gathered Ria into his arms.

Lola slid her glance away, took a sip. Welcome warmth spread out from her centre.

"I'm all right." Ria cleared her throat several times. "Truly." She touched the side of Charlie's face, gave him a soft smile.

Charlie, pink-faced, returned behind the bar, poured another cup for Ria and placed it in front of her. He gave them a look of apology, took up a tea carafe and a tray of cups, and stepped out from the bar.

"He work here?"

Ria nodded. "New bartender. Just started tonight." She paused. "Last night."

Lola surveyed her best friend closely. Dark hair, dishevelled. Dark eyes, bloodshot. Shoulders, slumped. Clothes, borrowed.

"You jake?"

Ria returned the scrutiny. "Are you?"

"Touché." Lola raised her cup before taking a drink. She rubbed surreptitiously at her chest with a fist, disliking the hollowness that had settled there.

"Sam's gonna want someone else on this."

Lola looked over. Ria stared down at her mug, chewing on her lower lip.

Lola carefully replaced her coffee on the bar. "You ready for that fight?"

Ria shook her head. "I'm not giving up this story. I don't care if she says I'm too close." She gripped her mug. "I won't."

A commotion rippled behind them. Ria turned around. Lola followed suit after another swallow of coffee.

The uniforms on guard saluted crisply to two men standing at the entrance of the room. The man on the right wore a blue-and-green striped tie with his sand-coloured suit. His companion wore a light grey suit with a tie of pale blue. Both wore slightly cocked trilbies and bland expressions. Their flat glances swept the room.

The newcomers stepped lightly down the three stairs. Officer Chin approached them, snapped out a salute and gave his report.

Lola made a sour face. She watched with a feeling of inevitability as Chin gestured toward the bar. The suits looked over at Ria, then Lola. They returned their gazes to Chin. The suit in grey nodded, then moved along to another uniform. The other suit followed, notebook in hand. Lola made her way behind the bar and poured herself more coffee. She considered another shot of brandy.

"Here they come," murmured Ria.

"Cha cha cha," muttered Lola. She gritted her teeth, returned to her stool next to Ria.

"Miss Monteverde? Miss Starke?" said grey suit. "Detective Inspector Charles Leung at your service." He gave a small bow. "This is DS Chester Eng." The latter nodded. "I sincerely apologize for delaying you here. I know this must be an extremely frightful situation. Please know that the Crescent City Police Department is deeply appreciative of your cooperation during such a distressing time."

Lola kept her face impassive, inclined her head. Ria stayed rigid beside her. Leung looked from one woman to the other and back again. DS Eng stood immobile, his face unreadable, eyes sharply focussed on Lola.

"Is there anything more we can do for your injuries?"

Ria shook her head. "We've been taken care of, Inspector. Just minor cuts and bruises." She paused. Lola heard her take a deep breath. "We were several feet away when the shots occurred." Her voice held the slightest tremor.

Leung nodded. "Of course. I apologize for the redundancy. Eng and I just need to hear your version of events for ourselves." He paused. "And, I'm afraid, we must ask you to step outside with us."

Ria inhaled sharply. Lola had a moment of vertigo. She felt a hand on her elbow, steadying her.

"I'm truly very sorry." Leung's grip was kind, firm. "This is an extremely difficult request, I understand that. But we need every scrap of information we can wring from your memories if we are to apprehend the murderers."

Lola nodded curtly in response to his solicitous expression. He let go of her elbow.

"You think it's more than one person?" Ria frowned.

"Ah, that's right." Leung flicked a glance at his partner. "You're with the City desk at the *Herald*. Well, all I can say is we have no comment at this time. Now, please, if you would?"

Lola concentrated on walking with her spine straight and her shoulders back. They passed a seeming gauntlet of saluting uniforms and staring people. Then Eng was efficiently helping them through the ruined doors. Lola heard Ria's breathing coming fast and shallow. She took her friend's hand and squeezed.

Glass shards glittered everywhere. The dark patch on the sidewalk glistened. Lola stared, knew it would be tacky to the touch. She found herself calculating how long it would take to dry completely. Then she realized Gillian would have someone cleaning it up before it ever got a chance to dry. Rubbing her goose-fleshed arms, she stepped gingerly around broken glass until she stood a few feet from the doorway.

She turned to find the two detectives watching her, eyes cold. She was fine with that. Coppers always did their watching with flat eyes.

Lola said, "You want to know how it played out?"

Leung nodded. "Again, I apologize most sincerely. I know this must be distressing for you. But we must do what we must do." He gestured to Ria. "Please. And take it step by step, if you would."

Ria blew out a breath, began. Leung asked questions at every conceivable ambiguity. Eng scribbled in his notebook continuously, his strokes meticulous and efficient. Lola craned her neck and saw a neat sketch, complete with notes, emerging from Eng's steady hand.

Leung took Lola through the final moments, poking at it from different angles, trying to get a comprehensive view.

When Lola finished, Eng looked up at her, cocked his head. "So you understood that it was gunfire?"

Lola considered her reply. "I can't honestly tell you *what* I understood in that moment."

"But you knew it was dangerous." Lola looked at Leung. He said, "You knew that something was wrong. That's why you pulled Miss Monteverde down."

"I suppose."

"All right. Why?" At Lola's look, he said, "Why do you recognize the sound of gunshots?"

She stared at him blankly.

"Why didn't you think it was a car backfiring, for instance?"

"I'm a trained private investigator."

"Any guesses then? As to the type of gun?" Leung leaned in.

"Just a regular piece of heat." Lola paused. "Not a chopper."

"Not a submachine gun." Eng eyed her intently. "You're sure about that?"

"The shots weren't rapid enough," she said slowly, thinking back. She cleared her throat. A trickle of sweat ran down the back of her neck. Lola shivered as the ocean breeze blew across her skin.

"How long would you say the car had been at the curb?" said Leung.

Lola shared a glance with Ria.

"Fifteen, twenty minutes? We weren't keeping track," Ria said, voice low.

Leung gave a brief nod. "Did you note anything about the car?"

"When it pulled up, Ria and I made a crack about it. I know it was a Packard." Lola hesitated, tension coiling up her neck and the back of her head. "I'd forgotten it was there. By the time we came back from the beach."

The sound of Eng's pencil strokes filled the silence.

"We both forgot it was there," said Ria. Tears spilled down her cheeks then, fragile and bright. She covered her mouth, suppressing her sobs. Lola put an arm around Ria's shoulders, keeping her own emotions tightly in check.

The detectives offered handkerchiefs simultaneously. Ria kept her chin tucked down as she took Eng's square of navy linen. Leung absently tucked his back into his pocket, making a careless lump in his jacket.

Leung gave a short bow. "My apologies, ladies, and my thanks. You've both been through a terrible and trying time. You may go home."

Eng raised his head from his notes. "Just a moment. You have a Ghost, don't you, Miss Starke?"

She nodded, took a deep breath. Waited for the inevitable question.

"We shall require your Ghost to answer some questions in the presence of one of our Catchers. I'm sure Officer Chin was clear on this?"

"Yes," she said. "I've got the card."

"Later this morning then. Shall we say, eleven? At Central."

"You know he wasn't with me then?"

Eng nodded. "And he's not with you now, correct?"

She nodded wearily.

"Investigations hinge on the most surprising things, Miss Starke." Eng turned to Ria. "Miss Monteverde, I'm afraid your gown has been taken into evidence."

Ria shuddered. "Keep it."

Eng nodded. "If you recall anything more." He handed each woman a card. Leung did the same. "We'll have your car brought around. Good day." They tipped their hats and walked away.

Ria straightened up, out of Lola's hold. She tightened her borrowed shawl around herself. "I need to go home," she muttered. She sighed, looking out at the water, then spoke without turning back. "Give me a lift downtown?"

Lola hesitated. "They'll understand if you take the day off."

"I just need to work it out with Sam," Ria said. "And a telephone call won't do. You know her. I need to argue my case in person."

As Lola reluctantly acquiesced, four men in tuxedo pants and shirtsleeves came out from the Club. She recognized two as waiters. Buckets, stiff brushes and push brooms were set down with a clatter. One of the waiters began sweeping glass shards together into a pile. Another man poured water onto the pavement. The remaining two threw down some thick towels, kneeled on top of them and started scrubbing.

Lola turned away, but she couldn't escape hearing the harsh sound of stiff bristles scraping on concrete.

THREE

L ola drove deftly, weaving amid the morning's commercial traffic. Trucks ground their gears and belched black smoke, roaring down the broad avenues of Crescent City, morning deliveries well underway.

Under ten minutes and Lola was dodging just a few more late newspaper trucks as she parked in the alley behind the *Crescent City Herald*. She imagined smoke blowing out the windows and doors, as the morning edition was finally done and the presses lapsed into a few hours of well-earned rest until it was time for the afternoon run.

Ria had her head leaned back on the seat rest, her eyes closed.

A chill spread across Lola's shoulders. She tightened her grip on the steering wheel.

"What's happened?" Aubrey's voice was tense.

Lola turned in her seat to face Ria. "You sure you're jake?"

Ria's eyes opened with a flutter. She rolled her head to the side. She blinked once, twice, abruptly sat up straight. Her eyes narrowed as she looked closely at Lola. "Is Aubrey back?"

Lola studied her friend's face. "Yes."

"Promise you'll tell him everything."

"Everything about what? What's going on?" said Aubrey.

Lola ignored her Ghost's impatience. She spoke to Ria. "You're bearding the lion in its den, you know."

"You're telling me, sister." Ria scrubbed at her face.

"Want I should wait?"

Ria shook her head. "The least Sam can do is order me a taxi." She gathered the overly large shawl, straightened her shoulders. One hand on the door handle, she hesitated. "Listen, you've got to tell Aubrey what happened, all right? I can't even begin to understand your arrangement, I admit it. But I know it'll go easier on you if you just spill. Don't keep it bottled up."

"Only if you do likewise."

"Deal. Now, get gone."

Lola watched her friend walk steadily to the loading dock door and slip inside. She closed her eyes, gathering her strength for the drive. A sudden bang set her jumping, eyes flying open, her wrist hitting the steering wheel. Cursing, Lola looked around. She saw a worker pushing a hand truck around the corner of the building.

"Will you tell me once we're home?" Aubrey sounded cautious.

Lola shook her head. She turned the engine over, checked her surroundings, and started off.

Aubrey waited three blocks.

"Why was Ria wearing borrowed clothes?"

Lola clenched her jaw.

"The more you stonewall, the more I ask."

"Where were you?"

There was a long pause. "With your mother."

Lola felt a muscle twitch at her temple. "You told her yet?"

"That's between me and her. I'm sorry, but it's none of your business."

"You are spying on my mother. I'd say that's a damned good reason to make it my business."

"We've been friends practically our entire lives. Don't you think I've got her best interests at heart?"

"If that were true, you'd tell her. Nothing to hide between old friends, isn't that right?" Lola spat out each word with precision. In the resulting silence, she heard her own ragged breathing.

"Lola," Aubrey said, voice quiet, calm, "take Ria's advice. Tell me what happened."

Pressure built up in her chest, threatened to explode out of her mouth. She breathed through her nose slowly. She thought of Ria, the lines around her eyes and mouth, the earnestness in her eyes. Then she spoke, keeping her tone flat, reaching for objectivity.

There was a long silence afterward.

"Dear gods. I don't know what to say."

Lola refrained from the obvious retort.

She drove the rest of the way to East Town in silence.

Where the scrabbling classes lived and died, the streets were already bustling. Young mothers and middle-aged *amahs*, holding toddlers' hands or with babies tied to backs, crowded the sidewalks, doing the morning's shopping. Bus stops were thick with men in suits and the occasional young office lady. Lola smiled a little to see all the copies of the *Herald* among them.

Her smile died when she thought about the coming afternoon's headline.

Leaving her coupe on the curb, Lola swiftly walked the half-block to the Aunties' building. A number of people looked askance at her, eyes travelling from her face down to her rumpled evening wear and back up again. She ignored them easily. It was far from the first time people had stared at her *gwai* features in the City.

Lola automatically noted that Betta's consulting rooms were dark. Too early for even the most desperately ill to visit the best Healer in Crescent City. Lola let herself into the foyer off the street and climbed the steep stairs to the Aunties' flat. She smelled dark tea and fresh baking. She paused for a moment on the landing, knocked softly.

Veronica opened the door, her silver-white hair pulled back into its usual tight bun. A dark green apron covered a pale green sweater set, paired with brown wide-legged slacks and ballet flats.

"You look right out of Central Casting," said Lola, "'well-to-do widow.'"

Veronica laughed. "Good morning to you, too. Or should I say good night?"

Lola kissed her Auntie, hugged her tightly. "Is everyone up?"

"Of course, darling. We're much too old to bother with lie-ins anymore."

"You never did anyway, as I recall."

A strident voice called out from the inner rooms. "Stop nattering in the doorway and bring her in here."

Veronica pressed her lips together into a thin line. She threaded her arm through Lola's. "Come on. She's in a fine one today. Oh, and good morning, Aubrey."

Lola slipped off her heels and slid into the slippers the Aunties always kept for her on the mat next to the door. She remembered with surprising clarity the very first pair: a girl's size medium, pink, topped by a bow with tiny white polka dots. She'd always been careful to treat those slippers with utmost contempt. Lola smiled a little now as she recalled the sober, navy slippers that eventually replaced the little pink monstrosities.

Veronica led Lola into the rest of the flat. As they stepped from the front hall into the main living space, Lola's stomach growled loudly.

"Just in time," said Viola. She stood in the kitchen, white flour dusting her purple apron. She wiped her hands carelessly on a kitchen towel. Lola hugged her close.

"Oh, little one, you'll get flour over your beautiful gown."

"Gown?" The owner of the strident voice neared. Lola pulled back, kissed Viola on the cheek, and gave her another squeeze before letting go. She turned around.

"Good morning, Auntie Vivian," said Lola.

Vivian returned the greeting briskly, wearing an impatient expression. She pulled out of Lola's hug and eyed the younger woman critically. "That's not a good colour for you. Where were you? Why are you here so early?"

Vivian took Lola's hand and led her toward the kitchen table. Viola brought a chipped blue-and-white tea cup to Lola, followed by an ashtray. Vivian sat down in the chair across the table and lit a cigarette in a holder. She nodded as Viola placed a cup of tea on the table for her.

Lola wrapped her hands around her own cup, careful to turn the chip away from her lips. Lola felt the smoky tea heat her entire body as it went down to her stomach.

"Bad luck, using that cup," said Vivian.

Veronica sat down. "Leave her be. I'm fond of that cup myself."

"I can't believe it's lasted this long," said Viola.

"Twenty years," said Vivian. "And chipped as soon as I bought it."

"Sorry, Auntie. I was a clumsy child," said Lola.

Vivian grunted, took another drag from her cigarette.

Viola smiled. She stood behind Vivian's chair, one hand on its back, the other at her hip. "I remember so clearly how small your hands looked when you first started using that cup, darling. You were so determined."

"Stubborn," said Vivian.

"Persistent," said Veronica.

"Stubborn," said Lola.

"And Butch wanted so badly to buy you a new one," said Viola. "But you, determined, beautiful child that you were, you said no."

Lola shrugged. "It seemed a waste of money. It was perfectly usable." She took another sip. "Still is."

Vivian smiled. "You must be the most frugal heiress in the entire City."

Lola felt a small measure of tension in her shoulders melt away.

"I always said Butch did well by you. He never lived beyond his means and he taught you how to respect money," said Vivian. "Not a lot of rich girls can say that about themselves."

Lola attributed the sudden heat in her cheeks to the strong tea. She cleared her throat. "I'm sorry, Aunties, but I have some bad news." She swallowed, shoving away vivid memories. "It's about Stuey, Uncle Keun's son." She loosened her grip on the tea cup. "He...he died this morning. He and Tommy Chu."

The older women gasped. Vivian opened her mouth, then closed it with a snap.

"They were gunned down this morning, in front of The Supper Club."

Lola shook her head, trying to rid herself of the sudden ringing in her ears.

"Tell them everything," murmured Aubrey.

"Ria and I, we were there..." Lola looked away.

"Are you all right? And Ria?" said Viola, her voice tight.

Veronica grabbed Lola's hand. Lola nodded, soothed them with reassurances.

"Start from the beginning." Vivian spoke softly.

Lola kept her voice calm and level as she gave a brief account. The older women listened, silent and unsettlingly still. When Lola finished, no one spoke at all.

Street noises seemed close and loud within the flat. Lola heard laughter, deep and rumbling, followed by a high giggle and that distinctive loud babbling of young boys excited about something. She imagined a small family. Or, perhaps, two groups entirely: a small crowd of boys darting down the sidewalk, coming to a couple walking hand in hand, milling for a few moments around them and then parting. Their footsteps faded, replaced by the roar of starting cars and trucks. Lola knew that if she went to the window, she'd have just seen the traffic signals change.

Lola carefully unwrapped her numb fingers from around her chipped cup. She lit an Egyptian cigarette.

"Use a holder, girl," said Vivian absently.

Lola obediently rooted around her clutch for it, popping out a white card in the process. It landed face-up in her lap. Stuey's name and a phone number. She slid her lit cigarette into the ebony holder, hands trembling. The holder's mother-of-pearl inlays flashed as she stuffed the card back into her purse.

Veronica said, "Thank you for coming to tell us. We'll ring Keun and Liliane later this morning."

Viola nodded solemnly, checking her wristwatch. "The rites will have to start this afternoon."

Vivian said, "I'm sure they'll call us first. Keun won't forget us."

Veronica and Viola exchanged glances.

"Oh, don't look like that," said Vivian. "I've not gone off. I know it was a long time ago. He may no longer be my brother-in-law, but Keun's a good man. He'll ring us soon. I'm sure of it."

"I'm sorry this has brought up unhappiness for you, Auntie," said Lola. "I thought you would want to know as soon as possible."

Vivian waved her hand dismissively. "I won't lie. I never liked that boy, Stuey, whatever sort of name that is. Had a dishonest look about him. Always did. A sly child. Oh, I know we aren't to speak ill of the dead. I'm not. It's truth. There's a difference. And besides, what does it matter to them, the dead? They'll be on to their next life soon enough."

Viola gently laid her hand on Lola's. "You did right, little one. Viv is being obstinate. And ungracious."

"As usual" hung unspoken in the air.

"You must be exhausted," said Veronica. "Do you want to stay?"

Lola shook her head.

"Wait, wait, wait." Vivian plucked her nearly spent cigarette out of its holder and dropped it into the ashtray. "Tommy Chu. Did you speak with Lucky then?"

"No, I...Aubrey wasn't with me."

"What do you mean?" Vivian reared back against her chair. "It's not possible that he wasn't there."

"We have an agreement, Auntie."

"Tread carefully," said Aubrey.

Lola kept her expression neutral. She could not afford to let the Aunties know the details of Aubrey's new situation. Her mother's safety depended on it. She was already skirting the line as it was.

"I've never heard of such nonsense," said Vivian. "Ghosts do not take...holidays from their Hosts. Nonsense."

"Tell her I'm not spying," said Aubrey.

Lola complied. Vivian sputtered.

"I said no such thing. Spying? What a terrible accusation."

Lola said, "Aubrey says that's what you're implying, when you say he can't be elsewhere. Then you must think he's pretending to be elsewhere and the only reason for that would be..." She left off the rest.

"Ridiculous. I said no such thing." Vivian lit another cigarette. "Well, you look exhausted. Time to go home and sleep."

"Yes, Auntie." Lola was careful to embrace Vivian first. Veronica walked Lola down the hall. She touched Lola's arm at the door.

"Thank you for letting her be. She loved Stanley as much as she hated him. It's hard for her to bend. And I'm not sure she really knows what she's feeling right now, exactly."

"Stuey was different, Auntie. I don't think he was anything like Uncle Stanley. Least, not the way Auntie Viv says he was."

Veronica shook her head. "I'm sure they were like night and day. But the differences are difficult for her to see. She only sees how much he looked like Stanley and it reminds her." Veronica averted her eyes, sighed. "It reminds her that Stanley never gave her what she most wanted."

"Stuey isn't his son," said Lola. "And even if he were, it's not fair to be angry with him."

"I know. We know, darling." She gave a helpless shrug.

"He looks like Uncle Keun, too."

"Of course, darling." She raised her hands, palms up. "But."

"She doesn't see that." Lola sighed, rubbed her eyes.

Veronica wrapped her arms around Lola and hugged her tightly. "Be safe." She kissed Lola's cheek and closed the door.

FOUR

L ola awoke twisted in her sheets. She was flushed and sticky, her skin prickling from sweat. Her heart hammered at her rib cage like she'd just run up ten flights of stairs. She unclenched her hands from the sky blue sheets, unwound her legs, and tore off the sleep mask. Wincing at the pale sunlight, she stumbled toward her private bath, splashed frigid water on her face, and dried off with a ruthless scrubbing. Resisting the urge to shred the thick blue towel in her hands, she carefully replaced it on its hook and stripped for a shower.

She came out to a remade bed and clothes waiting atop the smooth covers. Glancing at the bedside clock, she was shocked that forty minutes had passed since she'd awoken. She dressed quickly in the pale grey dress, but she had to redo the small pearl buttons three times before getting them aligned. Slowly, she picked up the circle of white linen. Turning to face her dressing table, she watched her reflection slide the cuff past her left hand, pushing it up until it was wrapped around her upper arm. She tugged the dress material until the armband sat securely. She took a steadying breath, opened the door and strode out into the rest of the apartment.

"Good morning." Elaine placed a carafe on the dining table. A medium vase of cut crystal held bright violet irises tucked in amongst white peonies. Lola smelled dark tea and fresh baking. Her stomach rumbled as she recalled the fragrant *bao* Viola had been making just three hours earlier.

35

"Did they ring you?" Lola sat down, placed the napkin on her lap. She poured tea and inhaled deeply before drinking.

"The Aunties?" Elaine shook her head. "No. Miss Monteverde. She figured you'd forget to tell me." She served Lola slices of peach and melon, then plucked a *bao* from the platter. "She made me promise you'd eat, too."

"Don't see how that's your promise to keep," Lola muttered. She bit into the *bao*, fresh steam escaping, along with the rich fragrance of the rice wine sausage tucked inside. Lola ate it in three more bites, as well as the fruit on her plate, before reaching for another *bao*.

Elaine sipped her tea, leaning against the doorway to the kitchen.

"Where did you get this?" Lola gestured to her armband.

Elaine moved back to the table. "I know the traditions are important to you." She pulled out a chair and sat. "And I telephoned Viola. I'm sorry. I don't know the whole story, but what I've heard..." She ran a hand over her hair, touched the tight bun at her nape. "The Aunties spoke with his parents. They consider you all family. You have a right to wear mourning colours. I said I'd take care of it."

"Did you make it?" Lola's throat thickened. She swallowed past it.

Elaine nodded, her lips thinned to a line. "It's one of the first things you learn, in the factory. Sewing quickly." She looked away.

Lola stilled then replaced her coffee cup on its saucer with care. "Sorry. I'm making a mess of things today." She grimaced.

"Six was a long time ago." Elaine took a deep breath as she straightened up. "And I'm not a powerless child anymore." She gave a tight smile and disappeared into the kitchen.

Lola rubbed at her forehead, cursing herself for a hurtful fool.

⁂

Lola unlocked the door to the anteroom and hurried inside to her inner office, picking up the tray of envelopes off the floor. She rifled through them quickly, then binned the entire stack.

She unlatched the window locks and pushed up, letting cooler air into the room. It carried in the smells of exhaust and warming pavement, the sounds of morning traffic.

The telephone rang.

"Starke."

"Lola, my girl." It was an older man's voice, rough with use. Lola hadn't heard it in years.

"Uncle Nicky," she said.

"Stay right there. I'm coming up from the chemist on the corner."

Lola felt a pang at the English term. She thought of her mother's security man, St. John, and his rough working-class accent. Where was her mother now? France? Italy? Lola shook her head. It didn't matter. Whatever obscure corner of Europe she might be filming, Grace McCall would find out soon enough that her only daughter had witnessed two murders. Lola wondered how long she had before her mother would try to reach her.

She lit a cigarette.

The lift bell clanged. Lola laid her cigarette on the lip of the ashtray. She passed through the anteroom and waited for her old mentor in the doorway.

The doors to the lift rolled open with a clatter. Lola could see the shine on Nicky Lo's shoes from fifteen feet away. His starched white collar shone against his navy suit, pale blue shirt and dark tie. His trilby sat squarely, its band also light blue. He wore his white armband on the right.

Lola smiled a little. "You're pressed and powdered early today."

Nicky took off his hat, revealing black hair brushed straight back. He kissed Lola on both cheeks, embraced her tightly.

"Ah, it's wonderful to see you, my girl. Beautiful as ever." He pulled away, glanced at her armband, and looked into her eyes. They were of a height, even of a similar build. Despite his years, he remained slender with broad shoulders and long legs. Nicky's skin was a few shades darker than Lola's, the skin of peasant stock. Or so she'd been hearing from him since she was nine. "And proud of it, too," he'd always added.

Lola blinked, flushing slightly at her own inanity. Nicky smiled. He laid a palm on her left cheek. "I heard the news." His hand felt warm, dry, leathery.

"Let's go inside." Lola led him to her office, shutting the ante-room door and locking it with a click. Nicky walked to the windows and looked down into the street. Lola joined him, listening to the whoosh of vehicles and the clacking of heels below. She watched Nicky's profile, noting the deep creases beside his mouth, the lines fanning out from the corner of his eye. After a while, he turned to her. Lola felt dismay at the sorrow and weariness etched into his face.

"I'm so sorry, Uncle Nicky. I know you and Lucky Wai were friends."

"Shush. I know you were there." He studied her face. "How are you, my girl?"

Lola shrugged. She held his gaze briefly before looking away.

"I've seen worse." The words were ashes in her mouth.

"Liar," said Aubrey.

"Liar," said Nicky gently. He regarded her in silence for a few moments. "Come, let's sit."

He led her to the clients' chairs in front of her desk. The buttery leather club chairs were cold to the touch. Lola picked up her smouldering cigarette from the ashtray. It disintegrated into a cloud of white and grey. She rubbed out the stub and flicked her fingers, trying to dislodge flecks of ash.

The older man sat, patted his pockets, pulled out a pack of his own. Lola gestured to the lighter on her desk. Nicky fetched her a new cigarette from the box on her desk and lit it for her. He had long, tapered fingers, yellowed at their tips.

Seeing his hands, Lola recalled all the times he'd played at that old stand-up piano in his front parlour. She heard his wry tenor clearly in her mind. She knew he'd been glossing over whatever he thought were objectionable lyrics for a young girl.

She remembered her father's laughter filling Nicky's house. She thought of her father's baritone and the innumerable times he'd picked her up and danced, harmonizing with his mentor as they sang old-fashioned love songs to her.

Lola took a long drag of her Egyptian, blew it out slow and steady, just as she'd been taught all those years ago by the very man sitting across from her.

Nicky watched her, all trace of humour gone from his weathered features. It caught her by surprise, how many years it had been since she'd seen him. Every one of them seemed carved into his face.

He watched her through the smoky haze, long enough to finish half his cigarette, then abruptly dropped his gaze. He cleared his throat.

Lola knew that noise. She'd heard it over and over and over again in her years learning the trade from him. It was how Nicky Lo began his case summaries.

"Here's the straight goods. The flatfeet say Tommy had debts. A big gambler like him always has debts. They say he must've run up against Skinny Shu or Fatman Chow. Got caught short and the sharks needed to shed blood, send a message, et cetera. Dead men don't pay up, though, so someone must've got overly excited. Shot him dead instead of just hurting him."

Nicky shook his head.

"But I don't buy it. Don't get me wrong. I'm not saying the kid didn't like the tables. He liked them plenty. He was out almost every night. What doesn't make sense to me is that he'd get caught short." Nicky glared, gripped the arms of the chair. "No way Sebastian would've let Tommy short anyone. Bad for his reputation.

"He had that kid on a very tight leash. Lucky had his differences with Tommy, especially lately, but he always said the kid never lost his head at the tables. He knew his limits and stuck to them. Always."

Lola considered where to start. "I didn't know you and Tommy Chu were so close."

Nicky shook his head. "Lucky was my best friend for a long time. I know quite a bit about Tommy." He stubbed out his cigarette in two abrupt movements.

She narrowed her eyes at him. "Have you been asked to help?"

Nicky shook his head. "Haven't you been listening? I don't think the coppers know the first damned thing about it. They've gone down the wrong trail already."

"Yes," Lola said slowly. "I understood what you said. But I was asking about the Chus."

"I want your help, my girl. Simple as that. I'm too old to do this one alone. I need to know if Lucky was the target, not Tommy."

"And my being a witness ought to be a bonus."

Nicky's entire face reddened. "I can't deny I thought of that." He captured her hand in his. "But I could've just asked you about that. I wouldn't drag you into this if I didn't have need of your skills. I trust you. Plain and simple."

Lola assessed him in silence.

Nicky let go of her hand, sat back. "Lucky and Tommy, they weren't getting along so well. Every time I managed to grab the kid for a chat, he was impatient. Oh, he was polite, don't get me wrong. But he clearly had better things to do than indulge an old man for his Ghost. And I know they were arguing all the time. Tommy tried to keep a lid on it, but his face, you know his face, so expressive. Everything he thought was on that boy's face."

"What was he thinking about?"

"You read the papers?"

She shrugged. "Just the *Herald*."

Nicky shook his head. "I mean the industry rag, the one that counts all the money, that one. *The Show*. It's been full of Tommy's latest Next Big Thing." Nicky's lips twisted. "The kid wanted to move away from the old stuff, Lucky's bread and butter for twenty-seven years. Move into that whole *kung fu* comic shtick."

Lola thought for a moment. "Who else knew Lucky didn't approve? Other than you?"

"Sebastian must have. Tommy told him everything. Trusted his older brother to manage all the business, and Seb does a good job. Better than good. He took that little toughie and made him the hottest comedian in the world."

"I thought Lucky did that for Tommy," said Aubrey. Lola repeated her Ghost's comment to Nicky.

The older man nodded, hastily greeted Aubrey.

"Lucky was his big break, sure, no argument there. But Lucky didn't know the first thing about the business side. Never did. He had the timing, the gags, the jokes, all that wonderful talent." Nicky paused. His eyes glistened.

He cleared his throat after a moment, leaned toward Lola.

"Listen, my girl, this is more than an old man trying to distract himself from grief. Lucky and I were old, old friends. I owe it to his memory. He deserves the truth and I need you to help me."

Lola sat back and pulled more blue-tinged smoke into her lungs. She stared at her old mentor. This man had taught her father everything about being a gumshoe and then, after Butch had died, he'd taught her, too.

She was already involved, wasn't she? Would it truly put her out to help the old man?

Aubrey murmured, "You can find other ways to work through your grief, Lola. Stay clear of this."

She blew out the smoke and extinguished her cigarette.

"Where do you want me to start?"

Nicky's face shed a decade as he grinned. "I knew you'd come through for me."

A sharp rapping rattled the outer room door.

"Only coppers knock like that." Nicky rose from his chair, gathered his hat.

Lola motioned for him to stay where he was. As she entered the anteroom, she saw two shadows against the frosted glass of her outer walls. They were trying the door knob.

Lola strode over and swung open the door.

"Miss Starke," said DI Charles Leung. "We have some more questions for you."

L ola opened the door wide and stepped back. Leung and Eng crowded into her small waiting room. Movement out of the corner of her eye told her Nicky had stepped out from her inner office. The two coppers glanced at him. Lola remained silent, watching. Leung spared her a quick glance, then reached into his inner suit pocket and produced a card.

"Detective Inspector Charles Leung, sir."

"DS Chester Eng." Eng nodded, raised his hat.

"Ah, yes, of course. The Cha Cha Twins," Nicky said. At the identical looks on their faces, he gave a small laugh. "Please, forgive me. I'm old and I often forget my manners. Nicky Lo, at your service. I apologize for the nickname. It helps my poor memory. Which clearly I need help with, as I should have recalled how much you dislike that handle." He smiled his best charmer.

Lola said, "What can I do for you, gentlemen?"

"Additional information has come forward about Mr. Chu and that mysterious car you saw." While Leung spoke, Eng took out his pencil and black notebook.

"I'm sorry, Inspector, but as you know, I'm to bring my Ghost to Central this morning. I'm cutting it close as it is. I'm not sure I trust how that will look to them."

"Actually, we are capable of talking to you and Mr. O'Connell right here and now." Leung smiled politely. "It will save you the trouble of heading downtown."

Lola looked from one to the other. Leung's smile remained bland. Eng stared back at her.

"And this wasn't on offer earlier..?"

"It was a test," said Eng. "I didn't believe you actually had a Ghost." He paused. "I didn't know it was possible, frankly, for Ghosts to...disappear." He looked past Lola's shoulder. "Mr. O'Connell, I presume. I'm DS Chester Eng."

"Pleasure," said Aubrey, tone flat.

Lola gestured to the seating scattered around the low table. "If you'll take your seats. I need my cigarettes." Lola shot Nicky a swift look as she left. She snatched a cigarette and lighter from her desk.

"Well, I should be going," said Nicky as Lola re-entered.

"Actually, Mr. Lo, we'd appreciate you staying as well. We understand you were once great friends with Mr. Wai."

"Please, let's call him Lucky. He hated his family name."

Leung inclined his head. "As you wish, of course."

Leung and Eng sat in the two armchairs closest to the inner office door, leaving the two-person sofa for Nicky and Lola. A simple black ashtray sat in the centre of the low table between them all. She pushed it closer to the coppers. They inclined their heads in unison. Leung pulled out a pack of cigarettes and a slim, silver lighter. Eng kept his hands free for his notebook and pencil.

"Yes, let's begin with your Ghost, then, Mr. O'Connell. I was, I admit, confused to hear that you were separated during the time of the shooting. How is this possible, exactly?" DI Leung waved his hand to extinguish his match.

Lola compared his reaction against Vivian's outright disbelief and Chin's baby-faced confusion, and she was forced to admire his calm professionalism.

Lola said, "I'm not sure how, Inspector. Aubrey is the Ghost and he says he can't explain such things to me."

"Well, you see, Miss Starke, our problem is that we don't know why we should believe you."

Lola shrugged. "I can't solve that one for you, Inspector. I suppose you might have better luck with someone at the Temple of Spectral Studies." She turned to Eng. "So, you're a Catcher?" Lola eyed him with undisguised appraisal. "Most Catchers I've seen don't look much better than a street drunk on a weekend binge. What's your secret?"

Eng smiled.

Aubrey said, "What do you want to ask me?"

Eng shifted his gaze slightly away from Lola. "Let's start with where you were."

"I have a special arrangement with Miss Starke. She is, as you may be unaware, not a willing Host."

Eng's eyebrows rose.

"We require...a break from time to time," Aubrey said. "So, I take myself away. I do not stay to spy on Miss Starke. On my honour. As with any haunting, she is quite attuned to me. She knows if I remain."

"And why do you haunt her at all?"

"I felt an obligation to my oldest friend—Miss Starke's mother. We've been friends since childhood. She's worked hard and long to mend the rift between herself and Lola. I thought I could help...protect Lola. For Grace's sake."

"And have you?" said Eng. His face remained impassive.

"No," said Lola.

"No," said Aubrey.

"So you remain at odds then," Eng said. "As well as you, Miss Starke, and your mother."

Lola shrugged.

Nicky spoke up. "Why are you so interested in Aubrey? Do you believe a Ghost was involved?"

Leung turned his attention from the tip of his cigarette. "Normally, Mr. Lo, we discourage discussing ongoing investigations."

Nicky made a rude noise. "I'm no reporter."

Leung inclined his head a fraction. "Exactly. As one investigator to another, I trust you to be discreet."

"I'm flattered you know of me."

"You've been in the business a long time, sir. Your name, if not your face, is well known in the department." Leung offered him a small smile.

Nicky chuckled. "Nicely done, Inspector. I'm not only reminded of my age, but you also managed to veil a threat in there."

Leung nodded again. "Even so." He blew out smoke, placed his cigarette carefully on the edge of the ashtray. "We know that car was no taxi cab. We know it was not a private driver, as all the hired drivers of the people at The Supper Club have already been accounted for. We are looking at all possibilities."

"Surely, you know a Ghost couldn't have been driving. Or shooting," Nicky said.

Leung cocked his head to the side. "Mr. Wai was just as integral to Mr. Chu's success as anyone. Might not he have been the target?"

Nicky pointed at them. "That's exactly what I've been thinking."

Leung considered Nicky for a moment. "Do you have information to share with us, Mr. Lo?"

Eng eyed Nicky with curiosity, his pencil at the ready.

Nicky explained his theory. "We should be looking at who would want to harm Lucky," he said. "This gambling idea is rubbish."

"Our job is to separate the rubbish from the truth, Mr. Lo. We must investigate all angles."

"Exactly," said Nicky. "That's my point." He looked at Lola.

Leung narrowed his eyes. Eng stirred.

"Mr. O'Connell, when did you, ah, reappear?" Eng said.

"Not until Lola was driving Miss Monteverde to the *Herald*, downtown," Aubrey said.

"And you know nothing of what Miss Starke sees while you are...separated?"

"No. Nothing."

A pause. "Are you sure? Nothing at all? No memories, no wisps of thought?"

"Nothing, Sergeant. You know there's no mind reading here. And on my honour, I'm no spying sneak. It would break whatever small amount of trust we've painstakingly built together. That would hardly serve me in helping mend the fences with her mother."

Eng sat back and shared a look with Leung. The Inspector sighed. "Looks like we're back to you, Miss Starke."

Lola raised an eyebrow.

"What made you note it in the first place?" said Leung.

"It screeched to a stop at the curb and sat. No one got out. No one honked." Lola paused, thinking hard. "The window on the passenger side was already wound down."

"Did either Mr. Chu or his companion recognize the car?"

"No. The car was there before they came out. I don't know that they even saw it."

"And you couldn't see anyone inside?"

"There was a glare on the windshield. I didn't look too closely. We figured it was an irate spouse, come to drag someone home. We were turning back to the beach when...the men exited."

"Did you know them? Why did you interact with them?"

"I know Stuey. We share an aunt, Vivian Mei. She was married many years ago to Stuey's uncle, Stanley Lim."

Leung gazed at her steadily. "You don't look like you'd be related to Vivian Mei."

"Is that a question?"

Leung raised his eyebrows. "Surely, this can't be the first time someone has questioned your relationship with the Mei sisters, with any Chinese, for that matter."

Lola raised her chin. "Vivian and her sisters helped raise me from the time I was four. They were our family, mine and my father's."

"Your father, Butch Starke, died when you were seventeen." Eng referred to his notebook. "He was a studio player, like your mother, but turned to other work after a couple of films. This was back about twenty, maybe twenty-five years? Is that about right?"

Lola shrugged. "He wasn't as interested in the studio business as my mother."

"He did all right, by all accounts. Worked for Wu studios, with you, Mr. Lo, before striking out on his own." Eng looked up from his notebook.

"He was a good man." Nicky nodded.

Leung said, "You said Miss Monteverde wanted an introduction, so you walked back toward the doors of the Club. But that took you back toward the car, which you say had arrived before the two men had exited the doors. Now you're sure you didn't happen to peek inside? During the course of your conversation with the men?"

Lola shook her head.

"Then?"

"Then, we went for a walk on the beach, the four of us. Ria had an early meeting so we came back to say goodbye. There was no valet, so Stuey went hunting for my car keys. He came back outside with a handful." She swallowed, cleared her throat. "The glass shattered. I just...pulled Ria down. When I looked up again, I saw the Packard tearing out. It turned all the way around and took off down the street." A muscle in Lola's jaw twitched. She took another pull at her cigarette.

"Which way did it go down the street?"

"Down to Ming and turned right."

"You're sure?"

"No," said Lola. She ignored the slight tremor in her hand as she raised her cigarette to her lips. "It was a chaotic situation. I wasn't thinking about the car." She inhaled flavoured smoke. She let it linger in her lungs.

Nicky said, "I'm curious, Inspector. What would you think about a parallel investigation?"

Leung looked at him sharply. "This is a police matter. I cannot stress strongly enough that it is in everyone's best interest to allow us to do our jobs. Unhindered. Miss Starke is, while a well-reputed private investigator, nonetheless still a civilian. She has neither the authority nor the resources that the police do. That we do."

Nicky puffed his chest out. "I've been a private gumshoe for longer than you've been out of nappies, gentlemen. I know no one else is better than Lola. I trained her myself. She's never had your resources nor your authority, true, but neither is she forced to pander to politics. She will find the truth and that's what matters to me."

The two detectives shared a quick glance.

Leung said, "We're sorry for your bereavement, Mr. Lo." He paused. "We may not be as emotionally tied to this case, but we are sworn officers of the law in Crescent City. Whatever politicking may be happening behind the scenes, the fact remains that *we* are the police. We are entrusted with solving this murder and bringing its perpetrators to justice. Everyone in this City has an interest in discovering who murdered Tommy Chu."

"What about Stuey? Who's got his case?" Lola's throat tightened.

"Two of our best in Homicide," Eng said.

"I see. He doesn't merit Major Crimes."

Leung said, "That's not our call. You cannot deny that Mr. Chu was an enormously talented entertainer in a city full of talented entertainers. He was a shining star in Crescent City. The brass decided that we're the best ones for this case."

"And who are you to argue."

"Lola," warned Aubrey.

Eng and Leung both shrugged this time. "We stand by our record. We don't stop until we've caught our man." Leung leaned forward. "If you get in our way, you will undoubtedly find that out the hard way."

SIX

Down the street from the Lucky Bamboo mah-jongg parlour, Lola ordered a fast meal of *wun-tun* noodles and *gai-lan* greens. The shop owners offered her coffee, but she declined in favour of strong black *boh-lae*. They seemed amused at her Cantonese. Lola ignored their good humour. She spoke just like every other native of the City—hard and clipped. Not her problem that all they saw was a golden-skinned *gwai* girl.

She left her car at the curb and walked briskly down to the faded columns that marked the entrance to Sammy Lu's establishment. Lola knew from experience that the door weighed much more than its appearance suggested. It swung open silently on well-oiled hinges and excellent balancing.

Lola paused to let her eyes adjust to the interior dimness. She smiled at the young hostess, seated left of the archway that led into the main gambling floor.

"Miss Starke." The woman grinned, swinging her chin-length, black hair. A large white orchid, with a deep pink interior, was nestled behind her left ear. The cap sleeves of her *cheong-sahm* showed off her lightly tanned, finely muscled arms. Another peasant like Uncle Nicky, Lola mused.

"Miss Minnie," said Lola. "Fetching smock."

Minnie looked down at her shimmering green dress and dark heels. "Uncle Sammy thought it a bit much, but he doesn't pay me

51

enough to dictate my wardrobe." Minnie shrugged. "What would a middle-aged man know about dresses and heels anyway?"

"Depends on the man."

"Suppose you're right." Minnie laughed. "Looking for Uncle?"

Lola nodded toward the main room. "Mind if I go in?"

Minnie's eyes widened as she noted Lola's white armband. "I'm sorry for your bereavement."

Lola thanked her and slid a bill inside the glass fishbowl sitting at Minnie's elbow on the small hostess station.

"Thank you, Mistress." Minnie's voice was breathless, vacant.

"It's frightening how quickly you do that."

Minnie's empty expression transformed into a genuine smile of delight. "You really think so? My agent thinks I need to take a class or three with some high-priced acting teacher, but I'm not sure it's anything more'n a money machine for her."

"Go with your gut. At least you'll always know who to blame when it all comes crashing down."

Minnie rolled her eyes.

The room on the other side of the archway was large and open. There were skylights and windows, bright colours and dark furniture. The oppressive feel of many gambling parlours was absent here, as was the usual presence of hulking security men in too-tight jackets and large shoes. Lucky Bamboo didn't need those. It had the owner's niece and nephew, both lightning-fast and skilled in myriad varieties of *kung fu*. They also doubled as hostess and floor manager. It was an elegantly economical solution.

The early afternoon sunshine slanted obliquely through a line of windows across from the archway. Lola meandered around the edges of the tables and patrons as far as she could before being forced by the configuration of tables and potted plants to cut across the length of the room. She sidestepped a cigarette girl and stopped in front of a plain brown door.

In keeping with the owner's modesty, a rectangle of wood nailed at about eye level on the door simply read "Manager." She rapped smartly on the door, listened for Sammy Lu's grumbled reply. The door opened and the man himself appeared. His black hair couldn't quite hide the bald spot at his crown. His clothes, brown and pale blue, were immaculately pressed. He smiled when he recognized Lola, gave her a quick bow, and ushered her inside.

Lu's office suited him. Straightforward furniture, pale walls, neatly lined books, a single decorative painting. He spoke as he showed her to a chair in front of his tidy desk.

"Ah, Miss Starke. How lovely to see you. Can I get you a refreshment? An ashtray? I'm sorry, but we don't carry your brand of cigarettes yet. My supplier has been having trouble with his shipments on the other end, you see." Lu sighed. "The dangers of import-export, I'm afraid. Have you had a chance to see our newest dealer? Cassandra is a lovely girl. Came over just seven months ago. Dreadful sea crossing, but she was last woman standing—so she tells me. Strong stomach. Inherited from her people. Coastal fishermen from up northern way."

Lola smiled. "No thank you, Mr. Lu. It's business today." The smile faded as thoughts of her morning crowded in. "I'm afraid I have some bad news." She supposed Lu might find her recitation clipped and emotionless, but she kept her voice as bland as she could. At the end, she paused, wondering at her own motives, before adding, "Stuey and I were family, after a fashion. His father's brother was once married to my Auntie Vivian."

Lu pulled out his pocket square and wiped at his brow. "That's terrible news, Miss Starke. I'm deeply sorry for your bereavement."

Lola thanked him. "The coppers are pushing hard on this one, so I understand. However, I've been asked by someone close to Lucky Wai to do some investigating as well."

Lu frowned. "Are you certain this is a good idea? Are you all right with this demand?"

Lola's smile was faint. "I'm just as interested in justice as anyone. I want to ask a favour of you."

Lu nodded. "Of course. Please."

Lola explained as briefly as she could. "So, I need to know everything you can find out about Tommy Chu's gambling habits. Stuey's too. Anything and everything."

"I'll have Benny and Minnie help me."

"And please be discreet. I don't want the coppers giving you trouble."

Sammy Lu inclined his head. "We are in complete agreement on that, Miss Starke. Complete agreement."

❦

Lola took a deep breath as she drove down Orchard Street. A virtual sea of trees surrounded her, their fragrance heady and welcome after the layered exhaust of the City's eastern edges. She was grateful she'd thought to put on a scarf against the wind's tugging. It would have been such a shame to have left the top up on the car. She knew it would be brief, but she let herself enjoy the sensations as she drove past the acres of fruit trees that gave the street its name.

She caught glimpses of orchard workers dressed in green coveralls and dark green wellingtons. Under the June sun, every worker wore a wide-brimmed, conical straw hat. Trucks threw up billowing clouds of dust as they crisscrossed the orchard's internal roads.

Just as the low-slung hills on the northeastern horizon loomed, Lola slowed her car down as she came to a four-way intersection, manned by signs. She turned left onto Reservoir Road, away from the orchards. Harmony Lane was another eight miles west.

"What'll you do when the coppers are on to you?" said Aubrey.

"I've hardly been underfoot. If anything, I'm performing a civic duty."

"You may try for insouciance, but the stakes are too high for your usual brand of imprudence. They could take away your license, charge you with obstruction."

"You obtained a law degree somewhere along the way, did you?"

"Step carefully, that's all I'm saying. The Twins were surprisingly open with you and Nicky this morning. I don't trust it."

Lola shrugged. "This isn't my first rodeo. I know how to avoid the bull's horns."

As she drove on, the rural feel of Orchard Street disappeared and houses lined the northern side of Reservoir Road. Two-storey homes stood behind high walls and weathered wooden gates with iron hinges. The walls, made of baked bricks and painted bright white, shone in the mid-afternoon sunlight. Peaked, wooden archways spanned the gates, providing shelter from the rare rainfall or shade from the sun. At this time of day, the sidewalks were populated mostly by older *amahs* with their small charges.

Harmony Lane was short, just a block-and-a-half of well-tended homes that ended at a large park. The fences and walls were a little smaller than those on Reservoir Road, but the profusion of lush, tall trees more than made up for this. Lola drove slowly past the Lims' address and found a place for her roadster another three houses down the Lane. She got out, took off her scarf, and shook out her hair. She straightened her clothes, took a deep breath, and walked back toward the house.

People passed through the gate in twos, threes, some fours. Many of them glanced at her. Most, after seeing the white armband, looked at her face. Lola gauged it was fifty-fifty whether they glanced away or turned down their mouths in disapproval.

She lifted her chin.

As she walked through the opened gates, Lola noted the gleaming iron rings on the doors, their patina speaking of age and regular polishing. Strips of white cloth, tied to the overhanging corners of the wooden archway, twisted and flapped gently, catching the eye. Next to the open archway stood a long banner of coarse, unadorned white linen. Its top width was secured to a wooden pole anchored into a sturdy base. The bottom of the banner was attached at its middle to the pole behind it. Its corners snapped in the slight breeze.

A brilliant red Japanese maple stood in the centre of the rectangular courtyard. The Red Emperor, Lola recalled. The last time she'd been here, it had stood just past her shoulders.

"It's been a while, hasn't it?" said Aubrey quietly.

"I'm surprised you'd know." She looked up, searching for the top of the tree.

"You came with your father, isn't that right?" Lola remained silent. "Well, I remember Grace being concerned about his health then. He'd just begun treatments with Betta, if I recall."

"He wanted to visit with Uncle Keun. Sit in the garden. Be still and quiet." She paused, now staring sightlessly at the bright red leaves. "It was after the first treatment."

Lola craned her neck to look up through the maple's sun-dappled canopy. She took a deep breath, briefly closed her eyes, then brought her attention back to earth, exhaling. The benches and table that normally surrounded the tree had been removed, replaced by the tall wooden boxes meant for the funereal offerings.

Lola watched a group of three middle-aged women approach. They eyed her with curiosity as they emptied their bags of oranges into the boxes.

Lola cursed. She'd forgotten her offering in the car. She turned on her heel, hoping she wouldn't run into Keun and Liliane before she returned.

"Watch out," Aubrey said.

Too late. She turned straight into a hard shoulder. A man swore. Slightly dazed, Lola stepped back as she pushed the stranger away. The man swore again before he stalked away, glaring. Lola heard him mutter under his breath about clumsy, ill-mannered *gwai*.

"Easy there, Miss Starke."

Lola looked over to her left. She kept her tone cool and civil. "Bednarski." She rubbed at her forehead, addressed the other man standing with him. "Marks." Realization dawned. "They gave you Stuey Lim."

The first man doffed his hat. He was broad-shouldered, with a square head and no discernible neck. His suit jacket was a little rumpled, the brim of his hat just a tad misshapen. His green eyes were kind. "My condolences on your bereavement. I understand you and Mr. Lim were related."

His partner stood silently, watching Lola. His usual hooded expression was tempered, however, perhaps by the solemn occasion. Lola couldn't begin to imagine Marks compassionate.

Lola guessed these two had been up since they'd been called to Stuey's death scene, yet Marks showed none of the long hours since. His brown hat was crisp, the felt looking freshly brushed. His light-weight tan suit showed no crimps; his trousers held their knife-edged creases. While Bednarski's chin was slightly shadowed by stubble, Marks looked newly shaven. She contemplated the thin scar that ran from the left corner of his mouth to just below his left ear. He watched her assessing him, expression unfathomable.

Lola inclined her head slightly. "I forgot my oranges in the car. Please excuse me." They stepped aside. Lola heard them murmuring.

When she returned, the two *gwai* coppers were standing with Keun and Liliane Lim. Lola respectfully placed her oranges into the boxes around the maple. She held tightly to the now-empty bag as it fluttered in the light breeze. She looked upward again. Stepping within the circle of the funeral receptacles, she placed a hand on the trunk of the tree, motionless. She ignored the steps of other mourn-ers. She ignored the whispers and mutterings. Listening to the thump of oranges landing in the mourning receptacles, she felt the smooth bark of the maple's trunk beneath her hand, and breathed.

Then, she turned away.

SEVEN

C ustom required its due.

Lola saw with dismay that every pot, basket, and planter of Keun's beautiful flowers had been covered with black cloth. The servants had moved them away from the north side of the courtyard and clustered them in the southeastern corner. Only an upper edging of green ivy remained along the northern wall.

In the centre of the covered plants stood a small stone birdbath. Lola watched a trio of sparrows hopping in the water, nattering at one another. The chatty birds took wing, swooping and chasing each other. Lola craned her neck to track them until they were lost to distance and the brightness of the sun.

As she turned back, Lola caught a tail of grey cloth, flapping just inside the main door of the house, tucked into the northwestern corner. Banners of white linen hung from the second storey windows, their dark shutters folded neatly against the sides of the frames. The grey cloth peeked out again. Lola recalled a large, rectangular mirror in the entrance.

"What's wrong?" said Aubrey.

"The mourning covering. It's come undone from the mirror in the house."

"I'm sure the servants will sort it out."

After a pause, Lola continued toward the mourning area.

A large rectangle of black cloth hung on the northern wall, centred behind the casket, laid atop a dark teak table. There were three rows of mourning benches, draped in black linen and split by a central aisle. Mourners sat, facing the casket, murmuring prayers or sharing small talk. Some were silent. There were a few white armbands among them. Lola didn't know those faces.

She supposed they'd be thinking the same of her.

Wreaths of white flowers, supported on easels, lined the space around the central mourning area. An occasional deep blue iris was nestled among the white blooms. Condolences were written in stark black calligraphy on ribbons of orange silk trailing from the wreaths.

Lola walked solemnly up the aisle to the simple dark wood casket on the teak table. The wall covering fluttered at its hem. Lola felt the blood rush to her ears. She closed her eyes, recalling the image of the Red Emperor as she stood beneath its leaves.

She exhaled, forced away the images of glass bits glittering on a bloodied scalp, and looked down at Stuey Lim.

He was bound in broad strips of unbleached linen. The smell of anise and rosemary, soaked into the linen strips, countered the odour of decay. Lola had an urge to touch the linen strips, to feel the hard shell that now cocooned his remains.

A lacquered death mask rested on his face. Smooth depressions marked the eyes. A bland carving of nose, mouth, cheeks, forehead. Just enough to denote that the dead had been a man. The mask was white, unadorned.

"A straightforward reincarnation then," murmured Aubrey.

She tore her gaze away. It was bad luck to dwell on the face of death.

Lola forced herself to breathe normally. The sharp scent of the wrappings mingled with a thick, ashy smell. She looked over at a squat tripod brazier made from burnished bronze. Thin sticks of incense stood upright, anchored in pale grey sand. They would be kept burning, stick after stick, for the required forty-four hours until the cremation ceremony. It was one of the jobs of the monk, along with the funerary chant.

She let herself hear it then, the monk's voice. A monotonal drone, the words like a river of sound without discernible meaning.

She made herself relax, unclenching her fists.

"I'm sorry," said Aubrey, voice low. "This must be difficult. The memories."

"Memories?" Lola stepped away from the casket and continued walking beyond the mourning benches.

"Your father."

"I don't have any memories of his funerary rites." Lola tried to keep her tone calm, dispassionate. "He forbade me to attend and I missed the cremation as well." She couldn't avoid the bitterness, then decided it didn't matter. She had every right to resent the exclusion.

"I...didn't know that."

"Why would you? I doubt Mother would've gossiped about it. Even she wouldn't do that." Lola shrugged, trying to rid her shoulders of tension. "The Aunties took care of everything. And Betta, of course."

"You were...seventeen, weren't you? Perhaps he thought to spare you the pain." Another pause. He said quietly, "I can imagine I wouldn't want my child to see me that way, ravaged by illness."

"Don't," she said flatly.

Lola realized she'd been staring at the young monk. She turned away.

Seeing Stuey's parents a few feet away, she straightened her spine and walked over. The two detectives stood with them, murmuring in low tones. When they saw her approaching, Bednarski nodded to her and thanked the Lims. Marks inclined his head. Lola watched them step away. They may have made an odd-looking pair, but they moved with the same self-assured grace.

She forced her attention to the grieving couple in front of her.

"Lola." Liliane Lim's eyes filled. Her iron grey hair was pulled back into a tight bun. Large, dark eyes crinkled at the corners as she smiled through her tears. Lola felt the other woman's sharp, delicate bones as they hugged. "We're so glad you've come."

"I'm so sorry, Auntie." Her mouth suddenly dry, Lola swallowed. Hard. "I'm sorry for your bereavement."

Lola embraced Keun next, then kissed his cheek. He looked searchingly into her eyes. He shared Stuey's hairline, with its slight central peak, and a long aquiline nose. His eyes were kind despite the red rims and dark circles. Lola blinked, looked away.

The couple wore white linen. Loose tunics with traditional frog closures and high collars; flowing, wide-legged pants; and simple white cloth shoes with flexible soles. Lola towered over them both.

"Thank you for coming." Keun's voice was as gravelly as Lola remembered.

She scrabbled for something kind to say in return. Her thoughts stuttered. She looked down.

Liliane squeezed Lola's hand. "You were there when it happened. We know."

Lola shook her head, squeezing her eyes shut for a moment. "I am so sorry, Auntie." She blinked rapidly, struggling to keep calm.

"Detective Inspector Marks tells us you and your friend tried to help them. Stuey and Tommy."

Lola shook her head again.

"Will you sit with us?" said Liliane. "Just for a while."

Lola hesitated. "I don't know that that's a good idea."

Keun took her arm and led her to a front bench. "They've already seen the armband. They can say what they want."

Liliane sat first, motioning for Lola to join her. Keun waited until they were settled before sitting to Lola's right.

A large bowl of oranges, surrounded by wreaths, sat on a small table to the left of the benches. To the right, the monk kept the incense burning in a metal brazier. Lola watched grey smoke curling upward, into the bright sky.

An errant breeze swept into the courtyard. The incense smoke unfurled toward the casket before dissipating like tattered flags. Lola heard Liliane take a long, deep breath. The older woman let go of Lola's hand. She rummaged in her pocket and came up with a key attached to an odd metal ring with a short chain.

"This is the spare to his home." Liliane took Lola's hand and dropped the key into her palm. "Nicky said you were helping him."

"I—"

Liliane shook her head. "No, take it. This is our way to help." She wiped at her eyes with a crumpled handkerchief. "We're grateful for your efforts."

Lola looked down at the shiny key and its fob. It wasn't just a metal ring. It was an ancient coin, its centre an empty square surrounded by faint bumps, remnants of old characters. Lola rubbed them with a thumb. She sighed, closed her palm around the key and its coin. "Where is it? His home?"

Keun spoke quietly. "The Clipper on Peninsula Drive. It's a tall, beautiful building, just between Yew and Birch. He'd just moved there in February. He was so proud, said it was the premiere apartment building in the City." He cleared his throat, wiped his eyes. "Do you know it?"

"Yes." Lola paused, feeling uneasy. "Yes, I do." She looked up from her contemplation of Stuey's apartment key. "I live there, too."

The Lims shared a glance.

Liliane said, "A sign then."

Keun nodded.

Aubrey murmured, "Of good or ill?"

Lola shivered in the warm afternoon air.

❧

Evening laid claim to the sky when three strangers appeared at the courtyard entrance.

The two bruisers were obvious. Smashed noses and shoulders wide enough to span two of Liliane Lim. They kept their hats on. They may as well have been wearing signs that said "sugar boys." The *Tongs* weren't particularly known for subtlety.

Lola narrowed her eyes at the man standing between them.

Another gangster out of Central Casting. Taller by an inch or so than his guards, his suit was sharply tailored and subtly sheened, buttoned to showcase his lean body. He doffed his hat as he scanned the courtyard, revealing thick black hair neatly parted on the side and hawkish features dominated by a tall, straight nose. Lola guessed some mixed heritage in the man's background.

Keun stared for a moment before walking over to greet the new-comers. Lola scanned the people around her and was relieved to see Liliane far from the entrance. Stuey's mother stood in the doorway of the house, holding on to the doorframe with one hand, watching the gate with a curious expression.

Lola pushed away from the spot of wall she'd claimed between the black-draped planters and went to intercept Keun.

"No Ghosts," said Aubrey. Lola nodded.

The low courtyard chatter had died. The other mourners averted their gazes from the new arrivals.

The monk's chanting droned on.

Lola stepped up beside Keun just as he reached the entrance. "May I help you, gentlemen?" Keun said.

"Mr. Lim," said the tall one, "I am sorry for your bereavement. I am a friend of your son's." He produced a card, held it in both hands and bowed slightly, offering the card.

"Ah, thank you...Mr. Kam." Keun squinted at the card in the dimming light.

Kam turned to Lola. "Miss..?"

"Starke," she said. "A distant cousin."

The tall man bowed, fully this time. "My condolences on your bereavement."

"Won't you come in?" asked Keun. "All of you?"

Kam waved at his companions. They melted back toward the gate and disappeared into the deepening gloom. An expression flickered over Keun's face, too fast for Lola to read.

"They'll wait outside the gate," said Kam.

"They are welcome inside," said Keun.

"Thank you, sir, but they are better suited to be out there." Kam smiled politely, showing bright white teeth.

"My son would hardly have wanted...guards at his ceremony."

"I understand, Mr. Lim. However, my men will stay outside." His smile included Lola this time.

The sound of rustling cloth and footsteps broke the tense silence.

A tall boy, dressed in servants' mourning grey, moved around the courtyard, lighting the torches for the night's observance. A surge of sound invaded the space as people resumed their conversations and movements. The monk's voice threaded through the deepening twilight.

"It's time for the evening tea, husband."

Lola started at Liliane's voice.

"Mrs. Lim." Kam bowed. He offered her the ritual phrase and introduced himself, adding, "I was honoured to call Stuey my friend. We met at my club."

"Do you own a night club, sir?" asked Liliane.

Kam nodded. "Yes. It's called Figment. I was honoured to have Stuey play there frequently."

To Lola's surprise, Liliane nodded. "Stuey mentioned it." She gestured toward the tree. "You are welcome to pay your respects."

Kam inclined his head, murmured his thanks. He walked toward the towering maple, a netted bag of oranges in hand.

Lola stifled a curse. Where had those come from?

Keun gripped his wife's arm as the couple led Kam to make his offering. Lola trailed two steps behind. There were perhaps a dozen other mourners in the courtyard. Every last one of them seemed to be looking anywhere but at Kam.

"Can't blame them," said Aubrey. "Anyone willing to disrupt a mourning ceremony cannot be considered reasonable. Not that anyone expects a gangster to be reasonable," he muttered.

Lola imagined the Lims were likely of a similar mind as they watched Kam place oranges into the receptacles. He stood a moment, silently staring up at the tree. Lola felt an uncomfortable twinge watching him mirror her own earlier action.

The Lims accompanied him from the maple tree to the mourning benches and then up the aisle to the casket. They stayed a few feet back as Kam stood over their son. Liliane's profile was serene, composed. Keun had an arm around his wife's shoulders, a fine tension in his lean frame betraying his unease.

Kam moved to the brazier, its shallow bowl glowing with lit incense sticks. He laid the tip of an unlit stick on the brick smouldering in the sand. Once it caught fire, he held the incense between his palms, waving it slightly to make it smoulder instead of burn. Facing the body, he raised his hands and lowered his forehead until they touched briefly, repeating the action twice more until there was a haze of white-grey smoke around his head. He murmured a final time and inserted the incense into the sand surrounding the brick.

Kam was solemn as he approached the Lims again. Lola stepped up to stand behind Liliane. She saw Keun's knuckles whiten.

"I apologize if this has brought discomfort to you, Mr. Lim." Kam's gaze swept the courtyard. "Although, I can't say I'm a follower of such things." Voices around them lowered, some conversations dying out altogether. "Still, I understand how some of an older generation might take my presence as...ominous."

"If you were truly concerned," said Lola, "then why come at all, Mr. Kam?"

His expression remained sombre as he focussed on her. "Aren't we in the same boat, Miss Starke? Some would say the same of you."

"That's nothing I can help."

"As if being born *gwai* is any better than choosing to make one's living a certain way?" Kam shook his head. "No, I don't think that holds much water with those inclined to judge such things." He paused, assessed Lola with a clinical eye. Then he shrugged.

"I can change my lifestyle at any time. You, however, will always be what you are."

"Enough," said Keun. "She is family, not bad luck." He released Liliane, straightened to his full height. "Sir, thank you for your condolences and your prayers. I'm afraid, however, that your presence is upsetting our guests. I must insist that you leave."

"My deepest apologies." Kam bowed again. "However, there is another matter I must bring up, Mr. Lim."

Liliane stepped toward Kam. She barely came to the man's chest. Lola wanted to step forward, but the calm expression on Liliane's face stopped her. She'd only undercut the older woman's bravery. So she schooled her features into her best likeness of calm and forced herself to breathe slowly.

"What do you want, Mr. Kam?" said Liliane, her voice firm.

"To pay my respects, Mrs. Lim, as I said." He searched her face, his dark eyes glittering. "And to retrieve a certain item Stuey promised me but never delivered upon. A pocket watch. A very meaningful gift. Stuey was never without it."

"What?" Aubrey's outburst was equal parts anger and confusion.

"And what gives you its ownership?" said Liliane softly. She gestured for her husband to come closer. He did, taking her hand. Lola saw the tendons in Keun's neck. Her heart rate sped up as her own rage gathered.

"Your son used it as collateral, I'm afraid."

Keun pulled his wife back. "This is outrageous. This is not the time for such things. You must leave. Now."

Lola stepped forward. "Shall I escort you out, Mr. Kam?"

Lola felt Liliane's hand on her arm, cool and dry. "Our son has barely been gone fifteen hours." She paused, the tremor in her voice lingering in the short silence. "Sorting through his things has not been a priority. We shall telephone if we have something for you."

Kam assessed Keun and Lola with calm detachment. He nodded. "I'm grateful cooler heads have prevailed, Mrs. Lim. I apologize for the urgency, but business waits on no man's passing." He stared at Lola for several seconds. She held his gaze steadily. A twitch raised a corner of his mouth the barest fraction.

"I shall be in touch again."

He bowed deeply, then walked away. The crunch of his shoes echoed off the walls. Once he cleared the gate, the only sound was the monk chanting, his voice a low, resonant wave.

EIGHT

D o you suppose that monk is good enough to counter Kam's appearance?" said Aubrey.

Lola ground her teeth. "Just shut it, will you? I've had enough of your worrying. He's not any more bad luck than I am." She paused, waiting for a silver coupe to pass, then turned left into her parking garage with an awkward bump.

"Of course you're not bad luck, Lola, but that doesn't mean the quality of that monk isn't paramount."

Lola's knuckles whitened as she gripped the steering wheel. She forced herself to loosen up as she drove to her assigned spot.

She hated to admit it, but Aubrey was likely right.

Funerals were vital to the continued existence of the departed one's soul. Reincarnation or Ghosthood. Either choice was revered. What could not be tolerated was something to disrupt the soul's journey. Strict adherence to the intricate funerary rites ensured that souls went where they were meant to go. Entire schools within monasteries were dedicated to the study of funerary rites. If a monk made a mistake, it could mean the annihilation of a soul.

She shivered at the potential disaster the Lims had avoided.

"Still, for all of his posturing and implied threats, he didn't try to disrupt the chant in any obvious way. Didn't even look at the monk, far as I could see. His grief seemed real." Aubrey was silent for a few beats. "Perhaps he truly was a friend."

Lola jerked the car to a stop.

"Whether or not you buy into that sort of thing," Aubrey said, "having both you and that gangster at the viewing is...unfortunate. I'm afraid the Lims' reputation might not survive."

Lola slammed the car door shut and strode to the elevator.

If Frederick, the lift operator, found it odd that Lola asked for the eighth floor rather than the eighteenth, he didn't show it. He nodded, closed the doors, and pushed buttons. He stayed silent during the smooth ride up. Aubrey exchanged greetings with Marcella, Frederick's Ghost. Lola saw the old operator's face light up with a smile as he listened to his wife converse with Aubrey.

Lola kept her sour mood tightly reined in.

At the door to unit 818, Lola paused to take a deep breath.

"Must've paid top dollar for this unit," said Aubrey. "Most auspicious number on the floor."

"I doubt someone committed a double murder for an apartment."

"Stranger things have happened. You should at least check to see who's on the waiting list."

"Or get the flatfoots on it."

"Fair enough, considering you're not on the job officially."

Lola rubbed the coin Stuey used as his fob. She exhaled in a whoosh, and used the key to unlock his door.

She stepped into a small entryway with a closet to the right and a polished wood floor in a parquet design. Lola skimmed over her tired reflection in the mirrored closet doors with a grimace. She peered down a hallway to the left. A claw-footed bath in the first room and a couple of open doorways beyond.

She turned to the living room. Plump sofa and matching armchairs, all upholstered in deep green fabric.

A wall of windows across from the door.

Thick blue drapes had been pulled back, leaving panels of white sheers. Lola bunched up a handful of white cloth, creating an opening. She fought the urge to lean her forehead against the cool, pristine glass.

Blinking away the grit in her eyes, she scanned the streets crisscrossing the entirety of the City before her. Cars, like bright-eyed insects, scuttled on lit paths. Some dark buildings stood here and there, voids in the brightness. And, as ever, beyond them all, dark water glinting in the distance.

She experienced an unsettling familiarity, comparing this with her own view exactly ten floors up. With an inward sigh, she turned away.

"It's hard to fathom that you never saw him in the building," said Aubrey softly. "Although, as a musician, he must've kept even later hours than you."

Windows at her back now, Lola surveyed Stuey's home.

It was an open plan, with enough counters, furniture and half-walls to create nice flow patterns for good *chi*. The kitchen was tucked into a far corner to her right, an eating nook on the window side. A formal dining area with a six-seater in pale wood and ivory slip-covered chairs surrounding it. The chandelier was beautiful: crystals and frosted glass tulips. Lola flipped its switch to see its facets sparkle.

After a moment, she turned it off.

"He liked beautiful things," said Aubrey. "Eclectic too."

The paintings included bright abstracts as well as line drawings of people and still life objects, and even daguerreotypes from previous centuries. There were traditional jade sculptures scattered through the space, as well as ceramic and bronze figurines.

Lola walked into the kitchen, opened a few cupboards. Simple bowls and plates. Wooden chopsticks and ceramic spoons. Utilitarian mugs and tea cups. The electric ice box contained nothing, not even ice. A mound of lemons sat in a cut crystal bowl on the counter. Farther down, there was a vibrant white orchid, its waxy green leaves trailing over a faceted planter.

Skimming her fingers across the counter, Lola crossed to the hallway and paused. She turned to face the windows and realized there were living things everywhere.

Three jade plants in square golden-hued pots kept the furniture company in the sitting area. Another white orchid, small, accented with pink, perched atop the receiving table in the entryway. An orange tree, pruned into a shrub, took up space in the corner beside the wall of windows. As if seeing it had brought it into existence, Lola smelled its bright citrus tang.

She entered the hallway, rubbing at the pain in her chest.

In the bathroom, a large tub, black and white mosaic tiles, a white shower curtain tied into a column opposite the taps. A thick yellow towel hung haphazardly over the lip of the pedestal sink. Lola searched the small room, her eyes lighting on every detail. She checked behind the door. Nothing. Not even a bathrobe.

Lola imagined him walking around his home, towel wrapped around his hips. She rubbed her stinging eyes.

"You looking for something in particular?" said Aubrey.

Lola moved down the hall.

Next was a bright little room with yellow walls and five potted plants. A sturdy desk and chair shared space with two walls of bookshelves. She studied Stuey's taste in reading material. Tooled leather tomes mixed in with cowboy dime novels.

Lola glanced at the desk, ignored the chair. Blotter, pen, mono-grammed stationery, telephone. A brown leather appointment book laid open to the current week.

Stuey's writing was a surprise: spiky and inelegant, hurried. Lola flipped pages quickly.

"Why use English?" She cocked her head, thinking.

Pushing the chair back, Lola shifted until she faced the appoint-ment book squarely. She went back to the start of the month and scrutinized each entry.

"Plenty of 'TC's," murmured Aubrey. "Almost every day. No sur-prise there." The occasional sound of rustling paper filled the space as Lola continued turning pages. "Who or what is 'EV'? There seems to be a good number of those."

Lola stopped paging through the book. She turned to the first of the year and began again. "Looks like this 'EV' character was at least in his life as far back as the start of the year. Perhaps an old friend. Or a long-standing, regular appointment?" She flipped pages in si-lence. "Looks fairly regular. At least once a week. More in the last four months." She tapped the page. "A Healer, or a doctor? He didn't look ill and the times seem too irregular."

"You'll have to see if you can find his old books."

Lola pulled out a small notebook and her pen. She jotted down the letters as well as other names and sets of initials. She tapped her chin with the end of her pen. "No v's in Chinese," she muttered.

"Still plenty of *gwai* with those initials," said Aubrey. "Or *mixed breeds*, as they say so charmingly." A pause. "Person, place, or thing?" he mused.

Lola stared at the bookshelf. She gradually refocussed on the spines facing her, smiling a bit at one title: Small Cowboy, Big Horse.

"I'm sure he had plenty women in his life," she said. "If it *is* a relationship, it took a lot to keep it out of the gossip rags. Dating *gwai* or a half-*gwai* can still raise a stink."

She reluctantly turned away from the appointment book, still pondering the possibilities in those initials. She re-entered the hall and smelled fresh oranges. The last room loomed to her left. She huffed, forcing herself to cross the last few feet, at odds with her own emotions.

His bedroom was masculine, warm, elegant. It reflected Stuey's personality, just as she'd have guessed. She noted the untidy pile of clothes in an armchair, ties trailing over its back. She lightly touched a silver and jade cufflink on top of the teak dresser. The dark blue draperies had been pushed back here as well. Lola tapped the footboard of the unmade bed as she crossed to the long wall with its set of double doors.

She opened them up.

"I guess it's a lady friend, after all," said Aubrey.

Lola stared at the neat line of women's wear hung up in the closet. Day dresses and petite jackets, tailored trousers and silk blouses.

"Definitely a woman," said Aubrey, sounding distracted. "These are much too small for him."

Lost in her thoughts, Lola heard the scrape of a key in the front door too late. She went still.

Two sets of feet. Heavy treads. The door clicked shut. She heard a cough.

Lola quietly made her way to the door, peeked down the hallway. Bednarski rubbed his face with both hands. Marks placed his hand on the other man's shoulder. "I'll take the rooms," he said, his voice kind.

Lola held her hands out as she stepped out from the bedroom. "Don't shoot," she said, keeping her voice low and calm.

Marks whirled to face her, his hand on his revolver. Bednarski placed a hand on Marks's shoulder.

"Miss Starke." Bednarski's voice was bland.

"My apologies for startling you," Lola said.

"What are you doing here?" Marks narrowed his eyes. His cheeks went red. It might have been embarrassment, but Lola knew better. She saw a muscle twitching at his temple. The thin scar along the left side of his face stretched, drawing Lola's eye down to his mouth.

"His parents gave me their spare key."

"That's not an answer."

Lola exhaled, looked beyond them to the living room.

"I don't know." She clenched her jaw at the sound of her own ambivalence.

"Leung and Eng gave us the update," said Bednarski. He eyed her levelly. "You and Mr. Lo."

Lola nodded. "Uncle Nicky knew Lucky Wai a long time."

"That doesn't mean you're on this case," said Marks, his tone flat.

Bednarski nodded, his expression thoughtful. "But I'm willing to share information. With some caveats."

Lola blinked. "Did you just say 'caveats'?"

"Conditions," said Bednarski, "that are not negotiable."

"Go on." She glanced at Marks. He'd clenched his jaw so tight that Lola could see the muscles in his neck cording.

"I'm willing to assume we're on the same side," said Bednarski. "So I'm willing to help you if you help us. But no illegal activities, Miss Starke, of any kind. Whatsoever. Understood?"

Marks rolled his shoulders, stretched his neck.

"That's not a problem." Lola stared at Marks a second more before returning her gaze to his partner. "What do you really want?"

"I want to know everything you're doing. You and Mr. Lo. I want to know your leads, your contacts, your next steps."

Lola paused. "And what do we get in return?"

"I share information with you."

"That you deem worth sharing," said Lola.

Bednarski inclined his head.

"We're the coppers, Starke," said Marks. "We don't give out information about an ongoing investigation."

Lola waved a hand impatiently. "Don't try playing it loose. You want to keep tabs on Uncle Nicky and me. Make sure we're not blundering into anything."

"If that's how you want to look at it," said Bednarski. His face remained bland, impassive. "Those are the conditions."

"And if I refuse?"

Bednarski shrugged his wide shoulders. "I become less inclined to be friendly when next we meet."

"Do I have to say it?" Marks glowered.

Lola shook her head. "I get the gist."

"And if you continue on this case, you'll be meeting up with us. A lot," said Bednarski.

"In all sorts of unexpected times and places," said Marks.

Lola gave them what they expected. She made an unhappy face and pretended to consider her options.

"You're not seriously thinking about it," said Aubrey.

"Fine," she said to Bednarski. She glanced at Marks. "You should speak with the building manager, Miss Ting. Get names on the waiting list for this apartment."

The detectives shared a look. Bednarski shrugged. "Stranger things have happened."

Marks grimaced, taking out a notebook and pen. "Chinese superstitions," he mumbled, shaking his head.

"Is it true your Ghost wasn't with you this morning?" asked Bednarski. "He didn't see anything?"

Lola nodded, shrugged.

"You been down yet to Central?" asked Marks.

"The Cha Cha Twins said Eng would fix it. He took Aubrey's statement."

Bednarski's mouth twitched. "Do not tell me you called them that to their faces, Miss Starke."

Lola shook her head, lips twitching. "But Uncle Nicky did."

Even Marks raised a corner of his mouth at that.

Bednarski sighed, took a look around the apartment, stared out the windows at the City beyond.

"After you two left the viewing," Lola said, "a smooth-suited tough called Philip Kam showed up with two gorillas in tow. He claimed friendship with Stuey, but then leaned on the Lims for a pocket watch of some kind. Said it was collateral for something." She explained what Liliane had promised to get Kam to leave.

The detectives exchanged another look. Marks shrugged. Bednarski rubbed the back of his neck with a large, thick hand. Lola heard the scratch of stubble against skin. Or maybe it was his starched collar. He said, "Never heard of him. We'll ask Vice."

Marks brushed past Lola and headed down the hallway.

"Did you happen to take any of his old appointment books?" said Lola.

Bednarski assessed her with a flat gaze.

He said, "I know you and the deceased were cousins, after a fashion, but it wasn't by blood. How close were you?"

"Not very. Hadn't seen him in over five years. Whenever the tribute performance to the Mei Triplets was, at the Old Blossom Theatre."

"And yet you live in the same building."

Lola's cheeks flushed. "The first I heard, when his parents gave me this key. Guess he moved in about five months ago."

"And last night? What did you talk about?"

Lola levelled a clear gaze at Bednarski. She heard Marks opening drawers. Then hinges creaked.

"This your first time in here?" she said.

Bednarski's face tightened. "If it were, you'd be in for a much longer night."

"Why'd you come back? Forget something?"

Bednarski glanced down the hallway. He returned his attention to Lola. "What did you and Lim talk about last night?"

Lola considered the big man's expression. She shrugged. "Tommy wanted an introduction to Vivian Mei. Stuey thought I had a better sho—" Lola stopped, tried again. "He thought I had a better chance than he did at getting one."

"Why?" Bednarski watched her, face impassive.

"Auntie Viv doesn't like Stuey." She glanced down the hall at the sound of a door slamming shut.

Bednarski sighed again. "Miss Starke, we're all tired here. This'll go a lot faster if you'd just give me the goods straight." He raised his brows.

Lola stared at him for a moment. She fought the temptation to throw out a cutting retort. A series of thumps came from down the hallway. She focussed on Bednarski, ignored the sounds of Marks rummaging in a dead man's things.

"Vivian Mei was married to Stanley Lim, Uncle Keun's brother. It ended poorly. For her, at any rate. Stuey has—I mean," she swallowed thickly, "he had the misfortune to look just like Uncle Stanley. Every time she saw Stuey, Vivian was reminded that Stanley was a no-good, lying, cheating dog who didn't even have the decency to give her any children." Lola crossed her arms. "That may not be a direct quotation, but damned close."

"Where's Stanley Lim now?"

"He died years ago. I don't recall when."

Bednarski considered Lola for a few seconds. "And what makes Vivian Mei your 'Auntie'?"

"She helped my father raise me. She and her sisters."

"Fair enough," said Bednarski, nodding. "And no, we didn't. To answer you about his appointment book."

"Did he have an office somewhere?"

Bednarski shook his head. "He worked here or wherever Tommy Chu was."

"That makes the Chus' a likely place then." She considered his expression. "Which you've already been to."

"This is not our first time around the block," he said drily.

Lola shrugged. "Can't take anything for granted. Nothing personal." She glanced down the hallway at the sound of another slam. The light in the office was still on. She said, "Do you know who 'EV' is yet?"

Another sigh. Bednarski jammed his hands into his trouser pockets. Lola caught movement from the hallway. Marks stood at the far end, just outside the bedroom. He stared at his partner, his arms loose at his sides. Lola looked back in time to see Bednarski nod once in acknowledgement. He said, "I'm sorry to be blunt, but we need you out of here."

"Is that a 'yes' or a 'no'?"

He gave her a blank stare.

Lola nodded, turned to leave. As she was about to cross the threshold, Marks said, "Call Central, Starke. They want that statement from your Ghost."

"They can get it from the Twins," said Lola. "I'm going to bed."

NINE

CHU TRAGEDY STUNS CRESCENT CITY

City Desk, Valeria Monteverde—Police are still baffled by the tragic death of Tommy Chu, Crescent City's beloved comedian and budding cinema star. It happened in the predawn hours as Mr. Chu, and best friend Stuey Lim, were about to depart from their regular evening haunt, The Supper Club.

Club owner Mrs. Agnes Au could not be reached for comment. At the request of the authorities, Club manager Mrs. Gillian Gee has closed The Supper Club indefinitely.

In the interest of full disclosure, it must be stated that this reporter was present, outside on the pavement, when tragedy struck. Along with a private citizen who declines to be named, I witnessed the following events, pieced together from what we remember, with corroboration from others.

Mr. Chu was smoking a cigarette alone, waiting on the sidewalk, while Mr. Lim went inside The Supper Club to retrieve car keys for friends. Upon his return, the murderous criminal or criminals driving a black Packard sedan, previously parked at the curb, opened fire. Witnesses who heard the gunshots attest to them being from a pistol.

The black Packard was last seen speeding away and turning right onto Ming Avenue.

Despite desperate efforts to revive them, Tommy Chu and Stuey Lim were pronounced dead at the scene by the emergency medical workers who arrived mere minutes later.

The present theory, according to Crescent City Police Detective Inspector Charles Leung, is that Mr. Chu is a victim of uncontrolled gambling habits and bad debts.

"We believe Mr. Chu made some poor choices and got involved with the wrong elements. We believe this method of killing speaks volumes about its perpetrators," said DI Leung in an official statement. "Mr. Chu was extremely well-known among the City's establishments. No man remains a winner night in and night out. Luck will always run dry eventually."

Despite DI Leung's heartless assertion, there are many who would argue that Mr. Chu was the exception to the rule. Born the youngest of seven in the sketchiest parts of Sai-Dong neighbourhood, Mr. Chu used brashness and wits to compensate for his small stature as a child. Feisty, sharp-tongued, and fearless—these are common descriptors for the City's late, great comedic genius.

Due to his own ambitions and a strong dash of good luck, Mr. Chu exemplified the rags-to-riches story. Raised by a widowed mother in the poorest of neighbourhoods, Mr. Chu nonetheless trained to become a stage actor and acrobat, the result of his driven and ambitious nature.

His good luck came in the form of the legendary Lucky Wai, visiting The Old Blossom Theatre where Mr. Chu, rehearsing some gravity-defying combat choreography, fell on top of Mr. Wai. The bad luck for both men—the older ended up with a broken ankle; the younger, with a broken elbow and cracked jaw—soon took a turn for the better. Mr. Wai, believing that Mr. Chu was his son in a past life, opened his home and his heart to the young star. This bond became so strong that it eventually impelled Mr. Wai to haunt Mr. Chu, to the young comedian's benefit.

In the seven years of their association, Mr. Chu, with Mr. Wai's mentorship, became the world's most beloved comedian and stage performer. Touring the world's stages, Mr. Chu brought his infectious laugh and broad talents to people around the world.

Tonight, Crescent City will get the chance to celebrate the life of the man who brought this joy into its citizens' lives.

Sebastian Chu, the late comedian's brother and manager, refuses to dwell on the tragedy of his younger brother's murder. He is relieved to have the police deal with finding the perpetrators of this heinous crime. Instead, the senior Chu is putting on a career retrospective for his talented brother this evening.

In an official statement, Sebastian Chu explained, "I've called in so many favours for tonight. I'm honoured and humbled by the response. The stage at the beautiful and historic Empress Dowager Theatre will not be dark tonight. My brother's spirit will shine on."

The list of performers includes the famed stage comedians Tsang and Chao, the aerial acrobat Mr. Keith Tshim, as well as world-renowned vocalist and close family friend Miss Evelyn Shao. Tickets have already sold out. A review of the show will be posted in the morning edition by Mr. Walter Yee, stage and cinema critic for the *Crescent City Herald.*

Sidekick Gets Equal Treatment

City Desk, Ronson So—Two of Crescent City's finest take their job very seriously. So seriously, in fact, that they could not be reached for comment. Detective Inspectors Truman Bednarski and Kestrel Marks have been given charge of a separate homicide investigation regarding the death of Mr. Stuey Lim.

Mr. Lim was an accomplished musician in his own right and a regular fixture at certain exclusive nightclubs around the City. Police believe he was not a target and that his death was a tragic accident.

Nevertheless, according to the brief statement by the police media liaison, an investigation is required to ensure that the police department has performed its due diligence and duty to a citizen of Crescent City.

If any member of the public at large has information he or she thinks relevant to the police investigations, please contact your local police station or telephone Central at Main 8989.

TEN

Lola switched off her car and sat in the deepening twilight, listening to the cooling engine tick. She heard the ocean just past the line of houses to her right, its crashing surf soothing, for all its relentless pounding. She allowed herself one deep sigh, got out.

Ria's house had deep blue siding, with door frames and window shutters so white they glowed in the dark of evening. Warm yellow light made a patch on the dark wooden boards of the front porch. Baskets of flowers, wicker porch furniture, window boxes. It always made Lola smile.

She entered without knocking, heard Ria on the floorboards above her.

"Just me," she called out.

She closed the front door behind her, strode down the short hall, did a dogleg through the kitchen, walked out the back door. She swept up the short train of her dark evening gown and sat on the top step of Ria's porch stairs. The beach was another five steps down.

Lola leaned against the stair post. She lit an Egyptian, careful to insert the dark cigarette into a holder first, and exhaled in a long, long breath, loosening the folds of the grey silk wrap around her shoulders.

No moon tonight, no one on the beach. The ocean waves pushed and pulled, set to their own hypnotic rhythm, bringing salt on the insistent breeze. Lola took off her heeled sandals and dropped them down beside her in a heap. Behind her, she heard Ria clicking down the stairs and through the house. The back door gave the smallest of squeaks before slamming shut.

"Uh oh. You look pensive." Ria rested a hip against the railing.

Lola took another drag of her cigarette.

"What's eating you?"

Lola shrugged. "Been a long day."

"Baby need a nap?"

"I took one. Didn't help."

"You, beautiful girl, need gainful employment. A calling. A vocation. Like me." Ria pointed to her face, put on a cheerful grin. "No nap. Still smiling."

"Not exactly the right tone for a funeral."

"We're not going to a funeral. We're going to a *retrospective*."

"Huh." Lola delicately tapped her ashes off to the side of the steps. It was too dark to watch them land.

"Who cares what they call it?" Ria said. "We show up. We cry a little. We laugh a lot. We try to get over whatever powerlessness and guilt we might feel. That is perfectly human, by the way, so don't go thinking you can avoid it. Now, where was I? Oh yes. We make enough noise to wake the dead. We toast Tommy Chu into the next life."

"I didn't see you at the Lims' today."

A pause. "Is that what's bothering you?"

Lola shrugged. She inhaled another lungful of smoke.

Ria sat down, pushing Lola's heels aside. She raised herself a little to straighten out a seam of her gown, then resumed her seat. She eyed Lola.

Lola eyed her back.

"What gives?" Ria said.

Lola considered, then told her best friend about Kam.

Ria rocked back as Lola finished. "Aubrey's right about them being shunned. There's no way any respectable Chinese family's going to associate with bad luck like that. Gods, I hope they'll be all right."

"I gave him up to Bednarski."

Ria stared.

"Even tough cookies know when the coppers have better resources. Bednarski and Marks," Lola paused, "they're jake enough, for coppers."

Ria shook her head.

"Faster to work with them. On this, at any rate." Lola shrugged.

"Never thought I'd see the day. That's the most reasonable thing I've ever heard from you."

Lola turned her face toward the ocean. She tasted salt on the slight breeze.

Ria sighed. Loudly. "All right, fine. Stick to the script. Where was I? Right. Did the monk do well? With the commotion and all?"

"A little young, but he kept the prayers steady. Didn't even falter when those three showed up."

Ria nodded. "A proper send off. Good. Stuey should find it easy to the next life."

"No retrospective for him, you'll note."

Ria shrugged. "People like the Chus, what do you expect? It's in their veins. The worst fate for someone like *that* is to be completely ignored." She took a deep breath. "Sam sent me to the viewing for Tommy. Didn't even get past the gate. No reporters. Family and close friends only."

"At least they didn't sell tickets to that," said Lola.

They sat in silence for a while.

Lola looked up at the sky, knowing the moon was hidden behind clouds tonight, but searching anyway. She leaned back onto her elbows and crossed her ankles. The swish of her gown was lost in the susurration of the waves.

"I wonder where Charlie ended up?" said Ria, her voice soft. "Said he was just behind the bar til he figured out what to do with his shiny new business school degree."

Lola glanced over.

Ria stared at the ocean, worrying a thumbnail between her teeth. "Feels like years ago. Can't quite believe it was just this morning."

Lola turned her eyes back to the beach. She deepened her breathing, grasping for calm against the memories that Ria's words dredged up. She focussed her mind on the water's movement, pushing all other thoughts away. If she squinted, she could make out the white edges of the waves as they swept into shore.

"I know it's not our fault, but I still feel guilty," Ria said.

Lola sat up, shrugging her grey wrap back onto her shoulders. "Reservations are for half-eight. We're cutting it close." She picked up her shoes.

Ria stared up at Lola for a few seconds, her surprised expression turning into a scowl. She got up and brushed sand from the hem of her pale gown. Lola slid her feet into the heeled sandals and adjusted the straps. In her peripheral vision, she saw Ria shoot her a dark look. She ignored Ria's muttering as they walked back through the house, turning off lights and locking up.

⁂

The bland-faced waiter appeared with a tea pot and delicate translucent porcelain cups. The pot was thick and beautifully painted with a picture of a mountain clad in wispy clouds. Gold threaded through the edges of mountain and clouds alike. Steam wafted out from the spout as the waiter poured for them, stopping precisely when the cups were two-thirds full. He bowed and retreated.

Lola closed her eyes as the intense smoky tea took over her palate. She sipped, felt her shoulders relax.

A second waiter, tall and bright-eyed, brought a tureen. Yan, the maître d', appeared, lifted the lid away. The velvety scent of sesame oil and the sharpness of herbs rose in a cloud with the steam. He neatly ladled clear broth out, set a bowl each in front of Lola and Ria, bowed, and left.

The women sipped their first course. Lola watched her friend closely. Ria narrowed her eyes at Lola a few times, but remained silent.

Waiters cleared everything away from the soup course and brought out the rest of the meal. Once the food was arranged according to Yan's particular standards, he personally filled their rice bowls, bowed again, and left them alone.

"Seven dishes," Ria said. "Your request?"

"Seemed appropriate." Lola looked over the table, counting the different dishes of glossy greens, meats, and seafood, to ensure the traditional menu for the bereaved had been followed.

"How old-fashioned," said Ria. "Is this for Tommy or Stuey?"

Lola shrugged.

Ria raised an eyebrow, delicately picked up a slice of black mushroom with her chopsticks. "Will the Aunties be there tonight then?"

Lola chose a piece of steamed fish in soy and flashed scallions. It all but melted in her mouth. "Of course."

Ria raised her eyebrows. "How's Vivian feeling about all this?"

Lola compressed her lips. "If I didn't know she has a heart deep, deep inside of her, I'd be tempted to say she's basking in the attention."

"But of course you'd never say such a thing."

Lola toasted Ria with her tea cup.

Following custom, they ate a bit from each dish. Lola did her best, but she had no appetite. When she judged she'd eaten enough to fulfill the traditions, she put her bowl down.

Ria did the same, eyed her narrowly. "Are you going to keep avoiding me?"

Lola propped her chopsticks precisely on a little porcelain block. "Flapping my jaw's not going to change what happened."

"There's no shame in sharing the sorrow and pain."

Lola took a deep breath, looked away.

"Oh stop it," said Ria, impatient. "We're best friends, aren't we?" She pointed her chopsticks. "At some point you'll have to stop fooling yourself. You are, in point of fact, not alone."

Lola kept her mouth shut. They'd been friends for over a decade. Ria could only be pushed so far.

Yan's silent waiters came again. They whisked away the remaining food. Lola knew they would pack it up, neatly and efficiently. A runner would take it all to a temple, one with a prearrangement with the restaurant, and it would be given as an offering. A monk or nun would spiritually cleanse the food and bless it before some deserving family would receive a meal. Lola had to admire the economy of the setup.

The bland-faced waiter brought oranges for the dessert course, eight bright segments so fresh Lola saw juice slide down their sides. Ria slid out her elegant mother-of-pearl cigarette case and a dark holder. A jade ashtray appeared on the table, as well as a young man waiting to light her up. She smiled her thanks and he left.

"Where's your next piece going?" Lola said.

Ria tapped some ash into the jade bowl. "I turned in a background piece. Just to fill the space until the coppers dig up something useful. Or I do." She exhaled cigarette smoke, eying Lola through the grey haze. "And I know you're changing the subject."

Lola cocked her head. "Do you have a line on something?"

"I could make you wait like everybody else," said Ria.

"You're not dying to tell me anyway?" Lola winced, hearing how forced her light tone was.

Ria sat forward. "For the record, I'm still steamed that you're being such a hard case. But—" she put up a hand just as Lola opened her mouth to reply "—I'm taking the high road on this one." Lola snapped her mouth shut. "As to my story," Ria said, "I know a set dresser for Tommy's stage show. And don't even ask 'cause I'm not givin' a name."

Ria waited until Lola nodded.

"Apparently, Tommy's been uncharacteristically distracted the past few months. Tripping over stage props, dropping his lines, missing cues. His sister was away last week, holidaymaking, they said. Leastways, that's what Sebastian blamed Tommy's distraction on. Said they both missed her."

"Didn't know he had a sister in the business," murmured Lola, thinking.

"Seamstress, costume maker, sometime errand girl. Not a performer like her brothers. My source says it was all a smokescreen though. Thought Tommy and Sebastian treated her like a servant, a slave. 'No better than a *gu lei*,' he said."

Lola gave a start. "A coolie? Their own sister?"

Ria nodded. "Ugly, I know, but his word. He said no way they were torn up about her being away. No, more likely it was Tommy arguing all the time with Lucky."

"Your source got a Ghost?"

Ria shook her head. "Didn't need one, he says, to hear the arguments. Just the one side was plenty hot as it was. Always about the same thing. 'The moving picture.'" She raised her brows. "Sounds like Tommy was mocking Lucky with that phrase. My source says they were always at it. Tommy and Sebastian on one side. Lucky on the other."

"But he was already filming, wasn't he? I thought I'd read something about hours of footage already shot."

Ria nodded. "And on stage every night. It was gruelling. Lucky ought to've seen how determined Tommy was to make it work."

Lola considered. "You can talk to Uncle Nicky tonight. Nicky Lo. He'll be at the theatre. I don't know that he'll agree to be quoted, but I think he's worth speaking to."

Ria narrowed her eyes. "Is there something more?"

Lola hesitated, then explained the visit from Nicky that morning. Ria's expression was hard to read.

When Lola was done, Ria nodded, started another cigarette from the end of her first. Replacing the spent one with the new, she deftly crushed it out in the ashtray even as she inhaled more smoke. Lola caught the fine tremble in her friend's hands.

"You sure you're jake?" she said.

"You're not asking me now, are you? Not after your big show of denial?" Ria exhaled a plume of smoke.

Lola felt her face heat. "Chain smoking isn't normally your thing. Just thought it was worth asking." She kept her voice level.

"I'm jake," Ria muttered. "Just peachy." She blew another mouthful of smoke at Lola.

"So," said Lola slowly, piecing together what Ria had been saying earlier, "you must've found something. In Tommy's past."

Ria was silent a long beat. Then she shook her head. "Damned if I do," she muttered. "Fine. Yes, yes I did."

"Are you gonna tell me?"

Ria sighed dramatically.

"You know you wanna spill."

Ria sighed again. "Tommy may have two birth certificates."

Lola raised her brows. "That's gonna blow some wigs."

"Tell me about it. Sam practically kissed me when I told her. Dreadfully awkward, that."

"How?" Lola prompted Ria with a gesture of her hand.

"Found a source." Ria shrugged. "She found me, actually."

"And...?"

"Two different hospitals. Sai-Dong Memorial and Oceanside."

Lola frowned. "Oceanside? That may as well be the moon from Sai Dong. Was he sold? That's the only need a baby has for a false certificate. Or are you saying he had it falsified, as an adult?"

"My source claims to be the baby broker." Ria ground her cigarette into the ashtray. Lola noted with satisfaction that she didn't light another.

"That's the perfect reason to doubt her. Besides, if he was born at Oceanside, the mother came from money. Why involve a broker? The orphanages are full to bursting with the wealthy's unwanted get.

They just drop them off at the back." Lola scowled. "Did you ask her why the family wanted money for Tommy? Is that even his name?"

"Yes, it is, as a matter of fact. And it seems our baby broker didn't ask a lot of questions. Tends to scare the families away."

Lola stared at her.

Ria scribed a circle on the table linen with her finger. "The girl was maybe sixteen. Probably not more than forty-five now. No idea of the father. Maybe she needed the money to hide her actions from her family."

"How did your source get involved?"

"She was a nurse at Oceanside. Says it was her first time selling a baby." Ria's lips thinned. "But her name got around. She turned it into her full-time business. Apparently she's retired now."

Lola scowled. "She got a hold of you right quick. He's not even been gone a day."

Ria took up another cigarette. She inhaled sharply, fired it with Lola's lighter until its tip glowed an aggressive orange. "Says she feels the time is right. She doesn't think the siblings will raise too much ruckus. Their parents are long gone. Tommy won't care." Ria stopped. "That sounded callous. I didn't mean it that way." She raised her cigarette, stared at it as she exhaled, then mashed it out in the ashtray.

"Did she just happen to contact you when she heard the news of his death?"

Ria shook her head. "Stop right there. This is my story. As far as the source is concerned, the last thing I need is you blundering in and throwing your weight around. I need her and her old network. It's my only lead on finding the mother." She picked up her cigarettes again, tossed the case down onto the table with a huff.

"How do you even know her story's true?" Lola said. "It's full of holes. Why would the girl go to the hospital close to home if she didn't want her parents to know? Better to try the east side hospitals if she wanted anonymity. And if her parents were involved, even more reason for them to shunt the girl to somewhere far from their home."

"They're a hospital," said Ria. "The people who work there aren't wealthy even if the neighbourhood is. Can you see them turning away a scared young girl, pregnant, about to give birth? And maybe she didn't have time to get to the east side. Maybe she wasn't even from a wealthy family. She might've been a servant girl, knocked up by Number One Son or some other twit." Ria tapped the table. "The point is, I need to find out."

"Gods, I hope she was smart enough to lie anyway." Lola shook her head. "Then at least there's a chance she's a survivor."

"Mei Ling Wong," said Ria. "As good as an alias. There must be thousands of girls with that name and those are just the ones who actually live in the City. She may have moved away years ago. She may be married. Which is exactly why I need my source to be happy with me. If it was truly her first time selling babies, then whoever approached her next must have heard it from the girl or someone who knew the girl. I need that network of contacts." Ria looked balefully at Lola. "I don't need you playing the heavy."

Lola put up her hands. "Truce. I'm not trying to muscle in on your action. I've got enough on my dance card as it is. But if you find something solid, you've got to let me know. No, think about it, Ria. If this is true, the coppers will be peeved when they discover you held out on them. It's a whole new avenue of possibilities. Right now they've got nothing but a hunch about the gangster angle. I bet the

Twins are feeling the pressure already. One dubious lead, no sus-
pects. What they wouldn't give for another stream to fish. And
when they find out you knew all along, they'll put you through the
grinder, sister. I guarantee it."

"Your mixed metaphors are giving me a headache." Ria took a
drink of tea, replaced her delicate cup on the table, raised her chin.
"Like I said, I don't need you playing the heavy. I'm not afraid of the
coppers. This is my story. That source is mine. I'm going to use her
to find out the truth. Damn straight, she could be lying. I know that.
But the only way I'll find out is if I follow my instincts. There's a
reason she came to me with this. And I gave her my word that her
identity would be safe."

Lola bit back a sigh. "Just keep me in the loop is all I'm asking."

Ria snorted. "That is not all you're asking, and we both know it."
At Lola's expression, she held up a hand. "Listen, I'm perfectly capable of following up on leads and persuading people to give up information. In fact, that's my job, remember? *Crescent City Herald*, City
Desk crack reporter?"

"Ace reporter, yeah, I got it. But—"

"Keep your doubts to yourself. You just leave me to do my job
and you get on with yours. Your Uncle Nicky's got you at odds with
the coppers on two fronts. You've got more than enough to worry
your pretty little head over."

ELEVEN

Lola scanned the open air courtyard of The Empress Dowager Theatre. White banners stood throughout the square space, their edges blurring in the wavering torchlight. To the left of the main doors, a photographic enlargement of Tommy Chu's latest publicity still. The trademark grin greeted all.

"I've gotta give it to Sebastian Chu." Ria shook her head. "This is sure making some statement."

"And what would that be?" Lola raised an eyebrow.

"What else? The show must go on." Ria shrugged. "There aren't many willing to defy the infamous S.Z.K. Liu's architectural edicts." She gestured to the cluttered courtyard. "Wasn't the 'negative space' her one immutable commandment?"

"Perhaps he's not thinking straight," said Lola. "Grief has a way of...skewing things."

Ria glanced sideways at her. "That may well be true. But there's nothing a canny manager like Sebastian Chu does without there being an angle."

They continued past the photograph of Tommy, threading through the milling crowd, and stopped briefly at the box office, discreetly to the right of the building entrance. Tickets in hand, they entered The Auspicious Hall of Theatrical Wonders.

Ria gave a wry grin. "In any other theatre in any other city in the world, this would be called 'the lobby.'"

"Crescent City rules," said Lola.

Ria looked around, craning her neck. "There's gotta be a poster for every single one of Tommy's performances," she said. "The ones he headlined, I mean." She grinned. "I doubt Sebastian Chu wants to remind anyone of *The Lost Revue of Benevolent Father Siu.*"

"Don't tell me you actually saw that one."

Ria nodded. "I did indeed. It was a sad, sad night when I got pulled to cover for Walter that evening. He had a terrible cough." She cocked her head. "That's right. It was the same night I caught up with you and that artist, what's his name, that time at Lulu's. You were about to try your hand at dominoes."

"I can't recall his name, either." Lola paused. "You did seem a little worse for wear."

"It was painful, my friend, doubt me not. Tommy was definitely the bright spot. Like a new coin in a beggar's palm." Ria smiled. "I remember a spectacular singing solo while he balanced a spinning plate on a stick. Unbelievable. The absolute highlight of the show. Everyone in the audience—all ten of us—knew he was something special."

They fell silent as they scanned the posters. All but one showed that inimitable grin beaming out of Tommy's boyish, handsome face.

"Oh look." Ria pointed. "They even have the poster for *The Toil of Night.* Just goes to prove Sebastian truly is doing this out of love."

"How'd you figure?"

"I heard Tommy was very proud of it, his lone foray into serious 'thee-ay-tah.'" Ria shrugged. "His performance was generally praised, but the show didn't last more than a month. And that month was floated solely on the advance tickets."

"At least he gave it a shot." Lola grimaced at her choice of words.

The house lights blinked three times.

They moved on, passing behind the crowd at the doors, waiting to enter the Exalted Theatre Stage of Happiness and Amusement. They took the carpeted stairs to the first balcony.

"Front and centre." Ria surveyed their seats with obvious satisfaction. "Perfect for watching the action, on stage and off." She nudged Lola. "There's Her Worship."

Lola looked down to the prime orchestra section. In the front row, a broad-shouldered woman with grey-streaked hair chatted with her seatmates. She wore a demure navy *cheong-sahm* and earrings too small to see clearly, but they sparkled as she moved.

"I'm not surprised a desk reporter and a gumshoe didn't rate," said Lola, "but I guess being mayor doesn't get you a box seat tonight either."

"Tonight is for the entertainers," said Ria. She nudged Lola again. "The Aunties."

Lola observed them settling themselves in the box immediately up from stage left. Vivian stood at the front of the box and looked around the theatre, a pleased expression on her face. Veronica and Viola kept back, spoke to the tall usher who accompanied them. He smiled, shook his head, and gestured for them to sit in the closer row of three chairs. Vivian, in a deep purple *cheong-sahm*, took the best seat in the row, closest to the stage. Viola sat down next to her, looking around, her uneasiness clear. Veronica spoke again to the usher, but he shook his head once more, gesturing patiently for her to be seated. She smoothed her hands down her dark grey *cheong-sahm* and complied.

"Now those are good seats."

"Yeah," said Lola. "But only Vivian seems happy about it."

"Do you want to go?"

Lola rose. "I think I'd better." She began making her apologies to the people next to her. Ria pulled on her arm.

"Wait. Look."

Lola looked over in time to see Vivian hug Liliane, then Keun. Veronica and Viola followed suit. Vivian spoke to Keun, her expression kind. Then she kissed his cheek lightly and patted his hand. The Lims took the remaining seats at the front of the box.

"Who are they?" said Ria.

Lola explained as she retook her seat. After a moment, she said, "I just realized. Keun was Viv's brother-in-law for seven years."

"Um, yes. Is that significant?"

Lola hesitated. "I guess we really are family."

Ria patted Lola's arm.

The lighting gradually dimmed. A spotlight snapped on audibly, wavering for a second on the centre of the thick red curtains hiding the bulk of the stage. Footsteps echoed crisply on hardwood. They began at stage right, behind the curtain, and continued sedately toward centre stage. A pale hand parted the curtains. Lola's peripheral vision picked out movement as others in her row leaned forward.

A tall, slender man in an exquisite black tuxedo stepped out from the parted curtain. In the glow of the spotlight, the armband high on his left arm looked brilliant white. The man's thick black hair was parted on the left and swept away from a high forehead. His eyes were dark, intent, as they passed over the auditorium. He walked forward and stopped near the edge of the stage.

"My friends," he said, "I am so grateful to see you here tonight. Tonight of all nights, I feel blessed by the love you all share with me for my brother, Tommy." He surveyed the crowd. "Thank you, dear friends, for coming to celebrate with us. With my sister, Serene, and myself." He shook his head. "Not to mourn. To celebrate." He raised his left hand and closed his fingers into a fist. "Tonight is for toasting my departed brother, his accomplishments, his talents, his love of life, his love for you all." Sebastian Chu swept his hand out grandly to include the entire theatre as people applauded enthusiastically.

"Serene and I hope to share with you just a little of our thoughts about our brother. You know, we are the last three siblings left in the Chu family. Our mother, bless her soul, moved on many years ago. Her very last wish was that I take the best care of my little sister and brother. Even as Tommy's star was ascending, Mother knew that life would be full of obstacles beyond which suit to wear." He offered an indulgent smile.

"It was so important to him to look his very best. No matter if he was simply cycling to the corner chemist or arriving to watch the premiere of his own films, Tommy insisted on shining his very brightest. He depended so very much on our sister Serene and her skills as a seamstress. I am doubly grateful that we three siblings were able to live and work together in such harmony." More applause. Lola shared a look with Ria.

Sebastian turned toward stage right and gestured insistently. A young woman hesitantly appeared after a few seconds. He strode toward her and grasped her hand, tugging her along with him.

"Serene, everyone. Our sister, Miss Serene Chu." His voice trembled as he looked at her with a crooked smile. The applause increased. Serene hunched her shoulders at the wave of sound. Her hair was pinned back into a simple twist at her nape. Her black dress was severe in its tailoring and lack of adornment, showing Serene Chu to be an exceptionally thin woman, a few inches shorter than her oldest brother. A white band encircled her upper left arm. She wore no jewellery that Lola could see. Her shoes were flat-heeled and black. Her lips were compressed into a thin line, almost indistinguishable from the paleness of her face.

"She looks ready to bolt, poor thing," said Ria.

Sebastian leaned toward Serene and murmured. She nodded to him, dipped her head down briefly to the audience and walked quickly offstage once more. He watched her until she disappeared from the audience's view, then turned back to face the theatre.

"From the very first time my little brother saw the Mei Triplets perform, he was utterly compelled to become a stage performer." Sebastian raised his hand toward the patron box at stage left.

Liliane and Keun, seated in front of the Aunties in the box, turned and applauded. Vivian nodded regally to the entire theatre, a small smile playing on her full red lips. Veronica raised a slim hand. Viola smiled. Lola thought they looked as beautiful as she'd ever seen them.

"Please, ladies, stand and take a bow." Vivian rose immediately, smiling with pride. She waited for Viola and Veronica to stand too.

Lola's eyes filled with tears as she watched the Mei Triplets receive a standing ovation for the first time in more than twenty-five years.

❦

Thirty minutes later, Lola scowled as Sebastian Chu delivered another punch line.

Ria placed a hand on her arm. "C'mon, the joke wasn't that bad."

Lola forcibly relaxed her expression. "It's not that," she said, voice low. "It's the stories. Didn't your unnamed set dresser say they treated their sister like a 'gu lei'?"

Ria nodded.

"Then he's lying, isn't he?" Lola pointed to the stage. "With all these happy stories of working together."

Ria whispered, "Families are never only one thing." She shrugged.

Lola ground her teeth. Ria was right. These were not charitable thoughts. Every family had its arguments, its differences. She had only to look into the box at stage left to remember that. Love within a family had too many layers to judge based on a rumour.

Lola forced herself to sit quietly and listen to Sebastian wind down. Still, she refused to applaud when he exited the stage.

The spotlight went off and the auditorium was dark again.

A single note pierced the darkness, sung by a pure soprano. Lola recognized that voice. She wagered everyone in the audience did as well. An excited murmur spread through the auditorium. The spotlight brightened again, highlighting a painted Japanese screen at centre stage. Against the glowing white background, the stark image of three black cranes. A pale orange sun sat high in the painted sky and reeds shared the foreground with confident strokes of pale blue. Grey shadows stretched from plants and birds alike, reaching down to the bottom-right corner.

Lola couldn't tell if the painting depicted sunrise or sunset. There was a sense of melancholy in its lines and shadings, as inescapable as it was ephemeral.

The centre of the cleverly folded screen parted. A black-haired woman came into view as an unseen platform raised her up from below the stage. There was a collective gasp, then applause.

Evelyn Shao gracefully nodded in acknowledgement as she came to a stop level with the stage boards. She stepped forward as she continued singing an aria-like introduction to "Had It the First Time." Lola knew the song as a lullaby, something her mother used to sing to her, according to her father. Lola had a vivid memory of him, humming it as he shuffled around their little kitchen, making breakfast, lunch or dinner.

She swallowed thickly.

A coolness at her back. Lola just caught herself from flinching as Aubrey returned to her, bringing the cold aura distinctive to all Ghosts. She shifted, wrestling her attention back to the stage.

She focussed on Evelyn Shao and the most celebrated pipes in twenty years. That famous voice made the narrative soar and dive as the song wound to its bittersweet conclusion. The final note seemed to hang in the air, an invisible tracery of youthful dreams and fortune made bad by misguided love.

The singer's petite frame was accentuated in a silver, single-strap, mermaid gown. A pristine white triangle of fabric folded over from the strap and across the entire neckline of the gown, its downward point tastefully off-centre. It reminded Lola of a tuxedo jacket.

Evelyn Shao smiled shyly. "Thank you. Thank you for sharing with me tonight a little of your time and attention. I am so honoured to be here to celebrate and remember Tommy. He was the brother I wasn't born with, but was blessed with nonetheless." She paused to take a deep breath. "He and Stuey were very close to my heart, and I shall miss them both terribly." Her voice cracked.

She turned briefly away from the audience. A great heaving breath shuddered through the singer's slender frame. When she turned back, her shaky smile offered a silent apology. Her eyes were bright with unshed tears, and she nodded once, sharply, to the orchestra pit. The musicians struck up into the well-known first bars

of "Penny In My Shoe." The upbeat tempo forced her back into the
rhythm of her performance. Her smile came back by degrees.

Ria wiped at her eyes with a sniffle. "Damn."

Lola nodded, blinking, her gaze on Evelyn Shao as the singer
sang with joy and abandon about being poor and in love.

❧

Lola decided there must be an unwritten rule somewhere in the
manual of stage and theatre design that the back of the stage must
always look thrown together and transitory. Even here, in the jewel
of the coastal theatre community, wooden supports were bare and
unvarnished. Ropes that weren't already dangling down from the
rafters and tied off to waist-high wall hooks seemed to coil in every
available corner, like snakes napping in masses. Large painted backdrops were pushed against the outer walls. Green, forested corners
peeped out from behind city brownstones and starry skies. Blue
ocean swells poked out from behind the sides of swank apartment
views.

"Lola, my girl, over here."

Nicky Lo was immaculate in his evening clothes, dapper despite
the dark circles ringing his bloodshot eyes. He hugged her tightly in
greeting. "Is Aubrey here with you then?"

"Yes. Why?"

"Serene has a Ghost. Their *Mah-mah*. Thought Aubrey could take
stock of her when I introduce you." Nicky's gaze circled around Lola's head. "If that's all right with you, of course, Aubrey."

"Tell him I'm honoured to help."

Lola relayed Aubrey's reply. "Where are they now?" she said.

They paused to let a slight man pass, his hands full of ropes.

"Main dressing room. Tommy's room." Nicky rubbed his eyes. "Midnight seems later and later," he muttered.

"Are you still up to The Golden Boar afterward? My newspaper friend wants to speak with you," she said. Nicky scowled so she added, "Strictly background."

He nodded curtly.

Nicky led her through the convoluted passages made by standing backdrops and sets. The area was crowded with stagehands packing up, pushing dollies piled with wooden crates. People swerved and twisted to avoid being run over.

"It's normally much noisier back here after a show," said Nicky.

"Were you here often? When Tommy was performing?"

Nicky shrugged. "Lately, it seemed like I was always here." At her look, he sighed. "Lucky was very unhappy—I wasn't exaggerating about that. He asked. I came."

Aubrey said, "What will happen with everything here?" Lola relayed the question.

Nicky shrugged. "Storage? Your guess is as good as mine."

They made it through the maze of people, crates, and ropes, emerging at the mouth of a short corridor. At its end, a door with a large white star at eye level. Nicky rapped on it twice.

Sebastian Chu opened the door a sliver, blinked at the sight of Nicky. He pulled the door open fully, saw Lola, and stopped short. The skin around his eyes tightened.

Nicky stepped aside adroitly and held out his hand to shepherd Lola inside. "Sebastian. This is Miss Lola Starke."

"A pleasure to meet you, Miss Starke. Please come in."

"I'm sorry for your bereavement," said Lola. "And I'm sorry to intrude like this." She hesitated, noting that his stage makeup had begun to flake. She could just make out dark pouches beneath his eyes. The lines around his mouth deepened, seemed to draw the corners downward.

"Thank you. Please do come in."

Lola looked sharply at him, hearing his tone, but his expression was politely neutral.

"Yes, well." Nicky cleared his throat. "We appreciate it."

Sebastian inclined his head and led them into the room.

Lola noted a sitting area at the back with two small sofas, two end tables, two cuspidors, and three rolling racks of costumes, arranged end to end to end. She raised a hand in greeting as she saw the Aunties on the facing sofa. Viola was deep in conversation with the people on the other sofa, their backs to the door. Lola recognized the Lims but not the woman who sat between them.

As Sebastian led her and Nicky toward the back, she noted a rolling bar trolley, tucked against the far wall, and a few sketches framed on the wall opposite the door. A pale green statue of Kwan-Yin, goddess of compassion, stood beneath an enormous arrangement of hydrangeas on the far edge of the dressing table.

Lola's gaze travelled over pots of makeup and brushes scattered over the dressing table's surface. There were clusters of smeared cloths and swaths of extravagant fabric strewn carelessly about. She imagined Tommy absently wiping off makeup with the cloths and dropping them, his attention already on to the next thing.

She saw scissors in a matte black finish, as well as a straight razor, its strop hanging from a bolt jutting out from the side of the mirror frame. A stray feather lifted up, disturbed by their brisk passing. A pile of pocket squares sat on a chair. What appeared to be a script, one side curled back on itself, lay open in the centre of the dressing table. Lola slowed, read a few words, noted the graceful line of the characters, but she couldn't make head nor tail of the scene. It might have been the current script. It might have been another project entirely.

She caught sight of herself in the mirror on top of the dressing table. In the brightness of the light bulbs framing the glass, her skin didn't look much better than the grey of her gown. She resisted scowling, turned away.

They reached the others and Sebastian stopped, stepping to one side. Nicky made his greetings and leaned against an armchair.

Vivian gave Lola the once over. "You look tired."

"You do not," Lola said. Veronica hid a smile behind her hand while Viola glanced sideways at Vivian.

Lola kissed them each on the cheek, then greeted the Lims, together on the facing sofa. Evelyn Shao sat between them, eyes swollen and nose red. She offered Lola a tremulous smile and introduced herself.

"I understand you're a long lost cousin of Stuey's," she said, her voice kind, as Lola shook her hand.

"I had a schoolgirl crush on him once upon a time," said Lola. "He was a great sport about it."

Liliane laughed softly. "Oh yes, we recall." She looked over at her husband. He shook his head, wiped his eyes.

"I'm sorry for your bereavement," said Evelyn, her voice quiet, solemn.

"And I for yours," said Lola formally. She watched the other woman's eyes fill with tears, felt a responding sting in her own. She turned away, perched herself on the sofa arm closest to Veronica. The Auntie leaned into her.

"Evie's like a daughter to us." Keun squeezed Evelyn's hand.

Evelyn's tears spilled over. She spread open the handkerchief clutched in her hand, wiped her face roughly. Lola absently noted the lack of makeup streaks on the rumpled cloth while she considered Keun's words. They pinged something in the back of her mind. Nicky raised his eyebrows in query, but Lola had no insight for him. Not yet.

Liliane kissed Evelyn on the temple and held her hand.

Throat tight, Lola blinked rapidly and swiped a knuckle beneath her eyes. She forced her hands to unclench.

In her periphery, Lola saw the Aunties shift, dab at their own eyes. Viola reached across, placed a comforting hand on Keun. He pressed her hand with his own.

Lola looked at Sebastian Chu. Drawn face, thinned lips. He crossed his arms and took a few steps toward the dressing table.

A quick one-two knock sounded before the door swung inward and a hand dolly came through the doorway, followed by three men in dusty green work uniforms. The shortest of the three took a long drag at his cigarette and squinted at the gowned and suited occupants in the room. Behind him, the other two fanned out and began pushing the costume racks together. Another group of men came through with portable wardrobe trunks and stood them up near the costume racks. They opened each of the trunks, eight in all, then left. The first three men left the hand truck next to the far corner of the dressing table and also exited. The first man tipped his cap and departed. They left the door standing open.

"Seb," said Evelyn, voice gentle. He startled, turning to her. She stood. "You've got so much to do yet. And my train's in a few hours. I must get back."

"Serene will miss you," Sebastian murmured. He took her hands, kissed her cheek.

"Tell her I'm sorry I had to go. I'll ring her tomorrow."

Everyone stood then, and Lola heard variations on the theme of departure. She stepped back to allow Vivian to walk over to the Lims and Sebastian Chu. A hand closed on her own and pulled her away from the others.

"May I have a word?" Evelyn's gaze was direct, urgent. "It's about Philip Kam."

TWELVE

Evelyn led the way to a curtained alcove Lola had missed earlier, just a few feet farther down the hall from the dressing room. She left the curtains open, speaking in quiet tones.

"I heard he showed up today, looking for Stuey's pocket watch. You've got to help them. Keep Philip Kam away from them."

Lola started to reply when the niggling in the back of her brain finally became a connection. "Evie," she breathed.

Evelyn scowled. "Are you listening to me? You've got to keep Philip away from Stuey's parents. They tell me you're some sort of private detective, that you have training in these sorts of things. If you need money, I'll pay you to guard them. Whatever you want. I'll pay."

Lola put up a hand. "Do you know Kam then? Was he truly a friend of Stuey's?"

Evelyn nodded, her expression weary. "Not as close as they once were, but yes."

"Was it a falling out? Is that what the pocket watch business is about?"

Evelyn shook her head. "I don't know why Philip wants the watch." She squeezed her eyes shut. "Perhaps only because it was so important to Stuey. Philip can be strange like that, like one of those birds who loves shiny things. He's cruel, interested in other people's pain and suffering."

Lola mentally sifted through the singer's words. She said, slowly, "Why was the pocket watch so important? To Stuey?"

Evelyn pressed her trembling lips together. "It was a gift from his uncle, Stanley." She looked away, then back again. "Stuey never let it out of his sight or off of his person."

"Uncle Stanley?" Lola considered the angles on that one. "I still don't understand."

Evelyn waved a hand, dismissing Lola's comment. "I only know that it meant a great deal to Stuey. I don't know if his parents have it or not, but I do know that Philip wants it. Desperately. He'll continue to pester the Lims until he finds out who has it." She wrung her handkerchief in her hands. "I...I have a concert series to finish up, down the coast. I'll be back late tomorrow for the...for the cremation ceremony. Will you help protect them? Please? I can pay whatever you ask."

Lola shook her head. "I'll protect them anyway. And it's truth I want, not money."

Evelyn's expression shifted. "What do you mean?"

Lola glanced at the alcove entrance. All clear.

She lowered her voice. "I know who you were, to Stuey."

Evelyn's face paled. "We were good friends. We all were."

"Your name's all over his appointment book," said Lola. "'EV,' he wrote. That's you, isn't it?"

Aubrey let out a curse.

Evelyn stumbled backward a step, tripping on her gown. Lola whipped out a hand, steadied her. She kept her voice gentle, calm.

"It must have been difficult, keeping it secret for so long."

Evelyn shook her head.

Lola forced herself to speak the truth. "It must've been worth it."

"I have to go. I have a train at six." Evelyn took her arm out of Lola's grip. "You need to help the Lims. Keep Philip away from them. Please. It's what Stuey would've wanted." Her voice cracked, her features twisting as she cried. She shook her head and ran out of the alcove.

Lola didn't have it in her to give chase. Evelyn Shao would be back in the City soon enough.

She went back to the dressing room in search of Nicky. She found him leaning against an armchair, facing Sebastian Chu.

In front of one of the rolling costume racks, Serene Chu stood, back to the door. A wicker sewing basket sat at her feet. She ran a hand over a bright orange tunic. "*Mah-mah* says we'll speak to you tomorrow. I have to finish packing these tonight. Mend any that are torn before they go into storage."

"Seb, surely she can do this tomorrow. It's late. She's exhausted," said Nicky.

Sebastian shook his head. "I know, Uncle, but we only have tonight to get everything packed away. Yeoh is not fond of me. He won't hesitate to bin anything that's still here at nine o'clock tomorrow morning."

"Can Uncle Nicky and I help somehow?" said Lola.

Serene jumped and whirled around. Her brother scowled.

Surprise clear on her delicate features, Serene cocked her head, the familiar habit of Hosts as they listened to their invisible Ghosts.

"Yes, madam," said Aubrey in his most cordial tone. "I am sorry for your bereavement." A pause. "Aubrey O'Connell, madam, and Lola Starke. The daughter of my dearest childhood friend."

Sebastian looked from Serene to Lola. He said, "You are haunted, Miss Starke?"

Lola nodded. She extended her hand to Serene and introduced herself, adding, "I'm sorry for your bereavement. Please convey my condolences to your grandmother as well."

Serene nodded, head cocked again as she listened to her Ghost speak. "*Mah-mah* says thank you." She paused. "She also says Mr. O'Connell is very well-mannered." Her cheeks flushed. She looked down.

Lola guessed "for a *gwai*" had been left off.

Lola shrugged. "Sometimes I can even take him out."

Sebastian's scowl deepened. With a visible effort, he smoothed out his expression. "We really must get this packing done. Is there something specific you needed from us, Uncle?"

"His appointment book," said Nicky quietly. "Tommy's appointment book."

Sebastian glanced at his sister.

"Why don't I make myself useful here while you get whatever you need, Uncle?" said Lola. "You can pick me up on your way out."

Sebastian narrowed his eyes at her. "You are not to interrogate *a-Mui* while I'm gone. She's been through enough today." He held up a hand when Nicky opened his mouth to reply. "We all have. I understand you wanting to do right by Lucky, Uncle. That's why I'm cooperating. But I will not tolerate you upsetting my family. Is that clear?"

Lola exchanged a glance with Nicky before nodding.

"You can interrogate me tomorrow." Serene's smile was faint. "I'll put Miss Starke to work hauling costumes, all right, *Dai-goh*?"

Sebastian walked over, hugged her tightly. "Yes, my manners are appalling. But I have good cause." He led Nicky out. Lola caught a warning look from the older man before they disappeared around the doorway.

She returned her attention to Serene, noticed the gauze wrapped around the other woman's left hand. "It can't be easy packing these one-handed."

Serene angled her body, obscuring her hand as she walked toward the closest of the open packing trunks.

"Did that just happen? You weren't wearing a bandage on stage earlier."

Serene shook her head. "It's been a few weeks. My scissors slipped. It...it was a nasty business. I just didn't want to draw attention to it."

Lola followed Serene over to the racks. She caught the distinctive odour of healing tincture. She said, "My Aunties swore by the same brand of tincture. Dark brown bottle? Dark brown liquid?"

"The one that smells like rotten mushrooms." Serene smiled, shy.

"And you have to rub and rub until the colour's gone." Lola nodded. "I know it stinks, but it's strangely comforting too, isn't it?"

Aubrey said, "I always thought it was only for sprains and bruises. Never heard of it for cuts. I imagine it must sting."

Serene stiffened.

"Oh yes?" said Aubrey. "It is? Well, every family has its own traditions, doesn't it? Oh yes, of course. Your grandson must have been quite familiar with it. And, as long as it works, it doesn't matter what the bottle says, isn't that right?"

Lola heard him strain to be polite.

Serene's face went red. Lola looked away to spare the younger woman more embarrassment. Older Ghosts weren't always the most coherent.

"Where shall I start?" Lola gestured.

Serene pointed at the costumes farthest from the door.

"I'm finished looking those over." She paused, considering. "I'd better show you first. They're heavier than they look."

Lola noted the other woman's brisk movements, her slender hands rough-skinned, with swollen knuckles. Pushing aside a line of costumes on the rack, Serene used her good hand and an elbow as she demonstrated how to manoeuvre pounds of embroidered fabric without damaging intricate beadwork and delicate silk. Once Serene was satisfied with Lola's precise movements, she took her sewing gear and moved to the second hanging rack. The silence was soon filled by the sound of hangers scraping against rods, rustling fabric, Lola's shoes as she walked to and from the open packing trunks, and the occasional clatter of Serene rummaging in her sewing basket.

And the conversation between the two Ghosts.

"Quite beautiful, yes," said Aubrey. "How long did you say it took? Seven months? That's incredible. You're right to be proud."

"That sounds fast," Lola said to Serene.

"Well, I admit to making one of each of these," Serene said. "The copies were done by others." Her voice softened. "I've been making funny little outfits for *Yee-goh* since I was a child."

"These costumes are stunning work," said Lola. "Tommy must have been thrilled with them."

Serene shook her head, bent over a patch of green silk and golden embroidery in her hands.

Rapid footsteps neared.

"That was quick," said Lola. "I've barely moved a third of this rack."

"*Dai-goh* will help with the rest. You can just—"

"Miss Chu."

Lola whipped around at the sound of Philip Kam's voice.

"What are you doing here?" said Serene.

Lola turned to stare at her.

Serene shrank back. "You shouldn't be back here. You're not authorized to be back here. Who are you?"

Kam angled his head to the side, narrowed his eyes at her. He spared a glance for Lola.

Aubrey murmured, "Her Ghost is...apoplectic."

Serene's face paled. She hunched her shoulders.

Lola stepped closer to Kam. "Still angling for that pocket watch?" She watched him closely.

He assessed her openly without replying.

"What do the Chus have to do with it?"

"What do you have to do with it?" he asked.

"I've been tasked with protecting the Lims from you." Lola kept her tone casual. She moved subtly until she stood in front of him. "What makes this watch so important you'd bring possible disaster to Stuey's observances? You claim to be his friend. Why jeopardize his soul like that?"

"Don't tell me you believe in that bunk," he said.

A sound from Serene.

"Madame Chu, please," said Aubrey firmly. "Lola will deal with him. Perhaps you could convince Miss Chu to sit?"

Serene shook her head.

Kam made to step around Lola. She put a hand on his arm.

"What's your game here?"

He looked down at her hand, then up into her face. "They tell me you're a private investigator. Is that more of a vocation with you? You simply enjoy meddling in other people's business?"

"Your behaviour with the Lims hardly qualifies you as discreet."

"Your opinion of me hardly matters," Kam said. "You're even more of an outsider than I."

"Sticks and stones," muttered Lola. She stepped to the side, blocking him.

Kam took a step back, addressed Serene. "I'm simply after what's been promised me. I know there was deep sentimental value attached to that watch for Stuey. This is precisely why I need to secure it. He was my friend, too."

Lola made a rude noise. "First, it's a deal. Now it's altruism." She thought for a moment. "Why are you doing this? Pushing into their grief? Ignoring funeral etiquette? Is it a buyer? Is that it? You've already got someone lined up for Stuey's pocket watch?"

Kam's jaw tightened.

"Is it some sort of antique then?" she said. "Have you been eyeing it for a while now? Waiting for the chance to snap it up?"

"Stuey's watch was special only to him," said Serene. She'd come up behind Lola, stood next to her now. Lola glanced at her.

Serene's face was pink, her eyes wide. She thrust her chin out. "Stuey told me about that watch. It wasn't an expensive antique. Just a gift from his Uncle Stanley."

"Miss Chu," said Kam smoothly, "I'm afraid I have to disagree. Stuey showed me the assessment papers himself."

"Why would he do that?" said Serene, frowning. "He'd never think of selling that watch."

Kam paused before he answered. "He put up that watch in exchange for forgiveness of a debt. A good friend's debt."

Serene blanched.

"That's it." Lola gestured toward the door. "You're upsetting Miss Chu. If you approach us again, you'll be leaving with a police escort."

Kam looked to Serene then back to Lola. "As you wish. But I suggest you think hard about where that pocket watch might be. I have a legal claim to it. My feelings of grief notwithstanding, I will secure it."

Lola nodded impatiently. "Yes, yes, we understand. Now cut the drama and get gone."

She followed him closely and watched him from the doorway until he turned the corner at the end of the hallway.

"Is there a way to ring security from here?" she said, turning back.

Serene had clapped her hands to her ears, pressing so hard that the edges of her hands were white. Her shoulders rolled inward and her torso bowed until her back was a taut curve.

Lola ran to her side. "What's happened? What's going on?" She placed one hand on Serene's back, the other on the younger woman's shoulder. Lola could feel Serene's vertebrae sharp as jagged stones against her palm.

"Stop it," shouted Aubrey, loud enough to make Lola's ears ring.

Serene wrenched her head from side to side.

Lola reared back. "Aubrey, what the hells is going on? Is it the Ghost?"

Aubrey shouted again.

Serene shuddered and coughed, sputtering as she tried to inhale. Her breath caught in tight hiccups. Lola held onto Serene's shoulder, searching frantically for something to help stop the hyperventilating.

"Madame Chu." Aubrey's voice was a roar. "Get away from her."

Serene jerked, still trying to draw a full breath. Lola manoeuvred her into an armchair. Then she ran to the dressing table, tossing aside dirty cloths and crumpled scarves. Cursing, she ran to the door, but stopped short as she caught sight of Serene, one hand clamped over her mouth, the other pinching her nostrils closed.

Lola scrambled back to Serene.

"Dear gods, what are you doing? Stop it this instant."

Serene shook her head, squeezed her eyes shut. She curled into herself, elbows tight against her sides.

"Aubrey, damn it, is it her Ghost again?"

"No, Madame Chu is standing calmly now."

"Then what—"

A hand clamped on Lola's shoulder, shoved her to one side. Sebastian Chu glowered at her, his face dark with anger.

"What the devil have you done?"

THIRTEEN

Nicky sipped from a thick white tea cup, watching Lola over the rim. Ria observed the pair of them in turn. Around them, people laughed and talked and ate. The boisterous late night crowd at The Golden Boar paid the sombre trio no heed.

Lola scowled. "It's barbaric. The poor girl was suffocating herself, for gods' sake."

"You saw the room," said Nicky quietly. "No bag to breathe into."

Lola glared. "You're terribly calm about it, Uncle. Just how long has that Ghost been forcing Serene into fits?"

Nicky shook his head. "It may not make sense to those of us on the outside, but in the end, it doesn't matter, does it? Their family, their decision." He drained his cup, checked the pot, balanced the lid on the edge of the opening to signal for more tea.

Ria exchanged a look with Lola.

"Spoken like a man who's tried to do something about it before," said Ria.

"As I said, their family, their business."

Lola felt her face heat. "How many times did you try to satisfy your conscience before giving up?"

"Too many times to count, my girl. Stasha died when Serene was sixteen. Coming on ten years now."

"Tell him that we have to try something," said Aubrey, voice grim. "If he'd seen what she was doing to her Host, he'd be considerably less calm about it."

123

Lola voiced Aubrey's opinion.

"I've known that family as long as Lucky did. Sebastian is not open to discussing it. I'm sorry, but there's nothing we can do about Stasha."

Lola narrowed her eyes. "What's he got to do about it? Serene is a grown woman. We need to speak to her, not to her *dai-goh*."

Nicky waved a hand. "You have no siblings, you don't understand. Sebastian is the oldest brother, so he says what's what. Stasha is their grandmother, the oldest of the entire clan. She holds sway. They're a very traditional family."

"And that justifies Serene being abused by her Ghost?"

"Leave it, Lola," said Nicky, tone and expression weary.

They looked away from one another. Their waitress bustled over, sloshed some boiling water into their teapot, clanked the lid back on, and left.

Nicky refilled everyone's tea cup.

Ria said, "Look, it's almost half past one. Why don't we get started on why we're here?"

Nicky nodded. "This isn't much use, to be honest." He tapped the leather-bound appointment book at his elbow. "Nothing new. They were together for long stretches. Times varied but it was every day."

"Kam mentioned something about Stuey playing at his night club." Lola kept her temper leashed, forced a neutral tone.

"Stuey went to school just down the coast, in Bay City," said Ria. "Took a degree in teaching and music."

"A music teacher?" Lola imagined his easy smile and gentleness. "When did he have the time?"

"No, not teaching. Playing small gigs." Ria sipped her tea. "Clarinet. Some kind of jazz. Apparently he was quite the ace."

Nicky sighed, rubbed his eyes. "I didn't know any of that. I only ever thought of him in relation to Tommy."

Lola felt a keen ache in her chest. She pushed it aside. "When'd you have time to dig that up?"

Ria smiled slightly. "Crack reporter, remember?" Her expression turned serious. "I've been following the lead on that story."

Ria looked sideways at Nicky. Lola gave a small shrug.

"I need to ask you something, Mr. Lo."

"Off the record?" he said. Ria nodded. He gestured his consent.

"Why did Lucky Wai think Tommy was his son reincarnated? Was there something special about the timing of Tommy's birth?"

Nicky sat back, surprised. "You don't start soft, do you?" He scratched at the stubble along his jaw. "I don't think Lucky ever explained it to me, now that I think about it. He said that's what he believed and that was good enough for me."

"So there wasn't anything about Tommy's birth that factored in?"

Nicky shook his head. "Why?"

She smiled a little. "My turn to be off the record now. Someone approached me with a story." She swiftly summarized the baby seller's claim. "There are definite holes in this retired nurse's story, but I've got a line on someone who says he knows the doctor who delivered Tommy. Say something *was* hinky about his birth. Depending on what it is, it could be a powerful motive for murder."

Nicky was shaking his head before she'd even finished. "I don't see that at all, I'm sorry. I have a strong feeling Lucky is the key." Nicky tapped his tea cup on the table.

"As the target?" said Lola. "Or something else?"

There was a long pause.

Nicky tapped his tea cup again.

"Lucky had been married twice already by his thirty-fifth birthday, had three children, all stillborn. Nobody knew about that. And Lucky was able to keep it from the papers. I think even if they did, they'd never've printed it. Times were different then, they really were." Nicky paused, his attention turning inward. "He loved Tommy like a son. But Tommy was not a good Host, not really. Perhaps at the beginning yes, but not lately."

"How did you know Lucky was unhappy?" said Ria. "You don't have a Ghost."

"I could tell." He grimaced. "And I could tell when Tommy was lying to me about what Lucky was saying. Lucky was a scrupulous man. If he made a promise, he kept it. Period. End of story. He promised to make Tommy the best comedian in the world and he meant it. Lucky believed in Tommy, with everything he had." Nicky's expression hardened.

"When did it start going south?" said Ria.

"When Tommy started getting successful. His head filled with these new ideas for films. Seb encouraged him, of course. So what do you get when you have the two brothers scheming and planning? The end of Lucky's dream for Tommy."

"All due respect, Uncle," said Lola, "Tommy was a grown man. He was entitled to his own dreams. Clearly, he was ambitious before Lucky haunted him. It couldn't have been a surprise to Lucky that Tommy was strong-willed."

"No, of course not," said Nicky. "But Tommy didn't give a single thought to Lucky's *contribution* to his career. He didn't consider any of his Ghost's feelings nor his advice. He didn't consult with his mentor. Nothing. He woke up one morning, bathed, dressed, ate his breakfast and drove to the studio lot, ready for his first day on set."

Lola shook her head. "What about the paperwork, the contracts? Sebastian must've asked Tommy questions before they signed with the studio. There must have been meetings, in person. How could Lucky not have noticed any of that?" She looked squarely into Nicky's eyes. "If he told you he didn't know, then I'm sorry, but he was being wilfully blind at best."

"My friend said that's what happened and I believe him."

There was another long silence at the table.

"So Lucky felt Tommy was turning his back on everything he'd taught him," said Ria.

Nicky nodded. "I think he didn't speak to Tommy for weeks." He paused. "Lucky wasn't speaking to me either, then. Tommy wasn't keen on letting me near, kept making excuses and had that damned brother of his run me around until I gave up and went away. So, instead of being reminded, forcibly, of his duty to Lucky, Tommy ran wild."

"It's not as though he committed a crime," said Lola. "He made some career choices without his Ghost's agreement."

"He stopped any pretense of listening to Lucky's advice." Nicky glowered at Lola. "He argued with everything Lucky suggested. Argued, or outright ignored it."

"Disrespecting one's Ghost is hardly a felony," said Lola.

Nicky pointed at her, his chin at a stubborn angle. "Lucky was deeply, deeply hurt. He felt betrayed and abused. He'd foregone reincarnation for this boy, given up all hope of another chance to get it right, and for what? A few years more of being milked for every last ounce of his knowledge and experience and advice only to be discarded like an old slipper. Old and useless. Kept worrying he was going to get...thrown out."

Ria glanced over as Lola shifted. Nicky stared into his tea cup.

Ria leaned in, kept her voice low. "Lucky Wai thought Tommy Chu was going to try to Disperse him? But how did he tell you all of this without Tommy knowing?"

Nicky shrugged. "Been doing it for years. The simplest way is to wait for the Host to sleep. The longer a Ghost has been haunting, the longer their tether to the Host. They can travel, in a way."

Lola stared. "How do you talk then? A Conjurer?"

Nicky nodded. "Or someone we trust." He lowered his voice. "There are ways for Ghosts to speak through others without the touch. It's just not bandied about, you understand. But it's common knowledge."

Lola face flushed hot. How many other aspects of hauntings was she ignorant of?

Aubrey's voice was low, solemn. "Only the desperate and those with dubious ethics do such things, Lola." He paused. "Nicky's idea of normal is...coloured by the company he keeps."

Ria cleared her throat. "What you're saying, it's a serious accusation. You can't keep that to yourself. You've got to tell the police."

"They won't believe me now." Nicky shook his head. "They'll just think I've got a grudge against Tommy. Looking for a way to smear his reputation."

Lola tipped her head at Nicky's tone. "That was exactly your plan, wasn't it, this morning." She spoke slowly, working it out. "Why you antagonised Leung and Eng. You pretended to slip and use the nickname, didn't you?"

"I don't need them breathing down my neck, my girl. We don't need the coppers blundering about—" his mouth twisted "—trying to cover up that the great Tommy Chu was looking for illegal Dispersal spells in order to rid himself of his Ghost. This has got to be handled discreetly. For Lucky's sake."

Ria shook her head. "But you don't know that for certain. It was only what he feared. And aside from that, how would that lead to Tommy being murdered?"

Lola kept her voice low, but she couldn't tamp down on her anger. "Pride. That's all this is about. You're just out to protect Lucky Wai's reputation."

Lola and Nicky glared across the table at one another.

"You should've told me the truth from the start."

"I have my reasons, my girl. Don't push me on this. Your fa—" At Lola's rude noise, Nicky bore down. "*Your father* would've trusted me. You owe me at least as much."

Lola ground her teeth. "I'm still here, aren't I. You'd just better be clear what calling this debt's going to cost." Lola lit a cigarette and signalled for the waitress to bring their tally.

❧

Lola let herself into Stuey's apartment, quietly closing the door behind her. Her head was pounding in time to an invisible metronome, her body aching with fatigue. With grief.

"It's coming on 3:30," said Aubrey. "You need to rest."

She breathed deeply, exhaled slowly. The desire for another cigarette flitted through her thoughts, but it didn't feel right to taint the orange-scented air. She searched the dark outlines of the apartment, recalling the furnishings and plants by memory.

"What are you doing here, Lola?" said Aubrey. "The poor man's gone. The coppers have tossed this place twice, at least."

She stared out the window.

Silver clouds were now visible around a crescent moon, the rest of the sky a deep, velvety grey. Pale blurs hinted at distant stars.

"There's always something."

"I doubt that," said Aubrey flatly. "Bednarski and Marks strike me as better than average."

She scowled, the pressure in her chest increasing with every word Aubrey spoke. She strode down to Stuey's office. Everything looked just as neat as she recalled. The date book was even open to the current week, the pen neatly aligned beside it. She wasn't surprised Marks had put every single item back exactly as it had been. Walking over, she ran a finger along the dime novels again, smiling sadly. She assessed the room once again, wondered what the detectives took back to the station house.

Aubrey was right, damn him. The two *gwai* detectives were excellent at their jobs.

But she had to try.

Three-quarters of a fruitless hour later, Lola sat on the sofa and watched the sky above the horizon. Wearily, she reflected that her own view, ten floors up, would've been better.

She forced her brain to think over the past forty-five minutes. She hadn't found any hidden compartments or secret panels in any of Stuey's furniture. Nothing stashed in a neat little slit in the mattress. No loose floorboards or false walls behind the closet full of those beautifully tailored clothes.

She wondered if Evelyn Shao would simply leave her things for someone to dispose of. Otherwise, she'd have to confide in Liliane and Keun Lim.

Not her problem, she reminded herself harshly.

Lola slumped, letting her head fall back against the upholstery. She'd tossed Stuey's home ruthlessly and just as mercilessly put it back together neatly. There was nothing here.

She pressed the back of a wrist against her tired eyes, let her arm fall onto the cushions beside her. She stared at the plants in their stylish pots, the paintings and sculptures, the warm colours and fabrics. Stuey's character shone in everything around her. She stared at the table in the nook, readily imagined Evelyn Shao sitting with him, eating and laughing. Even Serene Chu had a better claim on memories with him.

For all that Lola knew him longest, it was clear now that she knew him least of all.

She rolled her head to one side, watching through glass as the night sidled up to dawn.

Outside the windows, the distant ocean remained dark even as the sky gradually, inexorably, lightened. Four o'clock had come and gone while she'd been rooting around the closet floors. In less than a full day, the formal cremation ceremonies would take place, releasing both men's souls into the eternal cycle.

At hour forty-four after his death, Stuey's remains would be burned to ashes, freeing his spirit to re-enter the queue for reincarnation and another chance to do it up properly.

Lola stared at the reflected dawn, chest aching and eyes dry.

FOURTEEN

It seemed like she'd only just closed her eyes when Elaine shook her awake. It was a telephone call. At seconds past seven o'clock.

"Good morning, Auntie." Lola coughed several times, trying to dislodge the frog in her throat. She sat down heavily in the chair at her dressing table.

"You sound terrible," said Vivian. "Sorry to wake you."

Lola swallowed, wincing at the pain.

Vivian cleared her throat. "Yes, well, final day before cremation. We want you to come with us to Liliane's. We'll meet you there at nine. It's important for family, yes?"

Lola held a sigh. "I paid them a visit yesterday, Auntie. I've got leads to follow up on today, but I'll be there before the ceremony begins tonight."

Vivian huffed a breath.

Lola shook herself, forcing her mind into wakefulness.

"But while I have you on the line, I need to ask you something."

Lola heard the strike of a match, Vivian's inhalation.

"It's about that pocket watch. The one Stuey was given by, er...his uncle."

"Stanley, his Uncle Stanley. It's all right. You can say his name. I'm not holding any grudges against the man. He's long dead, isn't he? And there's no point in begrudging the dead. That's what this newest tragedy has taught me."

133

Lola pulled the receiver away from her ear to stare at it for a moment. "Ah...what can you tell me about it? Why was it important to Uncle Stanley?"

Vivian exhaled forcefully. "It was an anniversary gift. From me."

Lola blinked several times. "Uh, which year?"

"First. I had it engraved. 'To Stan. From Viv. Love always.'"

Lola thought about that. "Did you know he'd gifted it to Stuey?"

Vivian made an impatient noise. "Of course not. Back then, I *was* still holding a grudge, silly girl."

"Yes, of course, Auntie." Lola considered her words carefully. "Was that gift...important to him? Would it have been significant that he gave it to Stuey?"

"By the time he gave it away? I haven't the faintest. But when I gave it to him, yes, it was important to him. We were still very much in love."

"And," Lola spoke slowly, "Uncle Stanley didn't have any children? After?"

"No, which is why, any fool can see, he gave it to his only nephew. Next closest thing. Besides which, I understand that Stanley was very fond of...Stuey." Vivian's voice softened. "I thought he'd pawned it when we split. For travelling money, you see."

Lola stayed quiet for a moment. "Auntie—"

"Now," Vivian became brisk, "about the ceremonies. You know you can't stay at Liliane's. You must attend the Chus with me."

"Auntie, there will be plenty of people you know. Uncle Nicky will take care of business over there. My focus is Stuey."

"I'm not merely looking for company, silly girl. It's our family pride on the line. We must put in a showing. Pay our respects, especially after his generous gesture at the theatre last night."

Lola thought over Vivian's possible motives. "The others aren't going, are they?"

"Pick me up from Keun's at nine o'clock tonight."

Lola rubbed her face, thinking quickly. "I'm going to split the difference. I'll be at the Lims' until Second Rites are completed. Then I'll meet Uncle Nicky for Final Rites at Tommy's cremation." Lola spoke over Vivian's grumbling. "I won't miss Stuey's cremation, Auntie. This is as much as I'll compromise."

"I'll tell the others." Vivian rang off.

"Any theories yet?" said Aubrey.

"About what?" Lola crawled to the top of her bed.

"Take your pick. Vivian's command that you accompany them this morning. Why Nicky Lo needs you to run interference with the coppers. Whether Kam's going to show today or tonight." Aubrey paused. "How to tell Nicky his theory makes absolutely no sense whatsoever."

Lola grabbed a pillow off the floor, punched it into submission, tossed it back onto the bed.

Aubrey said, "If you can explain to me how Tommy hiring someone to Disperse Lucky turned into getting himself gunned down in the street, then I concede you're a better man than I."

Lola stuffed herself back under the sheet, pulled a pillow over her head and squeezed her eyes shut.

⬖

She'd opened all the office windows in the hopes of catching some fragment of a cross breeze. A rumbling truck passed in the street below. A horn blared. She heard a shout of masculine laughter. The scent of cigarettes seemed to strengthen for a moment then dissipate. China's Best. Their pungent, sweet clove aroma reminded Lola of her father.

"Sorry," she said into the horn, "care to repeat that?"

The servant on the other end of the line remained blandly polite. "Miss Serene is available at two o'clock."

Lola thanked him and replaced the telephone receiver on its cradle. She sipped from her cup of coffee, listened to the faint squeak of the motor turning the fan blades in the corner. She slid a dark cigarette out from the inlaid box atop her desk.

"Ghosthood isn't quite the sunny picture they paint, is it?" She tapped the end of the cigarette against the heel of her palm.

"Becoming a Ghost doesn't negate one's personality."

"So if you were a pain before you died, you'll still be one after?" She lit up, took a drag. "Never mind. I don't need you to answer that."

Lola listened to another round of traffic stopping, then starting up again. She absently counted the sound of footsteps as someone walked down the sidewalk, his jaunty whistling fading as traffic roared past and he got farther away.

When she finished her cigarette, she picked up the telephone again.

Sammy Lu was polite and to the point.

"Listen, Miss Starke, we haven't heard a darned thing about either Tommy Chu or Stuey Lim. And we asked everyone. Discreetly, of course. That's not gonna be a big deal amongst us parlour owners. We've all gotta know what's what, if you understand me. So I don't think anyone's holding out. But I did hear some noise about the girl, his sister."

"Serene Chu?"

"She's got a Ghost, right?"

"Her *Mah-mah.*"

"Yup, that's the one. The Ghost."

"The Ghost." Lola thought back to Tommy's dressing room. Did Kam hold the debt over Stasha Chu? Did Stuey put up the watch to cancel her debt?

"Something wrong with my phone," muttered Lu. He raised his voice. "The Ghost. Ah…Anastasia Chu. Strange name. Apparently, they call her 'Stasha.'"

"Do you have a number, for the debt?" said Lola. "It must be rather high."

"No, it's not like that, Miss Starke. Ghosts don't bet with money. It's an Ether debt."

Aubrey cursed.

"Ether debt?" Lola said.

"Yes, it's the only thing they have, isn't it? Their Hosts may, of course, have money debts as well. That's actually often the case, both being indebted, I mean. It's difficult for a Host to fend off their Ghost's addiction." Lola was surprised to hear the sorrow in Lu's voice. "We don't allow Ghosts to gamble at Lucky Bamboo. It's a dodgy business, Miss Starke, collecting Ether from Ghosts."

"I'd imagine it would require an unscrupulous Conjurer."

"It's an evil business," said Lu. "Ether addiction is impossible to overcome. By allowing Ether bets, an owner is profiting from misery, plain and simple. The Ghosts who bet and the Ghosts who work for him or her."

"I'm sorry, Mr. Lu, I don't understand."

"Houses that allow Ghost bets must, by necessity, also employ Ghosts themselves, you see. The house Ghosts make sure the Hosts who are gambling aren't lowballing their Ghosts' bets, and they also put up the energy when guests win their bets."

"But, that's...a sort of vampirism, isn't it?"

"It's an addiction, Miss Starke, yes. Although I suppose cannibalism would be more accurate."

"Wait," said Lola, "we're talking about Ghosts feeding off other Ghosts'...what? Their substance? A part of the Ether?" She paused. "I've never heard of that before."

"I'm no Spectral scholar, Miss Starke. All I know is it's an evil business, any way you look at it. If you're thinking of nosing around this joint, the one that holds Anastasia Chu's Ether debt, I...well, frankly, I'd advise against it. These people, we already know they're unscrupulous. There's no telling what sorts of trouble you're liable to find. Are you certain you still want to do this?"

Lola found Lu's grave tone unsettling.

"The man has a point," said Aubrey.

"Thank you for your concern, Mr. Lu," she said. "I've promised a friend I'd help." Lola jotted everything down, promised to stop in when time permitted, and rang off. She sat motionless, staring out her office window.

"That would explain Kam last night," said Aubrey, thoughtful.

"And why Serene pretended not to know him. I can't imagine Sebastian being jake about his *Mah-mah* gambling with..." She shuddered, her skin prickling with goose bumps. "They must be keeping it from him."

Lola locked up, turning to head for the lift when she heard her telephone ring. Swearing, she hesitated, then fumbled with the locks and ran back inside.

It was Ria.

"Just about to come see you," said Lola.

"Checking up on me, you mean." Ria laughed, sounding weary. "I bet I'm doing about the same as you are, doll."

"To pump you for information, actually," said Lola. "The coppers may be on the right track after all." She summarized her chat with Sammy Lu. "There's nothing illegal about this Ether betting, for all that it makes my skin crawl."

"It takes all kinds, Lola, whether we understand them or not. You can't save everybody. Leastways from themselves."

There was a heavy silence. Lola reviewed everything she'd seen the night before: the interplay between Serene and her Ghost, Serene and her brother.

"There's something rotten with that family," she muttered.

Aubrey surprised her with his reply. "Yes and we'll do something about it."

Ria sighed. "I'm still not convinced someone would shoot Tommy to send her a message, though."

Lola felt a sudden stab of anger. She stared out the window, focussing on the shop front across the street. She pressed her hip into the side of her desk. After a moment, she cleared her throat.

"Maybe they were balking at the amount. Maybe they were behind on payments. The betting is legal, but you can't very well jump a Host in broad daylight and start siphoning her Ghost's Ether energy without someone raising a fuss. And last I heard, kidnapping's still not copacetic."

"That might explain the out-of-town trip she took," said Ria. "If this Kam character was turning up the heat on Stasha Chu."

"What d'you mean?"

Lola heard a door slam down the hall from her office.

"Remember the 'holidaymaking' my set dresser mentioned? Well, Serene really did go somewhere. Left the City for a week. I'm still tracking down where. She only returned two days ago."

"Day before the shooting," murmured Lola. "I doubt her brothers would've allowed Serene to leave for a vacation in the midst of a big film project. Not that a week's going to make your neighbourhood 'sugar boy' any less aggressive. Probably the opposite."

"Wasn't making any sense to me neither," said Ria.

Lola ran through some possibilities in her mind. "I'll let you know after I find out from her this afternoon."

"Where did Sammy Lu say this gambling joint was again?"

"Eastern Promises. Somewhere around Sai-Dong."

"I know it," said Ria. "Cheap place on a dodgy street. Muscle on the door. Two months ago, a boy was found stabbed on their doorstep. Of course nobody saw nothin'." Ria paused. "What the hells would make a Ghost force her granddaughter to a place like that in the first place?"

"I doubt Stasha Chu cares much about that." Lola paused. "Maybe it was familiar. Serene and her brothers grew up there, right?"

"Or perhaps no one else would take her bets anymore."

Lola felt her guts twist at Aubrey's words. "Or maybe Kam warned off every other gambling joint. Forced her to come to him."

"Everyone knows the *Tongs* rule that part of the City," said Ria.

"What the hells were they thinking? Messing around with the *Tongs*? Trying to outsmart a gangster." Lola scowled.

"I don't know that we can blame Serene for her Ghost's actions," said Ria.

"Serene, I can understand, after a fashion," said Lola. "It's Stuey Lim I don't follow."

FIFTEEN

There were only three homes at the pinnacle of the North Hills Enclave, site of the most spectacular views anywhere in Crescent City.

Two belonged to the City's oldest families, ancestral enemies who had brought their feud across the ocean from Shanghai. Instead of imperial appointments and favours, however, the Wongs and Changs had played their game out anew with the rough-and-tumble gold prospectors of a century past.

During the heated gold rush into the area then known only as "the Crescent," the Wongs plied essential wool and cotton goods. The Changs spent their time and energies on establishing a network for their poppy trade. Eventually, the Wongs expanded into every imaginable kind of gear manufactured for camping and mining high into the forested hills surrounding the crescent-shaped bay. The Changs came to dominate the market for every conceivable vice desired by the lonely, desperate people who streamed into the Crescent looking to strike it rich.

Close to eleven decades later, the Crescent was called the City by its citizens, and the two families held strong to their respective footholds. Lola, a reluctant student of the historical lectures her father used to give her, readily understood why the Changs and Wongs had built their mansions here. The power of symbolism was impossible to ignore.

So what did it say that the Chus bought the house in the middle?

Perhaps it was the quality of the light, she mused as she drove up to the Enclave. The tall, whitewashed walls up on the pinnacle were certainly not novel. All the homes she'd passed driving up the winding road to get here had been hidden behind similar structures. *These* walls, however, seemed to radiate white light, creating a halo effect that softened their corners and made the sky seem achingly blue.

After that first glimpse, passage through to the Chu mansion grounds was surprisingly mundane. A gate, a guard, a visual inspection, then Lola was told to follow the gravel driveway and park by the fountain. She got out into the heat of mid-afternoon, holding a cloth bag of oranges and her purse.

The former home of a European director of the silent film era, the house was two storeys of pristine white adobe walls topped with bright terracotta tiles. Two rows of sashed windows reflected every available shaft of sunlight. Lola squinted behind her sunglasses. The main door was in a recessed archway. The door opened and a man walked out toward her.

The servant wore dove grey silks and a bland expression. He had a white band high on his right arm, the narrowness appropriate for his station in a grieving household. He bowed low. "Miss Starke, this way please." His English was nasal with an east coast inflection.

"Cantonese is fine," she said. The man bowed again and turned back toward the house.

"Not bad," murmured Aubrey. "Not important enough for Chu himself to come out, but he did send someone so you'd not have to knock."

As Lola expected, there was a great deal of marble in the main foyer. Pale grey stone was highlighted by the natural light coming through the large half-moon window atop the main entrance door.

The ceiling was high and vaulted. In the middle of the foyer, atop a wood table covered by white linen, stood an arrangement of white flowers, larger than Lola could encompass with her arms.

The servant stopped to the right of the main door. A rectangular table of deep mahogany and stout, carved legs stood against the wall. He bowed, gestured toward the table. Lola relinquished her bag of oranges. He emptied the fruit out into an alabaster receptacle with short cylindrical incense burners on either side. Fragrant smoke drifted upward.

Lola counted three mirrors in the foyer, all covered according to custom by dark grey cloth. The servant led Lola up the winding staircase on the left side of the foyer and then down a long hallway. Their footsteps were muted by the deep blue carpet that ran the length of the hall. Interior doors stood closed, their dark wooden surfaces gleaming.

Lola glanced at a frame as she walked past. A traditional depiction of Fu Lu Shou, done in fine silk needlepoint. The colours of the three gods' robes were bright against the dark wooden frame.

The servant ushered Lola through a set of double doors at the end of the hall.

Sebastian Chu turned, backed by a wall of windows.

It was a panoramic view of the harbour and ocean in the distance, with most of the City laid out in the foreground. Lola stepped into the room and realized she'd been wrong. The windows were, in fact, an entire wall made of one seamless piece of curved glass.

"My favourite room in the house." Sebastian bowed stiffly.

"With good reason," said Lola.

He waved Lola toward the seats and gestured to the servant. "Tell Miriam we're ready for tea." The man bowed.

Sebastian offered Lola the long sofa facing the view. He chose an armchair at right angles. A maid entered with a tray, and deftly laid out pot, cups, a platter of cookies, small plates, and various serving utensils. She smiled at Lola, gave a small curtsey, and left.

Sebastian poured Lola's tea, then his own, and replaced the teapot with deliberate care. "I apologize for my conduct last night. Serene was quick to point out you were trying to help."

"I can easily understand your protectiveness. I hope your sister recovered quickly?"

He nodded. "Sadly, we're accustomed to her episodes."

Lola paused a beat. "Will Miss Chu be joining us as well?"

Sebastian used a set of small tongs and placed two crescent-shaped almond cookies onto a plate for Lola. "I know it was many years ago now, but please allow me to say I was quite sad to hear of your father's passing. I watched all of his films when we were children. Our favourite was his second with your mother, 'Don't Tell Me Now.' Tommy adored the chase scene down the steps of the windmill."

"It was a long time ago." Lola heard the abruptness of her words. She took a breath. "Thank you. I'm sorry to be intruding on your mourning period."

"When Nicky Lo gets a hold of something, he's unlikely to let it go without a fight. I prefer to choose my battles."

"Humour him, you mean?"

Sebastian took a noisy sip of tea. He replaced it upon the table with some force. "I understand he wants to feel he's doing right by Lucky, but I'm not clear what your obligation is. Since you were neither a friend nor obviously family to Lucky." He paused, openly assessing her. "Is Nicky paying you to work for him?"

"I understand obligation and duty perfectly well, Mr. Chu." Lola kept her voice calm. "My loyalties lie with Uncle Nicky. I made a promise to him, and I fulfill on that promise out of respect and love. Universal values, no matter one's outward appearance."

Sebastian shrugged. "What is it you think *you* can do that the police cannot?"

"Leung and Eng are the elite, I won't argue that. Uncle Nicky asked for my help so that's what I'm going to do. To the best of my abilities."

"I see that," said Sebastian. "Which is why we are talking now before I allow you to speak with *a-Mui*."

Lola gauged her host as she sipped at her tea. "I'm given to understand that your brother and his Ghost were at odds recently."

Sebastian sat back, shaking his head. He aged between one blink and the next. "Is this his angle?" He stared hard at Lola, black eyes fierce. "It's no secret Tommy was moving away from the stage and that Lucky wasn't happy about it. You should know, being haunted yourself, it's a complicated relationship. Lucky wanted what he wanted and Tommy disagreed."

"You sided with Tommy."

He nodded. "Of course. We both saw the future quite clearly. Oh, I'm not saying the stage will ever disappear. That's just fear mongering. Absurd. Film and the cinema—that's where our craft is headed."

"Spoken like a true believer."

"And what's wrong with that?" Sebastian arched a brow. "I'm not a religious man. Neither is Tommy. We give our devotion and energies to entertainment. We worship long hours at its altar and you should know yourself, having grown up in the business, it's a harsh mistress."

"Will you tell me the exact nature of the disagreement between your brother and his Ghost?"

"Lucky thought it short-sighted of us to focus so much on this film. Cheap tricks and acrobatics, he said. Lucky never acknowledged the artistry of Tommy's physical comedy. He loved the classic setup-and-punch-line gags, and the longer the setup, the more he loved them."

Sebastian shifted forward in his seat, his face animated. "Tommy was exploring the choreography of comedic fighting. He was incorporating incongruous objects for comic effect. Wine jugs and foot stools, even a dented chamber pot! You see, Tommy believed just as strongly as Lucky that incongruity lies at the heart of comedy. Lucky was the undisputed master of using incongruity in his routines. He did it better than anyone and he did it for a very long time.

"But that time is no longer. It's sad, I know, but our sorrow at the passage of things cannot prevent us from moving forward and continuing to grow ourselves and our craft. Tommy and I, we had a strong vision of the future of comedy. It's about *mixing* fighting with the punch line. Using the choreography of the martial arts to serve as the setup and the punch line, you see. Like a dance rather than just a dialogue." He sat back, shrugged.

"That is where Lucky and Tommy could not agree. The simple and profound nature of what makes people laugh." He paused. "But Lucky came around eventually." He trailed off, expression closing up.

Lola turned her gaze squarely to the stunning vista, giving Sebastian the illusion of privacy to pull himself together. She felt a twinge of guilt at the need to nose around in another's grief.

She watched the ocean sparkling in the distance, gathering her thoughts, reassessing her approach.

In the end, she forced herself to recall her promise to Nicky. This intrusion, now, was only the beginning. Serene Chu and her autocratic Ghost were still on the horizon.

She softened her tone. "Can you think of anyone who had a grudge against your brother?"

Sebastian shook his head. "As I told the police, we're in show business, Miss Starke. Feuds are played out with contracts and across marquees, not in blood and death."

"What about personal relationships?"

"Tommy was a popular man, but he didn't have time for any other mistress than his work."

"Even dalliances can go awry." Lola kept her voice mild.

"Not with Tommy. You don't understand. He was married to his career. There was no room for romance. Frankly, my brother was far from the romantic type."

Lola thought of the little dance she'd had with Tommy the previous night. It saddened her that this man seemed to think his own brother incapable of such a thing.

She assessed Sebastian Chu with a clinical view. He seemed extraordinarily self-possessed for a man who'd just lost a beloved sibling to a violent death. Lola surveyed the tight line of his jaw and the smudges beneath his eyes. Then again, perhaps he was simply using briskness as a mask.

She stared out the glass wall, calculating her next questions.

Far westward, the water was choppy with surf, its white breakers visible even from this distance. Large container ships were scaled down to the size of toys in a bathtub. They cut smoothly through the water along the horizon. Smaller pleasure craft wound around the bay, sails billowing.

"Do you think his death is connected to Lucky somehow?" Sebastian rearranged the cookies on the plate, straightened the teapot.

Lola returned her gaze to her host. A sharp vertical line formed between his brows as he frowned. His eyes were dark with intensity.

"I'm gathering as much information as I can. Questions lead to answers that lead to more questions, and so it goes. Somewhere along that path, we find the answers we need."

"What happens to the answers you don't need? Or want? Do you sell those?"

Lola paused, staring back with a bland expression until his face reddened. She said, "Personally? No. But you're correct to be suspicious. There are unscrupulous people in this profession."

"You haven't answered my question about Lucky."

"It's certainly a possibility."

"A meaningless phrase."

Lola shrugged. "I'm sorry, Mr. Chu. There's still a lot of ground to cover."

"All right." He drew himself up stiffly. "You should know that my sister was away for a week."

"I'd heard that."

"I'd like you to be discreet, so I am telling you myself, instead of having you hear some garbled version of the truth. Serene was at Sunrise Valley up north, by the Little Foothills. Do you know it?"

"A sanatorium. Exclusive and expensive."

"Yes, a private facility for rest and recuperation. We thought she'd been working too hard. She cut her hand, you see, and Serene is always so careful with her tools. We knew something needed to be done. Oh, she wasn't happy about it. But we are her brothers. Sometimes, she just needs to do as she's told."

"And how was she when she returned? Better, I hope?"

Sebastian hesitated. "Truthfully, I can't really say. Tommy's death happened the day after Serene returned. With that and some other troubles recently...I've barely seen her." He looked away a moment, then narrowed his eyes at Lola. "I will, of course, stay with her during your questions."

"As long as it's jake with her."

"She should be amenable." His tone turned brisk. "Although I haven't heard if she's returned yet from her visit to the Lims. We were to go together, of course, but I had pressing matters regarding the formal cremation ceremony tonight." He paused. "His parents wanted separate ceremonies, I can't fault them, but circumstances being what they are, we cannot be in two places at the same time. Serene felt strongly that she should see the Lims today. I don't have that luxury, I'm afraid."

"Were she and Stuey close?" said Lola.

Sebastian nodded. "Stuey was like another brother to her. To all three of us. He and Tommy met at the acrobatics school, as you know. They were eight and nine. Serene was six. I had just turned twelve when Stuey came to our house for the first time." He grinned slightly. "He was so polite in his pressed tunic and pants. Before him, we'd never even touched a silk *mien-lahp* before. But Stuey let Tommy try it on without so much as a pause to think about it. And of course, Tommy ripped it almost right away, jumping around and tumbling, making us laugh. Stuey was generous to a fault."

Sebastian's grin faded.

"Our small apartment was his second home, no matter that we had so much less than he did. It mattered little to any of us. My mother loved him as dearly as she loved the rest of us. His parents were always gracious and kind. We stayed with them many weekends off from school." His gaze drifted away from Lola and set on some distant point across the ocean.

He brought himself back with a visible effort. "So, to answer your question, yes, they were close. As close as we all were." He stood. "I'll see if they've returned. Please wait here. I'll have more tea brought up."

Lola inclined her head.

Aubrey said, "Why didn't you ask him about the gambling?"

Lola waited until Sebastian had closed the doors behind him. She walked to the windowed wall. There was something irresistible about standing right at the thinnest barrier between oneself and the sky. Her breath fogged the glass and she took a step back.

"She deserves a chance to explain first."

Aubrey grunted.

She spent ten minutes in silent appreciation of the view. A maid finally appeared with another tea-laden tray, followed by her young mistress.

Serene stood to one side of the door. Her eyes were underscored by dark smudges, and her gaze darted around the room, perhaps unwilling to settle on Lola.

"How are you, Miss Chu? I'm sorry for the intrusion." Lola gestured to the seats as she heard Aubrey greet the other Ghost.

"Madame Chu believes Serene should be fine. Just needs a spot of tea," said Aubrey.

Lola held her tongue. The maid settled Serene with a cup of hot tea and an assortment of small steamed *bao* on a plate. She gave Lola a fresh cup of tea as well, cleared the dishes from earlier, and departed. The door closed with a soft click.

Lola watched Serene take a bite of food.

"Are we waiting for your *dai-goh*?"

The plate rattled as Serene replaced it on the table. She threw a quick glance at Lola, fisting her trembling hands. "I'm fine," she said, then took a breath. "He had to take a telephone call."

"I don't see any need to wait for him, do you? The sooner we begin, the sooner we can be done."

Serene frowned a little as she listened to her Ghost. Her shoulders hunched inward. Her hands curled and uncurled repeatedly. After a while, Aubrey said, "Madame Chu would prefer that Serene finish her food first."

Lola nodded. "All right."

Serene took her plate up again with trembling hands. She ate, her face set grimly.

"This is an impressive room," said Lola.

"The view is, anyway," said Serene in a quiet voice. "It's hard for me to take much notice of the inside though. *Yee-goh*—" she swallowed "—had it changed every few months."

"Tommy did? Changed, you mean the colour?" Lola looked around at the furniture, all in varying shades of orange. She cocked a brow.

Serene nodded as she chewed daintily. "Colour, furnishings, flowers. Everything that could be replaced or painted, he wanted it switched."

Aubrey said, "Madame Chu thought it extravagant."

"I imagine it's quite a departure from your childhood," said Lola.

"Tommy hated being poor." Serene turned her face away.

"And how did you feel about it?"

Serene shrugged. "The view never changes, at least."

Lola couldn't tell if the past was too painful a subject or one beneath discussion. Her instincts screamed to shelter this frail young woman, but her training directed otherwise. She set her jaw. She could help this girl. She just had to stay the course.

Lola watched Serene push a few bits of food around on her plate, then set it down. She said, "I understand you were away for a week. Can you tell me about that?"

Serene's jaw clenched for a moment. "I had hurt myself while cutting out a pattern. Simple. I'd done it thousands of times before. The pattern *and* the injury. Honestly, using fabric scissors is always a hazard. They're extremely sharp and I am always in a rush because Tommy always wants everything done two days ago." She paused. "But my brothers thought—"

"—and Madame Chu agreed," added Aubrey.

"—I had been working too much."

Lola watched the other woman's face closely as Serene stared out through the wall of glass. "There are worse places in the world than Sunrise Valley. I'm grateful for my time there."

"I've heard of it."

Serene's lips compressed. "It's beautiful and peaceful. It's close to the Little Foothills. Sunny all day and cool at night. I spent a lot of time alone."

"According to Madame Chu," said Aubrey, voice tight, "Sunrise Valley is for very exclusive clients only. They have a strict vegetarian menu and they strongly recommend daily exercise. They have talented therapists in acupuncture and acupressure, instructors in *tai chi* and *qi-gong*." Aubrey paused.

Lola watched as Serene ate and sipped her tea with mechanical motions. Lola couldn't read her expression.

"She says Miss Chu was well taken care of." Aubrey's disdain was thinly veiled. Lola wondered how the other Ghost was reacting to it.

She brought herself back to her task. "Is that true?"

Serene nodded. "Of course."

Lola decided to switch up her direction.

"Did Stuey have a room here?"

Serene flushed. "No. Why would he?"

"He was family, wasn't he?"

"We were, yes, of course, but Stuey lived on his own. He liked his space. He had more freedom to compose his music, away from all the bustle here. And, I suppose it was what he was used to, being an only child." She took up her translucent blue tea cup and sipped delicately. "Being away for that week in particular made me realize that I'm far into my twenties, yet I've never lived alone."

Serene flinched, her face contorting. Tea spilled onto her hand.

"Madame," said Aubrey, his shock clear.

Serene replaced her cup on the table, wiped her hand unsteadily on her napkin. She offered a wan smile, the corners of her mouth trembling.

"Of course, it makes more sense for me to be close to my family." She paused, delicately cleared her throat. "My grandmother would like to continue with your questions, please. She'd like me to rest before tonight's cremation ceremony."

Her eyes shied away from Lola's concern.

SIXTEEN

A ubrey gasped in Lola's ear.

"How long have you been a Host, dear? You must not do much socializing with us." The reproachful tone was strangely familiar even if the voice was not.

"Is that you, Madame?" Lola spoke haltingly.

"Of course. Your Ghost is handsome, all right, but he's not very good at this."

"At what, exactly?"

"At social gatherings," said Stasha Chu. "You do know what those are, don't you, dear? Where people come together to drink tea or eat a meal and pass the time in pleasant chatter? You know, in this day and age there are many ways for Ghosts to participate with the living. This will make things so much more efficient."

"It's all right, Lola." Aubrey had regained his voice if not quite the smoothness in his speech. "I believe Madame Chu has...joined some of our energies together."

"I'm borrowing your communication system." Stasha chuckled. "I've never done this with a *gwai* before. It's not that different at all."

"I'll take that as a compliment," said Lola drily.

"I suppose it helps that you speak perfect Cantonese. Good for you, by the by. If it had been Mandarin, we would've been in trouble. Mine's so rusty. Oh yes, we can all hear one another now," said Stasha.

"Well," said Lola.

155

"Really, dear," said Stasha, "you should've already known all about this."

Lola had a moment of alarm. "Does this mean you can read each other's thoughts?"

"No, nothing of the sort. I've simply tapped into Mr. O'Connell's...oh never mind. It's really quite difficult to articulate in simplistic terms, you know, as it is quite complex."

"I can attempt to explain it later, if you like," said Aubrey. "We should be getting on, shouldn't we?"

Lola took a breath. "Thank you, Madame, for your cooperation. I'm sorry for this new bereavement."

"It's the lot of us old Ghosts," said Stasha. "We see everyone die, eventually. I thought I'd come to terms with Lucky's death the first time, but I suppose it's no surprise that Dispersal takes us all hard. 'There but for the grace of the gods' and all that. I chose Ghosthood at sixty-seven, and Serene is young yet. We'll see how I feel when it's my turn."

"Was Lucky having difficulties recently? With the haunting?" said Lola.

Serene startled as Stasha let out a cackling laugh.

"Feeling his bones, d'you mean? Don't we all?"

"What do you mean, Madame?"

Serene's expression was smoothly blank now.

"Lucky haunted Tommy for almost eight years," said Stasha. "A Host, any Host, will start to chafe eventually. Some of us like that challenge. Some just feel tired."

"I've heard there were some recent difficulties between them."

"Yes, for a good long time. But Lucky came around to their point of view. Sebastian is very convincing."

Lola shifted in her seat. "Did you agree with him?"

"Lucky didn't like quarrelling. I think he realized it was Tommy's life after all."

"What did you think of Tommy's new interest in film?"

"Tommy knew best. And I trust Sebastian to be careful."

"Did you agree, Miss Chu?"

Serene flushed a pale pink. "I think Tommy knew what he wanted and *Mah-mah* is right. *Dai-goh* would never let him take too big a risk."

"That went for his gambling as well, correct?" said Lola.

Serene nodded. Her gaze slid away.

Stasha said, "Yes. That was one of the few things my daughter-in-law taught them well about."

"What do you think of the police theory then? Do you think it's likely Tommy was in trouble with debts? Perhaps he was hiding his habit?"

Serene looked down at her hands, fiddling with a pale blue handkerchief.

"The police may be good for many things, but I assure you, they are mistaken about this gambling theory. My grandsons are responsible, smart men. They were never caught short." Stasha's tone raised Lola's hackles. She pushed down the sudden intense dislike.

Stasha said, "Surely, you must be considering that Stuey was the—"

Serene made a strangled noise, her body trembling all over. She quickly raised her handkerchief to her eyes, averting her face.

"I know you doted on him," said Stasha, "but sometimes we have to face harsh truths, especially about the ones closest to us."

Serene clenched her fists in her lap.

"Did you have something in particular to share, Madame?" Lola kept her tone neutral, though her heart rate had sped up.

"Well, not as such. I'm simply suggesting you keep your mind open," said Stasha. "It would be folly to be too narrow in your investigations."

"Of course. You must know that includes researching your grandson's acquaintances as well."

"I'm confident you'll draw a blank there."

Serene wiped her nose with the linen handkerchief and straightened up in her seat, her expression now stoic.

Lola calculated her next words. "I'm given to understand that you, Madame, have incurred some rather precipitous debts."

Serene's eyes widened.

"Who's been saying these lies?"

Lola winced at the volume of Stasha's outrage.

"Madame, step back please. Now." Aubrey's anger was clear as a bell to Lola's ears.

"It's what I've heard in the parlours," said Lola.

"Tell me who. I want names."

"Isn't it true, Madame?" Lola said mildly.

She heard Stasha muttering, quite close, then the Ghost's voice faded. Lola guessed she had moved over to Serene. Lola watched the younger woman closely.

Serene fidgeted in her seat, folding the handkerchief in her hands into smaller and smaller squares until it could not be made any tinier. Then she let it spring out of its forced shape. She stared at it for a moment, then began twisting it between her fingers. She spoke under her breath. She shook her head several times, her movements jerky.

Lola didn't need to hear the words to recognise an argument.

Serene raised her chin. "No. We can't keep it secret any longer." She forced out a sharp laugh. "Too many lies. It'll all come down on us anyway."

"Please, Madame," said Aubrey. "We're here to help."

"I sincerely doubt that," Stasha said. "Are you just here to scare up some more gossip? Are you really working with Nicky Lo? Or just scavenging for some newspaper?"

"Take care with your tongue, Madame," said Aubrey. "We do not stand for bullying."

Lola said, "I assure you we're here on good faith." She watched Serene as Stasha sputtered about *gwai* manners.

The younger woman slowly straightened up in her seat, her shoulders now square, spine erect. She precisely folded her handkerchief into fourths and placed the square of linen back into a pocket in her skirt. Serene met Lola's gaze.

"What did you hear?"

Lola made an easy guess. "That Philip Kam holds your grandmother in Ether debt."

"Yes, that's true."

"Why did you pretend not to know him last night?"

"We can't let anyone know about our situation."

"But surely, your brothers know? Or, at least, your *dai-goh*? How long has this debt been running?"

Serene's cheeks turned ruddy. "They both knew about the money. But the Ether debt, no."

"Sebastian covered your money debt?"

Serene nodded. "He did, yes. We had to start paying the...other debt six months ago."

"Why didn't you tell your brothers about the Ether debt?"

"I forbade it," said Stasha.

Serene said, "Please, you mustn't tell. She couldn't bear it if everyone knew. And we're already taking care of it."

"How's that?"

"I have weekly appointments."

"*You* do? What do you mean? I thought this repayment was only between Ghosts."

"Because the amount is so large, I made a deal." Serene cleared her throat. "To speed up the repayments, they take energy from me as well."

"My granddaughter is a good girl. She knows her duty."

Lola calculated the amount of debt incurred requiring continuous weekly payments for six months. She pressed her lips together tightly, carefully schooling her features to reflect nothing. Showing her inner seething would net her little in return.

Serene raised her chin. "It's what must be done. *Mah-mah* has promised me no more gambling. And I'll keep her to it this time."

"You must," said Aubrey. "Your Host cannot sustain this forever, Madame. It's clear to any observer."

"And Kam hasn't tried to shake you down for even more? Surely he's figured out you're keeping it secret from your brother," said Lola. "Did he charge 'interest' to keep it quiet?"

"No. I've barely seen him beyond that first time. And the...when we made our deal." Serene began twisting her handkerchief between her slender fingers. "We never spoke of my brothers. *Dai-goh* gave me money to settle the debt. He never asked me who held it. I took it personally to Mr. Kam."

"So he could deny it, I bet," murmured Aubrey. "Clever."

"Is it possible that Tommy's death is a warning to you, Madame?" said Lola.

"How dare you," said Stasha coldly. "As if these horrible deaths have anything to do with me. It's preposterous and insulting."

Serene's hands stilled. "I don't think so. *Mah–mah* is in serious debt, I do not deny that. But Mr. Kam is a businessman and ruthless, above all else. I recognize that, trust me. They cannot collect Ether against our wishes. Murder would not change our arrangement. We're already cooperating."

Lola considered Serene's words, her change in demeanour. The frightened little girl had evaporated. Now a proud young woman of means sat before Lola, confident in her assessments of a merciless gangster. Not even mention of the murders had shaken her.

Lola wasn't quite sure what to make of it. She thought back to the previous night's encounter.

"Why do you think Kam hasn't called off your debt?"

Serene shook her head. "I don't believe him. Stuey would never, ever give up that watch, and especially not for me."

"Why not?" said Lola. "You were as good as siblings. If he had eyes, he could see what it was doing to you. He had the means to protect you."

Another head shake. "No, he didn't know about the debt."

"I wouldn't put it past Kam to mention it to him, however," said Aubrey.

"Stuey would've talked to me first." Serene gripped her hands tightly. "That watch was too important to him."

"Let's say, for the sake of argument then," said Lola, "that Stuey did, in fact, make this deal with Kam." She paused. Serene nodded, reluctance clear in her expression. "He hasn't forgiven your debt entirely, though, presumably because he wants that pocket watch in hand first." Lola cocked her head to one side. "But why would he think you would have it?"

Serene blanched, and the dark circles beneath her eyes stood out starkly.

"Your theory is ridiculous," said Stasha. "Stuey would not make any such deal, and certainly not without telling us."

A knock sounded at the door. Sebastian entered. He caught sight of his sister's ashen face and his expression hardened.

"What have you done, you ignorant *gwai?*" he said, striding over to Serene. He put his arm around her shoulders. "*Mui-mui,* I'm here. You're all right." He glared coldly at Lola. "Get out."

Serene clutched at his hand. "No, it's all right. I just...felt faint. From hunger, most likely."

"Of course," said Lola, rising. "I've taken up enough of your time. Rest assured, Madame, Miss Chu. Uncle Nicky and I will be following up on those leads I mentioned. We *will* discover the truth. You can bet on that."

Lola inclined her head and left the room.

SEVENTEEN

Once they'd exited the main house, Lola listened to Aubrey swear a good long streak. After a pause, he said, "That was some big talk from you."

Lola shrugged. "Maybe it'll shake something loose." She hesitated, cleared her throat. "What about you? Everything extricated properly? There's no chance she's eavesdropping?"

"No, she's gone." He paused. "It was...an interesting experience."

"Any insights into the old woman?"

"No, she adroitly kept her thoughts to herself, just as I did mine. And, apparently, that sort of connection doesn't transmit emotions, either."

"Her voice did that well enough," said Lola.

"Something was off with Serene," said Aubrey slowly. "Timid as a mouse, then roaring like a lion. All in the space of a few seconds."

Lola hesitated, pondering the changes she saw in Serene's demeanour. She felt a deep unease, tried to shake it off. "Grief makes people strange."

Lola reached her car just as she heard the sound of another vehicle on the gravel drive. She stood next to her door and watched as a dark blue Packard pulled up. It stopped with a rumble. She heard the parking brake being engaged.

The Detective Inspector wore dark grey today, accented with a pale green tie and matching feather detail in his trilby. His Detective

Sergeant was in black and grey. Dark colours but not a drop of sweat on either of them. Lola felt the sun on her head all the more keenly.

"Miss Starke." DI Leung tipped his hat to her. "I am not, unfortunately, surprised to see you here."

"The pleasure's all mine then, Detective Inspector. What brings you out to the Enclave?"

"May I hope that this was purely a social call?"

"I'm afraid I can't speak to your hopes. But I'm just leaving, if that makes a difference." Lola opened her door. A wave of heat surged out. She rolled down her driver's side window then did the same for the other three doors. The Twins observed her with contemplative expressions.

Lola considered what she'd learned from Serene and Stasha Chu. She came to a decision.

"Would it interest you to know that Philip Kam holds a substantial Ether debt over Serene Chu's Ghost?"

"Where did you hear this from?" said Leung.

Lola shrugged. "Doesn't matter. I'm telling you so you can check into it. Put some pressure on this Kam character. I mentioned him to Bednarski." Lola spread her hands. "As you say, I've got no official authority. But I'm concerned for the Lims. They're good people who've just lost their only child. A gangster's got no business showing up at their home and threatening them."

The Twins shared a look. Eng spoke this time. "Tit for tat then, Miss Starke. No one's been willing to admit to holding any debts on Tommy Chu." He glanced at his partner. "But we're still waiting to hear on Stuey Lim from our other team."

"Your information is appreciated," said Leung. "We'll be in touch." The detectives stepped away and turned toward the main house doors.

"No servant for them," murmured Aubrey.

Lola started up her Buick and drove back on the gravel driveway, through the gates, and out onto the long winding street, spiralling down and away from the best views in the City.

◈

"This is a long way to go on a hunch," said Aubrey.

"All you've got is time," said Lola.

"I could question the Ghosts helping Kam."

Lola thought that over. She supposed it was a damned sight better than his leaving to spy on her mother again. She checked her mirrors and watched the traffic on the highway. Long shadows stretched sideways from the distant foothills in front of her.

"You can do that?" she said. "Can they trace you back to me?"

"I'm no gambler, and you won't be there. They'll most likely be so startled, I'll get my questions in before they know what's going on."

"And if they're better than you give them credit for?"

"I'll make do, Lola. Don't worry."

"I've got good reason. And you didn't answer me. I have no idea what happens to me if you Disperse."

"I knew you cared."

"You aren't cut out for detective work, Aubrey. You were a dresser, remember? Not an actor, so you can't even act the part of gumshoe."

"Well, good thing I'm a quick study. I haven't been hanging around, buffing my nails. Nicky Lo trained you well, and I've been paying attention." He paused. "I don't need permission, you know."

Lola drove in silence for a good ten miles. She knew he was still hovering. She could feel his presence. But they were long past being courteous to one another, so what was he waiting for?

"When do we meet up?" she said at last.

"I'll find you." And he was gone.

Lola shrugged her tight shoulders repeatedly until the knot in them lessened. A sign passed on the right. Another five miles and she would need to make the turn. She thought about her approach for the upcoming interview. How much truth to tell. How much to hide. What would get her the best information?

All at once, the turnoff was upon her. She swerved and cursed herself for her inattention. The road remained asphalt and Lola made short work of the remaining half-mile to her destination. She used the time to settle her nerves.

She was soon driving next to a lush, manicured lawn of deep green grass. Lola slowed her car as she passed flowering shrubs and cacti, dotted between stunted desert pines. In the distance, a cluster of buildings, their white walls painted ochre by the setting sun, the only manmade structures for miles around. After a few more minutes, another sign announced her destination. She had arrived at Sunrise Valley.

Lola drove through an arch set over the roadway, noting the lack of traditional iron-handled wooden gates and any attached wall or fencing. The driveway meandered toward the main grouping of buildings, eight structures with similarly rounded corners and pale adobe walls.

As she parked in the visitors' section, she assessed the staff vehicles. Aside from one caramel roadster that gleamed in the waning light, it seemed that the staff liked modest cars. She locked up her own red beauty and headed toward the building marked "Sunrise Valley Sanatorium Welcome Centre."

The double doors led to an open space with windows and a high ceiling. A large reception counter of dark teak, its panelling carved in intricate patterns, sat about ten feet into the room. As she neared, she made out depictions of clouds, hills, trees, sun, and moon. A young man, black hair brushed up and back from a high, narrow forehead, raised his head, smiled, and stood up.

"Miss Starke?" he said. Lola nodded. "Welcome to Sunrise Valley. I spoke with you on the telephone earlier. My name is Will. How was your drive?"

"Fine, thank you."

"I'm glad to hear it. If you'll take a seat." He gestured behind and to his left. Lola walked forward, found a seating area of upholstered armchairs. "Manager Toh will be here momentarily. May I get you some tea? Perhaps water?"

"Yes, thanks. Tea would do well."

Will nodded, walked across the lobby to a door opposite the reception counter. Lola sat down, looking around the large airy lobby area. She was evidently the only visitor. She strained her ears, but heard only the sounds of clinking ceramics and, briefly, running water. A few minutes later, Will returned with a tray. The tea service was standard white ceramic, no designs. Lola allowed him to pour for her.

"Does Manager Toh usually work this late?" she said.

"She is just finishing her shift for today."

"And you as well?"

He grinned. "And me as well. If you'll excuse me, I need to attend to some final work before I can sign out." He gave a half-bow.

Lola picked up the promotional material set out on the low table beside her.

Welcome to Sunrise Valley

We know you'll find our traditional remedies and the setting of natural beauty the tonic you need to return to your optimal health and vitality. Our team of health experts include medical doctors, nurses, practitioners in acupuncture, acupressure massage, herbalists, and teachers in meditation and the ancient martial arts.

Lola silently calculated the cost of creating an oasis in the desert, gave up after she reached five figures. She heard the tapping of heels and looked up in time to see a tall woman with glossy black hair pulled back into a high tail. She wore a pale green dress cinched with a narrow brown belt that matched her smart brown heels. She was thin as a whip and sharp-featured. Lola could not imagine a better fit for the role of "high-priced administrator."

"Miss Starke, I'm Delia Toh. It's a pleasure to meet you."

"Thank you for seeing me on such short notice."

"Not at all. Shall we step into my office?" Toh led the way through the interior doorway and into a long corridor.

Immediately to the left, a sort of kitchen with a small ice box and a stove. A kettle still steamed faintly. Then three closed doors scattered on both sides of the hall. The last door on the right was open and Toh stepped inside. "Please, take a seat. May I get you more tea?"

Lola demurred.

Toh walked past her and sat down behind a medium-sized desk of the same dark teak as the reception counter. There were no intricate carvings here, but the wood was polished to a deep shine. Lola could smell a hint of wood oil and camphor. Toh leaned forward, a warm smile on her thin face.

"How may I help you today?"

"I'd like to know about Serene Chu's recent stay here."

"What's the nature of your interest?" Toh's expression was open and curious.

"As I explained on the telephone, I'm a private investigator. I'm working with a close friend of Lucky Wai. We're working on Tommy Chu's murder."

"Yes, I spoke with Mr. Sebastian Chu, as you suggested. He confirmed your involvement. How is Miss Chu's stay here related?"

"I'm exploring the possibility that her time here ties in to her brother's death."

"I'm sure you understand that our byword here is discretion. Our clients need to trust that we keep the details of their individual circumstances private." She raised a finger as Lola began to speak. "However, Mr. Chu has authorized me to share information about his sister in the most general of terms. Miss Chu stayed with us for one week. She came alone, except for her Ghost, of course. She was driven here by their regular driver, and he was the same person who picked her up." Toh's lips curved upward a little. "And you didn't answer my question."

Lola tipped her head. "I was told she had cut her hand while working on a costume. Her brother insisted this was unusual enough that she required treatment here. What can you say about that?"

Toh remained silent.

Lola allowed the silence to stretch out. A very slight furrow had appeared on Toh's brow. She clasped her hands before her on the beautiful desk. Lola could see a simple wedding band and long fingers that tapered into blunt, unvarnished nails.

"From what I've seen so far," Lola said slowly, "you're in the business of healing. So I would think you'd want to help someone like Serene Chu, rather than aid in her decline."

Toh's frown deepened. "Has something happened to her?"

"Other than the fact that she may be cracking under the pressure of her grief and the bullying from her Ghost, I really can't say."

"Your sarcasm hides a genuine concern, I'd guess."

"Oh, are you a psychoanalyst now as well?"

Toh smiled. "No, but I do recognize some of the frustration you're exhibiting."

Lola narrowed her eyes. "Frustration you've felt, you mean?"

"Yes." Toh's smile became apologetic. "We've seen the effects of Madame Chu's influence."

"I spoke with them today and there was just something...not quite right. It could be grief, I know. But something about her injury has been bothering me. Something I can't place." Lola paused, taking a deep breath, exhaling in a huff.

"I think the Chus are lying about her time here. Her Ghost went on and on about the medicinal tincture she was using, for gods' sake. It seemed a load of booshwash, frankly, but I realized that Stasha Chu got nervous whenever I asked about the injury. So here I am."

Toh nodded slowly, expression neutral.

Lola pressed on. "I understand your policy of discretion, but this is not the time for secrets, Manager Toh. I tell you honestly that I don't know how this information I'm asking for will help solve

Tommy Chu's death, but my intuition tells me it's important." Lola suppressed a quick slash of guilt for omitting Stuey.

Toh laced her fingers together atop the desk, assessing Lola openly. A telephone rang, muffled by the closed door. The women sat in silence, listening to the distant ringing. When it cut off abruptly, Lola saw Toh's shoulders subtly relax.

"It happens, Miss Starke, that I share your concern for Serene Chu. I'm not alone, here at Sunrise Valley, in that regard. And we've all been frustrated at differing times with her treatment by Madame Chu...as well as her brothers."

"Is she a regular client here? How often does she come?"

"Miss Chu has been with us three times in the past two years. Normally, she visits us in the winter for two weeks."

"So this last time was the anomaly?"

Toh nodded. "She had injured her hand, that part is true. However..." She looked away and sighed. "However, it wasn't a cut. Her wrist was broken. She refused to say how."

Lola thought quickly, pushing aside her fury to focus on her questions. "Did you have a staff doctor tend to her?"

"Of course. Dr. Mun is our specialist in joints. She examined Miss Chu upon her arrival and once more before her departure."

"A week seems short for complete recovery."

"It is. We have some very talented Healers. Coupled with daily intensive herbal treatments, we were certain her wrist would mend quite well. Our instructions from Mr. Chu were to use whatever means we had in order to speed his sister's healing."

"Tommy or Sebastian?"

"The elder. He's the only one of Miss Chu's brothers I've ever spoken with. Arrangements for her visits here have always gone through him." Toh shifted in her chair. "As it was, Miss Chu still had some deep bone aches to contend with. That sort of intense therapy by our Healers takes its toll from the person's own reserves. We tried to buffer the effects as best we could, but it's unavoidable in such a circumstance."

Lola mentally added the toll of weekly sessions with Kam's Conjurer to Serene's burden as well. Her lips thinned. "How was she when she left?"

"Exhausted. Our team was quite concerned. We wanted her to stay at least another week, but she was adamant about returning."

"She? Or her Ghost?"

"That I do not know. Miss Chu was determined to leave."

"And you let her go."

"We're not a prison nor a mental sanitarium. There's a reason we have no walls around our grounds. Our clients come and go under their own power. They rarely leave before they are ready. Forgive me if I seem arrogant, but the care we offer is unparalleled."

"Serene left."

"Point taken. But if you will allow me to defend our reputation, I would point out to you that there are times when it does more damage to argue than it does to concede. At any rate, I rang Mr. Chu. I relayed our concerns for his sister, but he was of the mind that she was a grown woman and able to rely upon her own judgment in these things."

"Seems a strange turnaround."

"How so?"

"Her brothers were the same ones who insisted she come here. All but packed for her and bundled her into the car, from what I've figured."

Toh steepled her fingers. "All I can say with certainty is that when I spoke with Mr. Chu, he didn't seem overly worried about it being too soon. Perhaps, as I understand they were all under a strict deadline, they couldn't allow any more delay."

Lola shrugged "I'll take it up with them later. Miss Chu was able to use her hand when she left?"

Toh nodded. "It was painful, I imagine, but possible. And there was a limitation on the full range of motion, of course."

Lola thought back to the heavy costumes in Tommy's old dressing room. Her lips compressed into a line. "Is there anything else you'd like to tell me?"

Toh loosened her fingers, placed her hands in her lap as she sat back. "I did not concede to Mr. Chu's request to prevaricate during this interview with you. As I mentioned, Sunrise Valley is only as good as the therapy we provide. And truth is our guiding principle.

"However, I would ask that you use the information I've imparted with discretion and respect. The Chus have their reasons for concealing her broken wrist. I do not condone the use of lies. I nonetheless must respect their desire for privacy." She shook her head, looked down at her hands, then met Lola's eyes. "I wish you luck in your investigation. The murder of one's flesh and blood is a horrible thing. I can only hope the truth of her brother's death will help her through her grief."

"Cold comfort," Lola murmured.

Outside the large window behind Toh's left shoulder, desert hills stretched across and away, their tops falling under darkness as the sun slowly dropped downward.

EIGHTEEN

Lola snatched up the note from Elaine and read it while she took out the ice and a pick. She tossed the paper back onto the countertop. Dinner out tonight. She stabbed at the block of ice until she got three chunks and threw them into a tall glass. Next came lemon and a long pour of gin.

"Rot gut," said Aubrey.

Lola pressed her lips together, a wave of goose pimples running along her skin, herald to his return. She felt something relax deep within her, and frowned.

"Only if it's cheap." Lola took a long swallow of her drink, then placed the sweating glass to her neck. "What'd you uncover?"

"Stasha Chu is in debt for more than she's made of, for one thing."

"Tell me something. How do you measure that?"

"Ether?"

"Whatever a Ghost is made of. It's not as though you can be weighed, right?"

"It's a simple spell. I imagine every Conjuration student is taught it in their first term."

Lola grunted.

"Apparently, Serene negotiated the terms of repayment with Kam on her own. Not even her grandmother had the final say."

"You believe that?"

"Can't see a reason the Ghost I spoke with would lie."

Lola collapsed onto her sofa. She downed the rest of her drink, kept hold of the icy glass. Elaine had left the draperies open, as Lola preferred. Here the sun was still visible on the distant horizon. Sunset painted the sky in vivid pinks and orange, turning the water beneath dark grey in contrast. Lola closed her eyes and leaned back.

"What's your take on Stasha? She likely to do it all over again?" She pressed her cold fingertips against her eyelids.

"Absolutely. They'll both be back in this exact same place in another six months, nine tops."

"You sound awfully certain."

"She mistakes control for power."

Lola couldn't argue with the disdain in Aubrey's voice.

She opened her eyes, sat up, and watched the sun disappear for another night. When the glass was no longer cool to the touch, she took it to the kitchen, and went to change.

⌘

Seven torches lined the entryway into the Lims' courtyard. The breeze wafting in did little to counter the heat of the flames. Lola imagined she could feel their heat on her back, for all that they stood on the other side of the space.

She stifled a yawn behind her hand.

"Long day?" murmured Veronica, sitting to her right on the mourning bench farthest from the front. Ahead of them, Vivian and Viola sat with Liliane, having a quiet conversation. Keun supervised the servants, who were packing the remains of their dinner for the monastery.

Lola smiled faintly. "I imagine Uncle Nicky's even more tired than I am."

"Hm. I bet he knows enough to steal a nap now and then." Veronica slipped her arm around Lola. "Is he coming tonight?"

Lola shook her head. "I think he's feeling Lucky's loss more sharply this time. He wants to be there for Lucky."

"Of course." Veronica sighed, turning to look at Liliane. "I suppose it can't be avoided. Forty-four hours is the same for both men, isn't it?"

"I can't think whatever's been put together by Sebastian for Tommy would suit Stuey or his parents."

"Not everyone holds her grief so tightly as you do, honey." Veronica squeezed her. "You may not agree with how the Chus mourn, but their sorrow is as real as yours."

"She has a point," murmured Aubrey.

Lola waited a beat. "Did Auntie Viv say anything about her plans tonight?"

Veronica hesitated. "Yes. We won't be joining her."

"Uncle Nicky is expecting me before Final Rites. I expect I'll take her with me."

Veronica shook her head. "No, she'll have to drive herself. No telling what you'll get up to and then she'll be stuck."

Lola gave Veronica a sidelong glance. As she did so, movement by the torches caught her attention. Two silhouettes wavered for a moment in the shadows thrown by the torchlight before resolving into the shapes of Philip Kam and a thick-necked guard.

Lola quickly searched for Keun. He stood by the central maple tree, brushing off his hands as he stared at Kam.

Kam stopped in front of the older man and bowed. "Good evening, sir. I apologize for the hour of my visit. I thought to spare you any unpleasantness in front of your guests tonight."

Liliane came to her husband's side. "I searched everything. We don't have the pocket watch."

Lola stood. She squeezed Veronica's hand. "Get inside. Take the others. Now."

Veronica gave Kam a wary look before ushering her sisters ahead of her toward the house.

Lola walked over to the Lims, eyeing the thug for any movement toward a weapon.

Keun shook his head. "Even if we did have it, you have no claim to it. It belongs to our son."

"I apologize for the vulgarity of this, sir. Stuey signed a letter, you see." Kam reached into his suit jacket and extracted a slim envelope. "A business transaction between friends." He offered it to Keun.

Lola smoothly stepped up. She held out her hand.

Kam raised an eyebrow at the Lims. Keun gave a sharp nod. Kam tapped Lola's palm with the envelope and let it go. She expected him to step back. Instead, he leaned in. Lola took a step sideways, putting herself between Stuey's parents and Kam. She made sure she had both Kam and his thug in sight.

She opened the flap, extracted a delicate sheet of paper, folded into thirds. Lola checked the envelope, gingerly opened the folded letter. It crackled loudly. Satisfied that there were no harmful powders or suspicious odours hidden in either envelope or missive, she passed the letter to Keun.

The older man held it out so the torchlight fell squarely on the dark, strong characters. Lola watched Kam and his companion. The thug stared blankly back at her. Kam watched Stuey's parents, his eyes dark. He flicked a glance at Lola and his expression tightened.

She narrowed her eyes.

Liliane gasped, drawing Lola's attention. The older woman had a hand to her mouth. Keun wrapped an arm around her shoulder, pulling her in tightly against him.

There was a sound like dry leaves crumbling. Lola looked down.

The letter trembled in Keun's grasp.

"Uncle?" Lola said. "Is it real?" To the hells with politeness.

Kam narrowed his eyes.

"Yes." Keun's whisper sounded harsh.

"Are you certain?"

Liliane nodded. Tears ran down her cheeks. "Stuey's chop, his stamp, it's unique. He carved it himself." She pointed at the letter. "It's there. He signed this. It's authentic."

"Auntie, anyone can—"

"I saw that very same stamp today," said Liliane, sobbing. "When I chose his things for tonight. I saw it today. I know it. I remember the day he finished it."

Keun swiped at his eyes, turned his wife into his body. He glared at Kam over her head, crumpled the letter.

Lola gestured at the gangsters. "You're leaving. Now."

"He was my friend." A muscle at Kam's temple twitched. "I have a right to attend his cremation rites."

Lola stared at Kam while she spoke. "Please take Auntie Liliane inside, Uncle. I'm sure she'd prefer to tidy up before the guests arrive." She took the measure of Kam and the thug as she listened to the Lims' footsteps recede toward the house.

"Will you throw us out bodily?" Kam swept his gaze over her with deliberate unconcern.

"Please leave now, Mr. Kam. Whatever your claim on this watch, it doesn't buy you a seat tonight. This is your last chance."

Kam took a step toward her.

Lola stepped back, turning. Kam's thug had tried to circle silently behind her, but she'd heard the scrape of his shoe. She cursed herself for leaving her gun inside her clutch, useless to her now as it sat within the house. She had a blade hidden against her upper thigh, but the thought of shedding blood in this courtyard was abhorrent.

A quick movement in her periphery. Kam lunged forward and grasped her wrist. Lola twisted swiftly in his grip until she was now holding his wrist. She pivoted as she placed her other hand on his arm. She pulled his arm around and behind him, pushed up at his elbow until he grunted.

Kam's bodyguard charged. Lola set herself firmly, kicked out at the side of his knee through the discreet slit in her long dress. She heard the heel of her shoe snap.

The thug howled. His left knee bowed sideways and he went down in a heap. Lola tightened her grip on Kam's arm. She pulled his back close against her chest. She heard his breathing, rapid and shallow.

Lola spoke into his ear. Softly. "It's time for you to leave, Mr. Kam. Call your dog to heel. I'll be happy to escort you out."

"*Gwai* trash still reeks no matter how much money you use to dress it up."

Lola tugged upward on his arm. "This is simply a friendly reminder. You could be on the ground, face in the dirt, my knee in your back. But it'd be a shame to ruin your beautiful suit."

Kam barked out a command. His man collected himself off the ground, growling as he put weight on his bad knee. He shot Lola a dark look before steadying on his good leg. He hobbled to the gate.

Lola kicked off her shoes, felt the cool tiles of the courtyard against the soles of her feet. She followed, keeping Kam's arm wrenched upward behind his back. She placed her other hand on his neck, careful to keep her fingers along his vulnerable artery.

"I press harder and you'll be senseless in seconds. Now, move." She used her grip to dictate his steps.

Out on the sidewalk, she followed Kam's man until they were halfway down the block. She scanned the neighbourhood.

It was an older area and the trees were beautiful and tall, their limbs wide-stretched and leafy. The street lighting was filtered and there were many shadowed areas. Lola picked one and stopped.

She tightened her grip on Kam's neck. "Why are you after the watch, really?"

She wrenched him to the left at a flash of colour in her periphery. Kam cursed. The thug stopped short, hopping backward on his good leg, his arms windmilling.

"Wanna try that again, genius? Your boss might land on his face next time with no way to break the fall."

Lola waited until the big man had limped back another few steps. He stood, his bad leg crooked, resting lightly on the ball of his foot. Lola twisted Kam's arm up and gripped hard on his neck until Kam gave a strangled cry. She looked at the thug.

"Your heater. Give it over. Leave it on the hood. Now get back. Other side of the cement." She sidled over, pulling Kam with her, then let go of his neck and snatched up the gun. She thumbed off the safety on the grip.

She spoke in Kam's ear again. "Why?" She pressed the nose of the gun against the back of his neck.

"It's business, that's all," Kam said. She twisted his arm again, pressed the gun into his skin. "And I have a buyer, yes."

"Did he offer the pocket watch or did you ask for it?"

"Stuey and I've been friends a long time. I only forgive debts if it's worth my while. He knew that."

"For what? To make some extra dough? That's beans to you."

"It's not personal gain. It's simple negotiations. I didn't need anything from him. But he offered up something intensely important to him. That meant he was desperate, and I had the upper hand. I took advantage of it and found a buyer."

"And now what? Your buyer getting antsy?"

"I have a reputation to uphold."

She wrenched his arm up another inch. He gasped. She let go and pushed him away in one movement. Stepping back, she eyed both men and held the stolen gun steady.

Kam turned to face her, rubbing his shoulder then his neck. He stepped back carefully until he stood next to his man. They were highlighted by a streetlamp. Lola stayed in shadow. She looked up and down the street. A line of three cars approached. She angled her body to hide the gat.

The thug stared at Lola. She was sure wheels were turning inside the man's bullet-shaped head, but she just couldn't tell at what speed.

"What's your name, sunshine?" said Lola.

He blinked.

Kam said, "Lee can't speak. His tongue is gone. An unfortunate run-in with the *Tongs* when he was young."

"Lee. I'll remember that when I hand over the gat to the coppers. I'm sure they'll be here any minute now." She gestured with the gun. "Goodnight, Mr. Kam."

He glanced down at the pistol in her hand. Lola kept it aimed at his chest. To her surprise, Kam slung Lee's arm around his shoulder, and together the men made slow progress down the block.

"Gangsters make bad enemies, Lola," said Aubrey.

"Thanks for the newsflash." She shook out her cramped fingers. She waited until she saw them get into a car and pull out. Then she waited a few minutes longer. She hid Lee's heater against the folds of her dress as she walked barefoot back down the block.

NINETEEN

The young monk, now silent, stood with his abbot, greeting mourners by a stand of black lacquered boxes to the right of the main mourning area. The chanting for Stuey's soul was complete, his spirit now tightly bound with prayers and magic.

Lola kept to the shadowy perimeter of the courtyard, listening to the night birds, shifting in a pair of flats she'd scavenged from the back of her car. She watched as mourners arrived, carrying symbolic black oak branches, the distinctive leaves like jagged six-fingered hands. The branches were offered to the abbot, then placed into the lacquered boxes by the young monk.

Bednarski and Marks came through the gate. Lola stepped forward. Marks scowled as he caught sight of her. He murmured to his partner and the larger man acknowledged her with a nod. She gestured for them to meet her at the cloth-covered planters. Marks's scowl deepened as he trailed after his partner.

"Good evening, Miss Starke."

Lola opened her purse. "Kam was here earlier. I picked this up from his man, Lee."

"Not exactly a rare name, Starke."

Lola eyed Marks narrowly. "He doesn't talk. Had his tongue cut out. Leastways, that's what Kam said."

Bednarski looked at the piece. "Not gonna get any prints off that now, Miss Starke. Why're you showing it to us?"

"You gonna take it or not?"

Marks was already pulling out a dark handkerchief. He laid the cloth in his palm, reached into her purse, and extracted the gun by its barrel.

"There's gotta be something on Kam," said Lola. "He's been around twice now, scaring the Lims. Maybe that doesn't warrant any action, but maybe finding a rod on that torpedo of his will turn up the heat under him. Distract him. Don't you have a laboratory full of poindexters, studying fingerprints and ballistics? This heater might've been used in some crime, just waiting to be identified."

Marks wrapped the gun inside his handkerchief. He raised an eyebrow at his partner as he slipped it into his suit pocket. "Sounds like desperate measures. Losing a slab of muscle like this Lee character won't mean squat. They're like weeds. Gangs are awash in 'em." Marks shook his head. "The only thing you've done, Starke, is made another enemy. And maybe you haven't heard, but gangsters make bad enemies."

"Yeah, I've heard," she muttered.

"We'll take it in," said Bednarski. "Pull some favours in Vice. The Lims don't need trouble to add to their grief."

"Thank you," said Lola. "It's not—"

"But Marks is right. This Kam can't be too happy with you."

"Better me than them." Lola looked over toward Stuey's parents. Lola could see their exhaustion as clear as a neon sign in the middle of the desert night. She nodded to the coppers and excused herself to join the Aunties, pulling at her dragging hem. She sat down heavily.

"Are you all right?" Viola grasped Lola's hand.

Lola nodded, distracted by the sudden rush of pressure in her chest. She pushed it down, blinking. She gave Viola's hand a brief squeeze then let go.

She twisted on the bench, did a rapid scan of faces. Some met her gaze blandly. Others frowned. Others still ignored her assessment. Bednarski and Marks stood close to the last row of benches, expressions respectful, hats held loosely in front of them. Lola turned back around to face the bier.

Conversation quieted, replaced by the rustle of clothing and discreet sniffles. The abbot walked to Stuey's body and turned to face the mourners.

He smiled gently, gestured to his assistant. The young monk came forward with a plain white bowl of rice wine. The abbot spoke blessings over the bowl and walked slowly around the bier. The cadence of his speech changed, and he began to chant as he poured the sanctified wine, drenching the linen wrapped around Stuey's body. The abbot stopped his circuit with his back to the mourners.

Lola sighed. First Rites were complete.

The young monk took the empty bowl and retreated to the shadows, next to a small table. His face was swallowed by the gloom as he turned away from the torches surrounding the platform.

The abbot raised his hands, readying himself for Second Rites.

He walked counter-clockwise around Stuey's remains, three and a half times, until he faced the mourners, the bier in front of him. He began his chant again and a fresh wind blew into the courtyard from the entry gate. It rattled the black oak leaves as it passed on its way deeper into the courtyard. Lola turned around. Torch flames flickered and shadows jumped wildly against the walls. The wind gathered itself around the Red Emperor maple, spinning around and around until the leaves shook and hissed. Lola saw Marks narrowing his eyes to slits, a hand pressed against his stomach to keep his suit jacket closed. Bednarski remained immobile, seemingly untouched, two blinks in rapid succession the only hint of the wind's effect on him.

Abruptly, the old maple tree went still and the wind sped through the crowd toward the abbot, leaving a wake of fluttering hair and tunic sleeves. The old monk coaxed the wind to him in singsong, dissipating its furious energy. It twined itself around his saffron robes and long moustaches, lifting and teasing with gentleness.

The abbot cupped his hands together and the wind allowed itself to be captured. He sang softly to the wind in his hands and then let his hands fall apart. Lola felt pressure building in her ears. She discreetly opened her mouth wide, trying to dispel it. The abbot closed his hands with a clap and the pressure disappeared.

Lola felt Aubrey's sudden nearness. She tensed, waiting for him to speak. After a moment, he retreated.

The old abbot looked up and out at the assembled mourners. The young monk took up a large wooden platter from the table beside him. Sprigs of rosemary were arranged around a mound of orange slices. He stepped forward, approached the benches. His first offer was to Liliane. She wiped at her eyes with a pale handkerchief, took a slice of orange. Keun was next.

When it was Lola's turn, she dutifully took her portion, as well as a small branch of rosemary. She held it tightly in her hand, brought it to her nose, and inhaled deeply. She welcomed the clean woodsy scent to help clear her mind of the thick smell of incense.

Lola's grip tightened as the scent excavated old memories. She fought her tears, methodically scraping her finger along the rough bark of the rosemary branch. She recalled her father's death and the painful, prolonged agony preceding it. The futile sessions with Betta to heal the growth eating him up from the inside. She thought of his weak smiles and terrible jokes. Her mother's tears. The Aunties singing softly to him, their three-part harmony pure and filled with love. Lola blinked and the images in her mind faded, replaced by the gnawing bite of loneliness.

The abbot gestured upward with his browned, wrinkled hands. "Please, everyone."

Lola closed her eyes, murmured, "Eternal life and the Cycle." She ate her orange slice, held herself carefully still as she waited to place the rind back on the rosemary-ringed platter. The young monk was there again, carrying the platter of orange rinds to the body and placing it at Stuey Lim's feet. The monk bowed solemnly, then stepped back.

He had completed Second Rites.

"Now, we wait." The abbot smiled with benevolence at the mourners.

Murmurs started up as people stood or stretched discreetly. Keun and Liliane rose and walked toward the abbot. The young monk bustled about unobtrusively, arranging bowls, candles, and tea cups on another small table next to the bier holding Stuey's body.

"Are you ready?" said Aubrey, voice subdued.

Lola nodded.

"Forty-four minutes between Second and Final Rites. Plenty of time to get there," Aubrey said, "if you're not ready yet."

"No," Lola said quietly, "it's time."

Viola turned, her expression sad. "Are you going?" Lola nodded. Viola exchanged a glance with Veronica.

"Where's your offering?" said Vivian.

Lola picked up the small satchel at her feet.

"Don't skulk off without giving it to the monk," Vivian said. "I'll be along."

"Yes, Auntie." Lola embraced them each in turn and stood patiently in line to be received by the abbot and his acolyte. Liliane and Keun stood with the monks, helping to accept the offerings and speaking with each mourner individually.

Lola slipped her hand within the satchel and brought out her funeral money. It was in two stacks, each tied with white silk ribbon. The paper squares were sepia in colour and thin as onion skin. A large square took up most of the paper, outlined in thick black. Red rectangles, embossed with gold characters, laid on two of the black square's sides. Lola reflected on the amount of time and effort put into this symbolic money, all so it could be burned to pay for smooth passage into the next life.

She held forth her stacks to the monk. He bowed over her hand and received her offering. Next to him was a tall metal barrel, its dark exterior reflecting the flickering torch flames. He laid Lola's offering inside the drum, on top of other stacks. Lola saw, behind the monks and Stuey's parents, a medium-sized box made of thin strips of unfinished pine. A pile of Stuey's clothes and belongings were packed neatly within, ready to be burned.

"Thank you." Keun's eyes glistened even as he gave a small smile. "We appreciate you being here to honour our son." He hesitated, clearly searching for more words.

Lola touched him on the forearm. "May he find peace in his next life." She hugged Liliane tightly before turning away.

Lola was near the gate when she saw a woman in a dark grey dress and cowled tunic standing under the Red Emperor maple, one pale hand on the trunk. The large cowl was pulled up, hiding the woman's features. Lola hesitated, sensing a familiarity in the silhouette. The woman raised a hand and beckoned to her.

As Lola neared the maple, the woman stepped farther into the shadows. The movement sparked the connection for Lola.

"Miss Shao."

"You're not doing your job."

"Oh?"

"I asked you to keep Philip away from Stuey's parents."

Lola raised an eyebrow. "Why are you hiding here? You've a right to be here, don't you, as a good friend?"

Evelyn stammered.

"I'm sure his parents would feel good knowing you made the effort to be here, when everyone knows you're so obviously a friend of the Chus."

"Lola," said Aubrey.

Lola's cheeks heated. She raised her chin.

Evelyn pulled down her cowl. Her face was pale and plain, without cosmetics. She challenged Lola with her stare.

"Well, what are you going to do about Philip Kam?"

"I showed him the pavement a few hours ago. And I've sicced the coppers on him. More than that, Miss Shao, I'm not prepared to do at this time."

Evelyn seemed to consider Lola's words. "Have you discovered anything more about the pocket watch then?"

Lola nodded reluctantly. She explained the letter, staying vague about Serene's role.

Evelyn chewed on her lip, her gaze on the Lims.

Lola said, "You ought to speak to them directly. You know they're good people." She paused. "And they already love you."

Lola didn't wait for a reply. She strode toward the exit, headed for the night outside the sombre courtyard.

A movement in Lola's periphery caught her attention and she turned her head sharply in the direction of the house. She squinted. It was a few more moments before she realized she was looking at a corner of fabric flapping intermittently out of an open window. Lola recalled the dark grey fabric from yesterday, the one she was sure was meant to cover an indoor mirror. She frowned.

Apparently, no one had secured it after all.

TWENTY

S top staring at me like I'm a lunatic."

Lola suppressed a smile at Nicky's grumble.

She stood with him in a long line of mourners. Behind them, the queue snaked down the three steps of the dais, wound around a grouping of flower beds filled with peonies, rhododendrons and lobelias—all white—then across the wide expanse of the Chus' front lawn until its tail disappeared into the darkness. It was not quite eleven o'clock. Torches were staked into the lawn, describing the path of the waiting line. Clouds filled the sky, blocking sight of the waning moon.

They stepped closer to the bier and its coffin. Lola could see Tommy Chu's remains, wrapped simply and thoroughly as prescribed by ritual, the one inviolable fact of funerals. Whether one chose reincarnation or the path of Ghosthood, the nuns had but one way to wrap the linen strips. To do otherwise risked the wrath of the gods and the path of the spirit.

Lola stared at the white linen strips, soaked with ceremonial liquids and glistening in the light of the many torches surrounding the bier. She smelled rice wine and rosemary, citrus and beeswax. She felt a mild pressure pushing against the front of her, discerned the edge of the protective spell which was the result of Second Rites.

Centred under the invisible dome of the spell, the lacquered coffin rested within a nest of silk drapery. Through the crush of people in line ahead of her, Lola saw intermittent, metallic flashes, close to the head of the bier.

"Did someone lose an earring?" Lola frowned. "I keep seeing a gold flash." She craned her neck, frustrated. "What *is* that?"

Nicky murmured, "We'll find out soon enough."

They took another step forward, only to jerk backward when the matron in front of them drew in a sharp gasp, recoiling from the coffin. The older woman hissed in disapproval and quickened her pace past the bier. Nicky and Lola exchanged a look. He shrugged. They stepped forward again and turned their gazes down into the casket.

"Damn it." Nicky rubbed at his forehead.

Lola blinked several times.

Tommy Chu's death mask was made from thick white ceramic, dusted with a fine sprinkling of gold, its edges marked with a thin line of filigree. Rather than the bland features of a man in peaceful repose, Tommy's mask was an exact replica of his face.

And he was grinning.

The matron whispered furiously to her companion. Lola glanced at Nicky. A muscle twitched in his jaw. He caught her gaze and she saw the effort it took him to smile.

Large branches of rosemary, each as thick as a housepainter's brush, were laid around the body. Orange rinds and silken satchels of anise were scattered in the fragrant boughs. On the other side of the black-draped altar was a round table of unfinished pine. Lola counted seven small dishes of food. She puzzled over the presence of the funereal meal at Final Rites. She thought the traditional seven dishes were only for the living.

Was this another of Sebastian Chu's unusual choices?

A nun in dark mustard-coloured robes, her head shaven and eyes closed, stood next to the table. She clasped her hands in front of her chest in a configuration of peace. Her lips moved in quiet prayer.

"Gods bless him," murmured Nicky. "May his spirit find peace."

"That's generous of you, Uncle." said Lola. "Considering."

"I wasn't talking about Tommy," said Nicky stiffly. "That nun's here for Lucky. She blessed that funereal meal for him and she's saying the prayers of peace for his Dispersal. The only damn thing in this gods-damned spectacle meant for him."

"I don't blame you for not noticing," said Aubrey. "See the second mask? That's for Lucky."

This second death mask was also threaded through with gold and limned with filigree. It was placed over the body's heart. Its features, however, were blankly uncontroversial.

At the head of the body was a tall, cylindrical candle, wide as an apothecary's bell jar. The flame was strong and unwavering, the nun's magic protecting it from the light breeze.

"The candle represents Lucky's spirit. It will be kept alight until the nun completes the Dispersal Rites, for peaceful passage of his spirit."

Lola and Nicky stepped back down onto the grass. They followed the line of people ahead of them and walked toward the seating area. There was one mourning bench draped in black crepe, set a few feet apart from the rest of the mourners.

"Have you seen Serene? Shouldn't they be sitting by now?"

Nicky's scowl deepened. "Seb has his own timetable. At this rate, I don't see how the viewing will be done in time for the cremation. It must already be half past."

Lola assessed the crowd. "They're almost done, I think."

"You haven't accounted for the scandal factor, my girl. Time for all the gasping and whispers and gawking. They don't even notice the second mask." Nicky rubbed his face. Lola heard the rasp of stubble. "Not your doing, my girl. That damned boy has the hardest ears I've ever seen. Won't budge a skinny inch."

Nicky glared into the distance. "As if what he spends has anything to do with Tommy's worth. I'm not sure he even recalled Lucky was a part of this. It's a good thing I asked about the nun. I know it in my bones, that boy would've let Lucky's essence go without a proper Dispersal."

Lola led the way to an outside aisle, midway down the rows of benches. "Here. We can make a quick getaway if we need to."

She scanned the crowd of people chatting solemnly as they waited for the Chus to arrive. She assessed as many faces as she could see from her outlying seat. There were plenty of famous mugs in the crowd, but she didn't see Evelyn Shao.

She wasn't sure how she felt about being relieved.

A servant ushered Vivian to the black-draped mourning bench. Lola caught a sidelong look from Nicky. She stayed in her seat, observed Vivian bow her head and clasp her hands in prayer.

Nicky said, "You ever think about what you'll do?" His gaze remained on the line of mourners, shuffling forward one by one.

Lola felt her stomach sink. "Let's not borrow trouble, Uncle."

He waved his hand. "No, no, I'm not saying it's gonna be soon." He paused, rubbing his chin. "I just meant it's something we all oughta think on."

Lola shrugged, belying her inner unease. "What's to debate? You die, you've got two choices: reincarnation or Ghosthood. You die with a Ghost haunting you, you've still got two choices."

"And your Ghost has none," said Aubrey.

"Your *Ghost*," said Lola, "already made that choice the first time."

Before Ghost or man could respond to that, Nicky shifted his attention away, toward the altar.

The nun, unlined face tranquil, took up a long-handled brass tool and capped the candle flame. Nicky sighed, used his handkerchief to wipe his eyes. Lola gripped his hand, alarmed by the sinew and bones so close beneath his skin.

She looked up to see the nun step down from the dais, holding the snuffed candle. A servant in dark grey mourning clothes followed her, carrying the funereal meal on a platter. Lola lost sight of them as they walked away toward the house in the darkness beyond the burning torches.

"Does Nicky know where they're going to burn that?" said Aubrey. Lola relayed the question.

Nicky nodded. "I made sure of it. Lucky loved the ocean."

"A beach then?" said Lola.

"Jade Cove. His favourite."

"The one with the lightning glass?"

Nicky nodded, expression strained. "I'm of a mind to join them."

A murmur ran through the mourners then.

Nicky's expression darkened as he shifted his gaze to the altar space. The Chu siblings approached. Serene was dressed in a traditional white tunic and skirt, her face pale and drawn with fatigue. She sat down stiffly next to Vivian on the mourning bench, her hands deep within the wide sleeves of her tunic.

Sebastian stepped up onto the second stair and turned to the crowd. He kept his face down. He wore a white tunic, wide trousers, and was barefoot. The traditional linen strip was wound across his forehead and tied at the back. He looked up, prompting some shocked whispers.

The flickering torchlight threw the angles of his face into harsh relief, deepened the shadows beneath his eyes, darkened the lines around his downturned mouth. His skull seemed ready to push through his pale skin.

"Finally caught up with him," murmured Nicky.

"The hours? Or the grief?" said Lola.

Nicky answered just as Aubrey spoke.

"Either."

"Both."

Sebastian held up his hands. "Final Rites are upon us. I take this opportunity to thank you all again for coming." He stopped, looked over the faces turned up to him. He took a deep breath. "It's been a long day, my friends. I'm sure none of you are surprised by that admission." He paused, looked down, then up again.

"What may surprise you is that I am out of words. I want nothing more than to sit and pray and think." He looked over his shoulder. "And say farewell." Silence followed as he walked to the mourning bench and sat down heavily. Serene shifted away from him, her face tilted up toward the bier.

Lola frowned as she watched Serene's profile.

A tall, thin monk dressed in saffron, his hair shorn and his face a rugged testament to hours spent in the sun, stepped up to the body from the right of the altar. A middle-aged servant held out a bundle of incense sticks to him. He accepted them from her with a murmur. He paused for a few beats, then started his prayers. As he chanted, he set out the incense in four groups, anchoring them in the sand within small pots of pale ceramic placed around the body.

The servant then placed a squat ceramic bottle in the monk's hands. He uncorked it and went around the body again, this time pouring rice wine into small cups that sat next to the incense pots, finishing with an additional cup at the head. The servant took the bottle of wine and disappeared down the far steps of the altar. The monk performed the same circuit with pale ceramic bowls of cooked white rice.

Then the monk took up a tapered candle. He closed his eyes, murmured, and the candle wick sparked to life in blue flame. He reopened his eyes and continued praying as he walked around the body, lighting the incense sticks. The sharp tang of the specially blessed sticks spread out from the bier. Lola tasted ash at the back of her throat.

The monk came to stand at the head of the body. He placed the lit taper in a ceramic holder in its own stand. He bowed his head, the signal for the mourners to begin their silent prayers for the spirit of Tommy Chu and his safe journey to the next life. Lola heard people crying quietly. She peeked at the mourning bench.

Vivian dabbed at her eyes. Serene clasped her hands together tightly, face tilted upward. Sebastian stared at the ground, his lips moving.

Lola said her private prayers for Tommy Chu and closed her eyes. She pushed away questions about her father's ceremony, memories of his death and his suffering. She shut out dark thoughts of her own ceremony one day. She listened to herself breathing, tuned into her heart beating.

A clear note rang out.

Lola concentrated on its echo, feeling its vibrations deep within herself. She opened her eyes.

The monk clapped his hands together three times, touched his fingertips to his forehead, then took the taper out of its stand. The steady blue flame sparked once with a white burst as the monk stretched his hand out toward the remaining incense, set in the bowl at the head.

As the magical fire touched the sticks, an arc of flame shot upward, lighting the other three pots of incense in quick succession. The growing fire popped and crackled beneath the invisible spell of protection created by Second Rites, while smoke began to stream upwards. The scent of rosemary, anise, and oranges blended with that of incense and burning wood, masking the odour of cremating flesh.

Lola looked over, furrowed her brow. Serene leaned forward, eyes wide, staring at the building fire.

"Something's wrong," murmured Aubrey.

"D'you see her?" Lola started to rise.

"No, it—"

Pressure, sudden and powerful. She winced at the mounting pain in her ears, noted that Nicky had slapped his hands against the sides of his head. Lola staggered to her feet. Then the pressure disappeared and Lola felt the sudden heat. She whirled, saw the fire reaching up toward the sky.

"Second Rites are broken," shouted Aubrey. "The protection's been destroyed."

Glass shattered. Lola turned her face away, raising her arms at the same time. She felt objects ricochet off her head and forearm. She waited a beat then looked up at the altar. The monk stumbled backward, arms flailing, falling away from the growing tower of bright orange flames that engulfed the dais.

TWENTY-ONE

Lola ripped the shawl from around her shoulders. She tripped up in her hem, hauled it up.

Following the path of exploded ceramics and incense sticks, flames had jumped from the altar to the lush lawn. The monk, his robes alight, fell from the altar into a line of fire on the grass.

Lola ran to him. She slapped at the flames with the fabrics in her hands, pushed and rolled him out of the fire. Screams filled the night. Someone bumped Lola from behind. She lost her balance, hands tangled in her shawl and dress. She landed on her knees and fell to her side. She tucked her chin down, trying to protect her face. One of her combs dug sharply into her scalp and then broke with a snap. She felt her hair torn out along with it.

Lola wrenched her hands out of the wad of burned linen that used to be her shawl. She stared at the bier and altar. An immense fire raged, fuelled at its centre by Tommy Chu's mortal remains.

People scrambled toward the driveway, their shouts and screams made incoherent by their terror. Lola looked down at the monk at her feet. He groaned, eyes squeezed shut, his face twisted. Lola grabbed his arm, ignoring his hiss of pain, and pulled him to his feet. His sandals looked unharmed, so she cajoled him into a shambling walk away from the fire.

A group clustered close to a large oak tree on the other side of the house. Some sat on the grass, holding themselves tightly. A few of the more elderly were seated in chairs. Others were prone, low

201

moans punctuating their restless movements. Grey-clad servants and a few mourners moved among the injured.

Lola set the monk down, with his back leaning against the great oak's trunk. He hung his head, panting, propped one hand down on the ground for support. Lola recognized the Chus' head matron, snatched at the older woman's sleeve, and left the holy man to the reverent ministrations of the improvised medical team.

She whirled, ran back toward the fire and collided blindly with a dark shape. She windmilled her arms as she tried to retain her balance.

"Damn it all to hells! Where the devil are you running?" Vivian glared. "Help me with him." She pushed Sebastian into Lola's arms.

Lola lurched under his weight. "Where's Serene?"

"I don't know. A wall of fire was about to collapse on us, and I had to push this idiot out of the way. I think he was trying to save the body, for gods' sake. Don't." Vivian grabbed her arm as Lola made to rush past. "You don't run *toward* the fire, stupid girl. Now help me with him or so help me, I'll dump him here and leave him."

Lola cursed, wrenched her arm from Vivian's grasp, and moved over to grip Sebastian more firmly under his arm. They dragged the unconscious man over to the tree where Lola had left the monk. The matron of the house gasped and called to the others when she saw Sebastian's face. A burly servant took Sebastian and laid him down carefully, under the matron's anxious supervision.

"Here, Auntie, let's sit you down." Lola found a chair, pulled it upright, and gingerly set Vivian onto it. She grabbed a running servant and asked for water. In the distance, clanging bells announced the approach of the fire brigade. Lola swiped at a line of sweat from her cheek and stared intently at the raging pyre that consumed the body of Tommy Chu. She snagged another passing servant to ask the time.

Twenty-three minutes past midnight.

Lola made Vivian drink a glass of water, then found a damp cloth for her. She scanned the grounds incessantly, searching for either Nicky or Serene. She startled at the sound of a thick, ragged cough.

Vivian slumped, eyes closed, the cloth held against her mouth. The shadowy light showed dark patches all over her dress. Her face was streaked with soot and sweat, and one of her earrings was missing. Lola felt her throat tighten up as she catalogued the scratches and burns on her Auntie's arms and legs.

She hugged Vivian close, felt how small the woman was in her arms. It was awkward, being bent over the chair. Lola felt a side seam in her dress give. She held on more tightly.

Vivian put an arm around Lola in turn.

Lola pulled back, held Vivian's hands. "I need to find Uncle Nicky. And Serene. Stay here. I'll get someone to take you home."

Vivian nodded wearily. Lola found another servant to watch over her and rushed toward the still-burning bier. She squinted at a familiar-looking silhouette in the distance.

"Detective Sergeant."

Eng whirled around, looking for the source of the voice. He pinpointed Lola and ran over. "Have you seen Miss Chu?"

Lola shook her head. "Vivian saved Sebastian, but she hasn't any idea about Serene. Were you here for the entire ceremony?"

"Yes, but we arrived late. We saw the fire start, but I lost track of Miss Chu once people started running. Vivian who?"

Lola's gaze darted over the scene of continuing chaos around them. "Where's Leung?"

"He found your mentor, Mr. Lo. They're helping the fire brigade get here. Do you see her Ghost, Mr. O'Connell?"

"No," said Aubrey. "I haven't noticed them since the Rites were broken."

Eng nodded curtly. "I'll keep searching."

"Eng." Lola grabbed his arm as he turned to go. "Vivian Mei. My Auntie Vivian. Will you please make sure an officer takes her home? When she's ready?" Lola pointed. Eng followed her gaze, stared at the soot-stained figure in the chair.

"What about you?" He turned back to Lola.

"I have to go back to the Lims' house." Lola grasped for calm amidst the panicky impatience gnawing at her.

Eng considered her. "In case there's sabotage there as well?"

Lola nodded, swallowed against the prickly dryness of her throat.

Eng looked back at Vivian. He gave her a brisk nod. "I'll take care of her." He touched her arm lightly. "Ring Central if there's trouble. Main 8989."

Lola ground her teeth against the rising unease in her belly. Her stomach soured at the mental image of a fire in Keun's beautiful courtyard. She agreed curtly and ran for her car.

⧉

Lola cursed as she worked the pedals with her bare feet. Her spare shoes were in the back, torn beyond repair. She stared intently ahead of her, calculating distances and speeds.

"How did they break down the barrier? Do you know?" Lola coughed, felt a rasping pain in her throat.

"I can guess," said Aubrey. "Tampering with the incense is the easiest way."

"Does it take a Conjurer?"

"Yes, it requires magic." He paused. "Sabotaging a spirit's passage is nasty business. It's safe to assume any Conjurer willing to do that is on the wrong side of the heavens."

Lola gritted her teeth, wrung the steering wheel.

"Steady on. You need to get there in one piece."

"It's got to be her," muttered Lola. "I saw the look on her face. She knew it was going to happen. She was watching for it."

Aubrey's silence filled the car as Lola sped past a traffic signal showing yellow, and through an empty intersection.

"That's a serious charge, Lola."

She thought of Tommy Chu's spirit, eradicated before its journey onward could even begin. "That was pure malice back there. It was wrong and evil." She narrowed her eyes. "She hated her brother so much she damned his soul. And I have no idea why." She slammed on the brakes as the signal ahead switched to red. Lola slapped the steering wheel. "Is she mentally imbalanced? Toh didn't seem to think so, or at least she wasn't willing to commit an opinion. But having a Ghost like Stasha..." Lola huffed out a breath. "I've got squat at this point."

"What will you do when you find her?"

Lola didn't reply.

Harmony Lane was quiet, the shadows cast by the trees still and dense. Lola waited, one hand on the hood of her car, listening to the engine tick as it cooled down by slow degrees. She sniffed the air, found it clean, tinged with the scent of old wood and the desert's night time chill. The tension seeped away from her jaw, slid down, away from her shoulders, until Lola became aware of the solid ground beneath her bare feet.

The gates were shut but unbarred. Lola pushed them open and slipped inside the courtyard. A small circle of five torches lit up the mourning bench reserved for the Lims. A lone figure sat, staring at the altar space. A quick glance told her the bier had been removed. She turned to close the gate behind her.

She faltered, her heart in her throat. She hung her head, one hand flat against the gate. The wood was rough to the touch. She forced herself to face the altar.

The bier was gone.

She looked up, blinking away a rush of tears. Stars blurred, reappeared diamond sharp and sparkling with light that would take eons to die away. Stars that were perhaps already dead themselves.

"Lola." Aubrey, voice ephemeral as cobwebs fluttering from a blown breath. She heard pain, too, and wondered if he was recalling his own death.

Lola shook her head, her throat tight. She put her palms together in front of her heart. As her eyes travelled from star to star, she offered up a silent prayer for Stuey's peaceful journey. She closed her eyes, wiped at the tears that spilled down her cheeks. She hoped he lived a long, happy time in his next life.

It took a few moments for her eyes to adjust to the torch-lit courtyard. She squinted at the solitary figure on the bench, realized it was Stuey's father. She thought over what she'd say, explaining the fire at the Chus', asking questions about Serene.

Her feet, nearly numb from the cold flagstones, remained unmoving. When she finally compelled herself to take a step, she turned around. She stole back out through the gates and left Keun Lim in whatever passed for peace in the throes of grief, to sit vigil in memory of his only child.

TWENTY-TWO

Marks stared at Lola, eyebrows raised.

She was acutely aware of her filthy bare feet, wrinkled, stained dress, and the stink of smoke in her sweaty, lank hair. She kept her chin up.

"Where's your better half?" said Lola.

A twitch at his jawline.

"Bednarski," she said.

"Not here yet."

"You got called in after the fire at the Chus'?"

He gave her a brusque nod. "In case there's trouble here."

"You really think the killer's gonna come back here?"

Marks gestured with his chin. "Get moving, Starke, before one of the uniforms snags you for a vagrant. Or a nutter."

A group of matrons sidled past her, shocked expressions turning into disapproving frowns and clipped remarks. Lola glared at them, baring her teeth.

"Easy," said Aubrey. "You're here to find Serene, not start a riot."

"Yeah, yeah." She flattened out her expression, and turned away from Marks.

The pavement in front of The Supper Club was now filled with flowers and banners, candles and brass bells, the offerings of a city in mourning. Small and large bouquets, ornate wreaths on tripod easels, bunches in vases. Blossoms in every colour save red. Bold calligraphy in black ink on large ribbons of orange silk, flowing prayers for Tommy Chu to find peace in his next life.

As Lola paced the length of the sidewalk, she saw the same sentiment repeated hundreds of times with thousands of flowers. But not one for Stuey Lim.

"Stop growling," said Aubrey. "Or your search for Serene will likely end fruitlessly in the hoosegow."

Lola clenched her jaw.

Coppers were thick on the ground, keeping people moving along in both directions. She avoided eye contact with the uniforms. Wooden sawhorses painted City blue were set onto the street. Traffic had been restricted to pedestrians only. A narrow corridor between the memorial objects and the crowd walking the street had been set up for people to stroll the length of the sidewalk.

"Got her."

Lola raised her head at Aubrey's exclamation. Triumph at having her hunch pay off was short-lived, however.

"I can hear Stasha." Aubrey was grim. "There. On the far left."

Lola pressed against a barricade to squeeze past the young couple in front of her. She felt her gown catch on the wood, yanked it, heard a rip. It didn't matter. She had to get to Serene. The younger woman's eyes were wide, her expression taut, as she whirled in a tight circle, looking for a way out. And yet, she shrank away from the people passing by, unable to make way for herself.

"Did you make out what Stasha was shouting?" Lola wove through the press of moving bodies.

"No." Aubrey cursed. "But I can guarantee that's her doing."

Lola rose up on her toes, her heart hammering now in her chest. She dodged past an elderly man in black, craned her neck.

Serene curled in on herself, face ashen.

Lola swore, pushed her way through a cluster of boys on the cusp of manhood. They snickered. She snarled at the lot of them.

Someone called out to Lola and touched her shoulder.

"Gods, are you all right?" Ria took in Lola's ragged appearance with wide eyes. "I lost track of you at the Chus'. Then Nicky Lo said that one of the Twins said you'd gone to the Lims. No one said you'd gone a few rounds with the fire. What the hells happened?"

"I was worried about the Lims."

"No." Ria gave Lola a little shake. "What happened to you?"

Lola frowned as Ria gave her a brief, hard hug.

"Wait. You were at the Chu house?"

Ria nodded. "It was my main assignment. Saw you, but everything was starting, so I sat at the back. Missed the viewing. I sent Soo over to the Lim cremation. Everything was jake there, she said."

"I know."

"What's going on?" Ria frowned. "Why would someone deliberately sabotage Tommy Chu's Final Rites?" She scrutinized Lola, her expression thoughtful. "You know who it is, don't you?"

"A hunch, anyway." Lola shook her head, shrugged angrily.

There were too many threads to pull.

The pocket watch. The debt. Evelyn Shao. Serene Chu's erratic behaviour. Her broken wrist. Stasha Chu's abusive conduct. Uncle Nicky's conviction that Lucky was the target. Lucky's rift with Tommy. Tommy's birth. The disruption of his cremation. Kam.

Lola was certain she was forgetting something. Although at this point she had no idea if it'd be crucial or not.

She cursed, hoping Nicky had dug something up. They badly needed a break.

She made to push past Ria. "Listen, I've gotta go—"

"This is serious business," said Ria quietly. "You can't keep this to yourself."

"I know."

"And I don't mean spilling for a story. I mean, if the coppers know you're holding out on them, they're not likely to call it a brodie and be done."

"I said I know."

"Stop that," Ria said. "I don't care who's watching. I'll shake some more sense in you if I have to."

Lola felt tension climbing up the back of her neck. She mulishly clamped her jaw closed.

"Well at least you didn't haul off on me," said Ria. "All right. I've gotta meet up with the camera jockey. Remember. You're not alone in this." She shook Lola gently then and pulled her in for another tight hug. Lola felt some of her tension drain away.

Ria let her go. "Better." She pointed a finger at Lola. "Don't be a tough guy. Watch yourself and find time to sleep, you got me?" She pointed for another beat, then turned and walked away.

Lola watched Ria disappear into the crowd. The whispers around her grew as she stood, motionless in a filthy dress and bare feet. Lola grit her teeth against a sudden tide of weariness, sudden as a desert night, pushing her to go home. She rubbed at her temples, dropped her face into her hands.

"Hurry, Lola." Aubrey was a cool presence against her side.

Lola scrubbed at her face, makeup be damned. She was already a sight. She forced her head back up and straightened her shoulders, looking over at the barricades.

Despite the heavy crowds thronging the street, there was a small clearing around Serene. Her thin arms were wrapped around her waist. Her tunic and skirt were wrinkled but clean of soot.

Lola glared at Serene's clothing, the linen still white. She recalled Vivian's soot-streaked face and dress, her Auntie's brave efforts to save Sebastian. Lola's blood pressure spiked. Her fatigue burned away—along with her pity.

She strode over, heedless of the people staring, and grabbed Serene's arm. Serene gasped. Lola leaned in, trembling with anger.

"You're coming with me. Now."

Serene jerked her head up. Lola took a small step back. The younger woman's face contorted, lips stretched over her teeth, eyes squeezed so tightly her temples were blanched.

"Gods damn it," Aubrey said. "Stasha's gone off her nut."

Lola cursed her temper.

"What is going on here? What are you doing to her?" A middle-aged Chinese man glared at Lola.

"I need to take her to a Healer. She's having a seizure. It's her Ghos—"

Lola broke off as Serene thrashed, catching Lola in the chin with a sharp knuckle.

The younger woman screamed, a high thin sound.

Lola swore. The man said, "I'm getting the police."

Aubrey's voice was frigid. "Stop it, Madame. You're making a spectacle of your granddaughter."

Serene stilled.

Lola waited, breath held. She loosened her grip slowly.

Serene went limp and slumped to the ground.

⟨✸⟩

Lola wove the car through dawn traffic, passing heavy produce trucks and newspaper lorries making their deliveries with the coming of the sun.

"Madame," said Aubrey.

Lola glanced at Serene, slouched in the passenger seat, her head against the window. Either Stasha was in a nearly similar state or—

"She won't speak to me," said Aubrey.

Serene stirred. "Where are your shoes?"

Lola looked over again. Serene pulled herself up against the seat. She coughed, hurriedly reached into a pocket, and brought out a light blue cloth to cover her mouth. Lola saw dark spots of sooty saliva bloom on the pale handkerchief.

"Long story," Lola said. "How are you feeling?"

"Where are you taking me?"

"To a Healer in East Town."

Serene frowned. "I want to go to the Dowager."

"Why?"

"Packing. I have to finish packing."

"I thought the theatre manager forced you out last night."

Serene shook her head, vehement. "The Dowager. Take me to the Empress Dowager."

Lola hesitated. She checked her mirrors, changed lanes. "You know, Detective Inspector Marks released you to me because I promised to take you directly to the best Healer in the City. Who also happens to be a personal friend."

"What did you say to me earlier?" Serene said, hesitant. "I have these...episodes sometimes. I don't remember things clearly."

"Blackouts?" Lola glanced at her sharply.

"Yes," Serene whispered. "I...*Mah-mah* helps keep me safe when they happen."

Lola slowed behind a fruit truck.

"Well that explains why the family might put up with this haunting," murmured Aubrey.

"You're going the wrong way. You have to turn left up here."

Lola frowned. "I didn't know you drove."

"I...well, it just seems so familiar, except I made that left back there..." Serene's answer trailed off.

"Madame, please. This is hardly the time—"

Lola drummed her fingers on the steering wheel, then stopped. That was Aubrey's impatience, not hers, blanketing the inside of the car.

"Yes, yes, fine. You think your granddaughter is confused."

Serene watched the streets pass by without expression.

Lola considered her options. She had no proof that Serene was the saboteur of Tommy's cremation. The younger woman was calm now, if not wholly healed. Lola had no idea how long this peace would last. She had to take advantage of it. Especially if it hastened Serene's rescue from her crazed Ghost.

She took a deep breath, quelling her internal doubts and disgust.

"Serene," she said, "I need your help." Lola gave a sidelong glance. Serene looked back at her warily.

"There's something about this pocket watch, Stuey's pocket watch. Something I can't quite figure," Lola said. "Do you know anything about that?"

"I don't know what you mean."

"Everyone says Stuey kept that watch with him every waking minute. But I don't understand why."

"He loved his uncle. Dearly. He was heartbroken when Stanley died."

Lola cocked her head to one side. "An uncle that was rarely in town? How often did Stuey see him as a child?"

"You don't have children. You don't know what they're like at all, do you?" She turned her head, looked out the window. "You could tell he was thinking hard about something because he'd rub it. Like a talisman."

Lola gauged Serene's tone. "Do you know where it is, now?" she said softly.

Serene kept her face turned away. "No."

The resentment in the reply rang Lola's alarms. She thought out her next question with care. "If he knew Philip Kam wanted that watch, would Stuey have hidden it or given it over for safekeeping? Perhaps...to your brother?"

"Never." Serene's mouth twisted. She shook her head. "He wouldn't have kept it safe."

"What do you mean?"

"*Yee-goh* never even kept a wallet. He had the luxury of losing things, forgetting things. He only had to focus on his craft." Her fists clenched. "*Dai-goh* took care of his money. Or Stuey did." She swiped harshly at her eyes. "But I'm telling you, he would not have parted with that watch."

"He trusted *you*, didn't he?" Lola pushed aside guilt at the blatant manipulation.

"Only with his precious costumes and clothes." Serene's expression shifted into an angry mask. "Never with his money."

Aubrey made a warning noise.

Lola filed away Serene's comment about Tommy. "I meant Stuey," she said kindly. "I think he must have trusted you more than many others."

Serene's cheeks coloured. "He did. He knew." She turned to Lola. "I know how to keep secrets." Her bitterness filled the car, turned the early morning sunshine harsh. And yet Lola sensed a tiny flicker of pride in Serene's admission.

"Don't," said Aubrey in an iron voice. "You will not harm her. She's your flesh and blood, for gods' sake."

Lola silently encouraged Aubrey against the other Ghost.

Serene bit her lip, looked down at her hands, smoothed the skirt of her dress. "Stuey told me how much it meant to him. Why he always wore it on the chain. Why it was so important."

Lola slowed, watched her mirrors, slid in behind an old open-bed truck stacked with cords of firewood. She sensed the cusp of a shift in Serene. She wrung the steering wheel, debating the risk in her next question. Would Serene crumble—or fight?

Lola took a deep breath. "Will you tell me? Now?"

A long silence. "Why do you want to know so much?"

Lola gave the glib answer. "I promised to look after his parents. To protect them from Philip Kam. The more I know about this watch, the more likely I'll find it before he does." She decided against bringing up Evelyn Shao by name.

Lola glanced over. Serene stared at the back of the truck ahead of them. The firewood swayed with the motion of driving, but every length stayed snug against its neighbour. Lola narrowed her gaze, discerned the knots of rope holding the top of the load down tight. The truck ground its gears, slowing to a stop.

Serene looked at Lola sidelong. Then she spoke, her voice light as spider silk. "Stanley was his father."

Lola jammed on the brakes. The car jerked forward then back. Lola hurriedly mashed down the clutch and pushed the gear shift into neutral. The car rocked back and forth. Lola watched the cords of firewood in the truck sway in front of them, her skin prickling with perspiration.

Serene stared straight ahead. "I...was having a bad time, working on those costumes. Isolated, resentful. Feeling like a slave." She paused. "Nothing new, I suppose, but I must've said something out loud in his hearing."

Lola shivered at Serene's blank expression.

"He took pity on me. Which was also nothing new. He said he understood about families, more than I knew. That it was important to choose one's family, especially when one felt there was no choice at all."

Serene smiled faintly. "I told him to stop flapping his gums. I was happy he'd made the effort to cheer me up. But he was serious. He leaned in and...told me. Just like that."

The truck changed lanes, rumbling into a lower gear to make a right turn. Serene shifted her attention to Lola.

"So you see, he lived a lie, a lie he was happy with. His real father was a wanderer. His mother, killed in an accident before he was out of diapers. And he ended up with the best of people anyway. A family that was easy to choose, easy to love."

"That is uncalled for, Madame," Aubrey said, voice heavy with disdain. "He showed kindness to your granddaughter. You only emphasize your own character with such malice."

"Wait, wait." Serene braced one hand against the dashboard, body rigid, face pale and streaked. "What time is it?" She looked out the windshield, the side window, craned around to face the rear. "Is the sun up? Is it?"

Lola kept one eye on the street, the other on Serene's frantic movements. "What are you looking for?"

"The sun. Is it up? Is it past four o'clock?"

"Yes." Lola frowned. "The sun rose just past four."

Aubrey cursed. "We missed the bells."

"No." Serene's wail raised the hairs on Lola's arms. "The ringing of the bells. The forty-eighth hour. I missed them." She pounded her thighs with clenched fists. "That was the whole reason I was there with all those horrible, mindless, stupid *gifts* for the great Tommy Chu." Her face twisted into an ugly mask. "All for nothing."

She let out a short scream of frustration, hit the dash with the flat of her hand.

Wincing, Lola searched the street ahead for a place to pull over safely. Vehicles were parked tight, one after another, as far as she could see. She reached a hand over to calm Serene. The younger woman slapped it away.

Serene's eyes went wide. "I did it. Thanks to *Yee-goh*, so clever, he and *Dai-goh* found a way to talk without Uncle Lucky knowing. That's how they made the deal with the studio. I knew all about it. Do you hear me, *Mah-mah*? Do you understand? I did it, right under your nose. I paid a Conjurer to sabotage the incense sticks and you had no idea. Tommy made my life a horror. He was hateful and cruel and he deserved what he got. If I could've traded Stuey for him, I'd've done it in half a heartbeat."

Aubrey's shouts filled Lola's head. She squinted through the pain, determined to keep her eyes on the road. She spied a gasoline stand a few blocks up, checked over her shoulder to make the lane change.

Aubrey grunted in pain. "Get away from her." Lola heard him struggling, the sounds of laboured breathing close.

"I should've done it when I had the chance. Useless girl."

Lola froze, stunned by the sound of Stasha Chu's voice in her mind.

She felt ants crawling over her face and neck, spreading down onto her torso. She slapped at her arms, her neck, fighting to drive straight. She risked a look down at herself. Her arms were red from her own violence, the skin puckered into goose bumps. Then a frigid cold descended, starting at the crown of her head. It spread downward, an invisible coating of ice. Lola's vision blurred at the edges.

"Get away from me," she shouted, thrashing. "Get out of my head, you filthy twisted haunt."

The sound of fist meeting flesh and the cold lifted. Lola shuddered, the memory of Stasha's presence an oily film on her mind. She tried to relax her white-knuckled grip on the steering wheel.

A car honked from behind and Lola startled, ramming her foot down on the gas pedal. She steered with stiff hands while trying to tap the brake.

"No," yelled Serene. "Leave her alone." She lunged forward and grabbed Lola's hand, wrenching the wheel. Lola pulled at Serene's fingers, trying to pry them off. Serene punched Lola in the arm, the ear, the leg. She slid herself back, angled her body and kicked out with her feet.

"What the hells are you doing? You're going to get us both killed." Lola dodged every which way, trying to block Serene's flailing assault without causing an accident on the street. The car juked and shimmied as Lola did her damnedest to keep to their lane.

She saw movement in her peripheral vision and instinctively arced her elbow out, planning to let go of the steering wheel, to snag Serene's foot and push the younger woman away.

Instead, Lola felt something snap in her arm as Serene's kick landed. She cried out, shoving the smaller woman away from her. A horn blared. She grabbed the wheel left-handed and straightened out their path. The screech of brakes. The rumble of a large truck downshifting gears.

Serene grabbed a handful of Lola's hair. Lola convulsively tightened her grip on the steering wheel. A spear of pain from her injured elbow, tucked in close to her body.

They veered into the next lane. Serene's twisted, yanking Lola back the other way. Lola let go of the steering wheel too late. The car barrelled to the right. Lola grabbed Serene's wrist, reaching across her own body with her left hand. She screamed as her right elbow collided against the seat.

They slammed to a stop against the curb. Lola's neck wrenched and her elbow smashed hard into something, her vision blanking. She scrabbling for something to hold, to regain her bearings. Her vision cleared.

Serene's face was slack, her eyes shut. Her head lolled to one side. The window behind her was cracked in a spider web pattern.

Voices were raised. Lola's door opened. She tried to turn her head around. She forced her eyes to focus. Her sight contracted again, blackness crowding in. She coughed thickly, felt a warm gush down her chin.

Then she was out.

TWENTY-THREE

She came to with a start, reaching for the pistol under the pillow next to her head. She flexed her fingers, twisted her shoulder, and realized she wasn't moving at all. Her arm was immobilized, bound tightly to her chest.

She groaned, felt a spike pierce her brain, behind her left eyeball. It throbbed in time with the ache in her elbow.

Lola struggled to open her grit-filled eyes, frowning with the effort. She groaned again. Her face hurt. Then, a rush of blood to her head. The air around her erupted in sound. Unfamiliar sound. Her eyelids finally unglued.

Nicky sat at her bedside, peering at her with bloodshot eyes and deep lines carved into his face.

"You gave me a real scare, my girl."

Lola grunted.

"Here, they said to give you water." Nicky put a hand behind her head and tipped a glass against her lips. Her tongue and the inside of her cheek stung. She would have hissed, but the water was too important to waste. She kept her mouth open and swallowed until Nicky took the glass away.

"Serene?" Her voice was little more than a croak.

Nicky nodded, turning the mechanical bed crank with smooth, slow motions. Lola's head and torso lifted.

"Banged her head. But she was conscious. Seb took her home already. Didn't want the heat."

Lola surveyed the room. An internal window against the wall next to the door. Its drapes were drawn. The door was closed. Another window opposite let in bright sunlight. No other occupants. No other beds.

"He made sure you had a private room," said Nicky. "Seb did. Got here before anyone else. Took care of all the arrangements." He paused. "Stasha said you caused the accident. Telling every Ghost and Healer within earshot."

Lola grunted again.

"Said you were harassing Serene with questions and tried to scare her. Lost control instead and almost got her killed."

Lola stared at Nicky through half-open lids. He shrugged. "You oughta know what's being said."

She pointed for more water, her finger wavering. After another long drink, she cleared her throat, coughing at the sensation of steel-spiked cotton scraping up and down.

"Easy there, my girl." Nicky took her hand, patted it.

She took a deep, shaky breath.

"Found out she'd missed the temple bells. Went off her nut."

Nicky furrowed his brow. "The deaths, they're too much for her." He hesitated, squeezed her hand. "Was she trying to kill the both of you?"

"Don't know," Lola croaked. "Stasha tried something with me and then Serene attacked." Nicky gave her more water. "May've been trying to protect me." She let her head fall back on the pillows.

Aubrey's cool presence pushed at her from the left. "You mustn't tell anyone, Lola. That Stasha tried to possess you."

Lola shivered, recalling Stasha's alien presence in her mind.

"People will panic if you do," said Aubrey.

"Cold?" Nicky peered at her, fussed with the blanket until it draped both her shoulders. He refilled her water cup, took his seat.

"She was livid," said Aubrey. "When Serene admitted to the sabotage, I had to hold Stasha back. Then she turned on me. *Kung fu.* I was surprised. I let her go. She…used me, as when we spoke with them. Used me to access you."

Lola shuddered. The blanket slithered down, pooling at her lap. Nicky jumped up to fix it.

"The look on her face." Aubrey paused. "She was ready to kill someone."

Lola frowned, looked at Nicky. Her mentor took up her hand.

Aubrey said, "I'm sorry, I know you can't speak to me now, not with Nicky in the room, but this is out of our hands now. It's time to bring this to the Council. I must tell them about Stasha before she does more harm. Possession is forbidden, Lola. If she tries that again, she'll bring the Council down on her and on Serene. And there will be repercussions for us all."

"Wait, Aubrey, wait. Need more time. Don't go…" She didn't care what the Council would deem necessary to keep Stasha in line, but she knew they would have little mercy for Serene. The Council ruled all Ghosts and kept their secrets. They would count the death of one woman more than worth the cost.

She struggled to think, but the pull of pain and the pace of the previous night dragged her down. Lola closed her eyes.

When she woke, she opened her eyes to find Viola peering at her, expression intent.

"I'm still here," said Aubrey quietly. "I haven't left."

Lola went limp, her eyes fluttering closed.

Her Auntie smiled and kissed her forehead.

"Oh darling, are you all right?" Viola stroked Lola's hair.

Lola smiled, opened her eyes. "I may not be the best one to ask."

Nicky tsked. "You've got a cut inside your mouth and you bit your tongue, looks like. That's gonna be sore for a few days. Your elbow's broken, but it was a clean break. It's bound up for a very good reason, so don't go moving it around. You got knocked pretty hard on the noggin. You blacked out, so they want you in here another day. And something about your neck. Another sore spot and it's gonna hurt for a coupla weeks."

Veronica smiled. "Betta will have you right as rain, honey."

Lola nodded, then winced. "Weeks?"

"I think he said whiplash." Nicky was apologetic. "What did that little girl do to you?"

"I don't recommend stopping a car with a curb." Lola grimaced, suddenly aware of every lump in the mattress. "Any chance I can have something stronger than water?"

"Water they say, water it is," said Viola.

Vivian poured from the glass pitcher, switched places with Viola, and helped Lola drink. She said, "Now then, what's this I hear about you trying to kill someone?"

"I think she's serious," said Aubrey.

Nicky explained in Lola's stead. Vivian harrumphed. "Stasha always was overly melodramatic."

"How are *you*, Auntie?" Lola tried to look Vivian over, could only slump against her pillows instead.

"I'm in much better shape than you." Vivian waved a hand in dismissal. "What did you say to her? Stasha claims it was an interrogation. A botched one. That Serene was lucky to come out of it alive."

Lola shook her head, then groaned. Vivian clucked at her. "Be still, stupid girl. Your head's only going to hurt more. And you'll need your wits about you. Stasha's always been histrionic, but that doesn't mean she won't cause you some serious trouble. Look what she's done to that poor girl, her own granddaughter."

"Aubrey says she's more interested in control than care." Lola coughed.

Vivian wagged a finger. "If someone at the Temple had been doing their jobs, Stasha Chu would never have been allowed to haunt anyone, let alone a sixteen-year-old girl. Lucky tried to speak to someone about that. Long before he ever met Tommy. He just knew *her*. That was enough."

Veronica leaned against Viola's chair. She nodded. "Stasha was always pig-headed."

"Ambitious, too," said Vivian. "Back when she was a chorus girl, she set her sights on Lucky. Knew he'd be something big." Vivian shook her head. "Damned if they didn't last all of six months. Just long enough for him to see past her looks. Oh, you should've seen her then. Legs that went forever, thick, black hair, a face like a goddess—beautiful, cruel. Every man drooled when she walked past, and she knew it. Couldn't dance her way out of a rice sack, but one look at those legs was enough. She used what she had for as long as she could. Got knocked up by Anson Chu, though, and that ended the so-called stage career. He was just a stagehand, dumb as an ox. Handsome as a devil. You can see him in the eldest one, Sebastian."

"It was hard for her, when her husband died," Viola said. She glanced at Vivian. "Stasha had a two-year-old son and no money. Her husband's parents were dead. She was forced to go back to her own family."

Veronica nodded. "You know how it is now. Think back to Stasha's youth, in the old country. Ten times worse. She was disgraced, and her parents were ashamed."

Vivian pulled a face. "Of her misfortune to be a widow."

"To be a woman." Veronica's voice was hard. "A so-called burden." She huffed. "Utter rubbish."

Lola's sight wavered. She felt her hand being taken up. Shifting her gaze, she forced her eyes to stay open. Vivian stroked her hand. Lola pulled her face into a weak semblance of a smile.

"When Stasha found out she was dying, she was desperate to haunt someone, anyone. Couldn't bear the thought of leaving this life. She ran that entire family with her iron will, her ambitions. Got accustomed to having her way." Vivian made a rude noise. "That should've rung a few alarms. Lucky tried to talk to the monk performing the ceremony, I remember. But Stasha convinced everyone that it was just spite on his part. We all knew better."

"Unfortunately," said Veronica, "no one at the Temple wanted to stand between a dying woman and her granddaughter."

A long pause. Lola realized her eyes had closed. Her ears worked fine, however.

"After Lucky took in Tommy, she became his biggest fan."

"Lola," Aubrey said, "we have to intervene. *I* have to intervene. With the Council. When Stasha tried to possess you, she crossed a very serious line. I'm not sure what they're going to do to her, but I have no choice. She's harming her Host, and she tried to kill you."

Lola snapped to full wakefulness.

"I have to warn Serene." She struggled with the blanket left-handed, trying to leverage herself out of bed.

Nicky and Vivian spoke simultaneously.

"Hang on there, my girl."

"Don't be stupid." Vivian kept a tight hold on Lola's hand.

Viola stepped up and laid a gentle hand on Lola's shoulder, pushed her back down. "Darling, there's nothing we can do for her. The Chus won't allow interference."

"Not for lack of trying," said Veronica. "The Chus are proud as well as stubborn. If nothing else, those traits they've inherited from Stasha."

Lola closed her eyes for a moment, marshalling her strength. "Uncle, help me. Please. I need to warn Serene."

Nicky shook his head. "There's nothing for you to do, my girl."

"Lola," said Vivian, "stop your nonsense. They won't thank you for your meddling. Aren't you listening?"

"Then you promise me." Lola paused, catching her breath. "Promise you'll warn Serene, Uncle. Stasha wanted to kill her."

"Her?" said Aubrey.

"Promise me, Uncle. You'll go. Now."

Nicky shushed her. "Yes, of course, my girl. You just calm yourself now. I'll go as soon as you're calm. I promise."

Lola heard murmuring, saw Veronica at the door, calling out to someone. A nurse entered a few moments later, a round woman with a haggard face and hair streaked with grey. She smiled perfunctorily, moved briskly.

"There now, Miss, you're all right here. But we can't have you getting out of bed just yet. Not until Doctor Higgins gives his say-so."

Lola felt a sharp jab in her left arm. She looked down groggily at the syringe in the nurse's hand.

A curse formed in her mouth—

TWENTY-FOUR

B etta looked at Lola with concern etched deeply on her beautiful face. Lola grimaced as she manoeuvred herself into the front passenger seat.

"Thanks for coming to get me."

"I know I said I'd help you, but I'm not sure this will go over well with my landlords."

"I'll handle them."

"I'd like to see that."

Lola grunted as she folded a part of her that she should've stretched instead. "What the Aunties don't know won't hurt them."

"Ah, but I'm quite certain it will hurt me."

"Look, I'm sorry to drag you into this, but you're what I've got."

"After such a resounding vote of confidence, how could I refuse?" Betta held up a hand at Lola's look. "If your doctor says you're free to go, then I'll take him at his word."

"Well, he did. To me. About an hour ago."

"Are you sure I don't have to sign you out or something?"

"Ask Aubrey if you don't believe me."

"I'm taking his silence as agreement with you." Betta cocked her head to one side as she assessed Lola's face. "But you do look a bit green around the gills."

"Can we just get out of here? Please? Fresh air will do me good."

"I know I'm going to regret this," muttered Betta. She closed the door and walked around to the driver's side. Lola clumsily rolled down the window left-handed. It was hot as all get-out. She needed to feel the breeze, any breeze.

She hissed when she bumped the sling around her right arm.

She took deep, calming breaths against the rising nausea. After a few moments of roiling queasiness with her eyes closed, Lola opened them and searched for something to watch instead. Betta navigated away from the hospital and westward toward Lola's office.

"So now that we're away from prying eyes and perky ears, tell me what's really going on."

"It's probably best if I don't."

"You only say that when you're in it deep, sweetheart."

"More reason to keep the danger contained then."

"You've already involved me." Betta glared at her. "I'm your getaway driver, remember?"

Lola swallowed, trying to stem a new wave of nausea. "Will you please slow down?"

A rude noise. "Your obstinacy will be the death of you."

Lola kept her eyes half-closed as she watched the car pull to the curb. Betta turned the car off. She placed a warm hand on Lola's forehead. Lola scrunched her eyes shut as Betta pushed healing energy into her.

It was usually a gentle affair.

"Ow."

"That's for lying to me." Betta took her hand away. "I could've done that anytime if you'd have asked. I'm not unskilled, if you'll recall. And I could've done it while you laid comfortably in your hospital bed. So don't be stingy, Lola. I deserve the truth."

"She's right," said Aubrey, voice subdued.

Betta frowned.

Lola's head felt clear for the first time in what felt like years, and the muscles of her face relaxed. She felt the tension in her neck and shoulders falling away. She took several deep breaths and opened her eyes. The sunlight was just as bright, but it no longer sent a spike of lightning into her brain.

Betta assessed Lola with a worried expression, her light brown eyes darkening the longer she stared. Her full mouth was turned down at the corners. There were more lines bracketing her eyes and her mouth than Lola recalled.

She suppressed a twinge of guilt.

Betta's gaze flitted over Lola's face. "Why did you call me to come? What do you need from me?"

Lola winced. "You're right. I should've been honest with you upfront. I promise to explain. But right now, I'm on the clock. Just drop me at my office. I need you to ring someone for me."

"Not bloody likely, to borrow a phrase from St. John." Betta glared.

"It's for Serene Chu, Betta. Please. The girl's in trouble. Aubrey says her Ghost is close to cracking and—"

Betta shushed her kindly. "All right, all right." She pursed her lips, thinking. "I'll take you to that chemist on the corner from your office. We'll get some soup at the counter. Once we get something into you, then you can do your explaining." She clucked her tongue. "You aren't nearly as strong as you think you are, Lola. The body and spirit need sustenance, and anger simply isn't enough."

Lola nodded shakily. She sank back into the upholstery and watched Betta fire up the car and pull back into traffic.

⟡

"And you're certain, Aubrey? You'd be willing to testify to a Temple adjudicator?" Betta didn't wait for a reply. "Because this is an extremely serious accusation."

"It's not an accusation, Betta." Aubrey's tone was cool. "I've watched it several times over just two days. Stasha Chu is abusing her Host."

"It's been ten years, surely, since she was originally tethered," said Lola. "And Stasha's attitudes didn't suddenly sprout up after she died. From what the Aunties said, she comes of a very traditional family, especially about girls." Lola scowled. "I doubt Serene ever knew a moment's peace even before the haunting."

Betta considered for a moment, expression grave. "Can I help her somehow?"

Lola felt a wave of relief. "You believe me then?"

"Why wouldn't I?" Betta met Lola's gaze with clear eyes. "What benefit is there to you to lie about this?"

"The Chus won't let you help. We have to come at them from a different angle. Official channels. I need you to put us in touch with someone who will listen."

Betta nodded. "It's a tricky situation, as I understand it. But I'm no expert in this. I can get you Janis Yiep. She still teaches the odd course here and there at the Temple. She retired as a full professor specializing in Ghost tethers. This covers the magical nature of the tether, as well as the softer psychological bond between Ghosts and Hosts. She's brilliant and a stickler for ethical conduct. She'll know all the rules and regulations."

Betta pointed a long finger at Lola.

"However, I must contact her first. It will help that Aubrey's with you. Janis is very partial to Ghosts, especially handsome ones."

A thousand rejoinders crowded Lola's mind. She was too tired to bother. She took a quick sip of water.

The tidy black-and-white chequered floors and creamy white walls hurt Lola's sensitive eyes. She squinted, regretted it immediately as her headache doubled in severity. Sweat trickled down the back of her neck, at her temples. She pushed away the half-finished bowl of spicy soup Betta had ordered for her.

The Healer pushed it back at her. "Finish it. You need to sweat out the toxins building up from your injuries." She gave Lola a plain grey linen handkerchief and refilled Lola's glass from the pitcher on the table.

Lola wiped at her face and neck, feeling flushed and sticky. She caught the counter man eyeing them again, the fifth time in as many minutes. She had a wry suspicion it had more to do with Betta's looks than with any concern for a customer in distress from overly peppered soup.

Betta sipped at her tea. "Janis can also help answer your other questions." She lowered her voice. "You truly believe Tommy Chu wanted to Disperse his Ghost?"

"That's Uncle Nicky's theory."

"But I'm still not clear how that could turn into what ended up happening."

"That makes two of us—"

"Three," said Aubrey.

"And given your history with such a spell, I'm not sure it's such a good idea for you to be sticking your nose into it, either."

Lola swiped the damp cloth over her face again. She didn't like remembering her role in the fate of the City's former Mayor. "I was cleared of any suspicion."

"I'm not accusing you of anything, for gods' sake." Betta leaned toward Lola, voice pitched even lower. "There's a reason it's not widely known, sweetheart. It's not just dangerous to perform. It can be dangerous even to know of it."

"Because the Council—"

Aubrey hissed.

"Aubrey's right," said Betta, "You mustn't speak of them so lightly. There are repercussions beyond just your safety, Lola. You know the rules. If we want to continue to live in harmony with our Ghosts, we don't speak of the ones who created those rules."

"And enforce them," said Aubrey.

"Betta," said Lola carefully, "we can safely say I'm past that point, don't you think? I made a deal with…them and I don't squelch. Especially not when it will cost my mother so dearly if I do. Their dirty little secret's safe with me, gods help me." Lola drank down half the glassful of water, wishing it were something stronger. "Right now I just need to understand if there's a way for a Host to Disperse a Ghost without his Ghost's consent or knowledge."

Betta fidgeted with her tea cup.

"I need the lowdown, Betta. Nicky's counting on me."

A crease formed between Betta's brows, her eyes searching Lola's face. Lola waited her out by drinking her soup. Clumsy with her left hand, she barely managed to get half a spoon's worth into her mouth. Beads of sweat popped out under her eyes. She replaced the spoon with a clatter against the bowl and reached for the now-sodden grey handkerchief.

Betta grasped Lola's hand. "If I tell you, you must promise me you will never tell another Host." Her grip on Lola tightened.

"Please. Promise on your father's grave." Lola looked down at her wrist, then back up.

"I promise on my father's grave I will never tell anyone anything I learn about this procedure."

Betta's grip grew harder still. "Aubrey, you'd better hold her to that. For both your sakes."

"You know I will," he said. Lola caught something in his tone, too fleeting to name.

Betta sighed, her eyes fluttering closed for a second. "Thank you. I need to know you understand how dangerous this information is." She looked down at her hand and Lola's wrist. "I'm sorry for that. Let me just—"

She closed her eyes for a moment, murmured under her breath, and reopened her eyes. She rubbed smoothly around Lola's wrist. A creeping chill slowly expanded beneath Lola's skin. As Betta continued rubbing, the redness disappeared. Lola's wrist felt encased in a cold compress.

Betta said, "The residual chill will last another half hour or so. If it goes longer, ring me immediately."

Lola took her hand back. She rubbed her wrist. It was awkward with her right arm in the sling against her chest.

"Are you all right?" said Aubrey.

Lola spoke to Betta. "I hope that was worth it."

"I'm sorry, sweetheart. I just...it's so important that you understand the dangers."

Lola nodded. She looked into the other woman's eyes. Betta looked deeply worried.

"Surely I can't be the only person who knows of this spell."

Betta waved her hands airily. "I don't want you to be the only one honest enough to admit it."

Lola didn't laugh at the attempted humour. "But surely Tommy wasn't the first Host curious about it."

Betta sighed. "Of course not. You're not the only Host I know who chafes at her binding."

"You're saying Ghosts aren't able to perform this spell."

"Ghosts are not allowed to practise any spellcasting," said Aubrey. Lola couldn't read his tone. But she did note his careful words.

"Betta, can a Ghost cast—"

The Healer raised a hand. "Enough of that. You know the rules," she repeated. "I said I'd give you Janis as a contact. Let me ring her." Betta slid out of her seat and walked to the public booth against the back wall. She nodded politely at the counter man, who ducked his head and returned to wiping at the countertop.

"She's taking a grave risk by helping you," said Aubrey.

Lola watched the counter man as he watched Betta. Poor sap. He was clearly already half in love. "I know."

"Uh huh."

A stocky man in a tan suit and straw boater slid onto a stool at the counter. He took off the boater, smoothed his black hair. The counter man tore his gaze away from Betta and moved briskly to welcome his newest customer.

Betta returned, a small smile on her face. "Janis is always happy to have visitors. Even if they bring trouble."

"I have another question," said Lola.

Betta raised a brow.

"Can a Ghost exist without a Host?"

"You truly can't leave well enough alone, can you?"

"This is about Lucky and Tommy, Betta. What if Lucky caught wind of Tommy's plan? What if Lucky was searching for a way to...not need Tommy?"

Betta shook her head. "Ghosts must be tethered to the living."

"Can they switch Hosts?"

Another head shake. "The ceremony is Host-specific. We all learn that in our first year at the Temple. It's a basic tenet."

"Yet Matteo Esperanza found a way around it."

"Lola," said Betta, "our recently departed Mayor should be no one's example of appropriate use of magic. He cheated."

"But the people of this city allowed him to," said Aubrey.

Betta looked over to Lola's right. "Yes, we did." She paused. "People bend the rules for very good reasons all the time, Aubrey. We ought not to judge them harshly."

Lola waved her hand, cutting into the weighted silence between Betta and Aubrey. "Back to Lucky, please."

Aubrey said, "If Lucky found out—"

"That's a big 'if.' As big as Nicky's theory in the first place," said Lola.

"If he did," said Aubrey, "then it's also possible Lucky arranged the shootings."

Cold shivered up Lola's spine. "Murder and suicide? Could Lucky Wai truly have been that desperate?"

"Old Ghosts do get strange sometimes." Betta's expression was sombre. "Perhaps Lucky felt he had no other options."

TWENTY-FIVE

Betta insisted on escorting Lola the one block to her office. Lola kept her spine straight and concentrated on walking steadily. Inside her building's lobby, she clenched her hands to hide the shaking, ignored the sweat that plastered her shirt to her back.

"Being stubborn isn't going to hold you up much longer," said Aubrey.

Betta held Lola's left arm, guiding her to the lift. Lola gritted her teeth and got in. She nodded to Billy, the lift boy. His eyes widened and his mouth clamped shut. He returned the nod and pinned his gaze to the floor numbers. Lola stared at the lift panel. She swallowed several times to keep her stomach calm. Betta made a small noise of impatience, placed a hand on the small of Lola's back. A soothing sensation spread through Lola's body.

She stifled a moan.

The lift stopped and Billy opened the accordion doors. He tipped his hat, face carefully blank as he closed the door. The lift disappeared downward.

"When'd they lengthen this hallway anyway?" Lola muttered.

Betta said, "Here, let me." She took Lola's keys and unlocked the door. When they entered the anteroom, it took Lola a moment to realize it wasn't empty.

"You oughta get that lock changed," said Ria. "I barely had to jimmy it." She was sprawled on the sofa, her feet propped on the low coffee table. She bent almost in half, crushed out her cigarette in the

239

ashtray next to her crossed ankles, and blew out a long plume of smoke.

"Guess I'm just a talented teacher," said Lola, voice fading.

"Valeria," said Betta. "It's been a while." Ria stood, dragged Lola to a seat, then exchanged hugs with Betta.

"Don't tell me she dragooned you into her escape." Ria looked at Lola with narrowed eyes.

"All right, I won't," said Betta, smiling.

"Don't you have better sense, doll? Betta has a reputation to uphold."

"Unlike me," said Lola. She fought to catch her breath.

"Don't even try to tell me different." Ria turned back to Betta. "I've got her from here."

Lola raised her eyebrows. It could wait, she decided. She said to Betta, "Before you go?" She pointed to her broken elbow. "I can't sit around waiting for it to heal, Betta. Please."

"Sweetheart, it's going to hurt like the devils if I do it all at once." Betta pursed her lips. "And you'll be close to exhaustion." She paused. "'Closer,' I should say."

Lola nodded. "I don't have any choice. Please," she repeated.

Betta's gaze strayed to Lola's right, complex expressions flitting across her face. She sat down next to Lola. "There's no gentle way to do this. It will certainly ache for hours afterward."

Lola gave a weary nod.

Betta carefully unwrapped Lola's arm, laying aside the long ribbon of cloth on the low table. She laid cold fingers against Lola's elbow and started to rub vigorously. Lola hissed as the first tendrils of searing cold blasted into her. Tears sprang to her eyes, left hot trails down her cheeks. Ria offered her hand. Grabbing hold, Lola closed her eyes. Fireworks of white exploded behind her eyelids, coming faster and faster until she swore she could hear them.

When Betta finished, Ria *tsk*ed. "I'm not sure you're in any better shape."

Lola hung her head, unable to move.

Betta hugged her with one arm. "Don't waste my efforts or the pain," she said. "Be careful with it. And take care of that head of yours. It's hard, but it's not indestructible." She left, her heels tapping down the hallway. The bell clanged. The lift doors slid open then shut with their usual racket.

Lola eyed Ria. "How long have you been in here?"

Ria snorted. "That's your first question?" She closed the outer door and locked it. "I'd think you'd be more interested in why I'm here at all."

Lola hauled herself up and staggered into her inner office.

Ria let out a long-suffering sigh. "I revise my estimation of your father up several notches. I bet you were never still as a child."

Aubrey gave a quiet laugh.

Lola stumbled to her desk, fell into her chair. She breathed heavily for a few moments as she stared at the inlaid box atop her desk. Ria came in, tossed a stack of envelopes onto the desk, crossed her arms and considered Lola. She handed Lola an Egyptian cigarette. "Need me to light it, too?"

Lola shook her head. "Get the windows?" She lit up with a slight tremor, closed her eyes. When she opened them after the first exhalation, she listened to the traffic noises coming in through the windows. Ria studied her.

"There was a big hullaballoo after you pulled a vanishing act. Luckily for you, someone mentioned Betta's name and they all assumed you'd been taken into her care for private Healing." Ria cocked her head. "Which, naturally, was your plan all along." She made a rude noise, dropped into a chair opposite Lola.

Lola took another long drag. "How'd that lead you here?"

"My powers of deduction. What else? I figured you were hot on some trail. You'd show up here eventually."

"Could've gone to the apartment."

Ria's eyes widened. "And risk Elaine's wrath. Puh-lease. This ain't my first visit to your circus."

Lola's burst of laughter turned into a wince. She focussed on breathing.

"As your official babysitter, sister, I gotta say you don't look so copacetic."

"Next time I ditch the hospital without my doctor's orders, I'll make sure to put on my makeup first."

"Couldn't hurt." Ria rummaged in the fabric bag at her feet.

"Where the hells did that bag come from?"

Ria paused. "If you missed seeing this bag, this *bright green* bag, there's a lot more wrong than even Betta can heal. But lucky for you, I've come prepared." She gestured with her chin. "Get a glass from out that magic drawer of yours." She held a bottle of orange juice. "And don't get any funny ideas about that fifth of whiskey. This here's freshly squeezed by Papa G himself. You dilute it, you ruin it. Got it?"

Lola dutifully pulled out two glasses and ignored the bottle in the bottom right drawer of her desk. She let Ria cut off the wax seal on the orange juice bottle and pour her a full glass.

"To my health." Lola downed her medicine in one long drink. The juice was bright and sweet and rich. Liquid sunshine. Lola banged her empty glass down on her desk. She flinched at the noise. Ria brought out a dark brown bottle and a spoon.

"What is this?" Lola frowned. "You've turned chemist?"

A corner of Ria's mouth lifted. "Time to take your medicine." She pushed bottle and spoon across the desk. "Two spoonfuls and that headache and neck pain ought to be more manageable."

"How do you know Betta didn't already Heal that?"

Ria raised a brow. "Did she?"

Lola stared at her.

"There you go, then," said Ria. "C'mon, don't be a pill about it."

Lola complied with ill grace, grimacing at the bitter syrup. Ria refilled her orange juice. When Lola had drained it, she pointed at Ria. "You plan on following me around the rest of the day?"

Ria rose, snatched up Lola's telephone. "Harmony 2818, please."

Lola fidgeted in her seat. She felt a restlessness beneath her exhaustion. She wondered where Serene was. If Sebastian would be smart enough to leave her at home. She wondered if Nicky had even bothered to telephone them.

"Elaine, it's me. Yes, we're at her office. Not very well, but you know how it is. All right. No, she's coming with—. Yes, I know. Good luck with that. I told you she would. Oh. That's perfect then. Tell him to meet us there. We're leaving now. Yes, thanks. Good-bye."

Ria fell back into her chair, sipped at her juice. She ran a slim finger around the rim of her glass. "You are officially tagging along with me now."

Lola raised her brows. "You can get muscle for a lot less than my going rate."

Ria gave a short laugh and finished her juice.

"I take care of myself just fine. And you'd be hard-pressed to take on a newborn kitten." Ria sat up, put her glass down on Lola's desk. "I'm going to Tommy Chu's wake at Golden Harvest."

Lola considered that for a moment. "You dug something up. About that birth story?"

"Ding ding ding. Give the lady a cigar." Ria smiled, self-satisfied. "I found the doctor who delivered them."

"'Them'? So he delivered all the Chu kids? So Tommy wasn't adopted?"

Ria shook her head. "Nope."

Lola thought hard. "How'd you find the doctor? Is she credible? Is Sam going to print the piece tonight?"

"I'll get it in tonight's edition only if I get an interview with Sebastian Chu. Sam would shunt me back down to the obits if I didn't."

"What about the doc?"

Ria's eyes shifted to the window. She uncrossed and recrossed her legs. "He's...problematic. Been suffering dementia for about six years. He's not real clear on timelines. But—" she cleared her throat "—he told me the story of the birth like it happened yesterday. Crystal clear memories of that one."

"So you're planning on confronting Chu at his baby brother's wake? In front of hundreds of industry people?" Lola frowned.

Ria glowered. "I've got better style than that. My plan is to corner him nice and quiet like. Have a civilized conversation. Set up the interview somewhere private. Say, his office. It's the perfect opportunity for him to set the record straight." She raised an eyebrow. "You get to come along and witness me in action."

Lola shook her head, cursing at the sudden dizziness. She gripped the edge of the desk. "I've got a schedule to keep. Two o'clock with a

retired Temple instructor. Nicky's depending on me. So is Serene
Chu's sanity." She explained as quickly as she could.

Ria gathered up the juice bottle and dirty glasses. "Nicky's been
waiting at your place. With Elaine. He'll meet us at the studio and
then he'll take you to this retired Temple instructor—whom Betta
was kind enough to tell him about when she tracked him down at
your apartment. And yes, the Aunties had a role in that and they're
angry with you, too. But don't let's borrow any more trouble than
we have to at the moment. I'm taking these to rinse down the hall.
You collect your strength while Papa G's nectar works its magic."

⟡

Golden Harvest Studios was encircled by a concrete wall standing ten feet tall and two feet thick. Its white stucco glowed in the
brilliant sunshine. Lola knew from her father that the top of that
wall had a channel carved into it, filled with gravel. And within that
gravel nestled pots of plants, their rims just barely visible to eyes
looking up from the sidewalk. Ivy and desert grasses draped gracefully down no more than three feet, while the vivid red flowers of
birds-of-paradise added colour contrast and distraction from the
discreet razor wire threaded through the plants. As walls went, it
was as welcoming as a structure meant to keep people out could be.

Lola thought it a fitting metaphor for the film industry.

She squinted behind her sunglasses at the long queue winding its
way out past the front gates and down the sidewalk. She saw white
armbands in various shades of cleanliness, each one properly tied
high on right arms all the way down the line.

She looked down at the white linen strip snug on her left arm.

Ria nudged her. "There he is."

Nicky approached from the other side of the gate. He wore a light grey suit, his shirt near-blindingly white. He captured Lola's hands in his.

"Right on time. How're you feeling, my girl? Betta said she healed you quick and dirty."

Lola shrugged, regretting it as her neck twinged.

Nicky gave her the hairy eyeball. "Uh huh." He shook his head as he looped arms with the women. "Come on then."

"What about them?" said Ria, gesturing toward the crowd with her chin.

"The wake's not open to the public. That's just the regular queue to get in for normal tours." Nicky nodded to the burly security guard standing just outside the gateway. The man returned the nod, flicking a glance at Ria as they passed him.

"This your first time inside?" Nicky said.

Ria nodded. Lola shook her head.

"Really? I'd've thought you'd be here on a regular basis, following a story."

"Maybe if you're writing fluff for the tourism pages. But the City desk's not much welcome here. We dig too deep and uncover too much. Studios are all alike. They like to control the flow of information." Ria grinned. "Admit it, before you retired from Wu Studios you would've been the one to show me the door yourself."

Nicky smiled.

He set a slow pace as they continued deeper onto the grounds. Lola grit her teeth as she shuffled beside him. They walked amidst large warehouse-sized buildings, easily forty feet tall and as large around as a city block. Most had their doors closed. Signs hung next to the doors, proclaiming filming within and demanding silence upon entry.

It was easy to spot the location for the wake. Streamers of white cloth flanked the entrance of one of the ubiquitous warehouses. To the left, enlarged poster-sized photographs of Tommy Chu. His signature, a dynamic flourish of flowing characters, embellished the space to the left of each photograph. Lola heard the dull murmur of a crowd from within.

Once inside, Ria looked upward. "It's huge in here." The sound of her words disappeared into the shadowy rafters high above their heads.

"This one's the smallest of the lot, actually." Nicky paused, scanning the people gathered under a tent-like structure of dark grey cloth and black-lacquered bamboo poles. "Come on. You've got time for some food, I should think."

"I'm not hungry," said Lola. Her stomach growled.

"You'll eat something all the same. Keep your strength up."

Ria arched an eyebrow at Lola, daring her to back-talk her old mentor. Lola frowned.

Nicky led them to a long table set out with a buffet of tropical fruits, steamed rice *bao*, and triangular, banana leaf-wrapped *djuhng*. Lola made a beeline for the urn of hot tea. It wasn't coffee, but it was strong and black enough to tide her over.

She considered the people solemnly standing about. "No one looks particularly distraught," she murmured.

"Tommy kept his work associates at arm's length."

"So his inner circle included his siblings and Stuey? That was it?"

Nicky nodded. "And Lucky, I suppose. For a while, anyway."

Lola assessed the crowd. They looked exactly as one might expect of a group of people mourning a business associate. Sombre, subdued, quiet.

"I'd like to think Sam and the others would be pretty broken up if I went suddenly," said Ria, looking around. "This seems rather...impersonal."

"The show must go on," Lola said.

A thickset man in a tan suit arrived and headed purposefully for the tea urn. She wondered if he was hoping for something stronger as well. Her fatigue returned in another wave and she wished she'd had coffee earlier, Betta's professional opinion be damned.

"Stop lollygagging and eat up," said Nicky. "Who knows when your next meal will be."

"Same as any other day," muttered Aubrey.

Lola itched to get up and walk around. Her pounding head advised against it. "Are they coming soon?" She rubbed at her temples, the back of her neck.

He shrugged. "Seb said one o'clock." He put down his tea cup and gave Lola his full attention. "I'm not sure you should be so eager to see them. Considering they think you tried to kill Serene."

"That's not what happened. She and I both know it." It was Lola's turn to shrug. "Besides, I was dragged here under duress."

"Speaking of enemies," said Ria firmly, "how did you get Lola past the gate? I'd think she'd be on their blacklist."

"That's why I had to meet you. They didn't ask me for your names." Nicky grinned.

"Good." Lola managed a tight smile. "Since I'm here, it's important that I speak to Serene."

"That might not be on the agenda today, my girl." He tipped his chin toward the opposite side of the tent.

Sebastian Chu spoke to a cluster of studio people. A white armband stood out starkly against his dark grey tunic. Lola craned her neck, searching for his sister. Sebastian stiffened, looked up. He started as he discovered Lola. He excused himself and strode over, his expression darkening with fury.

"What the hells are you doing here?"

"Please tell me your sister is safe at home." Lola kept her voice low and urgent.

"What business is that of yours?"

"Just tell me, gods damn it."

"Yes," he said, anger momentarily overshadowed by puzzlement. He pointed at Lola. "You stay away from her." He rounded on Nicky. "I know you had something to do with this, Uncle. You've abused your privileges at this studio. This woman is a danger to my sister."

Lola's anger burned away her weariness. "Not me. Your grandmother." She had no choice now with Serene absent. She had to get it through Sebastian's thick skull. "Her gambling debt is doing a much better job of it than I ever could."

Sebastian recoiled, his expression incredulous. "What the hells are you doing meddling in my family's business? *Lei-ah sei gwai poh.*"

Lola let his curse pass over her. "You paid off a substantial money debt for your sister. Ring any bells?"

"Keep your voice down," he whispered, stepping closer. "What? What are you blabbering on about?" He glared. "You leave my sister alone. I have clout here and I will have you thrown out. I don't care who your mother is."

"It's who my father was that oughta worry you, Chu." Lola glared back at him. "He worked for the studios long before you arrived on the scene." She stopped, took a deep breath. "But this isn't about you or me. If you'd just listen."

Sebastian's scowl deepened. He looked around then, spotted someone, and snapped his fingers. A man dressed in sombre navy came over, bowing and offering assistance. He barely came up to Lola's shoulder.

Sebastian pointed. "Get security here now. I want these people removed immediately." The little man bowed again and took off at a smart pace.

Nicky stepped into the space between Lola and Sebastian. He held up his hands placatingly. "Seb, we have our differences, but you know I'd never hurt you or Serene. Security's on the way. You can have us tossed after you hear Lola out."

Sebastian shook off Nicky's words, glaring at them all. His attention caught on Ria. "Who are you?"

"Valeria Monteverde with the *Herald*. I have some information I think you ought to know."

"And let me guess: I shall be honoured to pay a fee for this information?" Sebastian's handsome face twisted into a sneer.

Ria shook her head. "No, Mr. Chu, I don't work like that." She paused. "Perhaps we can speak privately for a minute or two. I promise you, as Mr. Lo said, we'll leave quietly after you hear what I have to say. But I'm certain you'll regret not listening at all."

Sebastian made an impatient noise. He pointed at Lola. "You, explain yourself and make it snappy. Your time is severely limited."

Lola forced her anger away, concentrated on keeping her tone neutral and business-like.

"Your sister is being abused by your grandmother. My Ghost has witnessed it himself. If it goes on much longer, with the stress of her latest grief, your sister may well be irretrievably harmed."

Sebastian crossed his arms, expression stony.

Lola suppressed an urge to slap him. "Fine. You still need to know that Philip Kam holds an Ether debt over your grandmother. Your sister has been helping her pay it off with her own life energy. In fact, the amount of the Ether debt is more than what your grandmother has. Do you understand? He's draining Serene too."

Sebastian's face contorted. "This is preposterous. Nonsense. *Mahmah* doesn't gamble anymore. *Mui-mui* told me that herself and she never lies to me. So there can't be another Ether debt."

"Gods, this isn't the first time?" The revulsion in Aubrey's voice was twined tight with anger.

Lola didn't have time to pierce Sebastian's illusions about his family. "You must keep your sister home. Make sure someone is with her—"

"I don't need you to tell me how to care for my family." His lips curled into a snarl. "She's got someone with her, tending to her injuries. Injuries she incurred when you tried to kill her. Injuries on top of the ones she received in another car accident the same day our brother died."

"What?" Lola felt her face go cold.

"What happened?" said Nicky.

Sebastian gestured, impatient. "She said she got into a fender bender, hurt her neck."

"Yes, but what happened?"

Sebastian glared at Nicky. "She stopped at the side of the road. Forgot to set the handbrake. Next thing she knew, the Packard had rolled down the other side of the hill, hit a fence. *Mah-mah* helped her get to a telephone and ring a garage for aid. They towed her car and she came home in a taxicab."

Lola felt as though her stomach dropped. "Gods, Chu. She'd just returned from Sunrise Valley, correct? She must've been in a lot of pain, given that a full healing wasn't completed. Broken wrists are not trifling. And the added strain of the debt and her grief—" Lola leaned in. "You've got to see how close she is to breaking."

Sebastian narrowed his eyes. "Of course my sister is under a great deal of stress. Your meddling only makes it worse. And your reckless driving nearly cost her her life. This deranged fiction involving non-existent gambling debts is nothing short of contemptible. As is your presence here."

"Dammit, Chu, just promise me you'll make her stay at home, safe with a servant or—"

"I'm not doing any such thing. And certainly not on the say-so of a meddlesome *gwai*."

With an effort, Lola swallowed her retort. This wasn't about her ego.

"I don't care if you hate me or if you hate my entire race, Chu. This is about keeping your sister safe, if not from her own family, then at least from a predatory gangster. Don't let your prejudices endanger her needlessly."

Sebastian chopped his hand downward. "Enough." Lola clenched her hands into fists, slowly released them. She looked away.

"You've warned him," said Aubrey, "the bloody scrub."

Sebastian pointed at Ria. "Say your piece. You have thirty seconds."

"I was approached by a woman claiming that your brother Tommy was adopted." Ria spoke calmly, compassion clear in her tone. "In my research, I discovered that, in fact, he was not. I'd like to sit down with you and ask you some more questions, specifically related to the information I unearthed concerning the true circumstances of his birth. And I think you'll appreciate privacy for our interview. My editor is set to run the evening edition with my story as-is, but I want your input, Mr. Chu. I think it's important to give you the chance to explain what truly happened. I think you owe it to the public." She paused. "And to your family."

Sebastian considered her with a cold look. "You've got ten minutes. After I finish at the wake." He gestured to a set of security men, standing patiently with the little man.

"There's our cue," muttered Nicky.

Sebastian gave his orders.

Ria gave Lola a swift wave before allowing a guard to escort her away. The little man trailed after them.

The two remaining men stepped forward, then stopped a respectful two feet away from Lola and Nicky. They were broad-shouldered, medium height, calm. Lola could tell they knew their business. She looked sidelong at Sebastian. He turned away.

Lola plucked at Nicky's sleeve. She spoke to the guards. "Don't trouble yourselves, fellas. We know the way."

TWENTY-SIX

They stopped at Nicky's car, a beat up blue Buick. Lola knew there were rust spots hiding beneath its thick coat of paint.

"Someday, Uncle Nicky, you will suddenly find yourself riding within a dust cloud of disintegrating metal on two axles and four wheels."

"I'll deal with that when it happens, my girl."

"If I didn't know you better, I'd say you were joking."

"There's nothing wrong with the engine. And there're plenty of reasons to look unassuming." He paused, took a deep breath, rolled his neck and shoulders. Lola leaned heavily against the Buick as she lit up a dark cigarette. The sun had started its descent from its zenith but Lola knew it would be hours before the heat let up even a smidgen. She exhaled a hazy blue plume of smoke and rubbed at her eyes.

"Damn it all to hells," muttered Nicky.

Lola straightened up and followed the direction of his gaze.

"What's the matter? Makes sense the Twins would attend the wake."

"I'm not surprised they're here, my girl. I'm cursing their timing. I'd hoped to miss them entirely. They're just going to tie us up with useless questions."

"No such thing. You taught me that, remember? Questions are always useful."

"Yes, *my* questions, cheeky girl. Not ones from the coppers." He squared his shoulders as the two detectives approached.

"Miss Starke, your doctor's quite vexed with you." Leung tipped his hat.

"Seems he's not happy that you checked yourself out of the hospital under false pretenses." Eng looked at her blandly.

"What are you doing about Philip Kam?" Lola explained the exchange with Bednarski and Marks the previous evening, as well as the letter, and the Ether debt.

"Kam's obsessed with this pocket watch," she concluded. "I've warned Sebastian Chu, advised him to keep Serene at home, but he didn't seem willing to listen to me. I doubt he believes that the Ether debt exists. But Serene Chu confirmed it does."

"I take it this was before you attempted to kill her?" said Leung.

Lola waved a hand, wincing at the slight twinge in her elbow. "It wasn't like that. She was overcome with grief, angry with the world. Her Ghost was distraught and caused Serene to overreact. Besides, she didn't press charges did she? Despite that harridan of a Ghost pushing her, I'll bet." She narrowed her eyes at the two coppers. "That girl has been through enough and her Ghost isn't helping matters. In fact, we're on our way to see a Temple official about it. My Ghost is willing to testify."

Leung swapped looks with his partner. He said, "We need you to come with us first."

Eng said, "We've discovered what we believe is the vehicle involved in the murders."

"Where? How?" Lola felt a shock of cold spread through her belly. She exchanged a glance with Nicky.

Leung inclined his head. "We can discuss this en route."

"We have an appointment, Inspector," said Nicky. "And Lola's tired enough as it is."

"The vehicle's down at Impound," said Eng. "This has to take precedence. I'm sorry."

Nicky exhaled heavily. "We'll take my car. We won't have time to get driven back here. And we'll have to ring our appointment. Serene's safety is at stake. We'll meet you there." Nicky hustled Lola into his battered Buick. He started it up after a few tries and pulled into traffic. Lola watched the coppers walk rapidly back the way they'd come.

"We need to talk, my girl."

Lola checked over her shoulder automatically as Nicky made a lane change. In the small side mirror, she caught a glimpse of the coppers, speeding to catch up, in a standard-issue black Ford. Leung drove, his usually bland expression replaced by a scowl. Eng scribbled in his notebook.

A man in a tan hat pulled up alongside their car for a few seconds, catching her attention. Then he slowed, turning off to the right. She squinted against the sunshine reflected off chrome bumpers in the opposite lane. The headache returned and she had a sudden yearning for orange juice.

"You have something to share?" She rubbed at her eyes.

Nicky puffed out his cheeks, released his pent-up breath. "Lucky was right. The cheeky little bastard lied to his Ghost about that film. Tommy told Lucky he was just rehearsing, there was nothing official in place. But, in reality, the studio had agreed to let him start before the official contract was even inked. Oh, they were smart enough to get the requisite insurance—and Seb helped with that, I'm told—but the paper for the film and the revenue splits were still in the works. They gave him resources and camera time before anything had even been typed up." Nicky shook his head. "If I didn't know that he stabbed Lucky in the back to make it happen, I'd admire the scheming little rat."

"I'm sorry, Uncle. In all the hullaballoo, I forgot. Serene said Tommy found a way to talk without Lucky's knowledge. That's how he signed his contract with the stu—"

Nicky slapped the steering wheel. "I knew it. This proves it. Tommy and Lucky did *not* mend things, as Seb claimed. My contact at Golden Harvest knew all about the arrangement. She was there when it happened. And so was her Ghost. They were clear on this point, my girl. Lucky did see Tommy sign that contract, you were right. But then he discovered Tommy'd lied to him about the so-called rehearsal time." Nicky shook his head. "So now we know how Tommy pulled it off."

Lola decided to focus on the issue at hand. She would have to tell him eventually, but right now, she had no desire to explain that Serene knew about Nicky and Lucky's clandestine communications, and that their example had spurred her to contract a crooked Conjurer to tamper with Tommy's incense.

Instead, Lola said, "How angry was Lucky? Did your contact's Ghost say anything specific?"

Nicky flicked a glance at her. "Angry enough to kill."

Lola considered her earlier conversation with Betta. "But Uncle, your theory is that Tommy was planning on ridding himself of Lucky. And now you've found a possible motive for Lucky to want to be rid of Tommy." She paused, weighing her next words carefully. "Would Lucky have been desperate or angry enough to damn himself in the name of revenge?"

She watched her old mentor closely.

Nicky chewed the inside of his cheek.

Lola said, "I asked Betta. She's adamant. There's no way for a Ghost to survive without a Host and no way to re-tether to another Host."

Aubrey said, "It's a complicated ceremony in the first place. I don't think performing a re-tethering without the original Host's knowledge is even possible."

Lola added Aubrey's argument to her own.

Nicky flexed his hands around the steering wheel. "I respect Betta. You know I do. But she's not exactly well-versed in the darker side of spells. Nor the underworld of conjuration and healing."

"Uncle, you realize you're saying that Lucky was willing to kill Tommy? His Host. The man he thought was his son in a past life."

Nicky rubbed his temple. "No matter how much I owed Lucky, if he pushed this into motion…I cannot condone murder. I need to know, my girl. For my own sake." The lines in his face seemed to deepen as she watched.

She nodded.

❧

The Crescent City Police Department Impounded Vehicles Lot, a huge area north of downtown, was secured by top-notch fencing, barbed wire, and regular patrols. When Nicky turned into the parking area, kicking up a cloud of dust, they had their choice of spots.

A muddle of black-and-tan dogs started barking. They were contained within a square corral between the main administration building and the exterior chain-link fencing. The dogs jumped wildly in time with their barking, the bright metallic tags at their collars flashing in the sunlight.

A window slammed shut in the building behind the dogs.

Lola jumped at the sudden blast of dirt as the Twins pulled up. The detectives hopped out of their car, and Leung inclined his head toward her. He gestured and led the way toward the gate.

"Thought you'd beat us here," said Nicky.

"You were barely inside that chemist's shop long enough to ring someone."

"Managed a smooth tail, I'll give you that," said Nicky, "but didn't you trust us to come as promised?"

"About as much as you trust us." Leung waved at the blocky building ahead. "You could've made your telephone call here."

An unintelligible yell sounded as the group reached the chain-link fencing. The dogs quieted, replacing their barks with low, rumbling growls. They paced their small square of hard-packed dirt, alert and watchful.

Leung greeted the gatekeeper, a uniform with "Kwan" on his tag. Badge numbers and identification were carefully checked and copied down. Kwan nodded once, returned to his gatehouse. The gate rolled sideways in jerky fits and starts, and came to an abrupt stop.

"According to the crew," Leung said, "the car's an enigma. As far as this case is concerned, that is. No clues to the driver's identity. We can't tell how many people may have been in it. Even the attempt at burning, though unsuccessful, charred most of the driver's side."

"We hauled it from the abandoned brickyard next to the Ping-Ohng Fisheries," said Eng.

"Burned," said Leung. "But mostly intact. They didn't use enough petrol."

"Amateur arsonists," murmured Nicky.

"Doesn't take a professional to kill." Eng's mouth thinned into a grim line.

No one disputed his statement.

"I'm curious why you're being so upfront," said Lola.

"I've always been upfront with you, Miss Starke" said Leung. "Can you say the same to me?"

Lola shifted her gaze to the maze of vehicles surrounding them. Waves of heat shimmered upward from the metal. She swiped at a bead of sweat at her hairline, clapped a hand to the back of her neck. Nicky pulled out his pocket square and roughly wiped his face.

They came to the end of a corridor of cars, in various stages of health and dismemberment. Leung stepped around a mound of old tyres and they rounded the corner to the left.

"That it?" Lola resisted the exhaustion pulling at her again.

"See any other burned out cars around here?" Eng said.

Lola threw him a glance over her shoulder. He wasn't looking at her, but rather at a spot beside her. Lola wondered if Aubrey looked as impatient as Nicky did.

It was clear at least that the car used to be a black Packard. Lola rifled through her memories, searching for something new. She stared at the car during a long silence.

"Anything?" said Aubrey.

Lola shook her head a fraction. Eng shifted, cleared his throat, closed in half a foot without seeming to move.

Lola stepped closer to the car, its acrid odour unavoidable. Paint had peeled and bubbled, leaving the surface looking like toad skin. Lola examined the interior. Cracked glass, blackened metal, and charred upholstery. The steering wheel had twisted from the fire's heat.

Leung placed his hands into his pockets and stepped back, examining the car from the side. "This used to be an impressive feat of ingenuity and engineering. Now look at it. There's a message in that, don't you think?"

Nicky grunted.

"I'm afraid philosophy was never my strong suit, Inspector," said Lola.

Leung nodded. "Can you identify this vehicle as the one you saw stopped outside of The Supper Club before the shooting?"

"I'm sorry. I can't. There was nothing remarkable about it then and there's certainly nothing I can see now to use for identification." She paused, considering the charred upholstery. "Though I suppose the front seat's a sort of clue."

Leung stared intently at Lola. "What's that?"

"It's up pretty tight. As though the driver were short."

Leung stepped in close to the car again. He looked in through the smashed-out window, even thrust the whole of his head inside. When he re-emerged, he looked at his partner with a deep frown. Eng returned the look with an impassive expression. Leung faced Lola.

"Thank you, Miss Starke. Your cooperation tonight is most appreciated. We'll speak with the crew, see if they moved that bench seat." He swept out his arm. "Shall we?"

Lola looked from Leung to Eng and back again. She caught Nicky's gaze. He shrugged. They let the coppers lead them back out through the maze of unclaimed vehicles, past the inscrutable Officer Kwan, through the gate and to Nicky's blue rust bucket.

"Can you keep Kam and his thugs away from the Chus and the Lims?" Lola said.

"We are not private security, Miss Starke. No matter our suspi-cions, we cannot arrest Mr. Kam without cause." Leung shrugged, apologetic.

Eng said, "Glad to know you came out all right last night."

Lola inclined her head. "Likewise. Thank you for taking care of Vivian."

He nodded. Nicky helped Lola into the passenger seat.

Leung slapped the top of the car, sending them on their way.

TWENTY-SEVEN

So it's either someone short or someone...short," said Nicky. "What does that tell us?"

Lola's mouth was dry. She swallowed several times before she could reply. "The Twins are thorough. They'll be up all night going through the books that Vice must keep on known sugar boys, looking for numbers on height." Lola shrugged, vision blurring with weariness. She blinked, focussed on the green Ford ahead of them.

"Good luck to them then."

Nicky drove toward East Town, making one quick stop while Lola waited in the car. She rode in silence for most of the drive, resting her head against the seat, eyes closed, body limp.

"I wonder what this Yiep will say about Serene's situation. She can't give much more and stay sane." Aubrey's voice was tense.

"I don't imagine her brother's that much of an idiot," said Lola.

"Aubrey worried about Serene?" said Nicky.

Lola nodded. "That girl's at the end of her rope, Uncle. Do you think her brother's smart enough to keep her safe?"

"Yes, but I won't lay any bets on her being happy about it."

"This Temple Mistress, retired or otherwise, is our best chance," said Aubrey. "I don't hold out any hope her family's going to do the right thing."

"If this play of yours doesn't pan out," said Nicky, "it'll cost Seb some obscene amount to cover her debt. Kam's got Serene between the devil and the deep blue sea, my girl. It's not illegal to hold an

Ether debt, just distasteful." Nicky grimaced as he shifted. "That little stay at Sunrise Valley must've cost her something extra because I don't see she had much time to renegotiate with Kam before her brothers bundled her off. It's not unheard of to have one's debt interest doubled for something like that."

"Gods, this is a mess, Uncle." Lola felt the need for a solution pressing down on her. "You didn't talk to Sebastian, did you?"

"He's stubborn as they come. We've done all we can."

"That's the attitude that's allowed this whole damned mess to continue, Uncle."

"Don't start. You honestly have no idea what you're talking about." He downshifted as the traffic signal switched to red. They sat in tense silence as they waited for the green.

Lola stared out the window, watching cars crisscross ahead of them in the intersection. She thought of something then.

"What about the pocket watch? Do you know where it is?"

"Me?" Nicky frowned at her. "Why would I know that?"

"You're close to the Lims. You knew Stanley, didn't you?"

"Stanley?" He paused. "Keun and Liliane were studio workers then, so I knew them, of course. But Stanley wasn't around very much. I was friendly with him, yes, but I'd never say close." He grinned at her. "Your father and I had our hands full with work—and *you*, if I recall aright."

Lola returned his smile, hearing the ring of truth in his tone. She collapsed back into the seat, content that Nicky hadn't been holding out on her about Stuey. She chose not to examine what her mistrust of her mentor meant.

⌘

Janis Yiep was a plump woman with iron grey hair and large black eyes in a face of rosy cheeks and smooth skin. She greeted them in her front yard, a medium-sized square of lush green grass and a rainbow of flowers. She held shears in one gloved hand and a wicker basket of long-stemmed flowers in the other. Her face was shaded by a conical straw hat and her feet were clad in bulbous shoes of bright yellow.

Lola bowed. "Thank you for seeing me on such short notice, Mistress Yiep, and for your patience in changing our meeting time. This is Mr. Nicholas Lo. My mentor. I mentioned him to you when we spoke." She offered the burlap satchel in her left hand. "Please, these are for you. They're from Shining Star Orchard, a little fruit stand Uncle Nicky knows of just this side of East Town."

"How delightful," said Yiep. "My parents used to take me out there, to the orchards, on weekends. It was even smaller then than it is now." She smiled, bringing out dimples in her cheeks.

"A pleasure to meet you." Nicky doffed his hat, bowed from the waist.

"This is my Ghost, Aubrey O'Connell."

"Yes, of course. How d'you do? It's a pleasure to speak with you. I don't have as much opportunity to work with Ghosts, now that I no longer teach regularly."

"Mistress," said Aubrey, voice warm. "It's an honour to meet you. Betta holds in you in high regard. However, she never mentioned you had such a talent for gardening. Your flowers are stunning."

Yiep inclined her head. "Now that I'm retired from lecturing, I spend most days out here, puttering about." She kicked out her foot. "Look at these. Wouldn't have been caught dead in these when I was at the Temple, but here? They're devilishly convenient. Made of actual rubber, clean them off with a quick spray of water. Slip on and off easy as pie." She shook her head. "Indispensable. Expensive too. European, you know. Ugly as sin, but it doesn't seem to matter out here. Shall we take this out back? I've got some lemonade ready." She smiled at Lola, her eyes sharp. "You look ready to take a break."

They walked along the light grey flagstones, passing the small house on its left. Bedding plants of creeping mint, flowering thyme, as well as tall herbs like tarragon, rosemary, and cilantro filled the space between the house and the pathway. Lola inhaled deeply, enjoying the fresh, clarifying scents. Rounding the corner of the house, she discovered an unexpected profusion of colourful flowers and shrubbery. Nicky swore softly as he bumped into her.

Yiep smiled. "Takes everyone off guard. I know the formal garden is all the rage lately, but here—" she inhaled "—here you can feel how futile it is to struggle against nature. You can smell it."

"It's remarkable," said Aubrey.

Yiep gestured, leading them to a round table of wrought iron painted white. Atop it sat a fat-bottomed pitcher and three tall, gleaming glasses. With a pronounced sigh, Yiep sat down in one of the two matching chairs. "Would you be so kind, Mr. Lo, to fetch that other chair over by the house?"

"Of course."

"May I?" At Yiep's nod, Lola poured the lemonade.

Yiep reached out for Lola's satchel of fruit. "Oh these look good." She pulled out a plump peach and bit into it, slurping noisily. "Stupendous," she said. "Please, pleasure before business." She passed the satchel to Lola. The trio ate their fruit in companionable silence.

When she was done, Yiep pitched the peach stone into a patch of wildflowers. Nicky shrugged and did the same. Yiep smiled again.

"Called 'composting.' Using food waste to enrich the soil." Lola followed suit.

"I'm glad I can help." Lola took a sip of her lemonade and set down her glass. It was sour, after the intense flavour of the peach, but she didn't mind. She rubbed at the smudge of fingerprints on her glass.

"I thank you for the gift of fruit, Miss Starke. And I do so appreciate your manners. It seems increasingly rare now for young people to do things in the traditional ways. I'm glad to know someone raised you properly." Yiep smiled. "Now, onto business."

"Betta mentioned our friend's problem?"

Yiep nodded, expression sombre.

"Will the Temple listen to me, if I approach on her behalf?"

Yiep narrowed her eyes. "The girl herself isn't willing to come forward?"

"She hasn't yet and I doubt she could stand up to her family," said Aubrey, grim.

Lola looked at Nicky then back at Yiep. "Uncle says that her family refuses to acknowledge there's even a problem."

Nicky nodded. "We've tried to help before, many of us who know the family. But they're extremely traditional, especially the Ghost, who is their matriarch. They see our concern only as interference." He paused. "I've told Lola this. Many times."

Yiep shook her head. "I'm afraid Mr. Lo is right. Your hands are well and truly tied, Miss Starke. Unfortunately, you don't have any standing in this sort of situation. The Host must come forward to file a formal complaint. Or the immediate family can. No one else. I'm sorry, those are the rules."

"I can't even file a complaint?"

"Well, you could. But without corroboration from the Host or the family, it'll go straight to a filing cabinet. I'm sorry." Yiep shook her head again.

Lola deflated, trying to think of any next step. She squared her shoulders, and pushed the issue to the back of her mind. "Thank you. I appreciate the information." She took a long sip from her lemonade, then reached for her purse. "May I smoke?"

"I'm allergic to cigarette smoke."

They sat in awkward silence.

Then Yiep took a deep breath.

"All right. So Betta tells me you also want to know how a Ghost can be Dispersed without killing its Host."

Lola shared a look with Nicky. He raised his eyebrows.

"Or whether a Ghost can survive without a Host. Or switch Hosts," continued Yiep. "You understand this isn't common knowledge? I need reassurances you won't banter about what you learn from me."

"I swear," said Lola, "upon my father's ashes that I will not spread this information around."

"I swear upon the memory of my wife," said Nicky.

"You already know I can't share it," said Aubrey quietly.

Yiep looked intently at all of them in turn. "Betta's already vouched for you, and that means a lot. But there's nothing like watching a person take their own oath to get a feel for their true intentions." She took a drink of lemonade, her expression thoughtful. "I've heard many rumours of your involvement with our former Mayor, Miss Starke. Of course, Betta has assured many of us, those within her circle, that you are innocent of any evil intentions." Yiep looked intently into Lola's eyes.

"And do you believe her?" Lola calmly met her gaze.

"You're here, are you not?"

"I'm grateful for your trust, Mistress."

Yiep made a dismissive noise. "Don't shine my shoes. Calling me 'Mistress' is all well and good the first time. But you're not the subservient type. I can tell." Her eyes gleamed with amusement. "I'm sure Mr. Lo, as your mentor, can confirm that for me."

"That I most definitely can," Nicky said.

Yiep turned her gaze back to Lola. Her expression sobered. "If you'd meant to be involved with that business, I'm certain Mr. O'Connell here would no longer be with us. And you'd likely be nothing more than a shell of living functions. If you'd be alive at all." Yiep narrowed her eyes, clearly waiting for a rebuttal.

Lola waited her out.

Yiep sat back, took a deep breath. Her gaze settled to the left of Lola's shoulder. "I'll tell you not because I think it's safe, but because I think it's more dangerous to keep people ignorant of such a powerful thing."

Yiep shifted in her seat, took off her hat and dropped it on the grass beside her.

"So now we get to it. The answer, in its simplest form, is yes. The spell you are asking about has three integral parts. One, a willing Conjurer. Two, a willing Ghost. And three, a willing Host."

"That's all? There's no special incense? No herbs or candles? What about a special location?" said Lola.

"It's not a ceremony. Just a spell. An intricate and dangerous spell, to be sure."

"Then it requires special permission from the Temple?" Lola glanced at Nicky. He leaned forward, intent on Yiep.

"Ah," said Yiep, "that's where things can get a bit sticky." She sat back, rested her elbows on the arms of her chair, set her chin atop her laced fingers. "Officially, of course, every important ceremony between a Ghost and its Host requires Temple permission. However, that's not the same as saying the *outcome* requires special permission, if you get my meaning."

Nicky nodded. "That's the part that's dangerous, then."

Lola toyed with her glass, working it out.

"Exactly. If everyone knew that Temple permission isn't a prerequisite to success—" Yiep opened her arms wide, palms up "—chaos. Not just about this, but about every spell, every ceremony. Everything."

Yiep's gaze shifted to Aubrey again before landing once more on Lola.

"This next is what you truly need to hear. For this spell you're interested in, you must have a Ghost wholly committed to its own death. There's absolutely no turning back on this. That Ghost must be utterly certain it wants out."

Lola looked at Nicky, confused. Nicky stared at the garden.

Yiep continued, "Then you must find a Conjurer not only capable of the complex mental discipline to create and hold the spell, but also one willing to do it. The Conjurer is required to help the Ghost apply to the Temple, you see, and this engenders intense scrutiny by the Temple for all three parties. This particular spell doesn't need a lot of pomp, but it does need absolute precision.

"Finally, you must have a Host who is willing to risk damage to her mental faculties, being thrown into a vegetative mental state, or even complete soul detachment. This last is theoretical, of course, because there has never been a report of such a spell being done, let alone being done successfully. But it is a well-reasoned and fascinating theory. After all, just consider. What would it be like to lose your soul, the very ethereal substance that allows you to partake in the reincarnative cycle? Your body might very well live on—at least, that's the current theory—but any Conjurer or Healer worth her salt would sense the absence of soul. Death would be a welcome alternative, wouldn't you agree?"

Lola tore her gaze from Nicky, set her confusion aside. "What happens to the soul, according to this theory?"

"We barely understand what happens now," said Aubrey.

Yiep raised a finger. She shook her head, smiled. "Not exactly, Mr. O'Connell, but it is true that the theories are wildly speculative."

"Theories," repeated Lola.

Yiep nodded. "No one other than Selby-Hwang has come up with a spell for this, and, naturally, she came up with the theories concerning Host Dissociative Soul Disorder as a possible result of the spell. But since her seminal work in this area, there have been others willing to put down on paper their theories on the dissociated soul, as it is called."

"And that group includes you?"

"Guilty as charged." Yiep inclined her head. "I am particularly interested in where these dissociated souls would be stored. Is it an entirely different plane altogether? Would they be visible to Conjurers, Healers, and Ghosts? And, if so, would they be visible in the exact same manner to all three groups? What, in fact, does a soul look like? I've never seen one, nor have I heard of anyone, anywhere in the world, documenting a sighting of one." She gestured with her hand, palm up. "Would anyone even recognize one visibly? Would any Ghost?"

"Well, if you can sense the absence of one, can you not sense the presence of one?" said Aubrey.

Yiep slapped the tabletop. "Exactly. But the teaching of that sensing is done entirely by using corpses to expose students to what the absence of a soul feels like. It's as practical a method as it is old. No one has ever come up with another way to sense a soul, Mr. O'Connell, and we've been using that old technique for centuries."

"If it ain't broke," said Lola.

"Yes, yes, it works well enough," said Yiep, "but it lacks a definite elegance, don't you see."

Lola glanced at Nicky. He chewed his cheek, staring at the wildflowers. She said, to Yiep, "Is there a way for a Host to contract a Conjurer without his Ghost's knowledge in order to have this spell performed?"

Yiep paused, eyes narrowed on Lola. "There are many ways, it is true, for Hosts to keep their Ghosts out of private conversations. And private moments, yes."

"And vice versa," said Lola.

Yiep nodded. "Conjurers are key for any Host or Ghost wishing to communicate clandestinely with others."

"So," said Lola, drawing out the sound, "if one wished to Disperse one's Ghost secretly...?" She gestured.

Yiep frowned. "It's not public knowledge. It's in your best interests to keep it so." She included Nicky and Aubrey in her sharp gaze.

"Understood." Lola took a sip of lemonade. "And the other? Is it possible for a Ghost to survive without a Host?"

Yiep shook her head emphatically. "Impossible. I'm sure Mr. O'Connell can attest to this, yes? The ceremony ties a Ghost intricately and inextricably to one living Host. One cannot change one's mind after the fact and change Hosts. There are no spells for such a thing."

"That you know of."

Yiep stared at Lola. "Yes," she said slowly, "that I know of. But my experience is not to be so easily discounted."

"Did Tommy Chu contact you sometime in the last year?"

Yiep blinked a few times. "No."

Lola waited for more. Yiep stared back at her.

Lola frowned as she swiftly considered what she'd missed. When the answer came to her, she suppressed a gasp. She looked quickly at Nicky. His gaze was still on the wildflowers. His brow furrowed, then his hands stiffened on the chair arms.

Lola kept her gaze on Nicky. She said gently, "Did Lucky Wai approach you?"

Yiep nodded. "I'm sorry."

Nicky covered his face with his hands.

Lola forced herself to continue. "What did he want?"

"He asked me essentially the same question that you did."

"Did he explain his interest?"

"He didn't need to."

"But did he?"

Yiep hesitated slightly. "Yes. He wished to have the spell performed for his own Dispersal."

"He was clear on that?" Nicky spoke up softly.

Yiep stared at him. "I'm sorry, yes. He was despairing. It sometimes happens. Young or old. Some discover that they are not as compatible with their Hosts as they'd believed."

Nicky said, "Did you dissuade him from this course? Did he seem set to go through with it?"

"I refused to perform the spell for him." Yiep pulled herself straight in her chair. "He refused to include his Host in the discussion. That was simply inexcusable. I would never even consider such a thing without the Host's consent. And here he was, hoping I'd do it 'on the sly,' he said." She paused, then raised her chin. "I'm sorry, I thought it despicable."

"How was he when you reacted to his request?"

"Put out, to put it mildly. It was clear to me that he hadn't truly thought it through. I daresay my lecture set him straight. There isn't a Conjurer within a hundred miles willing *and* able to perform that spell. They might be one or the other, but certainly not both."

"How can you be so sure?"

"I may be nothing more than a retired teacher puttering the rest of her life away in a garden, but I still have my brains. I remember all of my students. Our specialty is a very small one. They all keep in touch with me. I know where everyone is."

"And the new ones? The students you've never met?"

Yiep gestured impatiently. "Much too young to take this spell on. Trust me. It takes years of practice at the most mundane spells and ceremonies in order to get proficient at any of it. Oh sure, the Temple gives the younglings five years of study and controlled practice." She wagged a finger. "Entirely different animal. They don't teach this spell to the little ones, that's what I'm saying. I am the recognized expert. That's why Betta sent you to me. And I'm telling you there's no one within one hundred miles who could do this. Except me."

"So where did that leave Lucky?"

"He discovered the error of his ways. I impressed upon him the extreme danger to his Host, as well as the impossibility of finding a qualified Conjurer. Even without Temple consent. I told him he would not find any magic user able to perform that spell. Not successfully, and that was what mattered most to him. Botching that spell would mean unimaginable damage to him and to his Host. And I mean that. Unimaginable. No one knows what horrors would happen." She shuddered then pulled herself erect. "I told him he would simply have to wait."

"For someone with fewer scruples than you?" said Lola.

"For death. He would have to wait for death." She looked from Lola to Nicky. "Just like the rest of us."

TWENTY-EIGHT

I hate being right."

Nicky slumped in the driver's seat, his hat low over his forehead, hands tight on the steering wheel. He huffed out a breath, scrubbed at his face, mashed his palms against his eyes. Lola lifted off his hat, rubbed its smooth felt as she held it in her lap.

"I'm sorry, Uncle." She waved off the doorman to her building, gave him a tired smile.

"Why didn't he just talk to me? That's what I keep asking." He stared out the windshield. "Lucky and I talked when Tommy was asleep. He could've told me everything." His tone flattened. "I thought he had."

Lola chose silence over platitudes.

Nicky sighed, rubbed his eyes again. "Well, now we know for certain Lucky was desperate enough to look into it. We'll never know if he'd've gone through with it, though."

"You think he still loved Tommy enough to consider the risks to the Host?"

"I don't know...." His voice trailed off. "But if he didn't love him, my girl, I think he'd have simply contracted a killer. Same outcome."

"He'd've done that? Paid to have Tommy killed?"

Nicky exhaled loudly. "No. I can't see it. That's a whole different category of madness, isn't it? I can't believe my friend would do something terrible like that." He waved his hand. "I'm just—" He stared out the windshield. His jaw muscles bunched. "Damn it."

279

Lola kissed him on the cheek. "Get some rest, Uncle. We'll talk later tonight?"

Nicky waved her away.

She got out, resting his hat on her vacated seat.

"That was...difficult," said Aubrey.

Lola watched her mentor start up his rusting ruin of a car and drive off.

"That's one word for it when your best friend betrays you, I guess." She paused. "He'll be right as rain soon enough."

"And you?"

She shrugged, felt the weariness descending again. She thanked the doorman, entered the lobby and then the lift. Frederick smiled at her, closed the doors, pressed "18" on the panel. Aubrey exchanged greetings with Marcella, Frederick's Ghost.

Elaine stood in the living room, hands on hips. "Look what the cat dragged in."

"I'm sorry, and I'm beat. I'll beg forgiveness after I've had a nap," said Lola. "I promise."

"Good enough, mistress." Elaine's sarcasm brought a slight smile to Lola's lips. She waved in her maid's direction and staggered to her bedroom. She shed her jacket, went into her private bath, washed her face.

Aubrey cleared his throat quietly. "Did Yiep answer your questions then?"

"What d'you mean? You were there the whole ruddy time."

"Yes, but I'm not privy to your internal monologue." A pause. "I meant the ones you surely have about being rid of me."

Lola felt another tide of exhaustion threatening. She braced her hands on the sink, let her head hang down.

"I hope you've figured out it's not worth the risk to you, Lola."

"If you were truly so concerned for my welfare, you'd never have haunted me without my consent. You all knew I would never have agreed."

"Your father's wishes were very clear, Lola. And he knew you'd be unhappy about it. But a father's choices aren't quite as black and white as you like to think. He did what he thought was best for you. Seventeen's awfully young, no matter how much it feels differently at the time."

"I didn't need anyone to protect me then and I don't need it now. Least of all a former dresser, a costumer. If my father was so fired up to protect me, he should've done it himself." Lola clamped her lips shut.

"Well, Butch thought differently. As did Grace. And I was what they had." He paused. "Is that what's bothering you most? That he didn't haunt you?"

Lola fought against the old rage at Aubrey's words. She knew her father had loved her deeply. She also knew he'd constantly worried about her safety, even before she declared her intention to follow him into the job. They'd argued, but she hadn't known he'd be capable of going behind her back.

"That's not the point. That was never the point."

"I'm not afraid for me, Lola." He paused again. "Promise me, on your father's memory, you won't try it. He wouldn't want you to risk losing your soul. Don't spite him for making a choice he deeply believed would help you."

Lola threw her hand towel into the sink. "Understand this. I don't owe you anything. You or my mother. I know my father loved me. But you three made a grave mistake signing that Temple consent without my knowledge. I have every right to be angry." She scowled. "But it doesn't make me a sneak like Lucky Wai."

"You haven't promised me yet."

Lola shook her head. "Not going to. You asking proves how little you know me. But you keep bumping gums about it, I promise you'll be begging me for a Dispersal by the time I'm done with you."

❦

The Supper Club entrance had been so thoroughly cleaned, the pavement was shades lighter than elsewhere on the block.

"They didn't waste any time, did they?" said Aubrey.

"It's bad *chi* otherwise," Lola murmured absently. She took a deep breath, reminded herself that memories held as much power as shrines, and nodded at the doorman as he held the door for her. A swell of music and laughter greeted her as she doffed her evening wrap and handed it to the coat check boy.

She ate dinner alone, nodding to the many familiar faces of other regular patrons.

"Wouldn't we be better served if you checked in with Nicky? Or the Chus, for that matter?" said Aubrey.

"Uncle Nicky needs to be alone and the Chus would hardly take my telephone call, let alone welcome me through the gates."

"And so it's back to frivolity, is it?"

Lola raised her hand in greeting as she saw Gillian Gee enter the main room.

The Supper Club manager wore a deep purple *cheong-sahm*, with bright white peonies embroidered along the hem. A jade pin, trailing sparkling flowers from corded silk, swung as she moved her head, the overhead lights glinting over her glossy black chignon.

"How are you, Gillian?"

Gee inclined her head with a warm smile. "Fine, thank you. Mrs. Au and I are grateful for your continued patronage."

"Please, sit. If you have a few minutes, I'd like to ask you some questions."

Gee signalled a waiter. "Can we interest you in dessert tonight? It's *huhng dao saah*. One of Mr. Chu's favourites."

Lola demurred. The waiter returned with a fresh tea cup and ceramic pot, and poured for both women. Lola inhaled deeply, comforted by the smoky intensity of the dark tea.

"I wouldn't be surprised if you'd already heard," said Lola, "but it seems that Stuey Lim's treasured pocket watch is missing."

Gee nodded. "Yes. Philip Kam was already by earlier today asking after it."

Lola raised an eyebrow.

"He said that he and Mr. Lim had an agreement. The pocket watch now belonged to him."

Lola gauged Gee's neutral expression as she considered her next words. "And were you able to help Mr. Kam?"

"I'm afraid not. As far as I know, Mr. Lim never let that pocket watch out of his sight. If Mr. Kam hasn't discovered it yet, I'd imagine it's because Mr. Lim meant it this way."

"How well do you know Kam?"

"Not well at all, and that's by design. We try to keep our distance from the criminal elements."

"So it's common knowledge he's *Tong*?"

Gee smiled. "By his clothing, if by nothing else." She paused. "Although, to be fair, I'm given to understand his nightclub attracts some extremely talented musicians. Whom he pays well."

"And Stuey was one of them?"

"Yes." Gee cocked her head to the side. "May I ask you something?"

"Of course."

"What is *your* interest in Mr. Lim's pocket watch?"

Lola reviewed all of her possible replies. She shrugged. "I can't bear the thought of it going to someone like Kam."

Gee considered Lola for a moment. She inclined her head. "How may I help you?"

"I need to speak to the people he'd have been most likely to trust. I've seen the letter Kam has been waving around to prove his ownership of Stuey's watch. He has a buyer already waiting for it. For all we know, that letter is a fake, to prove a false provenance. I do think Stuey was generous enough to trade his watch to help a friend's situation. But I also think he was smart enough to keep that pocket watch out of Kam's hands until the friend was well and truly clear of danger from Kam."

A group of fresh arrivals snagged Gee's attention. She watched her staff for several moments.

"So you're saying Mr. Lim put up that watch to help a friend out of debt, a gambling debt to Mr. Kam?" Lola nodded. Gee's expression turned thoughtful. "So it's likely he hid the watch, or gave it into safekeeping, but then...."

"Yes." Lola swallowed past the thickness in her throat. "Stuey didn't have a chance to make good on the deal."

Gee wiped discreetly at her eyes with a silk handkerchief. "And now, someone may be holding onto the pocket watch, or it may be hidden somewhere." She was silent a moment. "Couldn't he have simply put it away at the bank, in a safety deposit box?"

"It's possible, but that doesn't feel right to me." Lola hesitated, trying to explain her intuition. "I think he'd've preferred a way to access it more easily. It would've been cumbersome to be visiting the bank so often."

"Not to mention awkward," said Aubrey, contemplative. "Too many witnesses."

Lola leaned forward. "For all that Stuey and I were family, I'm forced to admit I don't know his friends well. Can you help me get started? I'd like to speak to them, see if I can find a lead."

Gee nodded slowly, her expression filled with doubt. "I imagine Mr. Kam has already beat you to it."

"But the question is, would Stuey's friends have told him anything useful?"

"No, I suppose not." Gee reached across, squeezed Lola's hand. "I know you're a professional at this, Miss Starke, but even seasoned professionals can get hurt. Mr. Kam's not to be trusted. Please, tread carefully."

Lola nodded. "Gangsters and snakes. I'll watch my step."

Gee rose. "I'll write out some names and be back with a list."

Soon afterward, Lola was in the foyer, collecting her wrap and mentally mapping out her route for the night, when she heard her name. She looked up and saw Ria grinning at her from across the room.

Ria hugged her tightly, kissed her cheek.

"I'm glad you're all right. Are you leaving already?"

Lola nodded. "Trying to track down that damned pocket watch. What about you?" She assessed her best friend critically. The dark circles were lighter, at least. "Did you get that interview with Chu in on time?"

Ria's grin reappeared.

"It was a coup. Eggs in coffee. I made the evening deadline and Sam's happy as a clam. You haven't read it yet?"

Lola shook her head. "I was out cold half the afternoon and evening. And I've got to shake a leg." She dropped a coin into the boy's tip bowl. Throwing her wrap over her shoulder, she turned back and gave Ria another hug. "Congratulations. Let's get on the horn tomorrow. You can give me the lowdown."

"Wait, wait. Is everything jake?" Ria grabbed Lola's shoulders, peered intently at her face, then swept her gaze down and up again. "You cleared for duty?"

"Are you?" Lola gestured with her chin toward the main room. "I have a feeling it'll be a rowdy crowd tonight. Everyone's eager to toast Tommy Chu to the next life."

Ria's eyes filled with tears.

"Hey, hey, what's with the water works?"

"Grief," said Ria, trying to laugh. "It makes people strange."

"If I promise to read your big story tomorrow, are we square?"

Ria punched her playfully on the shoulder. "All right." She hugged Lola again. "And you'd better ring me to say it was the best thing I've ever written."

"For you, I'll lie any day."

TWENTY-NINE

L ola started with The Night Heron.

A hand-painted sign of graceful Japanese calligraphy fronted two storeys of dark clapboard siding. The upper floor was unlit. The main floor had a strip of windows across its width. Light seeped out from behind closed shutters.

No doorman. The heavy wood door creaked as she pulled it open.

A small stage was set in the corner farthest from the door. A woman held up a cherry wood stand-up bass. Her arms, bare in a sleeveless champagne gown, were corded with muscle. She turned the bass and started slapping at the strings. A pale man sat on a backless stool, using a pair of drum brushes to swipe and hit at his two-drum kit. The saxophonist stood to the right of his band mates, in shirtsleeves, purple suspenders, and shined shoes. His eyes were closed as he carefully rationed his heart into his instrument, creating a low, velvety note that filled the club.

Lola walked to the bar, sat at the end.

The bartender stood, elbows locked, hands resting on the bar with his thumbs gripping the edge. Lola caught the bartender's eye with a smile. He moved toward her with a relaxed stride and bright eyes. She noted a dimple in his left cheek as he smiled lazily.

She ordered a bourbon whiskey with ice. "Is the boss in?" she said.

The bartender nodded toward a booth in the far corner, closest to the stage. Lola saw a lean man dressed in a dark suit. The man acknowledged her attention with a nod, then rose and approached the bar.

"Good evening. I'm Toru Wakazono. How can I help you?"

Lola introduced herself. "I'm a friend of Stuey Lim and a private investigator. You've likely already heard, but I'm helping his parents search for his pocket watch."

"Philip has spoken to me of it."

"What did he say?"

Wakazono gestured with an elegant hand. "It was not a very plausible story."

"Did Stuey leave it with you, Mr. Wakazono, for safekeeping?"

"If he had, I am not sure I know you well enough to say."

Lola's face heated as a reply came to mind, wholly inappropriate to the situation. She turned her tumbler of bourbon in a full circle.

"Fair enough." She took out a piece of stationery from her purse. "I was given this list by Gillian Gee. Does that vouch for me?"

Wakazono held out a hand. He read the characters closely. "You are lucky I happen to recognize Gillian's hand so clearly." He offered Lola the list back. "No, I do not have Stuey's pocket watch. I would guess that none of the people on this list do, either, as well as the likelihood that Philip has already spoken to all of us."

"I figured as much. But I'm counting on getting better answers than he did."

Wakazono inclined his head, smiling slightly.

Lola found herself responding with a warm smile of her own. She glanced away.

"It is my opinion only," said Wakazono, "but if Stuey did give it over to someone, it would not have been one of our little society of specialized and highly itinerant musicians."

"Stuey didn't have friends that stayed closer to home then?"

Wakazono shrugged again. "Perhaps, but I do not know of any. Other than Tommy Chu and his siblings. Aside from which, you will not get anything from speaking with either Davy or Andy."

Lola looked at her list again. "That would be Last Call and The Anchor?"

Wakazono nodded. "They are both intensely loyal and naturally tight-lipped. Even with Gillian's handwriting, they would not trust you."

"What about Mimi Cheng? And...Maxwell Koh?"

"You might have better luck with Koh."

Lola caught something in his voice. She gave him a hard look. He smiled politely even as his dark eyes seemed to swallow the light.

❧

"This is the last shot tonight. The last name on the list." Aubrey paused. "What's the next step if this doesn't pan out?"

Wakazono had been right.

Davy Heung, a short man with a doughy face, had politely declined knowing anything at all about Stuey. Andy Siu, a bald man with a hard face, had pointed a finger at the door before she'd even said Stuey's last name. Mimi Cheng had certainly been more gracious, but just as unwilling to part with information.

Lola had to settle for the satisfaction of knowing that Kam wouldn't have got anything from them either, at least.

She drove north, on the coastal highway, its curves following the rugged coastline. Lola heard the pounding of ocean waves, the rhythmic crash as they hit the rocky headland far below.

"Lola," Aubrey said.

"Then I find a new list."

She kept a tight grip on the steering wheel and a keen eye on the road. The traffic was sparse but fast when it came on, headlights rounding a curve like a flashlight right in her eyes.

She zoomed past a blurred sign on the left.

About a quarter mile on, Lola slowed and made the turn into the lot for Moonlight. She hoped Koh, its owner, was as talkative as Wakazono had hinted.

The building was low-slung, facing the ocean with a wall of windows. A twin set of handsome men, the valet and doorman, attended to her with smiles showing bright white teeth.

Lola stood at the coat check, about to hand over her wrap when she heard a voice. She stopped, cocked an ear, then parted the bejewelled curtain and entered the club proper. She stared at the stage and finally understood the undercurrent of amusement in Wakazono's comment.

Evelyn Shao stood in the spotlight, eyes closed, expression so raw it made Lola's chest ache. She held a single note, the emotion unadorned and rough-edged. The note soared and dipped, then slowly, gently, faded. There was a long pause. Then Evelyn took a slow, tremulous breath and sang the mourning in her heart.

Lola felt exposed, standing rigid at the back of the room, though not a soul in the club looked at her. All eyes were fixed on Evelyn. There were no low murmurs, no rustling of silk and taffeta, no clink of glasses. This room full of people held its collective breath and lived the full measure of grief in Evelyn's song.

Pain, regret, anger, impotence, sorrow. They filled all the spaces in the room like air.

Lola blinked, trying to force the tears back into her stinging eyes, and trembled with the effort to stand up. She pressed her knuckles to her mouth as the emotions flooded through her and finally, over-flowed.

Denial was no longer possible.

For all that these people—these strangers—listened so intently to Evelyn's song together, Lola knew the truth of it. This was Evelyn's lament alone. The woman who'd loved him and had been loved in return. It was as simple, as powerful, as that.

Lola had no claim on Stuey Lim. She never had.

She cursed herself for a fool, to let jealousy blind her. It was clear as crystal now who held claim to that beloved, damned, elusive pocket watch.

When the song ended, a profound silence descended. Evelyn opened her eyes. They glistened as she refocussed on her audience. A slow blush coloured her cheeks. She nodded and left the stage, threading her way to the long bar against the right side of the room.

The house lights brightened gradually. Patrons blinked them-selves back into the present. They stood and applauded.

Evelyn turned and bowed, smiling prettily, her cheeks still pink. She raised her fluted glass in a salute. Waitresses in dark *cheong-sahm* circulated through the room. Quiet chatter and low laughter filled the air. The normal sounds of a busy nightclub resumed. Evelyn sat back down, facing the mirror backing the bar.

Lola rubbed the light wool wrap along her arms to gentle the goose bumps on her skin. She wiped at her eyes with a handkerchief, pulled back her shoulders, and forged ahead.

Evelyn perched gracefully on a stool, her slate grey *cheong-sahm* accented by a tangle of pink peonies and orange lilies. She stared at the top of the bar, her hands idly turning the champagne flute this way and that.

"Maxwell Koh, I presume," said Lola.

Evelyn glanced sidelong at Lola, smiled stiffly. Out of the spotlight now, the dark pouches underneath her eyes were even more pronounced, for all that her skin was luminously pale, her black hair lustrous. She looked a different woman than the poised singer on stage two nights earlier.

"Philip was here today." Evelyn sipped at her champagne, grimaced. She pushed the glass away.

"What did you tell him?"

"Nothing. I have nothing to tell."

Evelyn's gaze roamed the mirror, watching the room behind her. She closed her eyes, reached out and gripped the edge of the bar with both hands. Fine tremors ran down her arms. She exhaled sharply and smoothed out her dress, gestured to the barman.

"Felix, a pot of hot tea, if you please. The new kind."

The swarthy barman nodded.

"Forgive me, my stomach seems a tad unsettled." Evelyn offered a small smile of apology.

"Of course." Lola scanned the busy nightclub, spotted a woman with red hair, wearing a pale grey *cheong-sahm*, eyeing her narrowly. "May we speak in private?"

The barman set out a tea pot and two cups with smooth economy. He laid the cover for the pot aside, spooned in two heaps of dark leaves.

"Yes. Felix, have Grainne bring that in for me please. My office."

He nodded, gathered a tray from below the bar top.

Evelyn led Lola down the length of the bar toward a recessed doorway. They parted a set of dark silk curtains and went down a short hallway. A door stood open at the end.

The office was cheerful and bright, with flowers in large vases placed around the room. A slender chandelier of drop crystals sparkled from the room's centre, sending out refracted light. Halfway down one wall was a dressing table full of makeup pots and coloured jars, its mirror limned with bright bulbs. Along the wall opposite, rolling costume racks with gowns arranged by colour.

An *erhu*, its bow laid parallel to its neck, sat in an armchair, next to a light-bodied *pipa* on a stand. Sheet music was laid out in various stacks on different flat surfaces, as were piles of folded linens. In the corner, there was a small desk, one side piled with ledger books next to a slender black telephone.

"Do you have new information?" Evelyn sat in an armchair across from her traditional instruments. She tossed a pale yellow scarf onto a low table.

Lola quickly explained her evening's work. She watched Evelyn closely. "But I know where the pocket watch is now."

"Oh?"

A quick knock at the door. The red-headed woman entered. She assessed Lola openly as she brought the tea tray over. Lola kept her own face bland.

"My manager, Grainne Flynn." Evelyn smiled wearily at Flynn. "Thank you."

Lola exchanged polite greetings. Flynn poured the tea.

"Do you wish me to stay?" said Flynn.

"No, I'm fine." Evelyn sipped, her face relaxing.

"Are you certain?"

Evelyn nodded, offered a wan smile. "Miss Starke is helping Stuey's parents."

Flynn narrowed her eyes. "With?"

"Keeping Philip Kam out of their business."

Flynn stared a beat longer. She nodded curtly, turned her focus to Evelyn. "No more singing tonight. You're exhausted. I'll have Jess in to play the last set."

Evelyn smiled wanly. "Yes, all right, Mother."

Flynn glanced at Lola. "Don't keep her from her rest."

"Of course." Lola watched Flynn close the door behind her.

"Yes, she is always like that." Evelyn smiled over the rim of her tea cup. "The best friend one could ever ask for."

Lola pondered her approach while she took a drink of tea. She made a face at the acrid bitterness on her tongue.

"Sorry, I forgot. It's a special blend." Evelyn cleared her throat. "I haven't been feeling well. Nausea."

"I'm sorry to hear that. And this tea helps?"

Evelyn smiled. "So I've been told."

Lola studied Evelyn clinically. The woman's face was pale, her cheeks flushed, her eyes red-rimmed and bloodshot. It was an alarming decline from her appearance mere minutes ago on stage.

Lola forced herself to stay on course. "The pocket watch. I know you have it."

Evelyn went still.

"You're the only one he'd trust enough. And someone he could see regularly." Lola calculated swiftly. "Did you know about the trade? About Stasha Chu's debt?"

Evelyn stared at the *erhu* and *pipa*.

"How about Stanley's true relationship to Stuey?" Lola said.

Evelyn placed a hand at her throat. "You know?"

Lola nodded. "As does Serene."

"She does? How—?" Evelyn shook her head. Her hands fell to her lap. "Never mind. Stuey loved her like a sister. And Stasha would have no reason to care about Stuey's secret." She looked squarely at Lola. "She told you."

Lola nodded again.

"What else do you know?" Evelyn took a deep breath. She laid her hands lightly on her stomach.

Lola refilled Evelyn's tea cup. "Are you all right? Is it the nausea?"

Evelyn gave a weak laugh. "Yes, but it will pass. Please continue." She sipped her tea.

"Do you carry it with you?"

"The watch?" Evelyn shook her head. "It's in a safe place."

"Kam can't get to it?"

"No." She shook her head, expression grim.

"Does he know about you and Stuey?"

"We were the most careful around him." She hesitated.

Lola filled in the blank. "And Serene."

"We couldn't bear to hurt her." She looked down. "Stuey worried about her constantly. She's not had an easy life, being the only girl in that family. Her grandmother has always been traditional. Extreme."

"Is it true that Tommy mistreated her?"

Evelyn bit her lip, nodded. "Treated her like a servant, Stuey said. I've never seen that, but I was only ever with them in social settings. Or professional ones."

"Did you know about her broken wrist?"

Evelyn bit her lip. "Stuey tried to help, but Tommy was so angry. He lost his temper with her, grabbed her so quickly. And he was strong." She looked away. "Stuey said her brothers bundled her off too fast for him to stop them."

Lola felt a roiling in the pit of her stomach.

"Did you all know about her Ghost's ways? The abuse?"

"I...we...yes." Evelyn clasped her hands at her stomach again. "But they wouldn't listen to anything we had to say. For all that Stuey had grown up with them, they considered him an outsider. Stasha Chu did, for certain. She's extreme in her traditional views."

"Hating girls, exalting boys? That sort of nonsense?"

Evelyn nodded. "It's a terrible situation I don't understand. Stuey warned me against stepping in. So I...I kept my distance." She rubbed absently at her abdomen. "To be honest, we both did. We didn't want to be caught up in their family drama forever. We had plans of our own."

"Then why did Stuey make this deal with Philip Kam?"

Evelyn flushed. "He felt guilty for abandoning her. We—" Her eyes filled with tears. She shook her head, unable to speak.

"Lola." Aubrey's voice sounded odd. Tense and cautious.

Lola scowled. She was missing something, she was sure of it. Something about what Evelyn had just said. She reviewed the other woman's words, her demeanour. But the more she chased it, the deeper it hid. Shaking herself mentally, she forced herself to put it aside. Patience would let it come to the fore naturally. She just had to stay out of the way.

Evelyn cried silently, swiping at her eyes with her fingertips and the backs of her hands.

Lola got up to search for a clean cloth.

The dressing table was in jumbled disarray. Lola pushed aside various piles of makeup-stained linens, hunting for unused ones. She clinked around glass jars and moved little wooden tubs. She knocked over a stack of linens, grabbing them just as the pile toppled, scattering a pile of wire safety pins across the table and onto the floor.

Lola reached down, gathered the pins and the cloths that had fluttered down as well. She looked over at Evelyn, an apology at the ready.

Evelyn stared at what Lola held, wide-eyed, her hands clutching the armchair.

Lola looked down at the pins and the fabric. A sturdy cotton, unlike the rough towel-like fabric of the makeup cloths. She looked back at the cloths that were still folded. She picked one from the pile and examined it, noting its rectangular shape and curious layering.

Where had she seen this before? Lola unfolded and refolded the linen. Face cloths didn't need such elaborate folding. And Evelyn had a pile of those already, over there. They couldn't be for stage appearances. They were soft, but plain and too large. Lola stared at the little safety pins. Why would those be needed? How did they pin up the cloth? She turned the linen in her hands, folded the short ends together.

Lola gasped. She met Evelyn's shocked gaze once again.

"These are diapers, aren't they?"

THIRTY

Lola narrowed her eyes, thinking of Evelyn's behaviour, her words. "The nausea," she said slowly, "it's related to pregnancy, isn't it? You're with child." That ache in her chest again. "Stuey's child."

Evelyn's eyes popped even wider. "You mustn't tell. Please."

"What about his parents? They deserve to know they're to be grandparents."

"I know. It's just...I don't know what they'll think."

"Did Stuey know?"

Evelyn's face crumpled. "Yes. Those were his idea." She gestured to the cloth in Lola's hands.

Lola left it and the safety pins on the dressing table, sat back down next to Evelyn.

"The diapers?"

"He was very proud of himself for learning how to fold them, and pin them. We have a doll for practice. An ugly little thing, but we loved it." Evelyn sobbed, deep heaving cries that rebounded throughout the room. Lola took her hand.

The door flew open. Grainne took in the situation in one long look.

"Oh Evie." She sighed heavily. "I told you, didn't I? All those months ago. I told you it couldn't end well." She pushed aside a rack of dresses, revealing a small wardrobe. Reaching within, she extracted folded handkerchiefs, offered them to Evelyn.

299

Lola felt a stinging in her eyes. She grit her teeth. "You can't keep this from his parents," she said. "They have a right to know. And your child has a right to his or her grandparents."

"Don't think you can give the orders round here." Flynn glared at Lola.

"Hush, Grainne. She's not saying anything I haven't already thought myself." Evelyn pulled the linen handkerchief through her fingers repeatedly. "Gods, what will this do to Serene?"

"Better she learn from you than someone else," said Lola.

"She was already so fragile. I can't imagine how that newspaper story hit her. And now this? I don't think she'll be able to cope."

Lola frowned. "What story?"

Evelyn raised her brows. "You don't know? But it came out in the evening edition of the *Herald*. A reporter discovered the doctor who delivered Tommy. And she even managed a formal interview with Sebastian."

Lola recalled Ria's proud grin. "Why would that upset Serene?"

"Her grandmother, of course. Her traditional views," said Evelyn. "It's easy to read between the lines of Sebastian's comments. She must have been so angry when they were born."

Lola felt like her brain was smothered in wool. Her frown deepened. "When who was born?"

"Tommy and Serene."

Lola looked from Evelyn to Grainne and back again.

Grainne scowled. "They're twins. Do you get it now?"

Lola collapsed against the back of the sofa. "Oh gods." She thought about Stasha's treatment of Serene. It made a cruel kind of sense.

She refocussed on Evelyn. "Please. Tell me about the article."

Evelyn nodded, expression sad. "Their mother told Sebastian when he was twelve, after their father died. She asked him to keep it secret. Stasha thought it was bad luck, naturally, being from the old, old country. She didn't want others to know of their shame so she made the family move to a new neighbourhood. They pretended Serene was a relative's baby."

Grainne shook her head. "But as she grew older, Serene's likeness to her mother and brothers was too clear to ignore. So the old woman had them move again, this time into Sai-Dong. Serene was small enough that they could pass her off as years younger. Even though she was older than Tommy, actually."

Lola stared numbly at Grainne, then Evelyn. "You know they used to drown baby girls for this? In the old country?" She rubbed her forehead. "Bloody hells, they might still. What's Stasha going to do to her now?"

"I tried speaking to her. I telephoned as soon as I read the story." Evelyn shook her head. "They wouldn't put me through."

Lola jolted out of her seat with a curse. "This can't be good. I have to go."

Evelyn raised a hand to stop her. Grainne narrowed her eyes. "You gonna flap your lips on this?"

Lola nodded to Evelyn. "Your secret's safe with me."

"This feels bad, Lola." Aubrey's tone was grim.

Lola wound her way through the tables, careful of gesticulating arms and lit cigarettes. She reached the jewelled curtain at the same time as a stocky man in a white dinner jacket and red pocket square. He hesitated for a second, then parted the hanging strands for her, a polite smile on his plain face.

A memory at the back of her mind bloomed.

Lola's steps faltered and she stared at him for several long seconds. She mentally reviewed her day, recalling as much as possible.

"Are you all right, Miss?"

She considered her options hastily. She cursed the timing and made a choice.

"Yes, I'm fine. Sorry."

"Not at all." The man smiled. "Do you need a hand to your car?"

"Oh, thank you, but I think I'll just take a cigarette for a moment. Collect myself, if you know what I mean."

"Of course. Good night." He inclined his head and sauntered away.

"What're you doing?" Aubrey's confusion was clear, but she had neither the time nor the inclination to answer.

She walked in the direction of the cliff's edge until she cleared the bright lights of the entrance. She stopped and fumbled in her purse as though for a cigarette case. She grasped her knife, hooked her purse over her wrist, then turned casually as she listened to the man's footsteps, following him with her eyes to a car on the outskirts of the lot. A light-coloured coupe with a dark roof.

Aubrey repeated his question, angry now.

Quickly, Lola stepped farther away from the pool of light and stripped off her shoes, careful to hold them by the heels so they didn't clack together. She lifted the hem of her gown above her knees, her blade comforting in her hand. The gravel of the lot bit into her soles. Running lightly on the balls of her feet, she followed the metal and concrete barrier that bounded the lot on the ocean side, came up on the man from the rear of his car.

She heard him whistling under his breath, something light and bouncy.

Lola was grateful she'd chosen a simple grey silk gown. The neon of the club's sign did little to dispel the dark and there were only a few lights scattered on the perimeter of the lot. She was as close to invisible as she'd ever get.

The man slid into the driver's seat, pulling his door closed.

"Lola, what the bloody hells are you doing?" said Aubrey.

She sliced the air with her hand, commanding silence.

Given how she'd stared at him just moments ago, Lola thought it likely the man would simply start up his car and leave the lot. If he was good enough to tail her all day and not get made until nearly midnight, he'd be smart enough to see his odds were getting longer now that she'd had a good look at him.

She slid the wrap from her shoulders and the purse from her wrist, let them fall to the ground, ignoring the chilly night air. She took a firm hold on her switchblade, focussing past the pain in her feet.

She steadied her grip on her heels, then tossed them onto the roof of the man's car.

Running full out, she reached his door while he was still hunched over, his arms covering his head. Lola pulled open the door, dragged the man out by his collar. He tumbled out onto the gravel lot. She picked him up and spun him around, slamming him into the side of his car. His face was turned to the side, a cheek pressed tight against a window. She opened up her blade with a flick of her wrist, brought it within inches of his eye.

He stopped struggling.

"I'm going to check you for weapons. You might not see this knife while I do, but it'll be close enough to do some damage if you so much as twitch."

The man breathed heavily through his misshapen nose. Lola worked swiftly, the knifepoint sliding along his clothes, following the path of her search. She found nothing but a cheaply-made wallet.

She stepped back, just out of reach.

"Why are you following me?" She held the knife ready, kept to the balls of her feet.

"Hey now, steady there." The man attempted a chuckle. "I know, I know. You got me dead to rights. I won't give no trouble. We can talk, though, can't we? One professional to another."

"So talk already. Who hired you?"

The man rubbed at his chest, shook out his arms. Lola tensed. He smoothed down his black hair, brushed off his slacks and the sleeves of his tuxedo jacket.

"Next thing you know," said Aubrey, "he'll tell you he's got a bum ticker."

"The name's Dean Luhk. Nice to meetcha."

Aubrey grunted.

Lola stared. "Who hired you?"

Luhk grinned. "Ain't you figured it out for yerself yet?"

"You're not from around here."

Luhk nodded, affable expression just discernible in the dimness. "Just got into town three months back. From out east, near the mountains. Had me a lovely little private detection service back home. Wanted more excitement, though. So I packed up and came west."

"Uh huh. And now you work for Philip Kam."

"Now that's just a lucky guess, ain't it? You didn't even deduce nothin'."

"Why are you following me?"

"Keeping tabs for my client."

"What's he paying you?"

"Why?" Luhk's eyebrows rose. "You aim to buy him out?"

"Could be. Depends on the stakes." Lola glared. "You didn't answer me. Is he paying you? Or are you just working off a debt?"

Luhk's grin faded. "Now how'd you know anything about that?"

"Men like Kam don't pay men like you."

"What's that s'posed to mean?"

Lola shrugged, looked at him down her nose.

"Doesn't matter," Luhk grinned and shrugged. "You made me. My job's done."

Lola shook her head. "Still need to report in, though, right?"

"Well, yeah. But it don't look like you did much more than run all over town."

Lola raised an eyebrow. "He didn't tell you what he's after?"

Luhk's expression turned sullen for a second, then flipped back. "Ain't my business to know. I just follow whoever he tells me to follow." He flicked his gaze away.

Lola assessed him with a cold gaze. She hoped that gleam in his eyes was greed. It would make things so much easier.

"How'd you feel about making some extra dough on this deal?"

Luhk's grin returned.

"You tailed me to four clubs tonight, right?"

Luhk looked confused. His lips moved as he looked down, counting on his fingers silently. Then he shook his head. "Five. The Night Heron, Last Call, The Anchor, Mimi's, and here." He displayed his hand, fingers splayed.

"I'm afraid you've miscounted," she said. "I wasn't anywhere near a place called The Anchor."

"Sure you were. I got the notes to prove it." Luhk gestured to the inside of his car.

"Lola, what are you doing?" said Aubrey, puzzled.

"Work it out, Luhk. Slowly if you have to." Lola stared at him.

Luhk's brow furrowed then his expression relaxed. He grinned again. "Right. Four clubs. Gotcha." He cocked his head. "So I reckon a sawbuck for each of those clubs oughta smooth things out."

"You're paying this twit forty dollars?" Aubrey growled. "You know damn well he'll just double-cross you."

"So that's fifty," said Luhk. "On account a there were actually five." He held out his hand. "And in advance."

Lola smiled as she flicked her blade closed one-handed. Luhk's smugness faded. She motioned for him to get into his car, then quickly retrieved her purse from the ground.

"Come on then. I haven't got all night. Let's go tell your boss what he wants to know."

THIRTY-ONE

Following Dean Luhk through the door and across the large room, Lola was forced to admit that Kam's nightclub was beautiful.

Gleaming dark wood drew the eye to the bar. Polished to a burnished shine, it stretched along three-quarters of the long left wall. Two men in immaculate white shirtsleeves, held up by garters, were busy tending to drink orders, given to them by voluptuous women in tall heels and short dresses.

Crystal chandeliers dotted the ceiling. Linens in midnight blue and pristine white draped intimate tables for two. Chairs were covered in silver cloth and banquettes upholstered in dark leather. Lola trailed her hand over the side of one. The leather was soft, supple.

Muttering under his breath, Luhk continued down a corridor wallpapered in cream with subtle striping, the lighting soft and inviting. Lola glanced behind her. They'd picked up an entourage. Kam's thugs followed, two silent hunks of sentient, moving muscle. They met her gaze with expressionless eyes.

The office was at the end of the corridor. Lola thought it a strange placement for a successful Chinese man. Everyone knew it was bad *chi* to be at a dead end. Perhaps Kam had told the truth. He truly didn't care about auspicious signs.

Luhk knocked confidently, for all of his anxious grumbling, and opened the door. They stepped into a room that spanned the entire width of the club's space. Dark raspberry walls with burnished walnut wainscoting. Leather upholstery in a rich brown. A fireplace with a deep mantel. A seating arrangement to the right, with a long four-person sofa, two armchairs, and a shorter loveseat. A low chrome and glass table in the centre, with a swirled glass bowl serving as an ashtray.

"Dean, you bring unexpected guests."

Kam stood in front of a massive teak desk, papers clasped in one hand, a cigar smouldering in the other. A tuxedo jacket with a red pocket square was draped over a male dressmaker form in the corner. Kam's maroon waistcoat had a deep V-shaped collar. Ruby studs glinted on his shirt and at his cuffs.

Luhk looked back at Lola, his expression puzzled, then swung his attention back to his employer.

"She has a Ghost," said Kam patiently.

Luhk coloured. He thrust out his chin. The thug to Lola's left shifted. Luhk deflated.

"Miss Starke, I take it you found Dean out."

"Took me all day, but yes."

"Well, I suppose that should offset a few things."

Luhk straightened out his tie, smoothed his lapels.

Kam placed the papers on his desk, gestured Lola to sit.

"I prefer to stand." She angled herself to keep everyone in her field of view.

"As you wish," said Kam. "Dean?"

Luhk plopped down on the loveseat with a sigh. He plucked at his slacks, but there was no hiding the grime against the stark black of the cloth. He grimaced at Lola. She shrugged.

Kam balanced his cigar on the lip of the glass bowl and seated himself in the armchair facing the door. The goons stood on either side of the doorway.

"And what has Miss Starke been up to?"

Luhk faithfully recounted Lola's entire day. Then he paused, shifted his gaze to Lola. He smirked. "She didn't want me to tell you, Boss, about The Anchor. You know, Andy Siu's dive."

"True to form," said Aubrey. "The little bas—"

"You're a lying sneak, Luhk." Lola, playing her role, lunged for him. Kam's man grabbed her upper arm, jerking her back. She felt something pop in her left shoulder. Her vision filled with spots. The thug shoved her into the armchair opposite Kam. She gasped and tried to tug her arm out of the hold. She saw spots dance in her field of vision. She bit down on her lip.

Kam nodded to his man, who let her go with a final twist. He remained standing behind her.

"Hurting Dean would be a grave mistake, Miss Starke. He's a great asset to my businesses. We cannot afford for him to be out of commission for any length of time." Kam turned to Luhk. "Get back to The Anchor." He nodded to the guard still next to the door. "Search it tonight. If you don't find it, do his home tomorrow. Leave Siu intact. We may need him to answer some questions."

"Well done," murmured Aubrey. "Although Andy Siu won't be thanking you. Best if he never finds out you used him as a decoy."

Lola rolled her shoulder tentatively, testing it out. The pain was less intense this time. She breathed deeply, clenched her jaw and kept rolling. She couldn't afford her shoulder stiffening up.

Kam watched Luhk and the other man leave then retrieved his cigar from the ashtray and took a long inhalation. He stared at Lola as he exhaled a cloud of pungent grey smoke.

"I don't like meddlers, Miss Starke. Especially when they meddle in *my* affairs. So I've decided to make an example of you."

The man standing behind Lola laid a meaty hand on her left shoulder and squeezed. She cried out as he crunched the joint with his fingers. She punched at him with her right fist but the leverage wasn't there. It felt like hitting a stone wall.

He took her left elbow then and wrenched her arm outward, pressing down on her shoulder at the same time.

Lola screamed.

The thug let go, then picked up her left hand.

Lola twisted then, quick as she could, and punched him in the groin.

He dropped to the floor, grunting.

Lola sprang up, ready to stomp down on his head.

"That's enough."

Lola stepped away from the writhing man. Kam rose from his seat. She took another step away, holding her left arm tight to her side. She eyed the set of tools hanging next to the fireplace, rapidly calculated the distance.

Kam kneeled next to his man. "That's two of my men now. You're hard on my employees, Miss Starke." He looked up at Lola, gestured to her left arm. "Payback is a rough mistress, isn't she?"

He patted the thug on the shoulder, stood up.

"Consider us even now."

"What? Just like that?" said Lola.

Kam nodded. "Yes."

Lola gave him a long look. She strained to hear approaching footsteps in the corridor. She watched warily as the guard staggered to his feet, holding on to furniture for support.

"This isn't a Saturday matinée. I'm not going to twirl my moustaches and tie you to the train tracks." Kam shrugged, the movement elegant. "I like balance. You hurt my shoulder. Your shoulder is now hurt in turn."

"What about your bruisers? Lee and this one?"

"I can't speak for them. They're their own men."

Lola frowned. "What is this? You're going to make me fight my way out?"

Kam shook his head. "No, of course not. What did I just say about theatrics? No, this is about teaching you a lesson. You leave here because I permit it. For every hurt you give me, I will visit the same upon you. It's simple enough, isn't it?"

"And Serene Chu? What will you do to her?"

"Nothing. We have a business arrangement. Once I get that pocket watch, her debt is cancelled. Hers and that of her Ghost."

"And if you can't find it? If Siu doesn't cough it up?"

"Then we continue with the debt repayment until it's finished." He shrugged. "She's due for another repayment session day after next."

"You're not threatening murder?"

"If I killed my clients, then I wouldn't be able to recoup my investments, would I? It's straightforward economics." He picked up his cigar again. "Aside from which, attracting the notice of the police is bad for business. I understand that you've become rather familiar with a few of them. They might notice your disappearance and tie it to all the noise you've been making about me."

Lola shifted in tandem with Kam's beady-eyed thug. "And your antiques buyer?"

"That is none of your concern."

Lola gauged Kam's expression. "Got impatient, did they? The buy's off?"

He pointed with his cigar. "You have five minutes during which I guarantee your safety. After that, you take your chances."

Lola turned to go. She caught motion in her peripheral vision and jumped out of the way.

She raised her right arm to block the punch. It reverberated along her entire arm and spine. Her elbow flared with pain. She stumbled away, reaching for the fireplace poker.

"Myron." Kam's voice was mild. "Time."

His man stopped, straightened from his fighting crouch.

Lola forced her numb hand to close around the poker, carried it with her through Kam's door and out through the club.

The night had turned cloudy. She hoofed the three blocks to her car as swiftly as she could manage. She held the poker in the middle of its length, vigilant for anyone following her on foot.

"You can't drive like this," said Aubrey.

"I damn well better." Lola slid into the driver's seat, locked herself in. Five silhouettes appeared at the end of the block she'd just cleared. They ran toward her.

She jammed the key into the ignition and roared away as someone smashed at her headlight. Bricks landed on the roof of her roadster. Something cracked a rear window.

Lola didn't slow down until she found the nearest hospital.

❦

"You don't listen well, do you, Starke?"

"Can it, Marks. Are you going to arrest Philip Kam or keep standing around here, busting my—"

"You don't have an ounce of sense, do you? Just another stupid dame thinks she's bullet-proof."

Bednarski placed a hand on his partner's shoulder. "Sounds like it's his man, Myron, who did a number on you, Miss Starke. Kam didn't actually touch you, did he?"

Lola closed her eyes, let her head slump back. She hissed as the pain in her shoulder and elbow flashed.

"You should've gone to Betta." Aubrey somehow managed to sound sympathetic yet disapproving.

Lola opened her eyes to Bednarski's concerned mug. She smiled without humour. "No, DI Bednarski, Kam didn't actually touch me."

"You still want to press charges against this Myron character?"

"What good would it do me?"

"None against Kam."

Marks looked down his nose at her. "Net you another enemy, though. If you like collecting those."

"Trading in surliness for sarcasm, eh, Marks?"

"Lola, stop antagonizing him."

She clenched her jaw. She would not argue with her Ghost.

"I'll file." Lola sighed, pinched the bridge of her nose. "Since I went to all this trouble to ring you from the hospital and get photographed and all."

Bednarski nodded. "Let's get your statement from the top, then."

Lola kept it short and sweet. Marks wrote everything down with tidy, efficient strokes. He looked up once she stopped.

"Why'd you call us?" Marks gestured out into the hallway. "The uniform could've done this."

Lola hesitated. "I'd put you onto Kam. Maybe you were chasing a thread from him to the murders. I thought you'd want to know he had no motive to kill Stuey."

"Is that how it looks to you?"

"Ah, the surliness returns." She pointed at Marks. "I might be a low-life PI to you, but that doesn't mean you can play me. Any twit can figure it out. Stuey wanted to help Serene Chu, so he offered his pocket watch to Kam to forgive the debt. Stuey died before they could enact the deal. Kam already had a buyer on hand for the watch, but no watch to sell."

Bednarski rubbed his chin. "You're saying he'd never have killed Stuey Lim without that pocket watch in hand first."

"Not just that, but there was no need for him to resort to murder. Stuey was a man of his word." Lola's throat closed up. She swallowed thickly, shaking herself. "Whereas Kam is not." She raised her chin at Marks's expression. "I need to find Serene. I need to warn her."

"Tell them about Stasha, too. The more people who know, the better for Serene," said Aubrey.

Lola flicked her hand in irritation.

Marks narrowed his eyes. "Something your Ghost say?"

"It's about Serene's Ghost, her grandmother Anastasia Chu." Lola explained the abuse witnessed by Aubrey, the reason for the car accident. She stammered to a stop.

Bednarski scratched a stubbled cheek, exchanged a look with Marks. "Something wrong, Miss Starke?"

Lola swore. "I forgot to check the car." She stared at the opposite wall, thinking hard. "But even if it's true, she'd never—"

"Car?"

Lola shook off the chill in her gut. "Sebastian Chu said his sister had a minor accident with her car, a Packard, the same day as the killings. I don't believe in coincidence. I should've checked the car."

"Where's it supposed to be?" said Bednarski.

Marks stared at Lola for a few beats. "You think this other car's related to the shooting?"

Lola chewed on her lower lip, wondering how to explain without sounding like a madwoman. "I don't have any proof. And it doesn't make absolute sense. So don't go trying to poke holes in this. Just listen first." She glanced back at Marks. He frowned, then shrugged, and looked to his partner.

"Why don't you tell us what's on your mind?" Bednarski said.

Lola explained what she'd noticed at the impound lot and added her assessment of the Chu family dynamics.

"She killed her brother?" Marks glanced at Bednarski. "Why?"

"She hated him. After a lifetime of abuse, who can blame her?" Lola described her exchange with Serene before the car accident. "She sabotaged his cremation, damned his soul to nothingness."

"Did she confess to the gunning?" said Marks.

"No. Just to the sabotage."

Bednarski's voice rumbled from his chest. "Doesn't mean she didn't do it."

"But she would never hurt Stuey," Lola said slowly. "She was in love with him."

"Could've been an accident." Marks shrugged. "Maybe she never even saw Lim."

"We've lost count of the number of people who love the ones they kill," said Bednarski flatly.

Lola realized what she'd set in motion. "Please, you have to be careful with her. Her Ghost—"

"Yes, we understand. Her Ghost may harm her irreparably." Bednarski nodded at his partner. "Find the Twins. Eng can handle the Ghost."

Marks grunted an agreement.

He pointed at Lola. "The uniform stays with you 'til he delivers you home."

Bednarski cleared his throat. "We'll take care of Miss Chu. But the DA will need you in one piece to make this case. We don't want your gangster friends to get a hold of you first."

Lola nodded, weary to her bones.

Marks glared at her for another beat, suspicion clear as a beacon on his face. "No comeback, Starke?"

"I'm woman enough to admit when I'm beat, Marks. This is your show now. Soon as they put me back together, I'm going home."

An hour and a half later, Lola dragged the sleep mask off her eyes and threw it across the room. Twinges in her shoulder and elbows froze her for long seconds before she remembered she'd been healed. The pain was nothing more than her imagination.

The restlessness forced her out of bed and into the bathroom, to splash cold water on her face. She rotated her arms, to get limber and loose. She scrubbed at her skin to bring herself to full alertness.

"Where are we going?" said Aubrey.

"It doesn't feel right," she muttered. "I've missed something again."

She dressed quickly in slacks and a lightweight sweater, checked her weapons, slipped out of the apartment in soft-soled shoes.

Aubrey repeated his question.

Lola drove the silent streets, glad of her trusty beater Buick. She felt the need to move invisibly. Harnessing her unease, she let herself tune into her inner compass. She reviewed her conversations with Serene and Stasha, with Sebastian, with Nicky. She thought of the cremation ceremonies, of Serene again.

Twelve blocks later, it clicked into place.

"The Empress Dowager. It's where she asked to go yesterday. Why would she do that? They were supposed to be out of there the day before."

"You think she hid something there? Perhaps the gun she used to shoot her brother and Stuey?" Aubrey paused. "It would've been smarter to throw that gun away."

Lola shook her head, impatient. "I don't know." She changed lanes, pressed on the gas. "There's something unfinished there, though."

When she arrived, she was surprised to see the whole of The Empress lit up like it was a Friday night show. She cruised slowly closer, passing dark buildings on both sides of the street.

Sawhorses were set up halfway down the block. Half a dozen police cars were parked on the curb. Uniforms stood at the sawhorses, meant to keep busybodies out. Most of them faced the theatre, however. The sidewalks were empty.

Lola parked across the street, facing the wrong way. She got out and walked swiftly to the closest barricade. The officer on duty stood about five feet away, back turned away. Lola had an angled view into the alley next to the Dowager. She saw a cluster of uniforms and suits around the artists' entrance. The door was open, light spilling out in a bright rectangle. Lola recognized a tall figure in the group. She waved until she caught his attention.

The startled copper close to Lola saluted as Marks approached. Then she turned to watch as he jogged right past. The uniform scowled when she saw Lola. Marks did the same.

"Starke, damn it, why are you here?"

"Is Serene in there? What's going on?"

Lola saw the uniformed copper raise her brows.

Marks gripped Lola's arm, steered her away from the sawhorse and the curious officer.

"Go home, Starke. This is police business. Didn't you say you were done?"

"I was. But then it struck me that Serene was dead set on coming here, after Tommy's cremation. I couldn't understand why. It was a loose thread, kept bothering me."

Marks sighed, muttered a curse.

"What's going on, Marks?"

He swore again. "It's not your concern, Starke. Go home."

"Where's Bednarski?"

"He's not going to give you a pass, either, for gods' sake."

Lola craned around him to watch the coppers milling about. "She's inside, isn't she? Is she all right? Is there someone with her? Do you have a Catcher in there, to handle Stasha Chu?"

"This is police business. There's no room for low-life gumshoes, get it?"

Lola gestured impatiently. "Got it. Is Eng in there? It's the Ghost, isn't it? Is she the problem?"

Marks growled, a deep noise of frustration.

"Look, I'm here already. If you push me off, I'll just find another way to get inside. Just tell me what the bloody hells is going on, will you?"

Marks pinched the bridge of his nose. "Yes, she's inside. Scared the theatre manager so he called us."

"Is Sebastian with her? Is Eng?"

Marks nodded, face seeming to collapse with exhaustion.

"But they can't calm her down." He paused, exhaled hard. "She's threatening to kill herself."

"You've got to let me in there."

Marks pulled Lola back by her arm. She gasped. He released her, held up his hand. "Sorry." His expression hardened. "This isn't amateur hour, Starke. We know what we're doing."

Lola rubbed her elbow gingerly. "If that were true, you wouldn't be out here, twiddling your collective thumbs."

Marks leaned in, using his height to crowd her.

"Miss Starke," said Bednarski. He rubbed his chin. "I suppose I shouldn't be surprised."

Lola glared up at Marks for another moment. "Bednarski, you've got to let me inside. I can talk to her. She trusts me."

The big man raised his brows.

"Her Ghost lied about the car accident," Lola said. "I wasn't the one who lost control. I wasn't interrogating Serene. That damned Ghost tried to possess me."

"Lola, no," cried Aubrey.

Lola pressed on. "But Serene tried to protect me. Why would she do that if she didn't care about me in some way?" Lola looked from one stony expression to the other. "At the very least, she believes I'm on her side."

Aubrey hissed. "You don't know that for certain."

Lola refused to react to that. She looked at both detectives squarely. "Am I getting in through the front door or not?"

THIRTY-TWO

Lola stopped abruptly when she got to Tommy's old dressing room.

Trampled flowers, broken vases. Glittering glass shards. Smashed light bulbs, jagged mirror fragments. Slashed armchairs, overturned tables, toppled trunks.

And the costumes. The wondrous pieces of wearable art. Every damned one of them, shredded into piles of embroidered, sparkling trash.

At the centre of it all stood Serene Chu, clutching a pair of matte black scissors, point-down at her heart. DS Eng stood facing her, a good five feet away, his back to the door.

"*Mui-mui*, I beg you. Stop. Please."

Lola turned at the sound of the voice and discovered Sebastian Chu standing across from the ruined dressing table, behind an armchair. His face was strained, eyes ringed with dark circles.

Lola stepped forward. Glass crunched underfoot.

"No!" Spittle flew from Sebastian's mouth. "You stay away from her, you damned *gwai*." He strode to Lola, pushing her toward the door.

Lola pulled him to the side and ducked. A green mass smashed against the wall. Lola looked down at the broken jade bits of the Kwan-Yin statue.

"You're a filthy scheming liar. *Dai-goh*." Serene's face contorted with her rage. "At least this 'damned *gwai*' never lied to me."

321

"No, Madame!" Eng stepped toward Serene. "O'Connell, stop!"

Aubrey cursed. "I told you I wouldn't let you harm her. Not when I'm around."

Serene screamed. "She tried to kill me, don't you understand that? A helpless baby. She wanted to drown me, pretend I'd never been born." She pointed a thin finger at Sebastian. "And you all let her tether herself to me. You're despicable. And weak. I'm glad Tommy's dead. I'm glad I sent him to oblivion."

Serene pressed the scissors deep into her own flesh.

Lola gasped, reaching a hand out. "Please, Serene, I'm here to help. We've never lied to you, that's right, Aubrey and I. We're here to help you. We know a way to separate you from your Ghost. We know a powerful Temple Conjurer who will help. Please put those scissors down. Please. Don't hurt yourself."

Eng and Aubrey shouted simultaneously.

Serene convulsed. The scissors clattered to the floor. Her eyes snapped wide open, then rolled back, showing white.

"I've got her. I've got her." It was Serene's voice, underscored by another.

The disharmony set Lola's teeth on edge. The back of her neck flashed with icy cold, then the feeling of a thousand slashes on her skin spread from her scalp down over her entire body. She stiffened to keep from screaming.

"No, no, no, no." Lola felt the force of Aubrey's distress like a chill against her mind. "Lola, she's done it. Stasha's possessed her. I can't—"

Serene dropped to her knees, convulsed again, and collapsed.

Sebastian cried out and pushed away from Lola. He stumbled and fell to his knees beside his sister.

"This is madness." Lola glared. "Your grandmother just overpowered your sister. My Ghost saw it happen. She's gone too far this time, Chu. What she's done, what she's been doing for years, it's forbidden. Do you understand what that means?"

Sebastian cradled Serene's head with his arm. "Give me that cushion," he barked, snapping his fingers. Eng complied.

Serene groaned. Her eyelids fluttered.

"Is she still...controlling my sister?" Sebastian stared at Lola.

Aubrey said, "Yes, I think—"

Serene sat bolt upright, knocking her brother in the nose with her shoulder. He reeled backward, his hands flying to his face.

"No!" Serene thrashed her arms, hitting Eng in the ear.

"Stop!" Sebastian grimaced, his expression anguished. "*Mah-mah,* leave her be."

Lola caught a glint in Serene's hand a split second before Sebastian howled. Serene's raised her arm up, scissors in hand.

The tip was smeared with blood.

"Damn it, grab her." Lola closed on Serene from her side.

"Don't hurt her," said Sebastian on a gasp. Blood seeped out from between his fingers as he compressed the wound on his thigh. "She's not herself. Don't hurt her," he said.

"I won't let her take me again." Serene trembled, eyes wide, panicked. "I'd rather die first. You understand, *Mah-mah?* I'll kill myself before you do that to me again."

Lola thought furiously as she took in the standoff. She whispered to Aubrey. "Can you do anything? Keep her restrained?"

"I'm afraid if I try, she'll take over Serene again. I can't get to her fast enough. And the more often she possesses her, the harder it will be on Serene."

Lola cursed. "What about Serene? If we warn her, can she...rebuff the possession, like she just did? Give you enough time to handle Stasha?"

"I don't know," Aubrey said heavily. "This is unchartered territory for me, Lola. And we can't gamble with her life."

Eng jumped toward Serene. "No! Stop!"

Serene jolted violently, the scissors waving frantically with the motion. Eng cursed, holding his hand. Blood dripped through his fingers.

"She's done it again." Lola's heart clenched at Aubrey's grim statement.

"This charade sickens me."

Lola shuddered at the dissonance of Stasha speaking with Serene's voice. Serene's young face contorted. Stasha stared through her eyes now, glaring down at Sebastian.

"Your sister is right. You're nothing but a coward. Taking the easy choice to save face for yourself. But where does that leave the family? You've betrayed us all by telling Tommy's secret to that newspaper girl.

"Twins are a terrible piece of filthy bad luck, as anyone knows. But your mother didn't have the stomach to take care of it. I would have, of course, but she hid from me. Had the midwife distract me and help her disappear. We've kept this private for over twenty years, but now no one will ever remember anything about Tommy except this."

Stasha regarded Sebastian with contempt.

Sebastian's face was a mask of disbelief and pain.

Eng shifted, uttered a sharp hiss. He raised his injured hand. Lola saw blood running down his arm. He pulled out his pocket square.

Stasha narrowed her eyes at him. "I can make my granddaughter do anything I wish, Officer. Anything. She cannot escape my control. Do you understand? I shall have my say."

"Madame," said Eng. "We wish only to help you. You and your granddaughter both." He wrapped his hand with his handkerchief.

"I'm no fool. There is only one way for this to end."

"We simply want to understand," said Eng calmly. He pressed his hand against his trousers, hiding the trail of blood. "Your granddaughter claims her brother mistreated her. Was that behind his death?"

"You're coming at it all wrong." Lola gestured, impatient. "She doesn't care about Serene's mistreatment. She's the architect of it all."

Stasha lifted her chin. "This family thrives because of me. I created their future when I married Anson. I guided my daughter-in-law when my son died. I steered Tommy and Sebastian toward stardom. I made sure this useless bad-luck girl became of use to her family."

Eng glanced at Lola. She grimaced.

Stasha scowled. "Don't make that face. What do you understand of family, *gwai luey*, eh? You *gwai* with your mannerless children and divorces."

"I understand that killing a member of my own flesh and blood isn't the solution."

Stasha made a rude noise. "Then you don't understand anything at all about familial obligation."

Lola gauged the timing, pitched her tone to sound challenging. "Why did Tommy have to die then?"

Eng stiffened, aimed a frown at Lola.

"It was Lucky's fault." Stasha jabbed the air with the scissors. "Running around the City, asking for someone to put him out of his misery. Oh yes, I knew all about that. I have sources everywhere. Many Ghosts owe me favours." Lola's guts twisted coldly at the sight of Stasha's smugness on Serene's face.

"Just because my brilliant grandsons disagreed with him. Nothing but an overgrown baby, throwing a tantrum to get his way. It was only a matter of time before he finally figured out the way to go was to take Tommy with him."

Eng made a soft sound, though his face betrayed nothing. Lola noted a small pool of blood next to his shoe. She shifted her gaze to the doorway. Leung stood just out of Stasha's line of sight, mouth turned down at the corners. Marks and Bednarski crowded behind him. They pointed at Eng, movements urgent.

Lola racked her fatigued brain for some way to get medical attention for both Eng and Sebastian without forcing Stasha's hand. "Wait, wait," she said. "You think Lucky would have found someone to kill Tommy? Did he tell you that? Where's your proof?"

"It's the logical final step, isn't it? Lucky hated being second banana. He found out quickly just how talented my Tommy was. He couldn't stand being out of the spotlight. I told him not to haunt Tommy. I told him it was a mistake."

"I don't believe you," said Lola. She took a step closer to Stasha, angled so that Eng was in her periphery. "It was a big step in Tommy's career. Why would you have opposed it?" She signalled with her hand at thigh level.

Eng grunted. She could see him shake his head.

"My grandson didn't need Lucky Wai. He had enough talent for ten." Stasha poked the scissors in Lola's direction.

Lola shook her head. "But why did you kill him? Your own grandson? I don't understand."

Stasha growled, impatient. "I say what happens and when in this family. *My* knowledge of the business is what has allowed the Chu name to ascend to fame and success. Lucky was going to contract a killer to murder my Tommy in some filthy dark alley. Or poison him. An ignoble death, whichever way it was to happen."

Eng frowned. "So you saved him the trouble?"

"Exactly." Stasha nodded. "See, you understand, don't you? You're Chinese enough." She glared at Lola. "I control the narrative for this family."

Lola could not stop herself. "And Stuey, why him?"

"Bad luck. Nothing more. He came back out too soon."

"And you couldn't have spared him? For Serene?"

"Bah, useless girl. Falling for a man who would never love her." Stasha gestured dismissively. "She knows nothing of love, of grief. Just a stupid girl playing at sorrow."

"Does Serene know that she killed them? That she killed Stuey?"

"Some part of her, yes." Stasha scowled. "She's been unstable, unpredictable. Not like the other times." She puckered her lips as if to spit. "I created the perfect legacy for Tommy. I would have brought the girl to heel. Except for your useless blather to the newspaper." She pointed at Sebastian. "You ruined it all, you fool."

Lola felt a burst of cold swipe past her.

"Quick, I've got her." Aubrey's cry rang in her ears.

Serene staggered, eyes fluttering closed. The scissors clattered to the floor.

Eng sprang forward and kicked them away. They slid across the wooden planks and underneath a ragged pile of destroyed costumes. Bloody hands and all, he grasped Serene by her arm.

"Stasha Chu, you're under arrest," Eng said.

Serene struggled weakly, disoriented. "What?"

Lola turned to the door. "Medics, quickly." She turned back. "It's all right, Serene. Your grandmother has done something serious. Very serious. The police need to speak to you both."

"Lola, no." Aubrey pitched his voice low. "You may love the truth for its own sake, but the truth can only harm her now. Please, don't."

Serene stared at Lola, frozen. "What do you mean, serious? What's going on?"

Lola felt her heart clench at the vulnerability in Serene's pleading look. "I'm sorry, haunt, I can't start lying to her now." Lola raised her voice. "I think you may have already suspected. Isn't that right?"

Eng said, "This isn't the time, Miss Starke." He pulled gently on Serene's arm.

Serene shook her head, tried to extricate her arm from Eng's grip. "Don't patronize me. What's going on? What just happened?"

"Your grandmother, she...she took you over." Lola swallowed, gathering her determination. "She used you, Serene. She killed them."

"What? How?" Serene struggled against Eng. Crying, she thrust a hand into her dress pocket, pulled out a wrinkled mess of blue cloth.

"Damn it, Starke." Eng glared at Lola.

Lola looked around at the sound of shoes crunching on the glass shards by the door.

Eng let out a curse, pain clear in his tone. Lola spun back.

He held his hand close to his body, eyeing Serene warily.

She held a squat, square lighter in front of her, its yellow flame flickering as her hands trembled. She looked at Sebastian, set her jaw, and lit her crumpled handkerchief on fire.

THIRTY-THREE

Once the fire reached her fingertips, Serene dropped it onto an open trunk of ruined costumes. Marks pushed past Lola and leaped at Serene. Serene scrambled away, snatched up a random scrap from the pile of ruined costumes, ignited it, and threw it at the tall detective.

It landed on a different open storage trunk full of shredded clothing. Leung and Eng stamped at the fire.

"*Mui-mui*, this is insane. You must stop!"

Sebastian pulled himself up off the floor. Serene glanced at him, then dropped another burning rag on top of a mound of ragged costumes at her feet.

Lola grabbed the closest man's arm. "Get him out of here." She pushed Bednarski toward Sebastian and scrambled toward Serene. The fire raged within the closest trunk. Lola pulled up on one of the trunk sides, but the weight was too much to move and the fire too hot to bear. She jinked around the burning mass instead.

"Damn you, old woman. Stop struggling. We need to get her out of here to save you both." Aubrey's frustration fuelled Lola's own sense of urgency.

Marks circled, trying to get to Serene, but she'd set alight another pile of tattered clothing. He dodged around them, reaching with long arms to grab her. Serene moved swiftly. Marks cursed and snatched back his singed arm.

Serene backed over to the dressing table.

Lola thought rapidly, reaching for any ruse to stop the girl's madness. She shouted, "I found the pocket watch, Serene. Stuey's pocket watch, I found it. But it's being kept in a secret place, somewhere safe from Kam." Lola coughed. Black smoke rose from the burning clothing, dark and greasy. "I'll take you to it. Come out from there. I'll take you to it."

Serene scowled. "I don't want to know. If he hid it from me, he had a good reason."

"Please, you don't have to die like this. You don't have to put up with her abuse any longer. There's another way. We can help you separate from your grandmother, from your entire family, if you wish it." Lola beckoned. "Aubrey and I, we've found someone willing to help."

Serene glowered. "That's twice you've lied to me about that. I know the Temple won't help. Stuey asked them for me. They sent me a letter. *Mah-mah* said she'd never agree to it." She lowered her chin, glared. "This is my only way out."

Aubrey grunted. "Stop it, hag. You're not polluting her again."

Serene thrust the flame into the pile. Nothing happened. She pulled her hand out, looked at the snuffed lighter. She snatched up a wad of cloth, shook the lighter, and resparked it.

Marks jumped forward, reaching for her. His hand sent the lighter arcing away, onto a pile of make-up rags on the dressing table surface.

A bright yellow flame grew and the smell of burning grass filled Lola's nose. Serene struggled in Marks's grip, staring wide-eyed as smoke and flames flashed on the detective's sleeve. Lola kicked through a pile of burning costumes to get closer, scattering it into smaller fires that flared up as they found more fuel.

Cursing, she separated Serene from Marks and grabbed the other woman's arm.

"Come on!"

Serene stumbled. Lola lost her hold. The younger woman pushed and Lola collided with Marks, losing sight of Serene.

Marks clutched Lola briefly then released her. He slapped at his sleeve, coughing hard. Lola pulled him down to the floor and rolled him roughly.

"Lola." Aubrey's voice was tight, strained. "Get out. He'll be fine."

She dragged Marks back onto his knees. "Let's go, Marks. Now."

Squatting down, she started duck walking, pulling Marks for a few steps before her heel slipped on a scrap of silken scarf, sending her sprawling on her side. Marks clumsily helped her up, coughing and squinting through the thickening air.

Lola grabbed the hem of her sweater, pulled it up to her face and used it as a filter against the smoke. She risked a glance behind her.

Marks coughed and gagged, his eyes slitted, one arm barred across his nose and mouth. Lola searched for Serene as she made her way forward, in case the other woman was still stumbling for the door. The smoke was dense, grey and black and white. She had no idea how far the door was anymore, or if she was heading toward it.

She ran into the wall, hitting her forehead hard enough to see white flashes sparking in her field of view. She fumbled sideways until she felt the opening. Sparing another look behind her, she saw that Marks had stayed on course. He held his hand out, searching for the doorway. She grabbed his wrist and pulled him with her as she crossed the threshold.

"Hurry," said Aubrey. "Go right, then straight down the hall and turn left. I can guide you through the smoke."

The smoke was less dense outside the room, but the reprieve would be short-lived, Lola knew. This entire building was built of wood. The painted scenery, the ropes, the very walls. Everything would be alight in a matter of minutes.

Lola let Aubrey lead her and Marks, blinded by tears, through the maze of the backstage area. She held on tightly to his wrist, feeling the starch in his cuffs beneath her fingers. They emerged through the backstage door and into the alleyway.

Lola coughed, unable to stop despite the pain. A wave of tears accompanied the rough clawing in her throat. She spat black phlegm out and coughed again. Her nostrils were raw and streaming. She swiped at her nose with her sleeve. It came away streaked with black slime. Her eyes stung and watered hard enough to blur her vision. She heaved great breaths, the air seeming to stab at her as it sawed in and out.

"Serene," she said, gasping, "did she get out?"

"You need to see the medics, Lola." Aubrey spoke slowly, as if to a child. "You've got a bump the size of an egg on your forehead."

Lola reached up an unsteady hand, realized she was still holding on to Marks's wrist. She unclenched her fingers. His arm dropped like deadweight.

He cradled his right arm against his chest as he coughed. His sleeve was in blackened tatters.

Lola gingerly touched her forehead. Another fit of coughing overcame her. She doubled over, had a moment of vertigo. She pushed it away through sheer force of will until the encroaching blackness in her vision receded to the edges. Panting, she remained bent double to conserve her energy.

"Aubrey, where is she?"

Behind her, an agonized voice echoed her question. Lola slowly swivelled around.

DI Leung and a plump woman in the bright orange tunic of an ambulance medic were trying to restrain Sebastian Chu. He was on a stretcher, struggling to sit up. His face was streaked with black, contorted with pain.

"Aubrey." Lola's chest tightened. "Where is she?"

His voice was faint. "Lola, look to yourself. You need—"

Lola pushed off her knees and stumbled toward the backstage door. Smoke, dark and billowing, poured from within. Lola felt a hand pull at her shoulder. She shoved it away, got tangled in her own feet and collapsed against a hard body.

Marks shouted, inches from her face. "Too late. Look at the smoke. That thing's all wood. She's gonna go any moment." He roughly turned her around, dragged her away from the building.

"Serene's still in there." She looked around frantically. "Where's the fire brigade? Why aren't they here yet?" She grabbed Marks by his lapels and shoved him away. He grabbed her again, wincing. Lola found herself staring at his blackened sleeve, abruptly focussed on a patch of cloth that looked melted into his skin. She smelled the stench of burned flesh.

Lola pushed him aside, his grip too tight to break completely, and doubled over his unburned arm, retching.

"Move, move, move!"

Marks pulled Lola to the left and moved. Lola became conscious of clanging bells and several figures running past, toward the theatre. She scrabbled at Marks's hands. "Tell them. She's still in there. Tell them there's someone still in there."

"It's no use," he said, face grim. "They won't make it."

Lola looked up.

Four men ran back toward them, away from the building. They roughly herded Marks and Lola with them, down the alley toward the street. Other fire brigade members ran past, shouting over each other.

Unable to move against the tide, Lola was soon deposited with a medic and wrapped in a scratchy blanket. When she was able to raise her head, she discovered she was now half a block away from the front of the Empress Theatre.

"Gods, I hope they can save her," said the medic, the same plump woman that had been tending to Sebastian. "Looks like a close thing." She packed instruments and gauze into a large rectangular basket.

Lola warily touched her forehead. She felt a greasy smear of ointment, put her fingers under her nostrils.

"You won't be able to smell much but smoke for a while yet," said the medic. "It's just a homemade balm I use. I just sent someone for some ice. It'll help with that goose egg. Here." The medic gave Lola a gourd. "This'll help clear your mouth. I saw you retching."

Lola thanked her and took a slow sip of water, rinsed her mouth, and spat onto the street. She stoppered the gourd and wiped her mouth with a darkened sleeve. She felt movement around her, heard other medics speaking to other injured people. She stared at the flames now bursting out of the theatre roof.

She imagined the tiers, the dragons flaming and charring and burning into white-grey ash. The swirls of vibrant colour melting into one mass of black. As she watched, the neon sign cracked into two pieces and fell to the street, smashing with an awful sound that reverberated through the night. Lola instinctively turned her face away, raised her arms to cover her head.

A great shout arose.

Lola looked back in time to see the beautifully sculptured, tiered roof of the Empress Dowager Theatre collapse with a *whoosh* and a crash. She closed her eyes as a wave of debris blew into her face.

⚬⚬⚬

Lola rubbed her eyes again, but it didn't get out the gritty feel any better than it did ten seconds ago. She manoeuvred her car past an aging lorry, its rear and sides pocked with rust. Other than the two of them, though, the street was dead. No late party-goers, no stumbling drunks. The pavements were empty. The shops, dark.

Lola drove on automatic, her mind replaying the terrible fire of just a few hours past. Her hands, pale and streaked in the intermittent light from the streetlamps, started to tremble. She clamped them as tightly as possible on the steering wheel. Pushing past the pain, she focussed on the road in front of her, willing away the images of Serene. She abruptly pushed the heel of her hand against first one eye, then the other.

"You couldn't have saved her," said Aubrey.

"Why did you let Stasha go?"

"I didn't. She was torn away from me. She disappeared."

"Don't lie to me, haunt. You saw what happened. That fire was nothing to you. It didn't even exist for you in the Ether."

"Have you ever stopped to think that not all facts are helpful? Not every scrap of the truth serves you, Lola. Often, it's the knife that cuts deepest."

"You get cut either way." Lola coughed, her throat a throbbing mess. "Better to see the edge coming than to stumble around in the dark." She spit sooty phlegm into a handkerchief.

"Serene needed comfort, Lola, not the truth. It would've been a mercy, a small measure of comfort for her to be ignorant just a little while longer."

"Living isn't about *comfort*, haunt. Everyone lied to her. Her entire life. Can't you imagine for one tiny second the betrayal she felt? She deserved the truth, bitter or otherwise." Lola coughed again, her eyes tearing up. She took a deep, shaky, terrible breath. "Spill or don't. I already know you lied. The question is did you do everything you possibly could to save her?"

"No, you want to know if *you* did everything you could have."

She clenched her teeth so hard, her jaw creaked.

Aubrey's voice softened. "You did. I swear by all that matters to you, you couldn't have done any different."

Lola spoke slowly through her tight jaw. "Tell me the truth. I'll judge for myself."

She drove several blocks in silence.

She heard Aubrey sigh. "Stasha told me she would guide her to safety. I was worried about you. I had to trust her. I had no choice. I let her go. That's when I told you to go, that Marks would be all right. The smoke was getting thicker for you. You were coughing, your eyes were tearing up. But you started off and I glanced over to check on Stasha and Serene."

He paused.

"She was leading Serene the wrong way, away from the door. I ran over, tried to get her to stop, to guide Serene to safety. She laughed, told me to look to my own. I saw you crack your head on the wall. You were so close, Lola, so close to the door. I was worried you'd be too dazed to get yourself out of the building."

Lola heard him take a breath.

"I made my choice. I left Serene to fend for herself. I chose you."

"You what?" Lola gaped for a moment.

"You left her to fend for herself? With a madwoman as her guide? Whom you saw leading her back into the flames?"

Lola clamped her mouth shut. She reined in her voice. "You could have told me. You could have led me to her and I would have—"

"Died," said Aubrey, voice flat. "You would have died going toward the fire. You would have died trying to save her." He lowered his voice. "I know you, Lola. You would have died trying."

Lola felt the pressure building behind her tongue. Wringing the steering wheel, she swallowed the scream with a grimace. Bitterness chased it down to her belly.

"Serene Chu would be alive now if you hadn't abandoned her to her Ghost."

"It's the choice I made, Lola. And I will make it every time."

"I will not feel grateful, haunt. Understand me? Never. Not at the cost of another woman's life." She hit the steering wheel with the flat of her hand, welcoming the sting.

The street she wanted was crammed with cars at the curb. It was hours yet until dawn, although there was a tell-tale lightness to the east, the very gentlest of glows just beginning to encroach on the dark sky.

Lola parked between two green sedans. She rested her head for a moment then hauled herself out and up. She hobbled on her sore feet for a block to a three-storey apartment house. Its white wooden clapboard seemed to gleam faintly, even in the dubious light of the City streetlamps.

Lola plodded up the three steps to the main entrance and pressed buzzer 6. She waited a few seconds, pressed it again. And again. Then she leaned on it. Hard.

A clattering sounded from the front of the building. She stepped out of the alcove until she was visible from the upper floors.

"Lola?" Nicky squinted down at her.

"Can I come up, Uncle?" She swayed a little, disoriented from craning her neck up.

"Gods, my girl, you look terrible." He disappeared inside.

A low buzz from the door. Lola stepped inside. Silently cursing Nicky's fondness for apartments without lifts, she forced herself up, one weary step at a time, to the third floor. Nicky, undoubtedly aware of her pride, met her at his open door with a worried look. His hair was tousled, his face creased. He wore a dressing gown in faded blue over striped green pyjamas.

"Sorry to roust you." She slid inside, past the closet, then the open bedroom door on the left, and made a beeline through the short hall for the living room straight ahead. Her knees buckled as she reached the sofa. She reached out just in time to collapse onto the soft plaid. She clumsily kicked off her shoes, folded her legs up, and tucked her feet under.

"May I have something to drink, Uncle? I'm parched."

Nicky poked his head out into the hallway, checked both sides, then closed his door. He engaged all three locks.

"What happened, my girl?" He hurried over and sat on the lone armchair, at right angles to the sofa. "Were you in a fire?" He passed a worried gaze over her.

"Even City juice'll do, Uncle. Please."

Nicky nodded a few times, got up, and disappeared around a corner. He came back with a glass of water for her. She drank greedily. He refilled it and sat down.

Lola felt the chill of the water in her belly. She shivered.

"What's happened? Are you all right?" Nicky leaned forward, peering at her face. He sat back, looked her over again. "Have you seen a Healer? Been to the hospital?"

She dug a knuckle into her eye, rubbing away the tears. "I'm sorry, Uncle. I have bad news." She swallowed. "It's Serene." She rubbed her eyes again. "She died tonight in a fire at The Empress."

Nicky paled. He grasped the arms of his chair.

"There's more," said Lola, her voice dull. She recounted Stasha's confession, the mad Ghost's possession of Serene, the fires. She glossed over her escape with Marks in tow. She made damn sure to include Aubrey's decision to leave Serene.

Nicky rubbed at his face with both hands.

"I'm sorry, Uncle," said Lola. "About Lucky."

"I'm sorry too, my girl." Nicky sighed heavily. "I was so damned sure he'd never hire a killer."

"Stasha may not have been telling the truth," said Aubrey. "She was spiteful enough to lie about Lucky. And crazy enough to have made it all up."

Lola grudgingly relayed his opinion to her mentor. Nicky nodded. "Aubrey's right, my girl. If she was mad enough and cruel enough to murder her own grandson..." He trailed off, his face crumpling. He wiped his eyes roughly with the sleeve of his pyjamas.

"She would've killed her as a baby, Uncle. A baby." Lola felt her gorge rise. She swallowed several times, drained her water.

Nicky pulled out a white handkerchief from his dressing gown, cleaned his face, blew his nose. He sat, staring out the window at the dark.

"You know why I came?" said Lola softly.

He nodded.

Lola held his gaze for a beat. "I'll rest my eyes while you dress."

She crossed her arms on the arm of the sofa and let her head fall on top. She felt Nicky extricate the water glass from her hand, heard him place it with a click on the table and then shuffle away in his slippers. She closed her eyes.

"Lola, my girl."

She jerked awake abruptly. Nicky was on his haunches, his face level with hers. He smiled sadly, placed a hand on her shoulder.

"Up and at 'em," he said gently. His eyes filled with tears. "Time to tell the Lims who murdered their son."

He rose up and kissed the top of her head.

EPILOGUE

Another school, another ass trying to test the new kid.

I'm ready for him. I'm always ready for 'em.

This one's easily half a foot taller than me, wearing a stupid *mien-lahp* in navy blue. I can see the dumb fortune symbols on the fabric, probably chosen by his stupid *amah*. He has the look of a rich, well-fed bully. Thick, stiff lips. Hands like bear paws. Big nostrils and piggy eyes. Stupid smirk. Thinks I'm easy pickings. Me with my worn shoes, threadbare cotton shirt and twine belt holding up a pair of linen pants so thin, it's a wonder my underpants aren't peeping through.

Doesn't matter. I'll show him. I'll show every single one of 'em if I have to.

"Hey, I heard you ma's real popular. Yeah—" he looks around at his mates "—down at the docks." He huffs a piss dumb laugh.

I stare at him.

"Huh. You dumb or something? Slow *and* small." He laughs. I look around at the crowd of other kids. I recognize their hunger for a fight.

They always want a fight.

The big one speaks again. "You think you can give me lip?"

I roll my eyes. Big *and* stupid.

I hear some sniggering from the crowd.

The big one lumbers forward, aiming for a push. I sidestep and turn, careful to keep the crowd in view. I watch the big one stumble

341

to a stop. His face darkens and he scrunches his eyes up. This time he yells as he rushes me. I wait until the last possible moment before spinning away. His momentum carries him into the knot of his buddies. They all tumble to the ground, raising a thick cloud of dust.

The bully shoves his way to his feet, coughing and swiping at his eyes. The others pick themselves up, slapping at filthy clothes. They watch me warily. I bet they'll all get a tanning for that.

I stand, arms loose at my sides. I stare at each of them. They stare back at me, a couple open-mouthed, but no one looks ready to jump in. Movement from the corner of my eye.

The big one's brow is so low, his eyes have all but disappeared. "You just bought yourself a pounding, shrimp."

I shrug. The other kids burst into laughter.

"C'mon, *dai-loh*, you can take him!"

The big one charges again. This time, he swings out one of those huge paws and clips me behind the left ear. I whirl away from him, a starburst of pain exploding in my head.

When he comes at me a fourth time, I kick out, low. His heavy foot slams into me, but he trips, his arms windmilling as he tries to maintain his balance. I jump behind him, ignoring the pain in my calf and the hammering in my head.

I calculate carefully and then I kick his huge, round, mama's-boy backside.

He lands in a sprawl of meaty limbs and dirt-smeared *mein-lahp*. The kids laugh even harder.

Keeping my expression bored, I say, "Anyone else?"

The boy laughing the hardest comes over to me, his hands held palms forward.

"No, no, we got it. You'll wipe the park with us, squirt." He grins at me, then goes to help the bully up. "C'mon, *dai-loh*, come greet your new brother."

The bully's not laughing, but he comes anyway, rubbing the seat of his pants.

"You in charge?" I ask the laughing boy.

He grins even wider, beaming with good health and cheer.

"He gonna give me any more trouble?" I flick my head in the bully's direction.

The boy shakes his head. "Naw. He's pretty peaceful, when you get to know him." Another big grin. "He's just testing you out." The boy puts a hand on the bully's shoulder. "Right, *dai-loh*?"

"Yah," says the big one. "I'm oldest in class."

"And that concludes your official welcome to the Flying Tiger Acrobatics Academy," says the grinning boy. He puts out a hand, in the Western way.

"Put 'er there, pardner," he says, in English even.

I hesitate, shooting a glance at the other kids. They're all grinning now. Five boys, pushing and play fighting with each other. One cuffs the big one on the shoulder and jumps back, calling out a good-natured taunt. The boy in front of me waits, his hand outstretched.

I shake his hand. "Chu. Call me Tommy."

The boy's grin gets even bigger. He pumps my hand.

"You can call me Stuey."

ACKNOWLEDGEMENTS

Thank you so much, Heather Little of little h design works, for a second fabulous cover!

Thank you, Erinne Sevigny of Blue Pencil Consult, for your honest and thorough editorial consultation, and your enthusiasm.

Thanks, Kate Austin, for the rush copyediting job.

Thanks, Dr. Lindy Smith, for your generous help with my medical queries. You're totally my go-to source for medical research now, you know this, right, Lindy?

Thanks to my wonderful, eclectic Lady Mixers, all of whom are dreadfully funny, awfully smart, and terribly creative. Special big hugs to you, Caitlin Crawshaw and Danielle Metcalfe-Chenail. You know why.

Thank you, Kate Boorman. You're aces.

Thank you, Dawna-Lynne Duffy Power, sister of my heart.

Thanks, *Goh-goh*, for your unwavering support.

Thanks, Mum, for all the lovely craziness that is being Chinese.

Thanks, E and Wubby, for being so perfectly yourselves.

Thank you, Kevin, for everything I never knew I needed—and for all the things I did.

Dear Reader,

Thank you so much for making time to read this novel. If you've purchased this book, I thank you too for spending some of your money on my work. This might be the first time you've ever heard from me, but if you tool around my blog posts or website, you'll know that I am deeply grateful for the life that I lead, and especially, for the privilege of doing what I love: writing fiction.

This novel is in a series that centres on Lola Starke, but it's not a serial; the books needn't be read in order. I also write short stories which focus on characters other than Lola, but that take place in Crescent City. If you feel like dropping me a line about my stories, please write to me at sg@sgwong.com. I'm always curious to know what my readers think about my world.

I'm deeply thankful, too, for your support in additional ways: honest reviews of my books posted online, particularly on Amazon. Reviews helps indie authors like me (ones without big marketing dollars behind them) get noticed. Thanks! I truly appreciate it.

And finally, if you're interested in my behind-the-scenes creative machinations, I've got an email newsletter, too. You can use the sign-up via my Facebook Page. And I'm also on Twitter, so you can connect with me there as well.

Thanks again for reading my stuff! Let's keep in touch.

sandra.

ABOUT THE AUTHOR

SG Wong lives in Edmonton, Alberta, with her family and a whole lot of LEGO. She writes the Lola Starke novels and assorted Crescent City short stories in a lovely blue office where she can often be found staring out the window in between frenzied bouts of typing.

Connect with her via Facebook, @S_G_Wong on Twitter and at www.sgwong.com.

Made in the USA
Charleston, SC
13 January 2016